P9-CCY-586

Praise for Gaelen Foley

Her Only Desire
a *USA Today* and *Publishers Weekly* bestseller!

"Foley deftly adds an intriguing measure of exotic India to her usual classic Regency historical mix in the first of what promises to be an exceptionally entertaining and sexy new Spice trilogy."
—*Booklist*

"Foley's signature blend of wild escapades and steamy love scenes keeps her readership enthralled. Moving to sultry, exotic India, Foley fills her latest with historical color and cultural details, then adds suspense, passion, and hold-your-breath adventures."
—*Romantic Times,* Top Pick!!

"[A]n extraordinarily rich tapestry of events and emotions. You'll find humor and warmth amid the intrigue and danger and a relationship that manages to combine the sensual with the romantic. The plotting and dialogue are excellent, the characters vibrantly alive. . . . You can't go wrong with anything written by Gaelen Foley."
—*Romance Reviews Today*

His Wicked Kiss
a *USA Today* and *Publishers Weekly* bestseller!

"Foley maintains the delicious tension between Jack and Eden throughout; that, along with the mystery of Jack's past, propels the novel to an exciting conclusion."

—*Publishers Weekly*

"This is adventure romance at its best, a mix of *Indiana Jones* and *Pirates of the Caribbean* that stirs you and leaves you sighing with satisfaction."

—*Romantic Times*

"Compelling, absorbing and a delicious smorgasbord of different settings and characters, *His Wicked Kiss* is another nimble writing adventure from Gaelen Foley."

—romancejunkies.com

"Always fabulous."

—JULIA QUINN

One Night of Sin

"Delectably entertaining, lusciously sensual . . . an irresistible author skilled at blending passion and intrigue."

—*Booklist*

"*One Night of Sin* is pure perfection."

—The Historical Romance Club

"An absolutely fabulous romance! Don't start this tale late in the day, or you'll be up all night finishing it."

—freshfiction.com

"A compelling romance."

—thebestreviews.com

"*One Night of Sin* is a wonderful historical novel that takes readers on an adventure they will never forget . . . sure to be a favorite among readers."

—romancejunkies.com

Devil Takes a Bride

"With its wonderfully complicated, unforgettable characters, sharp wit, and a riveting plot rife with menacing danger and sizzling passion, Foley's latest Knight Miscellany historical Regency is simply superb."

—*Booklist*

"A truly sensual romance, possessing depth of plot and character."

—*Publishers Weekly*

"Complex and engaging characters . . . intense emotions and great depth of poignancy enthrall from beginning to end."

—*Romantic Times* Top Pick,
winner of the KISS Hero Award

By Gaelen Foley
Published by Ballantine Books

Books published by The Random House Publishing Group
are available at quantity discounts on bulk purchases for
premium, educational, fund-raising, and special sales use.
For details, please call 1-800-733-3000.

GAELEN FOLEY

HER SECRET FANTASY

A Novel

BALLANTINE BOOKS • NEW YORK

Sale of this book without a front cover may be unauthorized. If this book is coverless, it may have been reported to the publisher as "unsold or destroyed" and neither the author nor the publisher may have received payment for it.

Her Secret Fantasy is a work of fiction. Names, characters, places, and incidents are the products of the author's imagination or are used fictitiously. Any resemblance to actual events, locales, or persons, living or dead, is entirely coincidental.

A Ballantine Books Mass Market Original

Copyright © 2007 by Gaelen Foley

All rights reserved.

Published in the United States by Ballantine Books, an imprint of The Random House Publishing Group, a division of Random House, Inc., New York.

BALLANTINE and colophon are registered trademarks of Random House, Inc.

ISBN 978-0-345-49668-3

Cover design: Janet Holmes
Cover illustration: Aleta Rafton

Printed in the United States of America

www.ballantinebooks.com

OPM 9 8 7 6 5 4 3 2 1

CHAPTER
∞ ONE ∞

England, 1818

"The poor ladies! They're doomed, aren't they? Whatever shall they do now?"

"Sell the old manor, I suppose, though God knows it is a ruin."

"But it is their home—they've nowhere else to go!"

"Tsk, tsk, the ills of cards and drink, my dear."

"Yes, well, that is not the ladies' fault. Oh, it is so sad to see a once-great family slip into decline . . ."

The whispers were coming from a pew two or three rows behind her. Slowly the hushed exchange penetrated Lily Balfour's grief, drawing her attention away from the empty feeling in her heart, and the lulling patter of the rain against the tall, clear windows of their little parish church, and the droning eulogy from Grandfather's middle-aged heir, the new Lord Balfour—a stranger to her side of the family.

Behind the half-veil of black netting that gracefully draped her small hat, her dazed look of loss turned to shock and then pure indignation as the whispers continued.

What's this? she thought, listening in outrage. Someone was gossiping about her family, right here in the middle of Grandfather's funeral?

What a pair of busybodies!

She tried to recall which of her neighbors from among the local Quality had filed into the nearest pews behind her, but her mind was a blank. Indeed, she had spent the past two days in a fog, numb with sorrow and exhausted after months of caring for her dying hero.

For so many years, her grandfather, Viscount Balfour, had seemed larger than life. Being forced to watch him shrink day by day into a sick old man—being forced to watch him die—had been almost more than she could bear.

But he was gone now—at peace, she trusted—and as his heir's eulogy dragged on, her neighbors resumed their speculation on her family's fate. This time, Lily cocked her head slightly and listened with irked curiosity.

"Perhaps the new Lord Balfour will assist them. He seems a good-hearted fellow," one of the matrons suggested sympathetically, but the other snorted under her breath.

"Lady Clarissa would never accept it. The two branches of the family haven't spoken a civil word to each other in years. I thought this was common knowledge!"

"Yes, well, he can't leave them to starve. Oh, it's all so sad," her companion lamented softly. "First Master Langdon dead in India, and then the nephew in that horrid duel. Perhaps there *is* something to the old Balfour curse!"

"Nonsense. It's their own fault for being too proud. The answer is right before them if they would not turn their noses up at it."

"What answer? What ever do you mean?"

Yes, indeed? Lily frowned, wondering the same thing.

"One of the girls could still make an admirable match," the first lady explained in a brisk and reasonable whisper. "Well, not the elder cousin, perhaps," she admitted. "Miss Pamela is nearly forty, and very odd. But the younger one, Lily. Impeccable breeding, and she's got her mother's looks. I daresay an infusion of gold by way of the marriage mart could remedy their situation in a trice."

At these words, Lily felt the blood drain from her face; her entire body tensed, or rather recoiled, at the suggestion, and her fist closed hard around her crumpled handkerchief. *No.*

"But, dear, they could never afford a Season for her now. How they shall afford this funeral, I scarcely know."

"Well, it's now or never, if you ask me. The girl is nearly five and twenty. By the time she's out of mourning for her grandsire, she'll be on the shelf. Honestly, why she hasn't married yet is quite beyond all reckoning. She cannot lack for offers."

None of your blasted business, Lily thought, her jaw clenched.

"Perhaps Lady Clarissa did not deem any of her daughter's suitors fine enough for the old Balfour blood."

"No doubt. All the same, she is past the age of needing her mother's consent, is she not? I cannot speak for you, dear, but I should regard myself as derelict in my duty if I were in her shoes."

"Oh, come."

"No, really. What is she waiting for, a prince? A knight in shining armor? I had three children by the time I was her age."

Lily winced at their all-too-true reproach and ventured a tentative sideways glance at her mother.

Aged forty-four, Lady Clarissa Balfour was not yet ready to give up her reign as one of the most beautiful women in the south of England. Many also considered her one of the fiercest.

Her ramrod posture as she sat in the wooden pew assured her daughter that she, too, had heard the impudent whispers. But unlike the meeker and far more obedient Lily, Lady Clarissa slowly turned her blond head and leveled a withering glare at their gossiping neighbors. Her look must have struck them like an icy blast of Nordic wind.

How . . . dare . . . you?

Lily heard small mortified gasps behind her and was not at all surprised. She knew that look.

She sank down in her seat a bit, quite familiar with being on the receiving end of one of her mother's bone-chilling stares. She was only glad that this time it was not directed at her.

Her mother was the daughter of an earl—a fact that no one in her presence was permitted to forget—and was too well bred, thank you very much, ever to raise her voice. Of course, there was no need, when she could fling daggers from her eyes.

When Lady Clarissa Balfour turned forward again oh-so-serenely, her flawless face was a marble mask, hard and white against the black lace of her high-necked mourning gown. Having handled the insubordination from the locals, she slipped Lily a small sideward glance of cold satisfaction.

That's Mother for you, Lily thought.

She responded with a tiny, rather hapless nod. Then she tried to return her attention to the eulogy, but in truth, it was very difficult to listen to the new Lord Balfour's empty platitudes about a man he barely knew, a man whom Lily and everyone for miles around had loved.

Well, except maybe her mother. Lady Clarissa had been a dutiful daughter-in-law to the old viscount, but even as a child, Lily had sensed how they had blamed each other for her father's death. She had always felt caught in the middle between them. Indeed, sitting here, lost in her thoughts before her neighbors had so rudely interrupted, she had been woefully trying to decide which funeral was worse, this one or her father's.

In truth, it was no contest. Today her heart was broken, but it still could not match the loss that she had suffered fifteen years ago as a child of nine. Though she had loved her grandfather dearly and had tended him in his frailty day by day, she had been even closer to her father—two peas in a pod, her nurse used to say.

Besides, her grandfather had been old and ill, and Lily had known his death was coming. Years ago, she had been but a little girl, unaware of death, and had believed her marvelous Papa was off having a grand adventure in India, riding elephants and meeting glittering maharajahs. That was what he had told her.

He had promised to come back with a sack full of rubies for Mother and one full of diamonds for her. *"My little princess. Princess Lily! One day you'll be the grandest girl in all the land . . ."* Handsome, charming, and a thoroughgoing dreamer, Langdon Balfour had always tended toward hyperbole, but at nine, Lily had taken her father at his word.

About a year later, news of his death as a result of monsoon fever had brought her young world crashing down.

Perhaps that was why it was so difficult to listen to the new Lord Balfour's speech. It should have been Papa standing up there, telling everyone about his father, Lily thought resentfully. It should have been Papa inheriting the title and taking up his rightful role as male head of the family. They might still have been bankrupt, and mutually embarrassed of their family's decline, but at least they would have been together.

Instead, all she had left of him were fading memories of the fairy tales he used to tell her, and a garden folly that he hadn't quite managed to complete before he ran out of money . . . and time.

Now they were a household of women with precious little income to sustain them.

God help us, Lily thought as her gaze slowly fell.

Their anonymous neighbor was probably right. They were doomed.

That quickly, guilt set in. Familiar guilt. Maybe her gossiping neighbors had a point. *You could fix all this if only you weren't so selfish,* her conscience reproached her. *Why shouldn't you marry when it could solve everything? Just look at poor Mother. Hasn't she suffered enough? Look at her pride. She wasn't born to be poor.*

You can do this, it persisted, trying to rally her. *You can save them. You know you can, if only you'd forget about the past and stop being afraid.*

But she *was* afraid. Experience had shown that a healthy mistrust of people and the world was necessary for survival. Indeed, if her father had owned a measure of sensible fear, perhaps he'd be alive today. Fear was good.

Before long, the funeral service had ended. The gossiping matrons had fled by the time the grief-stricken congregation turned to watch the pall-bearers march out, somberly carrying their beloved lord's casket.

While the gentlemen swarmed into the adjoining church-yard to bury the viscount, the ladies climbed up into their carriages for the short drive over to Balfour Manor, where Lily's family would offer a modest reception.

Her mother marched ahead in regal fashion, lifting the hem of her black skirts above the mud puddles while one of their loyal family footmen—who had not been paid in several months, alas—hurried after her, holding an umbrella over her black-bonneted and sleekly coiffed head.

"Come, Lily," Lady Clarissa summoned her. "We must be ready for our guests."

She made no move to follow. "I'd rather walk, actually. I need . . ." Her words trailed off at her mother's exasperated glance.

"Lily, it's raining. Don't be absurd."

"I have my umbrella. I'd really like to take a few minutes alone, i-if you don't mind, Mother."

Lady Clarissa swept about-face and stared at her. "Of course I mind! I need you to receive our guests as they arrive. I shall be in the drawing room pouring the tea. You will stand in the entrance hall!"

"Aunt Daisy said she'd take my place. I'll only be a moment."

Lady Clarissa glanced dubiously at her stout and usually helpless but kind-hearted sister-in-law.

"Y-yes, I will mind the door," Aunt Daisy piped up.

Lady Clarissa rolled her eyes.

"Oh, let her be, Clarissa," Aunt Daisy pleaded. "The poor girl wants to say good-bye."

Lady Clarissa flicked a haughty glance toward the grave-yard, then shrugged. "Don't dawdle about it," she ordered. "In twenty minutes, we'll have a house full of guests, and I need you there."

"Yes, ma'am." Lily nodded, casting Aunt Daisy a grateful look as her mother turned away. Then Lady Clarissa and the two remaining members of her entourage—bustling and prattling Aunt Daisy and bookish Cousin Pamela, wrinkling her nose and drying her rain-flecked spectacles—all climbed into their weathered black coach and set off for Balfour Manor.

The grand brick house was only a stone's throw up the country road. The gabled roof was visible from here beyond the trees.

It's not a ruin, Lily thought defensively. So the roof had a hole or two. So what?

As she watched the line of carriages moving slowly toward it, she reflected in lingering amazement on the revelation in Grandfather's will. He had skipped her mother and left Balfour Manor, his one unentailed property, to Lily.

Of course she knew why he had done it. Not because she had taken care of him, nor even because she shared his blood, while her mother was only his daughter-in-law. It was because he had wanted to make sure that if indeed Lily stood by her vow never to marry, as well she might after what had happened to her, then at least she would always have a place to live, a home to call her own.

Not even Mother would be able to throw her out, as she had once threatened to do. Memories of her mother's cold reproach still made Lily tremble, though it had happened nearly ten years ago, when she was but a frightened fifteen-year-old. She still suffered keenly over the private shame she had brought upon her proud family; but under her grandfather's strict orders, they had closed ranks and kept her secret all these years, protecting her from any taint of scandal for the sake of family honor.

All of them had done their best to sweep it under the carpet. Not even her mother had mentioned it in at least eight years. But the knowledge of her sin was always there, beneath the surface in the polite and genteel war zone of her home. Life had gone on as it was wont to do, but Lily was left wondering if there was any way that she could *ever* be redeemed for her mistake.

This, in truth, was what she had lingered behind to ponder—not the loss of her grandsire, but the nagging guilt that still chafed after her neighbors' words.

"An infusion of gold by way of the marriage mart would fix their situation in a trice . . ."

Once more, the Balfour family honor was in jeopardy, not by scandal this time but by financial ruin. Years ago, it was she who had endangered the family's good name, but her kin had protected her. Now that they stood once more on the brink of disgrace, didn't she owe it to her family to save them if she could? Didn't she owe it to Grandfather?

As the line of carriages pulled ahead, she glanced over her shoulder at the men gathered in the churchyard.

Tears filled her eyes as she watched them lowering his casket into the earth. Lifting her fingertips to her lips, she looked ahead again while the rain softly drummed her black umbrella.

At length she continued walking homeward, setting each foot carefully in the precarious metal patens that barely kept her shoes above the mud.

What am I to do? I don't wish to be selfish . . .

She barely knew where to begin, thinking about how to pay for Balfour Manor's upkeep, a colossal expense even when its inhabitants dwelled meagerly. It was all hers now. Selling it was absolutely out of the question, but how she was going to pay the taxes, let alone fix the leaky old roof, she had no idea.

Maybe I *should* start looking for a husband, she thought uneasily. Whatever happened, she could not bear to lose her home on top of everything else. Her moldering house and this sleepy village were the only places on earth where she felt truly safe.

Besides, the whimsical folly that Papa had left half-built still stood at the back of the overgrown garden. If she had to sell the house, the new owners would probably demolish it, and that would be like losing her father all over again, along with most of her childhood memories, the innocent part of her youth.

On the other hand, if she didn't do something fast, she would lose the house for certain.

"One of the girls could still make an admirable match . . ."

At that moment, Lily heard a carriage clattering up the road and turned to look as she moved out of the way.

Through the gloom came a quartet of prancing white horses drawing a distinctive pink barouche with squat, rounded lines. When Lily saw the bright vehicle rushing toward her, she smiled for the first time that day. Her godmother, Mrs. Clearwell, had come all the way from Mayfair.

She knew her mother's faithful childhood friend had been invited to stay with them for a few days; eccentric as she was, Mrs. Clearwell always came in times of crisis.

Somehow the rain paused magically as the coachman, Gerald, drew the high-stepping team to a halt beside her. He tipped his hat with a cheerful, "Good day, Miss Lily!"

As she nodded to him, her godmother suddenly stuck her gray head out the window. "Oh, Zeus, I'm late! Lily, dearest, how perfectly awful of me! Have I missed the entire service? Get in, get in, my girl! You silly goose, what are you doing, walking in the rain?"

"I find the rain enjoyable, ma'am, and yes, I'm afraid you missed the service. But no matter." She could not suppress a wry grin. "You're just in time for tea and cakes up at the house."

"Well, thank goodness for that!" Mrs. Clearwell hopped out of the carriage and ducked under Lily's umbrella.

The short, plump, bejeweled lady held Lily by her shoulders for a moment, searching her face with a gaze that poured out the most heartfelt sympathy, and then, in a spontaneous rush of emotion, she captured her in an effusive hug. "My dear, dear girl. Poor creature! You bore the brunt of his illness, didn't you? Of course you did," she said with a sniffle. "You were there when he went?"

"Yes." Tears filled Lily's eyes at her warm-hearted godmother's kindness. "He would not take his medicine. He said he would meet death with his wits intact."

"Oh . . . a hero to the end."

Lily nodded. "He was in so much pain."

"Well, he's in Heaven now with your papa. There, there, sweet child. Are you all right?"

Lily managed a nod and wiped away a tear.

"Brave girl." Mrs. Clearwell patted her cheek.

She was Mother's cousin and was the only person that Lily had ever seen who truly knew how to manage Lady Clarissa. Their friendship had always rather puzzled Lily. The two women could not have been more different.

Her mother, for instance, would never have worn the star-shaped pins that twinkled in Mrs. Clearwell's hair. Especially not to a funeral.

"Oh!" the portly widow exclaimed with sudden vehemence. "Lily, child, you must let me get you away from this gloomy place! I know you are a thoroughgoing homebody, but come to London with me. I insist!"

She offered a wan smile. "I believe I have six months of mourning to fulfill, according to the dictates of propriety."

"Propriety, my foot!" her godmother protested with flashing eyes. "You've been in mourning since you were nine years old! No more, I tell you! Lord Balfour would not have wanted you to be unhappy, nor do I."

"Ah, you've always been so kind to me."

"That's because I see great things in you, Lily."

Lily shook her head at her godmother's nonsense, wiping a trace of moisture off her cheek and telling herself it was only a raindrop.

"Good, then," Mrs. Clearwell concluded out of the blue. "It's all settled. You will come to Town with me and we'll have a grand time! There are concerts and dinners and balls and soirees—"

"Honestly, I have nothing to wear," Lily interrupted wearily, a bit scandalized at her godmother's talk of her going into Society so soon after a death in the family.

"Pish-posh, Miss, life is for the living! As for your clothes, do not trouble your head a bit, we'll fetch a few dresses for you in a trice. Not a word about expense—I promise you, it is a trifling matter. I am your godmother and I can spoil you if I want! And you know my Norbert died extremely rich."

Lily gazed at her uncertainly. "It is hard to take your charity."

"La, girl! Chaperoning a young beauty in London, why, it would be the most excitement I've had in years! Now, don't be proud like your mama, or stiff-necked like His Lordship always was. Come, Lily, *I* know you are a practical young woman—and you know that I have always been on your side."

Lily's eyes filled with tears, but she turned away, making an effort to blink them back. "Very well . . . I will consider it. Just promise me one thing." She slid her wily godmother a sideways look.

"What's that?"

"You wouldn't be planning on playing matchmaker, would you?"

Mrs. Clearwell beamed. "Well, actually . . . now that you mention it, dear, there may be two or three *agreeable* young gentlemen I've happened across in London, who I think might just be *perfect* for you."

Lily groaned, then reconsidered, and abruptly blurted out a cheeky question: "Are they rich?"

"Lily, darling," Mrs. Clearwell chided with a merry wink, "rich as princes. Otherwise, I wouldn't waste your time."

"Hmm," she murmured, glancing over her shoulder at the big, cold, and gloomy Balfour Manor. The roof was probably leaking even now.

When Mrs. Clearwell gestured invitingly toward her carriage, Lily looked at her intently, then closed her umbrella and stepped up inside.

By the end of that very trying day, Lily's mind was settled on the matter. After all their visitors had left, save Mrs. Clearwell, who was upstairs in the guest bedroom at the moment, she called her kinswomen together in the drawing room.

She stood before the fire and faced them with her hands clasped behind her back. "There is something I wish to say to you all together. Something private."

"Yes, daughter?" Her mother lifted her chin.

Lily squared her shoulders and took a deep breath. "I have decided to accept Mrs. Clearwell's invitation to London. It's no use protesting," she informed them. "We all know something must be done."

Aunt Daisy frowned and cast an anxious glance at Lady Clarissa, then at Lily again. "But what about your mourning, dear?"

"I think in this case, Grandfather would understand," she said softly. She hesitated. "As the new owner of this house, I must take action if I am to keep a roof over our heads. So, you see, I shall go to London and find a man of means to be my husband—then none of us shall have to worry long," she finished hastily over the sound of their gasps.

The three ladies stared at her in shock.

"You're . . . going to marry?" her spinster cousin breathed.

"Oh, bless you, Lily, my dear, brave girl!" Aunt Daisy whispered, dabbing her eyes with her handkerchief. "I feared we were headed for the almshouse!"

Lily glanced at her mother to read her reaction. She waited on tenterhooks, searching her face.

Lady Clarissa was silent for a long moment. Then she lowered her embroidery needle and frame. "You are certain you can carry it off?"

Steeling herself to her task, Lily swallowed hard. "I can."

Her mother's sapphire eyes narrowed shrewdly. "*All* of it? A husband will have . . . certain expectations."

"Yes. I am aware of that, ma'am. I shall be prepared."

"But—Mother! Aunt Clarissa! Surely you can't let her do this!" Cousin Pamela burst out in alarm.

Nobody answered.

"I know we are poor, but you can't let Lily sell herself like—like an unmentionable female! It's perfectly macabre!"

"Macabre?" Aunt Daisy echoed, furrowing her brow.

"There must be some other way!" Cousin Pamela insisted. "I know!" She suddenly brightened. "I could sell one of my novels!"

"*No!*" both of their mothers said in unison.

"My God, you and your Gothic horrors, you will ruin

any shred of respectability this family has left," Lady Clarissa muttered with a dismissive shudder. "I will hear no more of such talk. Ladies *don't* write novels."

"But I could publish it under a pseudonym—"

"*We* would still know it was you, Pamela," Lady Clarissa said with great long-suffering. "Honor is honor. Marriage at least is a respectable occupation for a woman. You might have tried it if you hadn't wasted your youth on all your pointless scribbling," she added under her breath.

"Yes, ma'am," Cousin Pamela said faintly. She dropped her gaze, timid and crestfallen once more behind her spectacles.

A flicker of a frown passed over Lily's face. That was Mother for you. Always correct and straight to the point. Carelessly cruel.

"You needn't worry, Pam," she spoke up, trying to hearten her plain, rather pitiful cousin with a wan smile. "It might seem a little, er, macabre, but I don't mind it," she lied, "and besides, our mothers are right. It is merely the way of the world."

"Well, I, for one, never cared for the world very much." Regrouping after this slight encouragement, Pamela rose, putting the book she had been studying aside.

Marching over to Lily, Pamela stared into her face, her brown eyes piercing and intense behind her round, rimless glasses. Her breath stank of coffee—she never drank tea. "So, you're really going to do it, then?" she inquired in a fascinated murmur. "Even after . . . what happened? You're going to save us all from destruction by marrying a rich man?"

Lily lifted her chin a notch. "*Very* rich."

"Well, then, you'd better pick a stupid one," Pamela advised. "Easier to fool."

Lady Clarissa gave an idle laugh. "They're all rather stupid when you come down to it, dear."

The dry remark reminded all present that Lady Clarissa had never forgiven her husband for his ill-made scheme of running off to India to save the family fortunes. Not because she had been a particularly devoted wife, but because his death meant that she would never ascend to the title that she had married him for.

If he had lived, she'd have risen to the rank of viscountess. Instead, she was left with the mere courtesy title granted to her on account of her father's earldom.

"Yes, Lily, you listen to your cousin," she continued wryly. "Rich and stupid. Exactly the sort of man every girl needs."

"Right," Lily forced out softly, masking her dismay. She was determined to emulate her mother's unsentimental cool as she faced whatever fate held in store for her in London. She knew full well this was her one chance to redeem herself in her family's eyes.

Rich and stupid it was.

After all, what smart man would ever want her?

CHAPTER
TWO

London, Two Months Later

*H*e was not what the committee had expected.

The nine Distinguished Gentlemen of the Appropriations Sub-Committee for Eastern Expansion took their seats at the long, elevated table at the front of the moldy medieval chamber and readied themselves for the parliamentary hearing they were about to conduct. Each secretly relished the prospect of an afternoon spent at their favorite game of the old slice-and-dice. Ah, yes, it was ever so pleasant to while away the hours grilling, insulting, browbeating, and badgering whatever unfortunate career officer had been dispatched from the front lines to report back to them, the civilian authorities—answering their questions, providing explanations, in short, scrambling to dance to their tune.

After all, it was *they* who held the purse strings for the army. Besides, such occasions presented ample opportunity for all the speechifying that no politician could resist.

Having done this many times before, the gentlemen knew what sort of spineless young weasel the commanders in the field always sent: some obsequious fop, no doubt, an aristocratic younger son who would rather have been at the gaming tables at White's. The sort of unctuous, dandified aide-de-camp who was careful to hang back in the shade of the generals' tent when the bullets started flying.

But that was not what Colonel Montrose had sent them this time from the front lines of the latest nasty little war in India—the one they largely preferred to forget.

No, indeed.

The chairman nodded to the armed bailiff, signaling their readiness to let the games begin. This worthy, in turn, hauled open the ancient creaking door as if to drag some poor, cowering Christian in to face the lions.

But then, the strong, ringing rhythm of polished boot heels striking the ancient flagstones just outside the door gave the committee their first inkling that their expectations may have been a bit . . . off.

Then *he* appeared in the doorway—and half the committee drew back in alarm. A few actually gasped. All of them stared, their gazes traveling over him in awed confusion. They took one look at the bona-fide warrior who had been sent to deal with them and knew that this sun-baked, towering savage was not going away until he got exactly what he came for.

A magnificent specimen in full-dress cavalry uniform, Major Derek Knight stalked into the chamber, and when he passed the long table where the committee members were arrayed, they were forced to note his impressive height, for although their table sat on a raised dais, he was still on eye level with them. He stared forward as he marched in, but was not too humble to look the canny old chairman, Lord Sinclair, straight in the eyes when he passed him.

It was a cool, metallic glance of warning—or a brief, disgusted glare. He ignored the earl's muttered, "I say!" and prowled on, moving with controlled power and grace, all menace and rippling muscle.

Upon reaching the smaller, lower table set up across from theirs, he stopped, pivoted with crisp precision, and did not salute them but stood at attention, his plumed cavalry helmet under his arm—rather like a Roman centurion, some thought.

For a long moment, none of the Gentlemen knew what to say, quite how to begin. Even the aged chairman was a bit stymied. They could only stare, marveling in spite of themselves to remember that such men existed out on those distant battlefronts.

The major's indigo coat fitted snugly across his broad chest as he waited. Gold epaulets gleamed on his shoulders. A black silk sash girded his lean waist, the long ends brushing the side of a solid thigh encased in cream-colored breeches. His ebony knee-boots were buffed to a spotless sheen, while his shining silver dress-sword caught the light. His smooth, black hair was bound back in a queue like a horse's silky tail. His sun-bronzed skin was tough and dark, but the small lines etched around the corners of his pale, wolflike eyes gave him the look of desert nomads used to peering out over long distances of bleak terrain. The proud angle of his chin, his unyielding stony stare, not to mention the startling girth of his biceps all proclaimed the warrior a force to be reckoned with on the battlefield.

Or off it.

"Ahem," he said, jarring the Gentlemen out of their daze.

The chairman coughed quietly while a few of the others shifted in their seats as they all began to recall with dawning uneasiness that they were accountable to men such as this, being, as they were, in charge of the money the army in India needed to function, and perhaps they had been a tad . . . remiss.

Watching them with infinite patience, Derek Knight sincerely hoped they felt uncomfortable.

These bloated slugs did not know the meaning of the word. "Uncomfortable" was going into battle knowing that you had so few bullets in your ammunition case that you'd have to load your gun with little rocks after a few shots and pray to God it worked. Or perhaps "uncomfortable" was better described as having the surgeon dig a ball out of your back without at least a swig of whisky to take the edge off the pain. *Ah, what is wrong, my dear gentlemen?* he thought, hiding his cynical amusement as he watched the subtle signs of a guilty conscience play across each haughty face.

He could almost hear the excuses running through their greedy little minds. To be sure, it was difficult for any man to think of parting with three million pounds sterling, and after all, they were only human. No doubt urgent requests for more funding were easily misplaced, what with all the business such important gentlemen had to conduct each day.

Now and then they received a tally of the casualties, but these were sloughed aside in favor of the mounds of treasure that British generals sent back from India, with new maps staking out the most recently conquered territories.

For all this, Their Lordships were swift to take credit. But in fact, the consistent success of the army in India must have led them to conclude that the task of subjugating the hostile maharajahs must not be all that hard! In which case there was no real rush to send the army the gold and supplies it kept whining for, now, was there?

At bottom, Derek supposed these chaps were all very sure that, come what may, the Indian army would do what it always had done—it would manage, with or without the gold that Parliament had so inconveniently promised.

And so it would. But that was not the point.

Unfortunately for the roomful of politicians that he faced, a promise actually *meant* something to men like Derek Knight. He had been sent by his crusty old commander, Colonel Montrose, to inform "them demmed cheese-paring bureaucrats" that an army marched on its stomach, not on its feet, and the men would want to be paid.

For his part, Derek was not happy. His boys had been promised this gold and it had not appeared.

Somebody had some explaining to do.

He raised his eyebrows politely. "My Lords. Sirs. Shall I begin?"

"Er, m'boy—right, yes. Please do."

Apparently they would be skipping the niceties today. What a shame, he thought dryly. It seemed he had shocked the lovely Gentlemen. There was more uneasy throat-clearing as he set his helmet aside and rested his white-gloved fingers atop the files from Horse Guards that he had brought as proof certifying his arguments.

He then proceeded to hand them their arses on a silver platter.

The Gentlemen would have dearly liked to find him an ill speaker. It would have been comforting, no doubt, to reduce the colonial-born barbarian in their minds to the mere killing machine he appeared to be, capable only of following orders. But he quickly dashed their hope when he launched into the explanation he had been preparing for some weeks leading up to this dismal assignment.

With the calm, strategic cunning of a seasoned chess enthusiast, he spent the next half hour explaining the nature of the enemy they faced; the Maratha Empire's considerable resources for repelling British attacks; what was at stake for the realm in all of this, the consequences of failure, and the benefits to be gained by success; and why the whole damned thing mattered, anyway.

"Gentlemen," he concluded at length, summing it up for those who had glazed over from too many facts. "The Maratha Empire is no trifling foe. It was founded by Hindu royalty of the warrior caste, and is currently ruled by a madman, Baji Rao. Baji Rao is known for his ferocity; he's killed several of his own family members in order to seize power and keep it. His own people live in fear of him, and now he seeks to unite all the forces he can muster to drive the British out of India. This is what we face. Our colonies are under threat. The army *must* have the resources we were promised so we can protect our people and our trade."

He took a long, slow, reproachful look around at them.

"I have been informed that Governor-General Lord Hastings issued his first request for the release of these funds nearly a year ago, but there's still no sign of the money in Calcutta yet. I implore the committee to understand there is no more time to lose. If we do not give this fight our all, we may lose our foothold in India entirely—and if that happens, our rivals in the region will be happy to take what we cannot hold."

"Major," the second-ranked member said complainingly, "Lord Wellington put the Maratha threat down years ago! If they were defeated then, how could they have been permitted to regroup?" The man waited, scowling at Derek as though the whole thing were his fault.

Derek looked at him for a long moment, certain that he had already answered this question several times, but, patient creature—no, saint—that he was, he resisted the urge to walk over and smack the man alongside his balding head to encourage the lot of them to listen.

It worked on the new recruits. Maybe he should try it.

But of course, this was not the Indian frontier. Civilization was ever so annoying. It would have been pleasant to bellow at them in full battlefield throat, but as a matter of principle, Derek did not allow himself to be drawn into arguments with men whose heads he could have crushed with his bare hands under different circumstances.

That would not have been exactly fair.

After all, they were only *civilians*. Civilized civil servants, who could not understand why he did not grovel and placate. Why should he? He had little respect for their kind. In his world, respect had to be earned.

And besides, he prided himself on his ability to tell the flat-out truth to anyone, so in a way, he was perfect for this assignment. He had always preferred blunt honesty to sparing people's feelings and he had never once danced around anyone's rank.

Somehow, though, he refrained from bellowing and did not resort to banging heads this time. Instead, he merely summoned up his blandest, lordliest smile—for indeed he was of aristocratic descent—and answered the question patiently, one more time.

God knew he wished he were elsewhere, preferably with his men in the thick of the fight, but alas, this dismal mission to London was his penance, his punishment. Some months ago, he had managed to vex his commander, Colonel Montrose, and now, for his "impertinence," the only way to get his old post back was to succeed in this horrid low mission of money-grubbing in London.

Damn it, he should have been sitting astride his horse right now at the head of his glorious cavalry squadron, *his* troops, whom he had personally drilled and trained to perfection. His elder brother, Major Gabriel Knight, had a matching squadron, and often they had used their might to squeeze the enemy between their forces, a classic cavalry wedge.

But now everything was changed.

Good God, to think of their boys out there without them, temporarily under the command of other officers who could not possibly possess the Knight brothers' own degree of expertise—well, it was best not to contemplate it too much, for such musings seriously darkened his amiable nature.

Just get the money, a silent, savage part of himself advised, the ferocious side that had grown strong through years of battle and helped him survive. *You'll be out of here soon. You'll get your chance to pay those Maratha bastards back.*

Aye, as if slaughtering some of his regimental fellows wasn't bad enough, in his last run-in with Baji Rao's henchmen they had nearly killed his brother, and this was a wrong that Derek could never forgive. Yes, serious wounds happened in warfare, but this had been different.

He wanted blood.

The sooner he made the Sub-Committee unhand the army's funds, the sooner he'd be restored to his old command. Once he was back where he belonged, at the head of his men, then he could hunt those Maratha bastards down and carry out revenge.

Eastern-style.

You touch my brother, I'll have your head on a pike.

Some hours later, when he walked through the door at the Althorpe, the fashionable address where he and his brother had taken bachelor lodgings, the familiar scent of the spices their Indian servants had brought along in the Knight family's migration to England infused Derek's nostrils. The familiar scent of home offered unexpected comfort after a decidedly trying day. Black pepper, cumin, coriander—the scents wafting through the five-room apartment informed him that dear old Purnima must be cooking up her famous chicken curry. He let out a low sigh and shut the door behind him.

"You're back! How was it?"

Derek glanced across the sitting room and spotted his elder brother reclining on the sofa by the fireplace, reading the London *Times*. As the wounded warrior slowly and gingerly raised himself to a seated position, Derek sauntered in, tossing the files from Horse Guards onto the demilune table nearby. "Remember that time we got lost in the desert west of Lucknow?"

"Yes. Why?"

"This was drier. God, I need a drink! I'll get it," he told his trusty servant, Aadi, who had just come padding out, barefoot and turbaned as always.

"Yes, sahib." Aadi removed Derek's coat smoothly from his shoulders, whisking it away to hang it up for him.

Tugging his white shirtsleeves back down about his wrists, Derek strode across the sitting room in his waistcoat and made his selection from the liquor cabinet.

"Join me?" he asked, glancing over his shoulder at his brother.

Gabriel declined with a wry shake of his head. "Purnima has forbidden me from drinking spirits yet. She's made me a pot of tea instead. Some ayurvedic business."

"Ah, well, you'd better do as she says. Purnima knows," Derek said sagely. "For my part, I find myself in need of stronger stuff." With that, he tossed back a large swallow of French brandy.

Perhaps no English officer was overly fond of that nation on the whole, but such fine liquor was rarely to be found on the other side of the world. Derek intended to enjoy all of Europe's pleasures while he could.

Especially those of the female variety.

"Went that badly, eh?" Gabriel prompted.

"Actually, no." Derek turned to him, lifting his glass to offer himself a deserved toast. "Damned vexing, but I am happy to say the mission is accomplished."

"What, already?" his brother exclaimed.

Derek nodded, a grin breaking across his face. "The vote

was taken, the measure passed. The army will soon have its haul of gold."

Gabriel stared at him in amazement. "Well done, little brother!"

"Ah, those chaps just needed a bit of persuading," Derek said modestly.

"I can't believe you got it done in one day!"

"I can't believe they only have one man on the committee who has any damned military experience," Derek countered with a snort. "Edward Lundy, nabob of the East India Company. He was once a field officer in the Company's forces, but now he works behind a desk. Fairly high-placed, I understand."

"So, they've got Company men on this panel, then."

Derek nodded. "Three. There are nine members in all, three from the House of Lords, three from the Commons, and three from the Company's upper echelons, like Father used to be. Far as I can see, the Lords are the ones who are really in charge. I'm supposed to check in with the chairman, Lord Sinclair, in a day or two to find out when the money will be ready for transport."

"God knows the army will be glad to finally have it. Three million pounds sterling, you say?" Gabriel mused aloud. "It must be killing them to hand it over."

"I know." Derek flashed a grin. "Of course, it's not like they have any right to keep it. Parliament merely put them in charge of doling out the army funds. I imagine they would've liked to hold on to it as long as they could. Probably hoping everyone would forget they had it," he added cynically.

"Let's just hope their tardiness hasn't needlessly cost too many of our men their lives," Gabriel muttered.

The brothers exchanged a grim, knowing look.

"It isn't real to them somehow," Derek remarked after a moment, swirling the contents of his crystal goblet. Then he shook off his brooding. "Bloody civilians."

"God knows," Gabriel agreed, and Derek poured himself another splash of brandy, blocking out the hideous memory of his last battle and the arrow that had gone through his brother's torso. The one that had been meant for *him*.

In the thick of the fight that awful day, Derek had been engaged with three other swordsmen, heedless of the archers. Gabriel had seen the threat but had been unable to push Derek away fast enough. Instead, he had done the only thing that there was time to do to shield him, and had willingly stepped into the arrow's path.

Derek was not sure he could ever forgive himself for not seeing it coming, for not being fast enough. Gabriel was not just his brother and fellow officer. He was also his closest friend, and as his big brother had always been, secretly, something of an idol to him.

Derek had spent months tending him day in and day out, especially after infection invaded the wound, praying as he had never prayed before and wondering how he'd go on if Gabriel died for his sake. God knew he did not give a damn about inheriting his father's fortune in his elder brother's stead.

In the ensuing months, thank God, iron-willed Gabriel had gradually made it clear that he had no intention of crossing the River Styx quite yet, but the whole ordeal had raised dangerous questions in Derek's mind. Was it worth it, this soldiering business? What was it really doing to him at the end of the day?

They were questions he refused to ponder in any greater depth, now that the whole ugly business was behind them.

Best forgotten.

Ignoring his doubts with a vengeance, he took another big swallow of the velvety libation, then turned to his brother. "How are you feeling today?"

Gabriel shrugged.

Derek waited, tilting his head expectantly.

His brother gave him a flat look. "As well as can be expected for a man who shouldn't be alive." Then he changed the subject, as unwilling to admit to physical pain as Derek was to admit to the mental sort.

"So, what happens next?" Gabriel asked.

Fair enough.

"The navy will assemble a flotilla to escort all that shiny silver off to India, where it belongs."

"Then that means you'll be leaving us soon."

Derek gazed at his brother, saying nothing.

"You do still plan to be aboard one of those navy transports when they set sail, don't you?"

Why was he asking? Derek wondered. He already knew the answer perfectly well. Same school, same regiment. They had barely been apart a day in their lives. *Uncomfortable* was discussing their impending separation.

"You know, we all wish you'd stay," Gabriel mumbled. "Father and Georgiana and I."

"Can't."

"It's a bad business, man. We were lucky to get out of it alive." Gabriel paused with a mild wince, pressing a hand vaguely to that section of his middle where the arrow had gone in.

"Are you all right?" Derek asked quickly.

"Fine." Gabriel ignored the twinge. "It seems to me we've been given a second chance. Why risk it?"

Derek studied him. If it were any other man, he'd have suspected that the brush with death had made him lose his nerve, but with Gabriel Knight, that was impossible. His brother had long been known as one of the most feared warriors in India, rather famous for his motto of *"No mercy."*

Derek was considered the nice one.

"Need I remind you, brother, that you are the firstborn?" he finally answered, adopting his favorite breezy tone to deflect the seriousness of the question. "*You* will inherit Father's fortune. As the mere younger son, the soldier's life is my only route to fortune and glory. Surely you would not have me doomed to obscurity?"

"Better doomed to obscurity than just—doomed."

"Have you lost all your ambition?"

"I'm just glad to be alive."

"Naturally. All the same, let's not forget who we are. You and I were not made for mediocrity, brother, and that is all civilian life can offer."

"Hang your ambition!" Gabriel started forward, a flash

of the old temper darkening his rugged countenance. "There is more to life, Derek, than fortune and glory."

"Pardon?"

"You always blame it on the fact that you're the younger brother, but we both know your trust fund is perfectly adequate for you to try some other mode of life, if you were so inclined."

"Like what?" he retorted.

"I don't know—you could buy land. Farm or something!"

Derek laughed none too kindly at his brother's advice. "Me? In a cow field? Sorry, mate, you've got the wrong man. Good God, oats and barley! I am hardly the agrarian sort."

"How do you know for certain? You've never tried anything else."

"I cannot turn my back on the men."

"But you'll turn your back on your family?"

Derek flinched and looked away.

"Father's old, you know," Gabriel said. "He won't be around forever. And what about our sister? Aren't you the least bit curious about meeting your future niece or nephew when her child is born? And what about Griff's little boy? Matthew, you know, he adores you."

"It's not as if I'm never coming back!"

"Well," Gabriel said slowly, "you might not."

Derek looked at him for a long moment, his expression darkening. "I've got a score to settle in India, brother. I will not rest until it's done."

"Not for me you don't," Gabriel warned him, shaking his head. "Hell, no. Just let it go."

"Let it go?" Derek's face flushed with anger.

"It was a fair fight. You only want revenge because you blame yourself for what happened to me, but I don't blame you, Derek. I did it willingly. You're my brother. Of course I'd give my life for you."

"You are so irritatingly noble," Derek muttered, studying the ceiling as he fought for patience.

"You'd do the same for me." With a low laugh, Gabriel

leaned back against the couch, beginning to look tired again. "I didn't save your arse just so you could go back to the battlefield and get yourself blown up. But there, no more. I've said my piece. Do what you want."

Derek just looked at him. "Has the mail come yet?" he asked, firmly changing the subject.

"Over there."

Derek took another swallow of brandy and strode over to the demi-lune table by the door, where he had buried the mail on its silver tray beneath his files from Horse Guards. He set the files aside and picked up the pile of new invitations and bills and half dozen prettily written notes in fine pastel papers scented with various blends of expensive perfume.

He frowned, ignoring the lot. *Damn it.* Nothing yet from Colonel Montrose. He wanted word of his men, but news was slow to travel between England and India. He would have to be patient a while longer, it seemed. Well, he could certainly find other ways of amusing himself in the meanwhile.

Leaving the bills and invitations on the salver, he took the candy-colored letters from all his new lady friends in Town and fanned them out in his grasp like a hand of cards, sauntering back toward his brother and feeling a bit more cheerful again as he inhaled their enticing fragrances with a sardonic smile.

"What, more of your bloody love letters?" Gabriel asked, arching an eyebrow.

"Love?" Derek laughed. "Not exactly."

He offered the fanned spread of notes to his brother. "Pick one. Go on."

"Why?"

"How else am I going to decide who to sleep with tonight?"

"You know you are incorrigible, right?"

"Life is short," Derek said.

Gabriel gave him a droll look and made a random selection, pulling a light green letter from the middle. He handed it to him.

"Ah, an excellent choice," Derek said mildly, reading the name. "Lady Amherst, then. Good enough."

"What about the others?"

"Oh, I'll get around to them before I leave Town, trust me." With an irreverent smile, he tossed the others carelessly aside for now. They fell like pale confetti and he dropped lazily into the chair across from his brother, where he cracked open the short but scandalous letter from the ravishing Lady Amherst.

He laughed softly at her clever innuendoes as he read, stretching his legs out before him.

"Oh, damn," he said after a moment as he reached the last paragraph. "I forgot about that masked ball I said we'd go to. It's tonight."

"We?"

"Didn't I mention? You're coming, too."

"The hell I am."

"Gabriel, you can't lock yourself alone in here forever," he informed him. "Besides, we have to celebrate my victory over the cheese-parers! I'm not talking about going in costume if that's your worry. It'll cheer you up."

"On the contrary, I'm sure it would annoy me exceedingly. Costume ball?" He scoffed. "No, thanks. You go without me. I trust you'll manage to have enough fun for us both," Gabriel added, nodding toward the scattered love notes from Derek's latest crop of feminine admirers.

"That's hardly the point. Tell me, brother." He leaned forward with a wicked sparkle in his eyes. "Did you know there was a census taken a few years back? They counted over a million souls living here in London."

Gabriel eyed him suspiciously. "So?"

"Figure half of them are female, and half of those of an age to be wooed. That leaves *two-hundred fifty thousand* ladies out there waiting for us." He nodded toward the door, then sent his brother a lazy smile. "That's over a hundred thousand girls apiece. I say we had better get started."

Gabriel shook his head at him, looking half annoyed and half amused. Derek knew the look well.

"Oh, come on!" he protested, laughing. "Honestly, if I

were you, I would want to make sure that everything still *worked* properly, if you take my meaning."

Gabriel's stern, elder-brother look turned to a scowl.

"Ah, never mind." Derek waved him off and rose to get himself another drink. "But I'm not going to let you sit around in here and rot all by yourself. You know what I shall do? I'll hire some gorgeous wench with no morals to take care of you. Now that would be amusing! An obliging little nurse to cater to your every whim. I am a most kind and thoughtful brother, am I not?"

Gabriel gave him a formidable stare from across the room and did not smile.

Derek laughed but did not press the issue. He took another swallow of liquor. "Killjoy."

"Derek, I nearly died," Gabriel said. "I *did* die, as a matter of fact. For several minutes, I tell you, I was gone—"

"Gabriel, that's impossible! How many times have we been through this?"

"The army surgeon told me that I didn't have a pulse!"

"Well, he must've been mistaken!"

"No, he wasn't. For God's sake, I saw you all around my body from several feet up in the air—"

"No, you didn't! Obviously, it was a dream."

"This was no dream."

"Whatever it was, I don't want to hear about it anymore. It gives me the gooseflesh, damn it. Dead is dead."

"Says who?"

"Oh, I don't know—natural law? The fact you seem to be missing here, brother, is that you *didn't* die. You lived. I know you've got a long road back to regaining your full strength, but sooner or later, I'd like to see you really live again."

"I know you would, Derek." Gabriel sighed. "But coming back from the dead, well, it makes a man rethink his life a bit."

Derek dropped his gaze, pressed with worry not just for his brother's health but dashed well for his sanity, and not knowing what to say. He stared at the floor, then looked at his brother again. "You're going to be all right, Gabriel."

"Of course I will. So will you."

"Me?" he asked in surprise. "You're the one who's wounded."

"Right." Gabriel gave him a shrewd look.

Derek dropped his gaze, feeling restless and uneasy in the silence that followed. What the hell was his brother trying to say? He was fine.

He was perfectly fine.

Or at least he would be when he was back where he belonged. With his troops. At the war.

Back in Hell.

CHAPTER
∞ THREE ∞

*A*fter two months in London, Lily's quest to snare a rich husband was moving along nicely according to plan.

Through Mrs. Clearwell's selective introductions, the great Balfour name had won her many an entrée into some of London's grandest homes, where, throughout the Season—at balls, at dinners, at concerts and routs—she had been presented to countless eligible bachelors, most of them rich and many blue-blooded, even a few titles in the mix. She had made it her policy to treat each one with cool reserve while she studied them surreptitiously to discover whether they fit her two main criteria for a husband: rich and stupid.

To be sure, there was no shortage of such men in Town, like those witless dandies forever lurking in the bow window at White's or admiring themselves in every mirror that they passed.

Unfortunately, in the meanwhile, the truth was, she had begun to have trouble reconciling herself to marrying a less-than-intelligent man. Taking advantage of an amiable blockhead with a large inheritance didn't seem fair, really. Beneath her. Grandfather would not have approved.

She felt bad about having nothing to give in return, only taking a man's fortune to save herself and her kin.

Perhaps such vain, idle fools deserved to be taken advantage of, but on the other hand, she did not know if she could endure waking up and having to face one every day for the rest of her life.

Perhaps, she reasoned, a lack of brains could be exchanged for some better flaw, something more tolerable. Indeed, she believed she might have found the perfect solution . . .

In any case, over the passing weeks, she had methodically winnowed down her list of possible mates until she was left with one.

"Oh, look!" Mrs. Clearwell exclaimed, gesturing forward into the crowd at the masked ball. "There is Mr. Lundy now!"

At first Lily did not see him, or rather did not recognize her suitor in his costume.

The thronged ballroom swirled with a fantastical array of mythical birds and animals, ghouls and grim reapers, numerous walking allegories, and more classical gods and goddesses than she could count. Even the footmen had been made to dress as harlequins in motley suits of gaudy gold and purple satin with jingle-belled foolscaps to match.

One of them presently glided up to the ladies with a silver tray, offering them confections that glittered with colored sugar.

"Ah, how quaint!" Mrs. Clearwell, disguised as Hera, helped herself to a miniature candy shaped like a pear.

Lily chose one of the tiny apples and thanked the servant with a nod; then she looked askance at her godmother. "Are you sure it was Edward you saw?"

"Of course I'm sure."

"But where?"

Mrs. Clearwell laughed. "You don't see him?"

"No," Lily said in confusion, searching the crowd for her big, brawny beau.

"Look again, my dear. I shan't ruin the surprise!"

"Hm." Lily scanned the ballroom again, determined to keep her demeanor outwardly cheerful, but in actuality, her mood was a bit off this evening. She was glad of the pale pink half-mask she wore, for it helped conceal her indifference to . . . all of this.

What the deuce was wrong with her tonight? All the curious sights and sounds and tastes of the night's flamboyant gala had been fashioned to delight, yet somehow she could not shake a strange sense of detachment.

The best that she could figure, she must be growing homesick, especially after spotting the garden folly on their hosts' moonlit grounds from the long, winding drive up to the mansion. This was the longest she had ever been away from gloomy, creaky Balfour Manor, and when she had seen the garden folly near the ornamental lake, it had brought back a lonely pang of nostalgia.

"Well?" Mrs. Clearwell prodded. "Don't you see your prince charming yet?"

"One moment, I will find him," she replied, ignoring the irony in her godmother's tone. She wouldn't have admitted it for the world, but in strictest truth, Lily was in no great hurry to visit with her suitor.

A few sinister-looking monks went skulking past, no doubt inspired by one of those horrid novels Cousin Pamela adored. She spotted one turbaned Saracen warlord and a nearly complete crew of pirates, young men getting drunk nearby while the orchestra played.

Then, all of a sudden, Lily spotted her suitor ahead—and nearly choked on her candy. "Oh, dear God," she uttered, her steps faltering.

Mrs. Clearwell laughed heartily, for they were not yet within earshot of her towering beau. "What's the matter, dear? Don't you like your Edward's costume?"

"Oh, God, it's monstrous!" Lily whispered, aghast. "Oh, *why* didn't he ask me first? What do you suppose he is?"

"The Minotaur, obviously."

"Ugh, yes, so it would seem." Lily blanched, took a large gulp of champagne, and braced herself to go and greet her suitor. Clearly, if she married this man, she'd have her work cut out for her.

She couldn't help staring at Edward as she and Mrs. Clearwell approached.

Ed Lundy's costume as the legendary Minotaur was apt.

Perhaps a little too apt. He already possessed the monster's hulking size and thick, bull-like neck all on his own, but between the wide, gleaming horns that bracketed the sides of his painted head and the makeshift brass ring that he wore in his nose, the likeness was slightly terrifying.

He had not yet seen her as he loomed ahead, half-man, half-bull—or possibly half-mountain. He swigged a gulp from his tankard of ale and made half an effort to suppress his loud burp as the ladies joined him. Lily struggled to hide her revulsion, but Mrs. Clearwell failed.

Edward bowed to them, offering a few gruff niceties, and Lily refused to be daunted. So what if he was a bit vulgar at times? After her mother's oppressive propriety, a part of her reveled in the big ex-soldier's unapologetic crudity. Besides, there would be time to work on his manners after they were wed.

To be sure, big, boorish Edward would never have been fine enough for her mother, but he suited Lily's purposes extremely well. Having started near the bottom of the East India Company's private armies, years ago near Bombay, he had saved the life of visiting British dignitary Lord Fallow in the midst of a bloody raid by Pindari bandits.

After Edward saved him from certain torture and death, Lord Fallow had repaid Edward's act of courage by helping him to advance in life through his steady patronage, and over the course of twenty years he had ascended into the highest ranks of the East India Company. But although he had grown rich in the process, Edward still found himself rejected by most of Society on account of his low birth.

Well, Lord Fallow had no intention of seeing his favorite shut out. Upon his recent retirement from public life, the earl had pushed through Edward's appointment to some important parliamentary committee so powerful that now everyone had to accept him.

He had been thrust into Society but now that he was in, God knew he needed all the help he could get to show him how to go about. What better ally could he hope for, Lily reasoned, than a bride whose aristocratic lineage was sufficient to impress the most arrogant nobs of London?

Of course, the ton would think that she was throwing herself away on Edward Lundy, but Lily had secrets to hide, and with her great family sliding into financial decline, to her it seemed a match made in Heaven.

Edward had money and Lily had class. He wasn't stupid, but he was very rich, and as a lowborn man on the rise, he needed a pedigreed bride, just as she needed him—a fair exchange. Because of that Lily found herself able to trust him—at least more than she could have trusted the silky, highborn rakehells who trawled the ballrooms of London looking for young ladies to corrupt.

Experience had taught her all too well to despise such men. Edward might be lowborn, but he treated Lily like a jewel, or like some sort of fragile porcelain figurine. Perhaps just a little in awe of her because of her loftier status and the aura of cool dignity that her mother had ingrained in her so well, he kept a reverent and respectful distance, and this pleased Lily very well. He did not touch her, and she did not want to be touched.

As he complimented her on the sparkly pink gown that was part of her fairy-queen costume, Lily noticed the knot of guests nearby casting haughty looks in their direction.

Edward followed her glance and took note, glaring them into silence. They obeyed the silent warning, hastily turning away, and Lily was pleased. Some in the ton might make fun of Edward when they thought he wasn't listening, but few dared openly cross the ruthless, self-made millionaire. When his Cockney came out and his military background showed, everyone knew they had better stand clear, for this bull would not hesitate to put his head down and charge.

Nevertheless, though Edward was as thick-skinned as his bullish disguise suggested, Lily knew every social cut he received had to hurt to some degree. He was fiercely determined to make these people respect him, and marrying her was simply part of his strategy.

For her part, she hated seeing the great raw fellow targeted as an object of sport by people born to wealth and privilege, people who had no idea what it meant to be poor.

It infuriated her and made her all the more determined to help Edward gain acceptance. It was the least she could do in exchange for his gold.

He looked at her ruefully as the now-cowering aristocrats slunk away. She gave him a wry smile in answer.

Almost at once, the silence turned awkward. Edward dropped his head and looked away, then he beckoned to a footman, who leaped to fetch him another tall tankard of ale. Lily didn't ask how many he had already drunk before she had arrived, but she noted that his eyes were fairly red. Edward liked his drink.

"Nice party, isn't it?" she inquired in a tentative voice.

"Right, er, yes. Very nice."

A pause.

"Glad to see the weather held. I thought it might rain."

"Perhaps tomorrow."

"Yes." Edward cleared his throat, Lily looked at the ceiling, and while they waited for the footman to return, their stilted conversation petered out entirely.

Edward cracked his knuckles, scanning the ballroom with a dark look, his big horns gleaming, and suddenly Lily wondered if something was bothering him. She recalled him saying that his committee was to have held some sort of important hearing today. Perhaps it had gone badly.

Chasing off a twinge of intense curiosity, she eyed him askance, but obviously it was improper for a young lady to display an interest in worldly affairs.

She dropped her gaze, unable to invent any new topic of discussion. As the excruciating silence stretched, she sent Mrs. Clearwell a pleading look—the bubbly woman was never at a loss for words, after all—but this time her sponsor let her flounder, smiling sweetly.

The silence dragged.

Oh, this was intolerable!

She longed to escape into the dark tranquillity of the garden. How lovely it would be to visit the garden folly right now!

Of course, it was not the sort of thing she could possibly

invite Edward to do with her. He would no doubt misinterpret her intentions, and that was the last thing she desired.

At least he showed no signs of requesting a dance. The last time they had attempted it, he had blithely flung and thrown and hurled her around the dance floor like a ragdoll. She had been lucky to come out of it with no broken bones.

At last, the footman brought the fresh tankard of ale and Edward immediately began guzzling it. In moments he would need another, at this rate. Goodness, Lily thought, watching him in trepidation, maybe something really was bothering him tonight.

At that moment, praise Heaven, a distraction arrived in the form of Edward's large, eccentric mother.

Mrs. Lundy sailed into their midst and saved the day with her usual garrulousness. "Oh, don't you look *beautiful,* my dear, dear Miss Balfour! Isn't she lovely, Edward? Oh, you are so fair! Good Lud, if I were half as pretty as you when I was young, I should have run positively wild! Goodness, why must it be so hot in here? Mrs. Clearwell, it's so much cooler on the terrace." While the big jolly nabob lady patted her face and fleshy throat with a handkerchief, beaming, though slightly out of breath with the exertions of her usual rapid speech and animated nature, Lily could not help gazing in wonder at her costume.

Bright turquoise robes swathed Mrs. Lundy's round bulk, but it was the woman's headgear that drew the eye. She wore a turban piled with artificial fruits: bananas, oranges, even a small pineapple poking up from the apex of her head, while large, gaudy earrings swung from her earlobes.

Meanwhile, she charged right on with her speech, barely taking a breath. "Hang me, have you ever seen a more elegant home? I am very sure that I have not. Very sure, indeed! Now, then, don't forget, tomorrow, one o'clock—you are both still coming over to help me plan the garden party, yes?"

"Yes, of course," Lily started.

"Thank heavens! Excellent! One o'clock it is, then.

Good, good. After all, this is to your benefit, as well, ain't it, dearie?" she added with a wink and a nudge that nearly knocked Lily over.

Lily stammered out an incoherent reply, her blush deepening, but the woman's point was well taken.

The social-climbing Lundys were hosting their first Society event, and with Lily and Mrs. Clearwell acting as helpers for the garden party, the ton would take note and begin linking Lily's name with Edward's. It was a respectable and discreet way to begin hinting at the possibility of a future connection between two unmarried persons.

"Then, my dear ladies, you will see all the elegance that I have planned for my bon voyage party! Everything is to be in the first, *first* stare. Extremely elegant, I can promise you that!"

"I am sure," Mrs. Clearwell said with amusement, barely concealing her irony, but Lily frowned.

"Bon voyage? I thought it was to be a garden party."

"Oh, yes—well—now it will be both, dear!"

"Where are you going away to?" Lily asked in surprise.

"Jamaica!" Mrs. Lundy pointed emphatically to her tropical fruit–laden headwear and let out a burst of laughter. "Couldn't you tell?"

"No," Lily and Mrs. Clearwell murmured in unison.

"Well, now you know! I can hardly believe it myself, to tell the truth! Me, in the lovely West Indies! I have never been there, you know—Jamaica. I have never been anywhere! Hang me, I've barely been outside of Middlesex, but my doctor says that it will benefit my health exceedingly to spend the winter in the islands. Oh, but I'm sure it will be too unbearably hot."

"Ocean breezes, Mum."

"Yes, Eddie, I know that's what you say, but—"

"I had no idea that you were unwell," Lily interrupted in concern. "Is there anything that we can do?"

"Oh, how kind you are, my dear! Such a lady, to the core. No, no. It is only *the gout*," she explained in a loud whisper. "No great cause for alarm."

"Thank goodness for that."

"Quite so," Mrs. Clearwell agreed.

"My doctor said that if my dear Eddie can afford to send his old Mum off to the tropics to escape the whole blasted winter here, then, why not?"

"Why not, indeed?" With a squeal of laughter, an intruder flung herself into their midst.

"Bess!" Mrs. Lundy exclaimed.

"I'm coming to the islands with you, no, I am, honestly!" As the tall, strapping girl threw her arms around Mrs. Lundy, Edward heaved a drooping sigh, well aware that he was the real target of her attentions.

Lily knew it, too, and clenched her teeth.

The daughter of a wealthy merchant who had lately bought himself a baronetcy, Bess Kingsley was not accustomed to being denied. Unluckily for her, not even Edward was dull enough to find the loud, spoiled, vulgar girl attractive. Unluckily for him, however, the more he tried to flee her, the more doggedly Bess chased.

She now positioned her rude self in front of Lily, deliberately blocking her out of the conversation.

Lily sent her chaperone a dry look. Mrs. Clearwell's eyes danced as if to say, *Now there's a perfect match!*

Not feeling the need to stay and vie for Edward's attentions, Lily excused herself from the group with a discreet murmur and took leave of them with a graceful nod.

Turning away, she walked at a sedate pace toward the grand curved staircase. In truth, she was glad to have a break.

Upon walking upstairs, she found the silk-hung ladies' lounge mobbed. Barely able to get to the looking glass, she checked her appearance as best she could, pleased by her whimsical costume with its pink tulle skirts dotted with silver sequins here and there. There was nothing particularly fairy-queenish about it, really, but it was pretty and light and it made her happy.

She took care to check the clasps on the diamond earrings she wore tonight, for they represented some of the last of the Balfour family jewels that had not yet been pawned for blunt. Carefully, Lily pressed the back on each earring, making sure they were securely fastened. The earrings were three generations old and had a tendency to come loose. If she lost one, she would never forgive herself.

Escaping the crush in the ladies' lounge a moment later, she drifted over to the gallery railing along the top of the stairs and gazed down at the colorful crowd. She spotted her party and knew that Bess would not be chased away anytime soon, now that she had cornered Edward.

Her gaze wandered to the line of French doors that opened off the ballroom to the terrace beyond. Perhaps this was the perfect time to sneak out and visit the garden folly . . .

Longing to explore the moonlit garden and the grounds, with a sudden surge of boldness, she decided to chance it. She lifted the hem of her sparkly pink skirts a bit and hurried down the crowded marble staircase. She employed all the stealth she could muster, determined that none of her party should spy her and stop her from sneaking away.

But then, as she was escaping, a ripple of excited murmurs spread through the ranks of the female guests clustered on the staircase and lined up along the railing.

"No, that can't be true. He made her *weep* with pleasure?"

"I heard that her servants couldn't decide if they should leave the pair their privacy or call the constable, what with all the screaming coming from upstairs!"

"Screaming? My word!"

"She told *me* he broke her bed."

"How very—energetic!"

"He's welcome to break mine," another purred, staring down into the ballroom.

"Better not let your husband hear you say that."

"As if he'd care. He still thinks I don't know about his latest mistress, fool."

Lily tiptoed past them in shock, trying not to let the ladies notice she was eavesdropping on their indecent gossip.

Who on earth were they talking about?

"Did you hear about his tryst with Lady Campbell?"

"What? No!"

"Tell!"

"Poor dear, she couldn't even go riding with us in Hyde Park last week because of that delicious pagan."

"You don't mean—?"

"Indeed. I don't know what he did to her, but she could barely walk, let alone sit her mount that afternoon."

"Good heavens!"

Scandalized laughter.

"Trust me, dear, she didn't seem to mind it."

Astounded by their wicked talk, Lily followed the direction of the ladies' collective gaze down to the center of the ballroom, and when she spotted the source of their excitement, she halted abruptly on the stairs.

Oh—!

Oh, my.

Lifting her fingertips to her lips, Lily stood mesmerized by the dangerous-looking man who had arrived, staring right along with all the other ladies.

No wonder all the women had gone mad.

He was . . . beautiful.

Sun-browned and raven-haired, over six feet tall with an iron physique, he wore his resplendent uniform with such pride that it was clear this was no costume for the masked ball. He carried himself like a military man, too—spine erect, chest out, shoulders back, his square chin high. And the self-assurance in the way he walked—a wary glide, part strut, part saunter—seemed to suggest that, indeed, he was master of more than one kind of conquest.

"Who is he, Mary?" some woman asked her friend.

Having walked in a sort of trance down a few more of the stairs, Lily now overheard the fevered conversation of another knot of gossiping women.

"La, dear, don't you know? He's only the stud of the Season."

Giggles followed, giddy and girlish.

"Shh! Do you want the world to hear you?"

"He's Major Derek Knight," the first woman revealed in

satisfaction. "The Duke of Hawkscliffe's cousin, newly arrived from India."

India? Lily's attention was captured all over again. That cursed place that had taken her father away from her?

"Ah, the Knight family, of course."

"Gorgeous, that lot. Yes, now that you've said it, I can see the resemblance. Aren't there two of them—brothers?"

"Yes, he is the younger. The elder one never comes into Society. I've heard they are both entirely fearless, though. Countless battles."

"What is their regiment?"

"I do not know, but they're in the cavalry."

Cavalry? Lily thought with a gulp. Oh, those cavalry boys had a wild reputation. Many of them were the younger sons of aristocratic houses, well educated and chivalrous, high-living and hot-blooded, eager to do battle over any point of honor. She knew that with its bounty of blue-blooded officers, the cavalry was deemed the most glamorous of the armed forces, England's military crème de la crème.

As Major Derek Knight moved through the ballroom, everyone seemed to want to know him, drawn in by the effortless charisma he seemed to exude. Men pumped his hand enthusiastically, while women here and there bent him down to greet him with worshipful kisses on his clean-shaved cheeks. He didn't seem to mind the adulation, but he appeared a bit distracted.

His restless gaze continuously scanned the crowd with an air of single-minded intensity, like a man on the hunt, but what was the prey he sought? Lily wondered. Then quite without warning, he looked up and saw her, and she found herself captured in his steel-blue gaze.

The moment his frank stare picked her out of the crowd, Lily went motionless.

She could not move, could barely breathe.

Pinned in his watchful study, she shivered at the force of unbridled sensuality in his magnetic eyes. From halfway across the room, the heat of him seemed to engulf her.

Then the hint of a devilish smile tugged at one corner of his mouth, and she felt her knees go weak.

Good God! She stiffened, appalled at herself and her thumping heart. She had never experienced such an immediate, visceral reaction to a man before. This was entirely bewildering and more than a little unpleasant.

She decided on the spot she did not like it. Who did he think he was to smile at her? It was *not* proper. He added insult to injury then, offering her a discreet bow from across the room.

Her heart lurched, but her demeanor turned instantly frosty—a habit, a knee-jerk reaction.

How forward! Mother would have been appalled, and so was Lily. At least that's what she told herself. She tossed her chin, but could not *quite* bring herself to look away.

Her heart pounded hectically.

I do not need this, she warned herself. "Younger son" equaled "no money." She had come to London for the express purpose of finding a wealthy husband—rich and stupid!—not to be seduced by a handsome soldier whose all-too-cunning smile made no secret of what was on his wicked mind.

Don't you smile at me, she warned Major Derek Knight in silent defiance, gathering up all her hard-won morals. *You're not going to break* my *bed, I can promise you that. Not in a million years.*

Oh, no, you won't.

His knowing smile widened, his stare staying fixed on her even as another woman sidled up to him and draped her arms around his neck, whispering in his ear.

His thickly muscled arm slid around the woman's slender waist, but he went on watching Lily with a patient, brooding gaze. As if he could see through her and her disciplined charade of virginal propriety.

As if he had all the time in the world to get to her.

And he could. She knew it the moment she looked at him. She had a weakness, and if the gossip was true, he was an expert seducer. Her heart slammed behind her ribs as a doomful warning within told her this man could ruin everything for her. He was dangerous.

Dangerous, immoral, and bad.

Deliciously so.

Completely unnerved, she pulled her stare away from his and took cover in the throng of guests, fleeing toward the row of French doors that opened out onto the terrace.

Really, boots to a ball! What a barbarian! Even Edward knew that much, she thought, casting about for any reason to find fault with the "stud of the Season" and reject him.

All the while, he continued watching her with a sort of detached amusement.

Nobody else at the masked ball paid her the slightest mind as she slipped out quietly, escaping the major's keen study. Her chest heaved. She gulped great lungfuls of the chill night air, relieved to be free of his stare, and yet strangely exhilarated by it.

It was as if no one had truly seen her in years until moments ago, when Derek Knight had looked at her. Truly looked at her.

For how many years had she made it her policy to try to stay safely invisible, hiding at home at Balfour Manor behind her iron-willed mother? Why? Simply from shame?

His stare had confused her. It seemed to pierce into the very core of her and find nothing that she should be ashamed of—ah, but this skittish overreaction was utterly absurd! He didn't even know her, nor she him.

And that was for the best.

That was how it must stay.

In seconds, she had crossed the terrace and sped away into the garden, reveling in the darkness, the solitude, the cool black stillness of the night.

Hurrying past parterres and flower beds and rustling stands of trees, she sought the little garden folly that had first attracted her attention, while patchy clouds above her veiled the moon.

What a funny little person, Derek mused, but the fetching blonde had vanished into the crowd, much to his perplexity. Women running *away* from him was not exactly the reaction he was used to.

Nevertheless, he put the mysterious girl out of his mind for the moment. Lady Amherst had wrapped herself around him and was demanding his attention.

"Good evening, Major," she breathed in his ear. "You're looking . . . healthy."

"Why, thank you, my dear. I am feeling full of vigor," he murmured, flicking a mischievous glance over her well-endowed figure. She giggled, and Derek bent to accept her lingering kiss on his cheek.

From behind her pale gold half-mask, her hazy-eyed stare devoured him. The woman was practically panting.

"So, what are you supposed to be tonight?" he asked, lifting the elegant young widow's hand and taking a step back to inspect her costume, a frothy, pale confection of a gown with a plunging neckline that drew his gaze to her finest attractions.

"What do you think?" she exclaimed, nodding toward the tall, hooked staff that she carried in her other hand.

Derek shrugged indifferently.

"I'm a shepherdess, you dolt."

"I don't see any sheep."

"I brought one, a toy, but I grew bored of carrying it around."

"You might as well put this aside, then, too." He removed the tall shepherd's hook from her hand and leaned it against the nearby column. He bent closer, lowering his voice. "I've got another staff for you to play with."

She suppressed a burst of laughter, her lovely face turning red beneath its dusting of white powder. "You are so wicked!"

"That's why you love me."

"You're a heartless flirt, Major."

"Dance with me," he ordered, taking both her hands.

"No—wait. I've a better idea." With a naughty smile, she crooked her finger at him.

Derek raised an eyebrow, his interest piqued. He leaned down, listening as she whispered in his ear.

"Ah, yes. Capital notion," he murmured.

"I thought you'd like it." She tugged on his shoulder and whispered again, this time flicking his earlobe with the tip of her tongue after she had given him his instructions.

Derek quivered. "When?"

"Now, silly. You go first," she added in a sly whisper. "I'll follow you out in a few minutes. That way, no one ought to notice that we're gone."

"Oh, they'll notice," he assured her, but she tossed her head.

"I don't care! Let them talk."

Derek smiled, amused by her brash independence.

"Go," she urged him, clearly eager for her private lesson in the exotic Eastern arts of love.

Far be it from him to keep a countess waiting. Happy to oblige, Derek gave her a discreet bow and withdrew.

Marching out onto the terrace, Derek paused and scanned the night-clad grounds, then jogged down the few shallow steps to the main graveled walkway, flanked by quaint topiaries. From there, he set out to find this garden folly that his latest paramour had named as the location for their rendezvous . . .

CHAPTER
∞ FOUR ∞

Jasmine vines had scaled the dark-green boxwood walls of the garden maze and gave off sweet perfume as Lily ran past, her steps light and fleeting over the cool, silken grass. The distant sounds of tinkling music and revelers' laughter from the ball floated out over the gardens from the sprawling manor house, but she did not look back.

Slipping through the shadows, she raced across the rolling parklands with a breathless sense of liberty.

The black velvet sky brimmed with stars, and the sound of the pond's center fountain lilted in the night as she neared. By the reedy shore, a graceful little gondola bobbed gently.

There.

To her right, she spotted the garden folly silhouetted against the starry sky. Her smile grew as she ran toward it, lifting the hem of her gown to skim the grass. Reaching the structure, she stopped abruptly, heart pounding, and stood before it, slowly tipping her pale satin half-mask up over her brow to reveal an expression of childlike wonder and delight.

Magical. The garden folly had been made in the shape of a giant pineapple.

How perfectly silly!

Delightful. She shook her head to herself in pure enchantment and walked on. To be sure, the folly was very different from the one she had played in as a child—ah, but the feeling was the same. Her own little secret world.

A time of dreams and innocence . . .

Laying her hand on the railing, Lily went up its three low steps in silent, effervescent joy. Inside, she took a turn about the wood-planked floor, her sparkly pink skirts swirling about her.

All of a sudden she threw her head back and laughed aloud. The sound was light. She whirled over to the delicate railing and gazed out at the vista of the man-made lake. She thought of her father calling her "Princess Lily" and for once, the memory of him did not hurt.

Leaning wistfully against one of the columns that supported the pineapple roof, she let herself soak in the pleasure of this stolen moment, simply enjoying the lavish gardens, the sweetness of the summer night, and the tranquil solitude.

Soon enough she'd have to be getting back to Edward, but not yet.

With a pensive smile, she leaned forward and rested her elbows on the railing. As an afterthought, she pulled her mask back down into place across her eyes in case anyone came along, but her thoughts lingered in the past, lost in nostalgic reverie. What a little silly-head she had been, she mused, a dreamer just like her father.

Her imagination in those days could turn a well-situated boulder into her own Camelot, a toad into a fire-breathing dragon, and a row of acorns into a cavalry of brave knights sent out to chase the beast away. Back then, she had still believed in heroes, and had known at least three magic ways to make a wish come true.

But these had proved false, bitterly so, when they had failed to bring her father back. Broken-hearted, she had put her dreams and her wishing powers away. By now, she had forgotten her made-up incantations, and as for heroes, she had come to learn that they were even scarcer than real dragons.

No, she thought with a sigh as she gazed out over the dark landscape, the cavalry wasn't coming. No one was going to ride to her rescue. It was up to her to save her clan.

An image of Edward the Minotaur rose in her mind with

a surge of distress. Oh, if any of those silly old spells still worked . . .

Knowing it was sheer foolishness, she closed her eyes and for one moment—just for old times' sake—made a wish with all her might.

Perhaps her need floated up to the stars and out across the ornamental water, as insubstantial as dandelion fluff, but you never knew. You just never knew . . .

She listened.

She waited.

She held her breath.

Nothing.

Well, naturally.

But then—her eyes still closed—she went stock-still, suddenly sensing a presence.

Her straining ears detected the scarcely audible creaking of the floorboards behind her.

"How did you get here before me?" a deep voice asked in a playful murmur that was all of a sudden right by her ear. Her jaw dropped as warm, strong arms smoothly encircled her waist.

Her eyes flew open and she looked down in wonder. Big, sun-tanned hands had wrapped around her with a tender motion, sturdy forearms sheathed in smart sleeves with handsome, gold-trimmed cuffs.

She stared down at them, slack-jawed.

How can this be?

Her wish could not *possibly* have come true. She wasn't even sure what she had wished for! *Is this real?*

Can this be happening? The tall male form behind her certainly felt solid and powerful, radiating warmth; she leaned back slightly against him, just to make sure.

Egads, there was a man behind her!

She was in somebody's arms! And it wasn't Edward.

The air in her lungs fairly evaporated from her astonishment. She started to turn around with great indignation and then stopped abruptly, afraid the dream might dissipate. For it was then that the greatest shock of all came: the realization that it felt splendid, achingly wonderful to be held this way.

How many years had it been since someone had held her?

"You were supposed to wait, my girl," he chided in a teasing whisper, leaning down to brush his lips along the curve of her ear. "But I suppose you couldn't contain yourself, hm?"

Lily tensed, tongue-tied and quite baffled. Her heart was slamming in her chest, just above the cloud of butterflies dancing in her belly.

Oh, dear.

It struck her with some nervous hilarity that her visitor obviously had the wrong lady and hadn't quite noticed it yet. Ah, yes—costume ball. Oh, how exceedingly awkward. Perhaps she should have been outraged, but his touch felt so, *so* good.

The big, sun-tanned hands had begun slowly stroking her bare arms, up and down, seductively. She swallowed hard and succumbed to a violent shudder. *Goodness.* His touch bespoke total self-assurance, and if there was any doubt left in her mind who had captured her, it fled when she caught the faint whiff of some exotic incense that clung to his uniform. Sandalwood, maybe.

Just arrived from India . . .

Dear Lord, she was out here alone with "the stud of the Season."

Major Derek Knight.

"So, are you going to kiss me or what?" he whispered, and Lily simply melted at the question. Her heated blood and her heart answered in reckless unison—*how could she not?*

This was madness.

She was not the woman he had come out to meet, but he had her full attention at the moment, and, God help her, her attraction to him was painfully acute. Oh, yes. In that moment, she made the conscious decision to let him do it if he wished. How wicked, how wonderful, what a perfect dream to be kissed by a handsome stranger in the moonlight, a bold hero from faraway lands—just this once, taking this one chance, before she had to do her duty by her family and marry someone she could never love.

There was no danger of him finding out who she really was—she wore a mask! she reasoned above the drumbeat of her clamorous pulse. Edward need never learn about this, nor anyone else in all of gossiping London. What else were masked balls made for but these kinds of naughty little adventures? It harmed no one. She could enjoy this secret, indulge the rampant curiosity this man had aroused in her on sight, and keep this memory locked away to get her through the cold, long years ahead.

Just this once . . .

With a gentle pressure on her waist, Major Knight began turning her around. She yielded willingly to his guiding touch, her pulse a staccato. When she faced him, she looked up and, oh, yes, to be sure, it was he—Derek Knight, conjured from a dream, looking truly like the embodiment of every woman's fantasies.

Now that they were so close, she could appreciate how impossibly handsome the man really was. Her gaze traveled over his chiseled face with its marvelous, strong bone structure. His eyebrows were thick and black, gracefully feathered, his sculpted lips fashioned for temptation. Most magical of all, however, were those magnetic eyes, piercing, pale blue-silver in the night and full of mystery. She looked into their glittering depths and saw the moment that Derek Knight realized his mistake.

He furrowed his brow, moving back slightly, then one eyebrow shot up as he stared at her in amazed recognition. "You!" he breathed.

Lily smiled mischievously at him, and his fine lips parted in surprise, a flash of white teeth in the darkness. He let out a soft laugh. "What a fortunate mistake!"

"Not who you were expecting, Major?" she taunted, lifting her chin.

"Better. Much better." His potent glance skimmed downward over her, but he seemed hesitant about coming close again. Somehow she found his sudden caution endearing.

"I saw you on the stairs," he informed her.

"I know. You were staring."

He frowned at her in mock reproach. "You ran from me."

Lily held his gaze. "Well, I'm not running now."

"Who are you?" Derek whispered, entirely bewitched. He couldn't take his eyes off her.

She shrugged her delicate shoulders and leaned back a bit against the railing behind her, swinging the folded fan that dangled from a strap around her wrist. "Nobody in particular."

"Oh, I don't believe that," he murmured in frank admiration, mesmerized by her languid motion and suddenly longing to kiss that elegant wrist. "Have you got a name?"

She favored him with a coy smile. "Of course I do."

"I see. But you're not going to tell me what it is."

She shook her head, her eyes dancing behind her pale-colored half-mask. "It wouldn't really matter, would it?"

"Why do you say that?"

"Your fame precedes you."

"Hm," he said sardonically, realizing that could mean any number of things. Still, Derek found himself charmed by her refusal to tell him her name. Any sort of denial from a female was indeed a novelty. Back in the ballroom, her beauty had first arrested his attention, but now that they were face-to-face, he quite liked her sly confidence and her air of cool grace.

He folded his arms across his chest and studied her in roguish fascination. "You seem to have the advantage of me."

"Yes. Major Derek Knight, newly arrived from India."

"I'll be going back there soon," he replied with a nod, offering the information as a pretty bald hint that if she wanted to know him, she'd better act fast and cough up her name.

"Why?" she inquired.

"Fortune and glory, love. Same as any man, Miss—?"

She shook her head slowly.

"Stubborn," he murmured, smiling. "Very well, then. Keep your lovely self a secret if you must." If he had to kiss it out of her, he'd learn her name eventually, but for the moment, he could enjoy playing along with her flirtatious game. Indeed, this whole situation appealed to the naughtier side of his nature, arriving for an illicit tryst only to find the garden folly already occupied.

Must be a popular spot.

He angled a discreet glance casually over his shoulder, but he saw no sign yet of a jealous suitor on the way, nor of his own companion for the night. He was suddenly in no hurry for Lady Amherst to arrive.

It wouldn't be long before she appeared, but in the meantime, Derek decided he certainly would not mind tasting this lovely vixen if he could get away with it—a most intriguing savory, a dainty hors d'oeuvre before the main dish.

He assumed she was here for the same reason he was, an illicit garden tryst, and he concluded without much thought on the matter that she must be either a widow like Lady Amherst or some ancient peer's neglected young wife.

Either way, she was fair game.

What a beauty. He let his stare travel over her in rich pleasure. The moonlight kissed her pale blond tresses with a white-gold glow, her upswept coiffure the height of elegance, with a few alluring tendrils kissing the curve of her neck. Above the floating cloud of her sequined skirts, her bodice drew his appreciative gaze to her slender waist and sweet round breasts, a lush, enticing body full of sensual promise. If he wasn't mistaken, she seemed to fancy him, too, the inviting arch of her body sending him cues that hinted at her willingness to let him come closer—despite, of course, her refusal to tell him her name.

Well, he could hardly blame her for that, he thought wryly. Mistaking her for another woman had not exactly helped him make a good impression. He felt a bit foolish for his mistake, but she did not appear offended.

"No costume for the masked ball, Major?"

"I would never misrepresent myself as something I'm not. What you see is what you get."

"Ah, an honest man? Fancy that."

"Brutally honest, according to my sister. Why do you sound so skeptical?" he inquired. "Haven't you met many honest men, Miss—?" he prompted, fishing for her name again.

"Nonesuch," she supplied with a lift of her chin. "Mary Nonesuch. At your service."

"Mary Nonesuch?" he echoed dryly, shaking his head at her cheeky jest. "Very well, then, Miss Nonesuch. As you stand there and lie to me with such a pretty smile, I suppose you're going to tell me that all men are liars?"

"Not all, perhaps, but certainly some."

"At least you're a fair-minded nonesuch."

"Major," she said softly.

Some breathy note in her voice brought all his senses to attention. "Yes, lovely?"

"Are you going to kiss me or not?" she whispered. "I don't have all day."

He stared at her, riveted.

Impertinent minx, throwing his own impertinent words back to him! Words intended for Lady Amherst.

Well, maybe he *was* a bit of a liar, because if he was perfectly honest, he would have to admit that this beautiful stranger's cautious smile turned him inside out.

No, he did not know her name. But if she thought that little mask concealed the hunger in her eyes, she was wrong. Her mask hid nothing, not from him. Nor did her practiced air of cool bravado. He saw her uncertainty, felt her longing to be touched; he sensed her trembling need and realized how much courage it had taken for her to utter her seemingly nonchalant request.

She wanted a kiss? he mused. Then she must have one.

He would give her a kiss she would never forget.

His pulse throbbing, Derek closed the space between them with one step, cupped her face between his hands, and captured her mouth hungrily with his own.

* * *

As his warm, silken lips caressed hers, Lily wrapped her arms around Derek Knight in a mix of helpless craving and wild relief. His kiss blurred the lines between reality and fantasy, but if this was naught but a decadent dream, then why did she feel wide awake for the first time in years?

Freedom sang through her veins. Joy thrummed along every tingling nerve ending. All the while, she could not believe she was doing this.

His hand curved tenderly around her nape, his gentle touch so skilled and reassuring it could have melted the defenses of the most reluctant maiden. His lips beguiled hers slowly, moving back and forth with such determined coaxing that she tilted her head back farther and parted her lips for the velvet stroke of his tongue. Her pulse was a reckless rhythm as she clung to him. She could feel his mighty heart pounding against her chest.

His desire was all-encompassing as he ravished her mouth, transporting her to a state of dazed delight. When his palm inched down her side and his fingers clasped her hip, she caressed the back of his hand, unsure herself if she was trying to stop him or urging him on.

She wanted this so badly, even though she knew that she should not. As his tongue glided against hers in warm, seductive expertise, heady intoxication bloomed inside her, clamorous want and throbbing confusion. The fiery need that rose up from the depths of her being took her completely off guard.

For so long she had managed to ignore the lonely ache to be touched, caressed, held. *Just like this. So dangerous.* He seemed to know exactly what her body yearned for. Her senses exalted in the masculine solidity of his broad chest pressed against her womanly softness. Her tongue reveled in his virile taste. She molded her hands over his massive shoulders adorned with the gold epaulets, and a moan escaped her as he lifted her up without warning and set her on the railing behind her, his hips crushing the tulle of her skirts as he pressed closer into the angle of her parting thighs.

He left her gasping his name as his wayward mouth descended along the side of her neck. She stroked his chest and flat stomach while his kisses traveled down the neckline of her dress. *Oh, God.* This was growing hotter and quickly going further than she had anticipated, but she could not compel herself to stop.

She raked her fingers through his silky black hair, mussing the neat queue that bound it. He didn't seem to mind, focused as he was on exploring her cleavage. This was a man who knew exactly what he wanted.

Entranced by his passion, she let him play. Dizzy with pleasure, she wrapped one hand around the nearby post and braced herself, arching against him slightly. He groaned down into the valley between her breasts. "Oh, God, don't do that," he said swiftly.

"Don't you like it?"

"I like it—far too much." He straightened up again and cupped her face between his hands, gently drinking once more from her lips.

Lily was on fire. The tender way he touched her now made her want to tear him apart.

"Let's get out of here," he suggested in a husky murmur. "There's a boat over there. I could take you out on the lake."

She looked into his flaming eyes and longed with all her heart to go with him. What did he mean by "take you," exactly? she wondered. In any case, she didn't dare. "I-I don't think that's a very good idea."

" 'Course it is." He gave her a smoldering half-smile, still panting a little. "I'll row, you navigate."

That smile was so hard to resist.

"Major, you don't *row* a gondola," she informed him, struggling for clarity, and fighting the urge to grab the delicious pagan and kiss him again. "You push it. With a pole."

"Right. Forgot."

Still breathless, Lily snapped her fan open and began

waving it in a valiant effort to cool her blood. "I believe it also involves some singing—in Italian."

"Singing? Now that falls beyond the call of duty."

"You won't sing for me?"

"You won't even tell me your name. Which is very cruel of you. Besides, I can't sing and I don't know a word of Italian. Only a little Latin—and *tempus fugit,* darling," he said urgently. *Time flies.* "If you're game for this, we've got to hurry."

"Oh, I forgot. You have a prior engagement," she teased in mild reproach, brushing off a twinge of jealousy.

"I can cancel, believe me. Let's go before she shows up. We'll sail off to the other side of the lake. And take a moonlight swim. *Naked,*" he specified with a smoldering look.

She laughed at the playful emphasis he gave the word, though she got the feeling that he was quite serious.

"You are a thoroughgoing rogue, aren't you? Major!" she suddenly exclaimed as he lifted her off the railing and swept her into his arms. "Put me down," she scolded half-heartedly.

"No. I am taking you with me," he announced, carrying her across the garden folly. "Somebody's got to help you escape, after all."

"Escape what?"

"You tell me. All I know is I'm here to rescue you."

"What makes you think I need rescuing?"

He snorted. Was it so obvious? "You can't have been enjoying yourself at the ball very much if you were out here," he pointed out.

"Well, you've got me there. For heaven's sake, put me down!" she ordered, laughing as he carried her across the garden folly. "I cannot possibly go for a moonlight swim with you. However intriguing your proposition might sound, I can't. I have to go back."

He stopped and looked at her, still holding her in his arms. "To whom?"

Lily just sighed.

"Husband? Lover?"

"Derek? Darling? Where are you?" A female voice softly

calling his name interrupted just then from somewhere in the garden, fair warning that they were about to have company.

Good God, Lily thought, realizing belatedly the danger to her reputation.

"Damn," said the major under his breath.

"Put me down!" Lily whispered.

He obeyed, but held onto her wrist. "Wait."

"Let me go before we're seen! I have to get back to the ballroom!"

"At least tell me your name," he insisted softly. "I want to see you again."

"No." Lily blanched behind her mask. "I can't."

"Why not?"

"I just—can't."

He stared at her. Lily gazed at him imploringly.

Awareness hummed between them, but when he reached out and took the edge of her satin mask gently between his fingers, intent on stripping it away, Lily stopped him in distress, laying a hand over his. "No."

She needed her mask more than he knew.

"So, you're just going to walk away and I never get to see you again? You won't tell me your name. If you won't let me see your face without that silly mask, then in future days, I could walk right past you and not even know who you are."

"I'm sorry. It's for the best."

His eyes asked why, but he shook his head and shrugged off what he apparently interpreted as a rejection of *him.* "Very well. Suit yourself."

"Derek, darling, are you there?" His companion was not yet in sight, but they both could hear her coming closer through the garden.

Lily sent a guilty glance in the direction of the woman's voice. Good God, if the lady discovered her out here alone with the "stud of the Season" it could lead to universal gossip, ruin, and the wreck of all her marriage plans. Failure. How would she ever explain it to Mother?

When she turned back to him in panic, he was staring at

her, as though memorizing every detail of what he could see of her face, her hair. She shook her head to discourage him and mouthed a regretful, *"No!"*

Then she yanked her hand out of his light hold and fled.

Derek furrowed his brow, watching his lovely mystery girl race away.

Everything in him wanted to chase, but he knew it would only upset her, and besides, still stung and rather put out by her rejection, he did not grovel and plead for any female.

She turned a boxwood corner by the maze, and even after she had disappeared, he remained mystified. What an eccentric young lady!

No doubt she was trouble. Her secrecy made him suspect she was some sort of schemer. She certainly seemed to have something to hide.

So, very well, then, she wanted no part of him. No matter, Derek thought with a snort. He had plenty of others to choose from.

He wasn't sure why he had bothered to use that final moment with her to memorize the details of her that were visible despite the mask: the exact wheat-blond shade of her hair, the elegant line of her neck, the shape of her honey-sweet lips, and the winsome curve of her smile. Now he had it, and God, she was beautiful. He did not think he could ever forget the likes of her.

Indeed, he might well know her the next time they passed each other in Society—though, no doubt, she would try to hide from him.

For his part, irked by her rejection, he wasn't sure how he'd react—if he would pretend to have no idea who she was or reveal his knowledge secretly and torment her with it for a bit of roguish sport.

The latter option was a lot more his style.

"Derek! Oh, darling!"

He let out a low, rather bored sigh as Lady Amherst's voice drew closer. He pondered escaping before she found him, but then, suddenly, a tiny sparkle on the floor of the garden folly caught his eye.

It lay glinting below the railing where he and "Mary Nonesuch" had nearly lost themselves in passion.

He walked over to the place, his gaze homing in on a small metallic object. He crouched down to pick it up.

Well, well, what have we here?

He dusted it off a little, held it up between his thumb and forefinger, and inspected the sparkling orb by moonlight—a diamond earring. Oh, yes, he recognized this little bauble. He had nearly swallowed it while kissing her ear. He quivered at the still-fresh memory of caressing her sweet little earlobe with the tip of his tongue.

Did she even realize yet that she had lost it?

Oh, how panicked she would be!

A sly grin spread across Derek's face as he realized what this meant, this little clue his mystery girl had unwittingly left behind. Sooner or later, she would realize her jewel was missing and then the frantic hunt for it would begin, a hunt that would force her to retrace her steps and lead her right back to him.

She knew who he was, after all. He wore no mask and was not difficult to find. A low, wicked laugh escaped him. *Oh, this ought to be amusing.* If she wanted it, then she could jolly well come and get it, he thought. But of course, if she wanted it back, she'd have to ask him nicely.

"There you are!" At that moment, the countess appeared.

As she ran to him, he slipped the sparkly earring into his pocket.

She was none the wiser. "Darling—at last!" He smiled at her, but when she embraced him, he glanced over her head in distraction. Far away across the garden, he saw a bit of pink go flitting into the house. The quality of his smile grew warmer, richer.

Good. She was safely inside once again. His mystery girl had gained the terrace and disappeared through the French doors into the ballroom. *But to whom?*

To whom did she belong?

Lucky bastard.

"Derek?"

"Hm?" Snapping back to attention, he turned to Lady Amherst and found her studying him at close range, her face etched with suspicion.

She pulled back and cocked her head, propping one hand on her waist.

"Something wrong?" he asked, all innocence.

Lady Amherst swept the area of the garden folly with a wary glance, then looked at him, one slender eyebrow arching high.

"Darling," she said as her gaze traveled over his mussed hair and thoroughly kissed lips, "what exactly have you been doing out here?"

CHAPTER
∽ FIVE ∽

*L*ily awoke the next morning after a long night of tossing and turning. She had no sooner opened her eyes than all the worries and fears that had kept her up nearly till dawn came rushing back. Her first thought was of Derek Knight; the second, of her missing earring.

She had been in an absolute tizzy since the horrifying moment she had come home from the masked ball, started to undress, and realized it was gone.

In the dead of night, Mrs. Clearwell's servants had helped her search the carriage and the floors all along the route that she had taken upon walking in the front door of her chaperone's cozy house in Mayfair, up the stairs to the little bedchamber that she'd been assigned. But none of their efforts located the diamond, and Lily was sure that she had lost it at the masked ball.

Indeed, her worst fear was that she had lost it at the garden folly—probably as divine punishment for her secret tryst with Derek Knight! She swore to herself that if not for her missing earring, she could make herself forget him in a trice. Unfortunately, now there was actual *evidence* out there somewhere, hard proof that she had been in an unsanctioned, unchaperoned location making mischief with a man whom she was not even supposed to know. Good God, how could she have courted ruin like this, flirted with disaster? Was she mad?

She could only pray that the major or somebody else might have found her lost jewel and had turned it in to their hosts of last night, Mr. and Mrs. Brooks. The sentimental value alone made the earring priceless, but even if it were an ordinary diamond, she could never afford to replace it.

Later today, during decent visiting hours, she would check in with the Brookses to ask if anyone had found the jewel, but the first order of business was her promised visit to Edward's house to help Mrs. Lundy plan her garden party. *Oh, Lord.*

Lily sighed, staring up at the ceiling, her forearm cast across her brow. She hoped it was easier to face Edward today than it had been last night when she had returned to the ballroom after kissing Derek Knight.

Her half-mask had been worth its weight in gold at that moment, for she was sure her guilt had been written all over her face. As far as she could tell, Edward hadn't noticed anything amiss, thanks in part to his indulgence in drink and his distracted mood over the committee hearing.

Meanwhile, the major must have remained outside with his lady friend, for she did not see him in the ballroom again.

She hoped that today, visiting Edward's grand castle-house, it would be easier to act naturally with her beau. All the same, she had better get herself in hand.

Pushing up from her alcove bed, she crossed her quaint little chamber with its soft pastel wallpaper and light chintz curtains and poured some water from the pitcher into the washing bowl. Then she bent and slowly splashed her face, trying to wake herself up, still musing on all that had occurred.

How strange it was that she had fancifully wished for a way out of marrying Edward, and Derek Knight had appeared. But she scoffed at herself. No doubt if the major ruined her, that would put an end to her marrying Edward!

Not exactly what she'd had in mind.

She reached for a towel and patted her face dry, then frowned at herself in the mirror, noting the dark circles under her eyes. After a night of sleepless worry, she was still in a state of dread over being found out, either by the major himself learning her identity or the insatiable gossips of the ton catching wind of their kiss. What the blazes had come over her last night? How could she have taken such risks, especially knowing how narrowly she had escaped ruin once before?

Sometimes she felt as if her whole life were a lie, but Derek Knight seemed to see through her. An honest man.

"Brutally honest, according to my sister."

Lily snorted as she recalled his words. They sounded nice, but she didn't trust him any farther than she could have thrown the big warrior. There was no way she would have taken off her mask last night even if he'd begged her.

Certainly she had reason to fear that he might still discover who she was, for if he did and was not a gentleman, there were all sorts of horrid ways he could use the knowledge against her. Blackmail her into doing whatever he liked . . .

Lily shuddered—not just from dread—and threw the towel aside in self-disgust. What a fool she was! What a wanton fool.

Kissing Derek Knight, she had dangled her future, her good name, and the welfare of her family off the side of a blasted precipice—and yet, for some reason, she could not even muster the proper good sense to regret it.

Gruesome dreams of war besieged his sleep.

Derek's head thrashed slightly against his pillow, his muscles clenching beneath the light sheet.

The damned cart kept breaking. In the middle of the battlefield. He had to get . . . something to . . . someone. Supplies, maybe, to the men. But the terrified horses wouldn't cooperate and the damned wheels kept getting blown off the supply wagon.

He could fix it, he told himself. He could fix anything, he was the handiest chap in the regiment, but the journey was endless, and Derek was near his wits' end with the knowledge that he was getting nowhere.

Nowhere.

All the while, the cannons roared so loud he couldn't

hear himself think, and the men couldn't hear his orders so they'd damned well better know what to do on their own. Had he trained them well enough? What if they could not survive without him? They could barely breathe with all the smoke and here he was, fixing a damned supply wagon wheel in the middle of a battle! Why wouldn't anyone help him?

He looked around through the hellish clouds of black powder smoke to get a hand with the stupid wagon, and instead he turned just in time to see a young private get his leg blown off. He choked back a shout, his first thought to get the kid into the wagon. Then he was racing toward the boy. He could hear him screaming through the clouds of smoke but he couldn't find him, and then all of a sudden he realized he was unarmed.

Jesus Christ, how could I have forgotten my sword at a time like this?

He awoke with a horrified start and shot up in bed, reaching about automatically for a weapon. His bleary eyes flicked open, his chest heaving as his panicked glance swept the room. Only then did he see that he was not in his tent and recall that he was not at the war, and there were no Marathas trying to kill him today.

Not here.

London.

Right.

God. He shut his eyes again briefly, rubbed his face, blew out a weary exhalation, and did his best to shake off the clinging confusion of sleep. It was only a dream. The same damned one as usual.

He shuddered, dragging his hand slowly through his tangled hair.

Lady Amherst slept on peacefully beside him, oblivious to his private hell.

Derek leaned back against the headboard, tousle-haired and bare-chested, the sheet falling across his naked hips.

Striving to get his bearings once more in reality, he idly scratched his jaw in need of a shave, but the ugly images still lingered in his brain. To distract himself, he turned his weary attention to the woman beside him, the sound of her soft snores. He stared at her in detachment.

Her voluptuous curves still drew his admiration by the flat gray light of morning, but Lady Amherst's face was buried in the pillow, hidden by her hair. Her tranquil slumber left him feeling all the more alone.

The evidence of their sport, meanwhile, lay scattered around his chamber. Strewn clothes everywhere. The small bottle of exotic fragranced oil that he had caressed into her skin and she his. Empty wine bottles. Candles that had melted into little pools, now solid disks of wax.

She had indulged his every whim and satisfied him down to the very bottom of the well, but if he'd had his fill of her last night, then why did he awaken feeling empty once again?

Derek gave a quiet sigh, then looked around, restless and uneasy until he spotted his discarded waistcoat on the floor beside the bed.

He reached down and fished the mystery girl's diamond earring out of the inside pocket. Reclining in his bed again, the sight of it sparkling like a star in the palm of his hand, the memory of "Mary Nonesuch" brought back a wistful trace of a smile to his lips.

Damned minx, who the blazes was she? And what had she been doing out there at the garden folly, anyway, if not waiting for her lover? He did not know. Nor could he explain why he cared or why the thought of her afforded cool relief like a soothing poultice for his wounded mind.

I'm going to find you, whoever you are, he thought, maybe too impatient to wait for her to come to him. He didn't even know her name, yet somehow he felt closer to that elusive nymph than he did to the woman in his bed.

When he caught a sudden whiff of Purnima's cooking, his stomach rumbled on cue for breakfast. Derek cast the sheet aside, taking care not to disturb his bedmate.

He rose and stepped into a pair of loose white drawers. As he tied the drawstring at his waist, he paused, startled by the lightly bruised teeth-marks that Lady Amherst had left on his stomach—a distinct love bite right by his navel. Egads, he had forgotten about that.

With a cynical twist of a smile, he shrugged on a loose banyan robe of dark-toned silk, then left his chamber silently, closing the door behind him.

He had things to do and, in truth, no real desire to be here when his latest conquest awoke, if he could avoid it. Not that he was trying to escape a conversation, but as a general rule, experience had taught him that the more discreetly he could take leave of his lovers, the smoother such partings went. He liked to keep things simple, make a clean break. He intended to get his day under way and pay a call on Lord Sinclair, the chairman of the committee.

He hoped that today the pompous earl would be able to tell him how soon the navy transports would set sail for India with the army's gold.

"Good day, sahib!"

Derek hushed Aadi with haste, glancing over his shoulder at the closed chamber door as his servant came hurrying toward him. No need to wake the tigress. "Morning, Aadi," he answered in a low tone. "Breakfast ready yet?"

"Yes, Major. Your bath, too. We, ah, presumed you would be going out this morning."

"Quite," Derek said ruefully, grateful that his loyal staff knew the routine. "You, er, will look after the lady for me when she wakes? See that she has all she needs after I've gone?"

"Oh, yes, sahib. As always."

Derek raised an eyebrow at his servant's cheeky bow, but he stepped past the Indian, following his nose toward the kitchen.

"Major, what shall I tell the lady if she asks us where you've gone?" Aadi asked after him in Bengali, nodding toward his closed chamber door.

"Oh, I don't know, tell her I've gone off on army business," he answered in his servant's native tongue and shrugged. "Tell her whatever you like, just make sure she's gone by the time I get back. Don't get too close, mind you," he warned with a sly glance over his shoulder as he walked

off down the hall, his loose robe flowing out behind him.
"She bites."

Before long, he was dressed and fed and striding down
Piccadilly, headed for Lord Sinclair's elegant Town mansion. He went on foot because it wasn't far and, admittedly,
he was keen to kill some extra time while his servants
worked on sending Lady Amherst on her way.

Pausing on the street corner, he ignored a newsboy selling papers and paced as he waited for a crowded stagecoach to rumble by. It was then that he noticed a florist's
shop behind him. Derek suddenly paused, turned, and
walked in.

He ordered flowers for the Brookses to express his
thanks for the invitation to the masked ball, but in truth,
his gentlemanly courtesy served a double purpose. While
the florist created the bouquet, Derek leaned on the shop's
counter, writing out a little note to be included with his offering.

After expressing his gratitude and complimenting his
hosts on their lavish event, a roguish smile played about his
lips as he wondered how to broach the subject of the earring. Then he dipped the quill in the ink pot and wrote:

> *I believe one of your lady guests may have lost an ear-*
> *ring in the garden, for I found such a bauble last night*
> *while admiring your grounds, but foolishly forgot to en-*
> *trust it to you before I left. Rest assured, I have the jewel*
> *in safekeeping. I presume you may hear from its rightful*
> *owner shortly. If you would be so kind as to inform me*
> *of the name and address of whatever lady lost it, I will*
> *make sure it is returned to her post-haste.*
>
> *Many thanks again for your kindness toward a new-*
> *comer to London.*
>
> *Sincerely yours,*
> *Maj. D. Knight*

Pleased with his inquiry, laughing a little under his
breath, he paid the florist and marched on to Lord Sin-

clair's. Mary Nonesuch was going to be so annoyed to find herself outwitted.

He puzzled over what her real name might be until he reached the chairman's towering residence, a venerable townhouse six stories tall, with no less than four bays of green-shuttered windows. He let himself through the black wrought-iron gate, ascended the few front stairs, and banged the brass lion-head knocker.

When the door was opened, he handed his card to the tall, white-haired butler and introduced himself with terse cordiality. "Would you please tell His Lordship that I've come on committee business?"

The butler looked at his card and then scrutinized Derek. "Very well, sir. You are here for the meeting?"

"Meeting?" Derek stared at him. "No."

"Oh! I see. Forgive me." The butler paled slightly and cleared his throat. "Please—pardon my mistake, sir."

"No matter. I am sure the earl will want to see me, in any case. I testified before the committee only yesterday," he added. He was not in the habit of explaining himself to butlers, but the man's slip, mentioning a meeting going on inside, alerted Derek that something was afoot. Best to be agreeable to win the man's trust. After all, it was in the butler's power to bar him from seeing Sinclair.

"Of course, Major. Do come in. I will advise His Lordship you are here."

"Thank you," Derek said warily, eyeing the man.

The butler still seemed a bit nervous, but Derek was admitted. He removed his hat as he stepped over the threshold, following the butler across the entrance hall's black and white marble floor to an elegant anteroom.

Here he was ordered to wait.

Something strange was going on around here, he thought with a familiar warning prickle on the back of his neck, the one he usually experienced before an ambush in the field.

So, the committee was having a meeting here in Lord Sinclair's house? What a pity he had not been invited.

While the butler went to advise His Lordship of his new caller, Derek surveyed the handsomely appointed anteroom with a growing sense of suspicion. Then he became aware of angry voices coming from upstairs.

He lifted his head and looked at the ceiling, trying to make out the muffled words of what quite sounded like an argument. The voices seemed to be coming from the room right above him.

"*Answer me!*" somebody bellowed.

Derek lifted his eyebrows as numerous voices joined the unintelligible reply. The butler must have intruded on the earl and the other gentlemen of the committee just then, for at that moment, their private argument suddenly ceased. Feeling increasingly uncomfortable, Derek took a seat on the nearby armchair and tried to look nonchalant as he waited.

A few minutes passed. He studied the room, on his guard, fully expecting the butler to come back and tell him His Lordship was not at home. Instead, when the door to the anteroom opened, it was portly old Sinclair himself who came tramping in, red-faced and seeming a bit out of sorts.

Derek rose from his seat as the earl came toward him, patting the sweat off his jowly face with a handkerchief.

"Major, m'boy, what brings you here? Haven't much time."

"Yes, sir. Thank you for seeing me." He nodded in respect, but he watched the chairman carefully. Something told him that asking about the meeting upstairs would get him nowhere. "I just wondered if you had heard yet how soon the transports might be ready to set sail for India," he said cautiously.

"What, since yesterday?" the old man snapped, rather startling him with his ill temper. "Cool your heels, lad! You're going to have to be patient. I know you cavalrymen are not known for that virtue, but there is an orderly *process* that must be observed before the funds can be released. If I were you, frankly, I'd expect delays."

"Delays?" Derek countered. "Why, sir? Is there a problem?"

"I'm not a magician, to pull a rabbit out of a hat, sir! Of course there's no problem. These things take time."

"How much time?"

"Weeks! Months? Hard to say!"

"Months?" he echoed in shock. "I . . . see."

But in truth, he did not see at all.

He could not envision any set of circumstances under which it might take *months* to send off the army's needed funds. Three million pounds had been specifically earmarked for military operations in India and was sitting in an account held by the Bank of England, waiting for the day it would be needed.

Wasn't it?

Suddenly, he had a sick sort of feeling in the pit of his stomach. His mouth went dry and he looked at old Sinclair. "Sir," he blurted out, "the men are counting on that money."

"Yes, Major, you made that very clear to us all just yesterday."

Derek cast about for any sort of logical explanation. What was Sinclair not telling him? Something was definitely wrong. "Sir, has something happened to the money?" he asked abruptly, blunt as ever, his tone grim.

The chairman looked him in the eye. "I would advise you to remember your place—Major."

"Sir?"

"I understand you are itching to get your old post back. Yes, I heard all about it. Your trouble with Colonel Montrose, the debacle at Janpur. If you ever want to be restored to your command, then you will mind your place."

Derek stared at him in guarded amazement, quite knocked down a peg by the insult. More important, he realized he had just been threatened with the loss of his career.

"I will send you word when I have news," the chairman said gruffly as he turned away and marched toward the door.

"My lord?" Derek took a single step in his direction.

"What?" the portly old politician shot back, pausing to glare at him.

Derek faltered, entirely taken aback by this unforeseen turn of events—perhaps naïvely so. *Careful.* He did not dare press his luck, for the only thing out of the man's mouth that he believed so far was the threat. "If there is, um, anything I can do to help the process along, sir, I am at your disposal."

His dutiful words and reassuring tone seemed to mollify the earl a bit, perhaps soothing his fear that the colonial savage was intent on causing trouble.

"Very wise, Major. Nothing now." The earl cleared his throat and adopted a slightly more amenable tone. "As I said, when I know more, I will send word. Till then, you may consider yourself on leave. Amuse yourself in Town like any young man may do. I hear you are a favorite with the ladies."

Derek dropped his gaze, as stung by the remark as he would have been by another out-and-out insult.

For he saw then that this man did not take him seriously.

This man thought he was an idiot soldier. Cannon fodder, made for taking orders.

Very well. We'll just see about that. With a look of dark tranquillity, he gave the chairman a nod edged with subtle insolence. "Aye, sir."

"Good lad." The earl banged the door shut behind him; a moment later, the butler reappeared and showed Derek out.

What the hell is going on? he wondered as he walked back to Piccadilly with slower, musing strides. Clearly, something was wrong, but what? Some sort of problem with the money?

He turned the mystery over in his mind all the way back to the Althorpe, but as he approached the back gates, a gruff voice from behind him called his name.

"Major! Major Derek Knight?" It was a man's voice, Cockney-sounding. He kept his tone low, as if leery of attracting too much attention.

Derek halted, turning around in wary surprise. "Yes?"

He saw a coachman leaning against a black carriage that was parked on the other side of the street and appeared to have been there for some time. Waiting for him?

A stocky, sinewy fellow of medium height, the coachman pushed away from the vehicle, approaching Derek slowly. The long, dark Carrick coat he wore could have concealed any number of weapons, Derek noted, though it appeared the man carried only a large driver's whip for his horses. Beneath the low, scrolled brim of his black hat, he had the weathered face of a bruiser.

"Can I help you?"

"Name's Bates, sir. My master sent me to collect you."

"Collect me?" Derek echoed. *Bloody hell.* Which of his recent bedmates had failed to mention she was married? He lifted his chin. "Who is your master, and what is his business with me?"

"I work for Mr. Edward Lundy, a Company man, sir." The coachman paused. "He said you might desire to speak with him about committee business."

Derek was immediately intrigued. On the other hand, this could be a trap.

Edward Lundy's fierce-looking henchman glanced down the street, as though keeping watch out for unwanted eyes on them. "Mr. Lundy may have . . . certain information for you, Major."

"Well, then. Let's not tarry." Derek nodded gamely at him, prepared for the risk.

God knew he had plenty of experience in defending himself if somebody had something nasty planned for him. Confident in his skills with his sword and pistol, he climbed into the coach. If Lundy had information and wanted to talk, Derek was willing to listen. Who could say? He might actually get some answers. It was better than being ordered to "cool his heels" and "amuse himself in Town" like some sort of meat-headed rakehell.

'Sblood, there was a war on. His boys were in harm's way. Damned right he wanted answers if Lundy could provide them.

The coachman shut the door with an ominous bang, and in another moment, they were off.

Beyond the mullioned windows of Edward's neo-Gothic castle of a house, the golden day beckoned, clear and cool.

From where Lily sat in the great hall, she could see the jagged gray shadow of the house's towers and turrets and its pointed gables outlined across the emerald grass.

Inside, however, the interior of her future home gave her the feeling of being in a cage. Perhaps it was all those diamond-shaped mullions crisscrossing the narrow windows. The décor was dark, too, heavy and oppressive, with its Gothic theme. Cousin Pamela would no doubt have adored it, she thought. Dark paneling stretched up to a vaulted ceiling of creamy white plaster, ribbed with dark beams. The three wrought-iron chandeliers that hung down from that great height looked as if they'd been pilfered from a dungeon.

Near the yawning fireplace, the furniture grouping where the ladies convened was upholstered in deep, jewel-toned velvets, perched atop spiral-turned legs.

Clad in a demure beige visiting gown with ivory lace trim, Lily sat beside her chaperone while the exuberant Mrs. Lundy rhapsodized on her plans for the garden party.

"We shall have all manner of athletics, cricket for the gentlemen, archery for the ladies, tennis for both, oh, and bowls on the green. Perhaps you would care to see the menu for the day, Mrs. Clearwell? I've got it here."

"May I?" Lily's sponsor graciously accepted the piece of paper.

Mrs. Lundy watched her anxiously while she read it with an appraising eye, but for Lily's part, she continually had to stop herself from staring at the large, gaudy, jewel-encrusted brooch in the shape of a rooster that adorned her future mother-in-law's gown. It looked like a giant glittering insect crawling up her shoulder. The hideous thing was probably worth a fortune. ·

"You may have a spot of trouble with the ice cream if the

day is overwarm," Mrs. Clearwell warned. "The almond chicken sounds lovely. And the salad."

"Oh, thank you for saying so!" Mrs. Lundy patted her sweating cheek with a handkerchief. "I *so* want everything to be perfect, for Eddie's sake. He works so hard, you know."

He was working now and could not be disturbed, closeted away in his study in another region of the sprawling house.

Lily didn't mind. She would just as soon not see her suitor until she had succeeded in erasing Derek Knight from her head.

Mrs. Clearwell passed the proposed menu to Lily to review, while Mrs. Lundy pulled out a little diagram of how the tables were to be arranged beneath the big striped tent that would be erected on the lawn for the day of the grand picnic.

While the two matrons continued discussing every detail of the garden party, Lily stared down at the scrawled sheet of paper in her hand, but her mind wandered.

Forget him.

She had known from the first second she had seen him that Derek Knight was dangerous. Nothing but trouble. The only thing their stolen kiss had accomplished was to further dampen her enthusiasm about marrying Edward.

Her duty.

Derek Knight was not for her. She had been betrayed by her heart once before, so this silly reaction to him signified nothing. Besides, even if she was somehow to snare him, Mother would kill her if she came home with a handsome half-pay officer. Rich and stupid. Those were her marching orders. Why should she torment herself with what was not to be? If she did not marry Edward or someone equally rich, then she'd have to sell Balfour Manor, and that would break her heart. It would be like admitting defeat, admitting ruin. Failing her family. The final nail in the coffin of the Balfour family's honor.

Everything rested on her success.

If only she could stop thinking about Derek Knight's hands. Those big, sun-tanned hands, raking through her hair. Tough and strong and capable—and yet those hands were gentle, too. She could still feel the magic of his touch when he had cupped her face, caressed her neck, her arms. It seemed her fantasies around the garden folly had taken on a very different theme, no longer a child's daydreams, but the needs and longings of a woman.

God. She shifted in her chair and passed the tip of her tongue across her lips. This would not do! She really wished she were better than this.

"What is your opinion on the matter, my dear Miss Balfour?"

Lily snapped back to attention, clearing her throat guiltily. "Pardon?"

"Ah, what's this?" Mrs. Lundy teased. "Was our young lady lost in some romantic fancy, hm?"

"Oh—I am sorry."

"Mrs. Lundy asked if you prefer the fife and drums or the brass band for the midday entertainment."

"Whatever you decide will be best, I am sure, ma'am." Lily forced a hapless smile. "Perhaps we should ask Edward which he'd rather."

"So, that's what you were daydreaming about, or should I say whom!" Mrs. Lundy beamed at having discovered Lily's presumed distraction over her big, strapping son. "Where is that boy, anyway? He should come and see you! It really is too rude!"

"Oh, I don't wish to interrupt him—"

"Nonsense!" Mrs. Lundy rang the silver servant bell beside her. "He is probably caught up in his ledgers. Perhaps he needs reminding that you're here."

In short order, a burly footman trudged into the great hall in answer to the summons. Lily could not figure out why all of Edward's servants looked like pugilists, but Mrs. Lundy did not shrink from ordering the formidable fellow around.

"Would you please tell my son to come and pay his respects to the ladies? They cannot be expected to wait around for his lazy bottom all day!"

"Yes, ma'am," the footman grunted while Mrs. Clearwell turned discreetly to Lily with a wide-eyed look over the woman's choice of words. Lily stifled a polite cough into her white-gloved fist.

"Well! We shall see him soon, I'm very sure," Mrs. Lundy said brightly.

Just then, a carriage came rolling up the drive, past the menacing stone lions that crouched by the gated entrance to Edward's estate. All three of the ladies glanced out the window; the sun glinted off the spotless coach as it clattered to a halt in the courtyard just outside the mullioned windows.

"I wonder who that is," Mrs. Clearwell murmured.

The footman's return interrupted them, his clomping steps echoing under the great hall's vaulted ceiling.

He stopped and clasped his hands behind his back. "The master wishes me to say he's about to go into a meetin' with an associate, madam. He gives his apologies and says he'll come as soon as possible. He told me to say that it shouldn't take long, but he does not wish to inconvenience the ladies."

"Bring us refreshments," Mrs. Lundy ordered the brawler. "Tea, biscuits. Chocolate, ladies? Lemonade? Something stronger? Fortunately for my son, we still have a few more details to iron out about the party. Tell him to hurry," she commanded her servant. "He's welcome to bring his 'associate' to take tea with us, as well. As long as the person's respectable, of course," she amended hastily.

"Aye, mum."

Mrs. Clearwell arched a discreet brow at Lily that seemed to inquire whether Edward actually knew anyone respectable other than the two of them.

Meanwhile, Mrs. Lundy had turned toward the window. "Oh! Oh, my. My goodness," she murmured admiringly.

Lily looked at her hostess in question, but now Mrs. Clearwell had also turned toward the window. Her eyes were wide.

"Heavens," her chaperone breathed, "if I weren't thirty years younger!"

"My word, that's a lovely piece of man-flesh if I ever saw one," Mrs. Lundy agreed with a lusty grin.

Astonished by their reaction, Lily looked at both women in shocked hilarity, then glanced out the window to see this "lovely piece of man-flesh" for herself.

The second she clapped eyes on him, she nearly shrieked and fell out of her chair—except that she couldn't breathe. Couldn't move. Couldn't even blink.

Derek Knight.

All color drained from her face.

Oh, good heavenly God, what could he possibly be doing here?

Sixteen different explanations barreled through her mind. Few made sense, and one was even more dire than the next. Her heart was pounding, her face had gone ashen, and the only clear words that kept tumbling through her brain were, *Oh, no. Oh, no! Why is he here? I'm doomed!*

He was in civilian clothes and ten times still more handsome than she remembered from last night, but as many times as she blinked, willing this certain hallucination to disperse, it proved to be no illusion.

It really was he; he was here, and she was doomed.

Obviously, her transgression had been found out. But how? How was it possibly—possible?

If his arrival wasn't bad enough, her terror turned to pure dread when, beyond the window, she saw Edward walking out warily to meet him.

Neither man smiled; they did not shake hands.

Good God! she thought. *They can't resort to violence!*

There was no question in her mind who would win that fight if they engaged in base dueling, but she needed Edward alive! He was no good to her dead!

Oh, this was terrible.

They walked away together, their faces inscrutable. They headed toward the stables, leaving Lily to try to decipher what was going on. Her overactive mind wasted no time in offering up a few choice, dreadful notions. Someone must have seen them together last night and told Edward. Maybe the other lady who had come to meet with Derek in the garden had witnessed the kiss and told others what she had seen. What if Edward had summoned Derek here to punish each of them separately—or, wait!

Something worse.

Far worse.

They both had spent time in India. What if they already knew each other from there—Derek and Edward? What if the major's light blue eyes and angel face hid the soul of a demon? What if he and Edward were in league?

Maybe Edward had put Derek up to it . . . to test her. She wouldn't put it past her erstwhile Minotaur. He had that ruthless streak. Maybe Edward could sense that she really wasn't quite as pure and proper as she seemed.

Oh, God.

She'd have walked right into a trap.

Lily sat frozen in petrified silence, completely at a loss, while the Lundys' servant wheeled in the tea cart with their refreshments.

I'm dead, she concluded, stunned. She felt paralyzed. Trapped. Strangely helpless before fate. Like one of those poor French nobles waiting in a line of wretched prisoners for his turn at the guillotine. *It's all over now. I am disgraced.* There was nothing left to do but wait and watch it all unravel.

She might as well have a spot of Darjeeling and try to calm down, she thought half-hysterically, though she still sat ramrod straight, masking her distress. What else could she do? Run away? What was the point, if her wanton nature had been found out?

The scandalous truth would only follow her.

That was why she had hidden at Balfour Manor all these years, why Grandfather had left the house to her—one safe place for her to hide the next time her world came crashing down.

She had not expected that day to come so soon.

For the moment, however, she could do nothing but try to recover her courage. Her heart pounded. In odd detachment, she watched Mrs. Lundy pour the tea.

But when Lily accepted a cup and lifted it to her lips, she nearly spilled it with the trembling of her hands.

CHAPTER
∞ SIX ∞

"Major," Lundy greeted him, gravel crunching under his boots as he crossed the courtyard to receive him. "Good of you to come."

"I didn't know I had a choice." Derek slammed the carriage door behind him and took a wary glance around at the landscape and the house.

With a hard look, Lundy nodded toward the stables. "Let's walk."

They did. As they approached the barn, the sound of vicious barking filled the air.

"Guard dog?"

"Monster," Lundy grunted. "Don't worry, he's caged. Did you have a nice visit with the chairman?" he muttered, keeping his stare fixed on the wide-open door to the stable ahead.

Derek glanced at him in surprise. "You know about that?"

"Of course. I've been ordered to befriend you."

"Really? Why is that?"

Lundy sent him a dry look askance and nodded in shrewd cynicism. "Hold on. Can't hear myself think. Maguire! Shut that dog up!" he ordered a groom as they walked into the stable.

The young laborer blanched. "Sir, all due respect, I ain't going near that thing."

"Oh, aren't you?" Lundy boomed. "Lucky I don't feed you to 'im. Where's Jones, then?"

Derek raised an eyebrow as he looked from the cowering groom to Lundy, surprised that he would accept the servant's refusal of an order.

"He's gone into the carriage house. Shall I get him?"

"Never mind. Dog only listens to me, anyway. Maguire," Lundy added in amusement, nodding toward Derek, "show the major what Brutus did to your hand."

The groom shifted the pitchfork he was holding to his left hand, and then held up his right, from which most of two fingers were missing.

Lundy sent Derek a matter-of-fact grin. "Come have a look."

Walking down the center aisle of the luxurious stable, Derek was secretly agog at his host's kingly collection of horses. Whoever was choosing Lundy's horses for him, the man knew what he was doing. There must have been two dozen of the finest warm-bloods that Derek had ever seen: Arabians, thoroughbreds, Hanoverians, Irish hunters.

Jealousy was extremely rare in Derek's nature, but as a cavalry man, horses were his passion, and looking around, it was depressing to see that this clod Lundy had already attained what *he* most wanted out of life. The lout probably couldn't even ride.

Well, I could sell my soul, too, and take a tidy office post with the Company. But then, who would keep his men safe out there in the field and see that they were properly trained for battle?

Still, he was only human.

Ah, damn. With naught but a sigh for what he couldn't have yet, Derek shrugged off envy and followed his host to the open doorway at the far end of the stable.

"Brutus! Shut up!" Lundy roared at the big, black dog penned in a large steel cage. Then he noticed a quartet of his thuggish henchmen loitering in the shade, smoking and dealing cards for an impromptu game. "You lot, back to work!" the boss bellowed. "How many times have I told you no smoking near my bloody stable?"

"Sorry, sir. Sorry." The cards were swept into somebody's pocket, the cheroots quickly doused in a nearby horse trough.

"Don't sorry me! You're goin' to burn the bloody place down one day and then I'll have you hanged!"

Lundy's rough-looking hirelings scattered, but their employer merely slapped Derek on the back. "Now, then! I believe we've got some business to discuss."

"Right," Derek said warily.

As they went back into the stable, his host couldn't seem to keep from gloating as he showed off all his pampered beauties, announcing how much each horse had cost him. Beyond that, Lundy didn't seem to know a lot about his bloodstock, but Derek kept his mouth shut.

The nabob was obviously hell-bent on impressing him— or torturing him—and if he wanted answers, then the most sensible thing to do was oblige the man and act impressed.

It wasn't hard.

The horses were outrageous. They stopped at the stall of a gorgeous dapple-gray Arabian. The mare nibbled at Derek's coat pocket, searching for a carrot. He stroked the horse's neck and cautiously steered their conversation back to the business at hand. "So, you've been ordered to befriend me. By whom?"

"Who do you think?" Lundy retorted.

"Lord Sinclair."

"Right-o. Tuppence for the gentleman."

"I paid him a call before your man brought me here. He was having some sort of meeting."

"I know. I was there myself earlier this morning."

"Ah. So, why does he want you to befriend me?"

"To keep you out of trouble, of course. Keep you busy and stop you from finding out about the committee's little predicament."

"Predicament?" Derek prompted.

Lundy stared at him. "They think I'm a fool. But they're not going to pin this on me. I had nothing to do with it. I don't care what they say."

"Pin what on you, exactly?"

Lundy searched his face with searing intensity, then

looked away, still playing his cards close to the chest. "Sinclair is hoping you will be content to amuse yourself in Town in a rip-roaring drunken haze, Major. That you'll use your time in London chasing skirts and raising hell like the typical cavalryman on leave."

"Is that what you think, too?"

"No. But it is useful to let Sinclair think so."

"Right," Derek agreed, though he was not yet sure where all of this was going.

Lundy leaned a meaty forearm against the horse's stall. "You see, I know firsthand the loyalty among fighting men, Major. I saw that loyalty yesterday in your impassioned speeches accounting all the army's needs. Very stirring. Makes me remember my own army days. The men in my unit. . . . I served in India, too, though it was only the Company's forces." He paused, a glint of the old rivalry between their two armies gleaming in his eyes.

The proud Regulars, commissioned by the Crown, had always been the envy of the East India Company's private security forces, which had been established to protect the Company's trading caravans in India. Whenever their day-to-day security tasks flared up into outright war, the Regulars were called in to lead and assist. The Crown's forces were assumed by all—especially themselves—to be the superior army, the elite. In war, the Regulars mingled with the Company's hired troops, usually in command positions. Of course they had better discipline, but in Derek's view the main difference was one of esprit de corps.

For the Regulars like Derek and Gabriel, the vocation of warrior was for honor, King, and country, while for soldiers of the Company like Ed Lundy, it was mostly just a job. Thus, while the Regulars tended to look down on the Company's troops, they, in turn, regarded the glamorous Regulars with a mix of resentment and begrudging admiration. Both emotions were visible in Lundy's gaze now.

"I know your kind," he continued, taking Derek's measure with a guarded glance. "In India, men don't last unless they're bold enough to take the initiative. A man learns how to think on his feet or he dies. So, no, I don't think you're going to sit around and do nothing but drink and woo the ladies while you wait for word from Lord Sinclair. But His Lordship certainly hopes that's what you'll do."

"Why? What's going on?"

Lundy smiled at him, savoring his information.

"Tell me!"

"Now, now, Major, this isn't India. You're in no position to be givin' me orders."

Derek narrowed his eyes at the man. "Stop wasting my time. There's some sort of problem with the money, isn't there?"

Lundy glanced over his shoulder. "After the vote last night, the committee met to review the books and close out the fund to be handed over to the army. But when we went over the numbers, we found three hundred thousand missing from the fund."

Derek stared at him in shock. "Three hundred thousand . . . ?"

"That's right. Somebody on the committee's been skimming off the cream. That's what Lord Sinclair doesn't want you to know."

Derek's mind reeled at the betrayal of their men out on the front lines, but he struggled to shake off his astonishment. "Why are you telling me this?"

"Because you're going to help me find out which of the others took that blunt."

"Oh, I am? Why?"

"Because we both care about the same thing, Major—the men. Besides, I know where I stand on that committee," Lundy said with a brooding look. "I'm the newest member and I'm an outsider. I've never been one of *them*. One of the highborn. They think I've no right to be there. They hate me for what I've accomplished in life, the fortune I've built. Oh, yes, I know it well. I know the way of the world. Whoever's done this is going to try to pin it on me. I can feel it in me bones. They'll gladly make the lowborn fellow the scapegoat if it will protect another of their class. I need you to help me find the truth."

"What exactly are you proposing?"

"An investigation, combining our efforts. They don't trust either of us entirely. We're both outsiders in this town. But if we play along with their misconceptions about us and meanwhile work together, then we may actually get to the bottom of this and find out where that money went."

"An investigation."

"Yes. They told me to manage you, keep you out of the way. We'll let 'em think that's exactly what I'm doing. Meanwhile, I'll be picking up whatever information I can on my end of it and passing it on to you so you can look into it more closely. But I don't want to be directly involved. It would arouse their suspicions, and I can do more good from the inside."

"Right," Derek murmured, scrutinizing him.

"If we can track down some hard evidence, then they can't unjustly pin this on me, and whoever took the money will have to put it back. That gold was earmarked for the men. The sooner we find it, the sooner we can get the money to them."

"Well, you're damned right about one thing," Derek said grimly. "I'm sure as hell not going to sit around and do nothing."

"I thought not. You'd better be careful, though," Lundy warned. "They're not taking any chances with you. They'll push back hard if they realize the two of us are working to expose the real embezzler."

Derek folded his arms across his chest and debated with himself, studying the man.

"You're very quiet, Major. Surely I haven't misjudged you?"

"No," he said tersely, sending Lundy a warning look, but he did not see fit to tell the man about Lord Sinclair's veiled threat a short while ago with the permanent loss of his command. Damned right he wanted to get to the truth, but he had a lot to lose.

More than Lundy knew.

Derek was silent, weighing his words. "How do I know it wasn't you who took the money?"

"You're welcome to review my personal accounts any

time. Talk to my banker if you like. I've got nothing to hide. We'll see if the others can say the same." Lundy paused. "I heard the Marathas nearly killed your brother."

Derek looked at him in guarded surprise, but of course, the story had circulated in Society.

"You know damned well we can whip those bastards, provided our army has what it needs to march and fight," Lundy said. "So, do you want us to beat the Marathas or not?"

Derek glared at him. Of course he wanted to beat the Marathas, but he did not appreciate Lundy's efforts to manipulate him.

"Ahem! Sir?"

They both looked over at the footman who had entered the stable.

"What is it?" Lundy demanded.

"Sir, Mrs. Lundy asks if you and the other gentleman would like to come and take refreshments now."

Lundy rolled his eyes. "God."

"I didn't know you were married," Derek remarked.

"He means my mother."

"Mrs. Lundy bade me say Miss Balfour and her chaperone have errands they must run. The ladies cannot stay more than another quarter hour, if you wish to see them, sir."

"All right, I'll be right there!" Lundy grumbled, then he turned to Derek with a long-suffering look. "Refreshments, Major?"

Derek arched an eyebrow and shrugged. "Why not?"

"This way." As they left the stable and walked across the graveled courtyard toward the house, Derek continued mulling over Lundy's proposed investigation.

He was a long way from trusting the man, but opposing him wasn't going to yield anything useful. Might as well go along with it—carefully—and see where it might lead. The man seemed fairly genuine, and besides, compared to Sinclair and the rest of the civilian Gentlemen of the Sub-Committee, Derek couldn't help harboring a slight bias in Lundy's favor, since he was a former soldier and had also

served in India. Lundy was certainly right about one thing:
They both were outsiders.

"So, who is this Miss Balfour?" he inquired, thrusting
the more serious business aside as he recalled the footman's
words about the ladies.

"A very beautiful creature and my particular friend."

"Oh, really?"

"Actually, she is my future bride," Lundy admitted with
an odd, almost secretive smile.

"You are engaged?" Derek exclaimed.

"Haven't asked her yet, but soon."

"Do you think she'll say yes?"

"She'd better." Lundy laughed. "You think my horses
are beautiful? Wait till you see her. My little jewel," he
boasted. "Even some o' them Patroness witches have called
her a diamond of the first water. She's gorgeous, man."

"Really?"

"More than that, a lady to the core. Old family. Old as
yours," he added. "Very high class."

"So, what is she after you for?" Derek drawled.

"My charm," Lundy retorted. "What do you think? Her
family's bankrupt."

"Right, so you are knowingly marrying a fortune hunter?"

Lundy shrugged. "Old bloodlines, like I said."

Derek shuddered. "You're brave."

"Bates!" he barked at his driver. "Get the carriage ready
to take the Major back to the Althorpe shortly. In here,"
Lundy grunted as they went in the front door. Then he
showed Derek into the great hall.

Ahead, three ladies were seated around a furniture grouping, silhouetted before a bank of mullioned windows.

In short order, Derek was presented to Mrs. Lundy, the
beaming lady of the house with a startling, ugly rooster
brooch pinned to her bosom, and to the girl's chaperone,
Mrs. Clearwell, an agreeable matron with star-shaped pins
in her hair. Last but not least, Lundy introduced him to the
elegant young woman who had sat quietly, motionless as a
garden statue, from the moment he had entered the hall.

"This is Miss Lily Balfour," Lundy informed him with

distinct pride. He went to stand by her chair and took her white-gloved hand possessively. "Miss Balfour, this is Major Derek Knight, newly arrived from India. He is a cousin of the Duke of Hawkscliffe," Lundy added, wasting no time in informing his "particular lady friend" that he had such a well-connected acquaintance.

"Major," she clipped out, not even lifting her gaze to meet his.

Well! She was a toplofty one, Derek thought, taken aback by her chilly reception. Did she deem herself too good even to bother looking at him despite his ducal cousin? Derek stifled a snort. No matter. Bloody London debutantes. He had met her kind before, fortune hunters; they always went for the firstborn.

They would not spare the time of day for men who didn't have at least a hundred thousand in the bank. Nevertheless, he greeted her with a gentlemanly bow. "Miss Balfour."

She continued to ignore him, studying the floor with her face frozen in a haughty mask devoid of emotion.

When Lundy released her hand, she tucked it back onto her lap, where it nested with the other.

The older ladies pulled Derek into a chair between them and began quizzing him eagerly with a hundred questions.

"What brings you to England, Major?"

"I was sent to testify before the committee on the state of the army in India, ma'am."

"Before Eddie's committee?"

"Yes, ma'am."

"And are you married?"

"No." He couldn't help laughing, for Mrs. Clearwell had wasted no time getting down to brass tacks. "Not me, ma'am."

"Well, we're just going to have to find someone for you, then."

"Mrs. Clearwell!" Miss Balfour uttered, her head down in apparent mortification.

"Quite so!" Lundy's mother chimed in, quite to Derek's

amusement. "Major, you must agree to come to my garden party. There will be an abundance of beautiful ladies."

"Then I would not dream of missing it," he replied. "Would you mind if I bring my brother?" His innocent query sent the pair to new heights of delight.

"You have a *brother*?" they fairly screamed.

"By all means, he must come!"

"Is he also a bachelor?"

"Yes, ma'am, I'm afraid that he is. Neither of us have been very lucky in love." Derek suppressed a devilish laugh. Gabriel would want to kill him for this. By Jove, he'd drag the man out of the house yet. "He was hurt in battle before we left India."

"Oh, how awful!"

"The poor man!"

"Yes, I know. I have been looking after him, but you know, I cannot match the tender solicitude of kind ladies."

"Of course not, Major. How sad!"

"Well! We will be certain to make sure your brother is carefully tended at the party."

"You are very kind."

To his amusement, the pair of matrons continued doting on him. He was used to this treatment, most females wanting either to bed or to mother him.

He was not used to being ignored.

Miss Balfour continued ignoring him.

Really, what was so fascinating out there on the lawn? She was staring out the window with such absorption one would think there was a unicorn out there grazing in the flower beds. Derek watched surreptitiously as she tore her seemingly bored gaze away from the windows and bent her head, peering into her cup as though the tea leaves might reveal the secrets of the universe.

The girl was outrageously rude—or perhaps she had a toothache, he thought sardonically. Or perhaps his male ego was merely piqued at being ignored by a pretty young woman, never mind that she was on the verge of becoming engaged to Edward Lundy.

And yet there was something strangely familiar about

her. He wished she would lift her head and look at him so he might figure out where he had seen her before.

Answering Mrs. Clearwell's next round of prying questions about his sister Georgiana's recent marriage to the Marquess of Griffith, he covertly studied Miss Balfour's ramrod spine and demure, white-gloved fingers.

Done with her tea, she set the cup and saucer aside and clasped her hands on her lap again.

Her prim, buttoned-up manner touched him somehow.

Her figure was slender and lithe; she had light blond hair all wound up tightly in a neat chignon on the crown of her head. Little wispy tendrils framed her face and played about her nape, which, in turn, was wrapped in lace from the high-necked collar of her day-gown.

Very pretty, he admitted to himself. Who'd have thought a clod like Lundy could've had such excellent taste? He was impressed.

At that moment, as if she had been acutely aware of his study all the while and simply could not take it anymore, Miss Balfour lifted her head and ventured a small, cautious glance in Derek's direction.

Their gazes met.

Locked.

The air exited his lungs with a whoosh. His eyes widened.

Good God.

Recognition unfurled in a flash.

It was she! Mary Nonesuch—his mystery girl from the garden folly!

Surely he was mistaken.

He could not move.

The two older ladies prattled on. Lundy was picking his thumbnail, and Lily Balfour stared at Derek in dread, in warning, indeed, in a silent plea for mercy, her face alabaster.

He could not believe his eyes.

His stunned stare traced the elegant line of her neck, that lovely neck he had memorized so carefully last night. It caressed the pale blond of her hair, her ivory skin.

She was Lundy's fiancée?

But how—?

He did not want to believe it was true, but as the seconds passed, he realized with a sinking feeling that there was no mistake. No, he recognized the gleam of those lavender-blue eyes from behind the pale satin half-mask she had worn at the ball; the memory of their bright sparkle was seared into his brain. And her mouth. He had memorized its shape too carefully to be mistaken . . . and its taste.

His gaze skimmed the lips that she had offered and he had claimed so passionately just last night.

She shot him a warning glare, as though reading the sensual direction of his thoughts. Now it was Derek's turn to drop his gaze.

His heart pounded as he did his best to conceal his growing bewilderment. What the hell was going on?

Considering the morning he'd had and all the people trying to play games with his mind, he couldn't help but be suspicious of her, too. Had last night been some kind of a setup? A deliberate trap to entice him? Was she a part of this mystery, the huge sum missing from the army's fund?

Lundy had already told him her family was bankrupt.

He remembered the diamond earring that he had in his keeping for her. Well, if she wanted it back, she was going to have to answer a few questions, plain and simple.

When Derek ventured another brief, wary glance in her direction, her eyes flashed out a warning plea not to expose her. He stared at her, obscuring his lips casually with his hand. He was sure their guilty wanting must be obvious to everyone in the room, but nobody else seemed to notice. It amused him to realize now that she had been sitting there not ignoring him, but trying desperately to escape his notice, as if she could hide from him.

Well, at least now he knew why last night she had refused to tell him her name. "Mary Nonesuch" had snared herself a rich nabob—and had risked it all last night for a few stolen kisses with *him.*

The realization pleased Derek and certainly helped to

allay some of his mistrust, but he would not be content until he'd had the chance to interrogate her personally.

"Let us get you some refreshments, Major. Lily, would you mind—?"

"Oh, er—of course."

"That's all right, I can help myself," he said, rising to join her at the refreshment table some ten feet away. It was probably his only chance to get closer to her.

Tense awareness thrummed between them as he stood casually beside her at the table, surveying the display of various biscuits and finger sandwiches. Their backs were turned toward the others.

"It all looks delicious," he drawled, needing nothing more than that to make her feel the innuendo in his words.

She edged away from him a bit.

"What do you recommend, Miss Balfour?"

With a haughty look, she turned her attention to the tray of biscuits and finger sandwiches. "You'd probably like most of it, Major. You don't seem too picky. Edward, dear, what can I get for you?"

"Give me the same as the major," he grunted.

Derek arched a brow at her, for he doubted very much that she had ever given Lundy what she'd given him last night. Lily Balfour slanted him an icy look of warning.

Derek fought back a devilish smile. "May I have the lemonade?" he asked gravely.

"I hope you choke on it," she said under her breath as she handed him the pitcher, an angelic smile pasted on her face.

"You'd better be nice to me—Miss Nonesuch," he taunted in a whisper.

She closed her eyes, pausing, as though she were still clinging to one last hope that he did not recognize her.

"Put some extra sugar in the lemonade for me," her suitor ordered. "I like it sweet."

Derek wryly handed her a spoon with which to do her future husband's bidding. But the moment their fingers touched, she yanked her hand back and the spoon clattered down onto the floor.

"Oh, my!" she gasped.

"No matter," Derek soothed, but they both bent down at the same time to pick it up and nearly bumped heads.

Lundy laughed with great, loud gusto at the near-miss.

"You have a talent for losing things, don't you?" Derek murmured under his breath as he picked up the spoon and offered it to her.

She looked at him sharply, a question in her eyes.

He gave her the subtlest smile, confirming his find at the garden folly. "Hyde Park in an hour," he breathed.

She acquiesced with the merest trace of a nod, though her look brimmed with worried mistrust.

They both rose again.

While he set the dropped spoon aside, she took a fresh one, plunking an extra rock of hard sugar into her suitor's lemonade. She stirred it noisily while Derek helped himself to a few biscuits and a cucumber sandwich.

They returned to their respective seats nonchalantly, but before long, Derek rose and took leave of their little gathering. It was turning into quite a busy day.

As his host showed him out to the front, where the same carriage and driver waited to take Derek back to the Althorpe, Lundy could not resist gloating over his latest acquisition. "She's somethin,' ain't she?" he boasted, grinning from ear to ear. "Beauty like I told you and a lady through and through."

"She's something, all right," Derek answered, climbing into the coach. He pulled the carriage door shut.

You have no idea.

The ladies left shortly after he did, riding with the top down on Mrs. Clearwell's pink barouche, the better to enjoy the summer's day.

Lily held a parasol over her head as the carriage rumbled down the country road leading back to Town. It was all very well to enjoy the sunlight, but a lady on the marriage mart had to have a care for her complexion.

God only knew she had so few assets of her own.

Mrs. Clearwell pointed out a pretty lake half hidden by

some woods in the midst of the meadows as they drove by, but while Lily nodded and managed to smile, her heart still pounded after her unexpected reunion with Derek Knight. Once more, the man had left her wits in an uproar.

Oh, she could not bear it. The suspense was agonizing. She had to know if he intended to tell Edward about her indiscretion last night at the garden folly.

Whatever happened, he could *not* be permitted to wreck her marriage plans—and she would tell him so at their upcoming meeting in Hyde Park.

Of course, it was dangerous to risk being seen in public with such a notorious womanizer, famous for breaking ladies' beds, but if they could talk privately, clear the air, perhaps she'd finally have some peace of mind.

There seemed to be reason for hope. After all, he had said nothing to incriminate her back at Edward's house, when he very easily could have. Indeed, he had looked as shocked at finding her there as she had been upon seeing him step out of the carriage. Perhaps she need not fear him, after all. But she was not taking any chances.

It was bad enough that she had put herself at his mercy this way. The old Balfour luck—all bad—had clearly struck again.

In the meantime, *Lord*, she could not believe the blackguard had managed to get himself invited to the garden party! Now that day was going to be all the more unpleasant.

"What did you think of the major, dear?" Mrs. Clearwell asked oh-so-casually.

Lily hadn't noticed her eagle-eyed chaperone watching her all the while, studying the play of emotions on her face, but now she looked over and saw Mrs. Clearwell's canny observation, almost as though the woman could hear the reckless thunder of her pulse.

Lily paled and dropped her gaze, trying to summon up an innocent tone. "He seems—pleasant enough."

"Pleasant? I thought he was perfectly charming. Honestly, I don't know why you can't find a man like that instead of Edward. Brave, well bred, and *so* impossibly handsome—"

"Mrs. Clearwell," Lily interrupted, finding her recitation of his virtues intolerable, "don't you know he has the most wicked reputation?"

Her chaperone's frown gave way to a chuckle. "As well he might, my dear. As well he might."

Lily looked at her, appalled. "Mrs. Clearwell, I fear you have been taken in by a rake's charm," she said severely.

"Haven't you heard, gel? It's a known fact. Reformed rakes make the best husbands."

Lily harrumphed. "Ridiculous cliché," she muttered as Mrs. Clearwell's carriage gained the genteel environs of Mayfair.

Airy laughter was her godmother's response.

Upon reaching Mrs. Clearwell's house, Lily hurried up to her bedchamber and leaned before the vanity, taking a hard look in the mirror. Well, she thought, meeting her own grim gaze in the reflection, he had unmasked her now.

There was no point in denying that she was attracted to him, but it did not signify. She only wished that she were not quite so eager to run off and see Derek Knight again.

It was nearly time for their meeting. She would have to hurry or she would be late.

Trying to tell herself that her urgency was born merely of her keen desire to rescue her poor earring from being held hostage by that barbarian, she smoothed her hair, pinched her cheeks to brighten their color, then ran back downstairs on slightly wobbly legs.

Mrs. Clearwell looked over in surprise. "Where are you off to, dear?"

"I should like to take my daily constitutional," she lied, ignoring a familiar jab of guilt for her lack of honesty. "I ate too many biscuits at the Lundys'. A bit of exercise would do me good."

"Ah, the energy of youth. For my part, I shall take a nap. That Mrs. Lundy is a dear thing, but she quite talked me senseless." Mrs. Clearwell offered her cheek, which Lily dutifully kissed. "Don't forget to take Eliza with you," her chaperone ordered. "This is not the countryside where you can walk alone."

"Yes, ma'am."

When Mrs. Clearwell retired to her chamber, Lily summoned the freckled housemaid, Eliza, who had been assigned to attend her.

Before long, she and her maid were in Hyde Park, awash in all the hustle and bustle of the Ring, though it was not yet as crowded as it would be by five. They stopped at the railing to watch the smartly dressed bucks and beauties pass in their fine equipages.

Lily scanned the park in search of Derek Knight.

Within a few moments, she spotted him. He came riding out from around a curve in the lane astride a glossy black stallion. The trace of a wistful smile touched her lips in spite of herself as she watched him. The consummate cavalry officer looked as proud as that high-stepping bit-of-blood that he sat with such splendor. The horse seemed to dance beneath him.

Ah, but she did not need a hero in shiny knee-boots and gold epaulets. The only kind of rescue she desired was of her family's dwindling bank account, and since she highly doubted that mighty Zeus was going to come raining down on her in a shower of gold, Edward Lundy was going to have to do.

"Lor,' look at 'im!" the maid uttered as the magnificent pair came closer. "He's beautiful, Miss."

"Yes," Lily murmured, thrusting aside a quiver of desire, vexed anew by her unwanted attraction to the man. She turned away to stop herself from staring at him. "Actually, Eliza, I'm afraid he is the real reason we are here."

"To 'ave a look at 'im, you mean?"

"More than that. I have to talk to him."

Eliza tore her gaze away from the major and turned to Lily in wide-eyed apprehension. "Is that quite proper, Miss?"

Lily looked at her in silent distress.

Eliza reconsidered, ducking her head with a humble glance that seemed to express her recollection that none of the staff had ever known Miss Balfour to do anything improper. "Well," she conceded at length, "if you *must* speak to that gent'l'man, then I'm sure you've got a good reason for it."

"Thank you, Eliza," Lily said softly. "I shan't be long."

With another wary glance in his direction, Lily saw that Derek Knight had spotted her. Just like in the ballroom, his watchful stare had picked her out of the crowd in the park and now homed in on her.

Her heart beat faster.

Sending her a forceful look from across the green, he turned the horse around and rode off at a handsome trot toward the graveled promenade that girded the Serpentine.

Lily noted the place he selected for their meeting. Tall bushes and stands of trees obscured parts of the walking path around the man-made lake. It was not as secluded as the pineapple folly, but then again, there would not be any kissing going on.

Pity, a cheeky part of her remarked. She repressed it with a twinge of self-directed shock. "Right," Lily said at length, her manner turning businesslike. She drew a deep breath and braced herself for the meeting.

While Eliza hung back obediently, Lily walked on toward the Serpentine to do battle with Derek Knight.

CHAPTER
∞ SEVEN ∞

"Well, well, Miss Lily Balfour," Derek greeted her, savoring her name now that he finally knew it. "We meet again." Smoothing his reins to the side, he leaned forward slightly in the saddle and surveyed her with an appreciative gaze as she marched toward him.

Having recovered from his initial shock of finding "Mary Nonesuch" at Edward Lundy's house, Derek paused to reassess his earlier suspicion that Lily Balfour might have something to do with the committee's missing funds. Sinclair's strange behavior and Lundy's shocking revelations must have made him a bit paranoid for a while there, but now he was in a much clearer frame of mind.

Looking at her now, seeing her for what she was—an impoverished aristocratic miss on the marriage mart—he realized his prior suspicion of her was absurd. What did well-bred young ladies know about embezzlement?

Besides, the whimsical girl he had flirted with last night at the garden folly was too much of an innocent to be involved in anything so nefarious.

No, she was merely a fortune hunter, he thought sardonically. *Little fool*. A garden-variety schemer, armed only with her feminine wiles.

She was making a big mistake, of course, throwing herself away on that clod, but Derek now dismissed the idea that Miss Balfour might know anything about committee business. He decided on the spot not to mention it to her. If he broached the subject, it would very likely yield nothing.

It would only give her cause to go to her dear Edward and ask questions, and that, in turn, would make Lundy more suspicious of *him*.

Best to keep her out of it.

"Dare I hope you've come looking for another kiss?" he taunted with a guarded smile.

"Hardly." The two clipped syllables were terse, no-nonsense. She stopped a few feet away from where he was seated on his horse and looked up at him. "I've come to get my earring back, as you well know."

"You shall have it," he assured her as he swung down off the horse, then turned to her, looking deeply into her eyes. "Just as soon as we've had a little chat."

She stiffened. "Major, please. Those earrings belonged to my great-great-grandmother."

"Patience, darling. Don't you trust me?"

She eyed him skeptically. "How do I know you really have it?"

Derek fished it out of his pocket and showed it to her. Relief flickered in her lavender-blue eyes as she stared at the diamond sparkling between his finger and thumb, but then she lifted her chin and merely let out a prim, "Humph."

He fought back a smile. "Come. Let us take a promenade." He offered his arm, but she did not accept it.

She hung back when he started to walk. "I cannot go far," she warned. "My maid is waiting. She'll report back to my chaperone if I'm gone too long."

"Oh, I don't think Mrs. Clearwell will mind," he said with a knowing half-smile.

Lily Balfour scowled at him.

Derek laughed. "You worry too much." With a gentle tug on his horse's bridle, he began strolling down the graveled lane, exasperating his companion but leaving her no choice but to follow.

When Miss Balfour fell into step beside him, Derek did not look at her, keeping his gaze fixed straight ahead. He spoke in a measured tone. "So, you have set your cap at the encroaching toadstool, Mr. Lundy."

"Don't call him that." she shot back defensively. "I thought you were his friend."

Derek made no comment.

"Besides, whether I've set my cap at anyone or not, I don't think that's any of your business."

"Of course it is. It became my business last night."

She dropped her gaze with a chastened look. In the fleeting silence, he could feel the heated awareness between them fairly vibrating on the air.

"At least now I know why you tried so hard to keep your identity a secret," he remarked.

"You claim to be an honest man, Major, so why don't you just come out and tell me what you want?" she demanded, stopping their forward progress and turning to him in exasperation.

He shrugged. "Merely to understand."

"Understand *what*?" she exclaimed, stealing a nervous glance about at the other people in the park.

"You, Miss Balfour."

"What about me?"

"I have the strangest feeling that the girl I saw at the Lundys' today was your usual disguise, so prim and proper. Last night, though you were masked, you showed me your true face, didn't you? A rare privilege, I suspect."

"Major, I have no idea what you are talking about," she replied in a withering tone.

"I think you do," he whispered with a wicked smile. "Naughty little liar."

She pulled back and drew herself up in regal indignation. "Did you summon me here just so you could insult me?"

"If anyone here has the right to be insulted, it is I," he retorted.

"What?"

"You used me," he accused her.

"You started it! I never asked you to sneak up behind me and grab me."

"Well, no, but you did ask me to kiss you."

She looked away, turning beet red. "Can I please have my diamond back?"

"Why are you marrying Lundy?"

"Why are you going back to India?" she countered, slanting him a scornful glance.

"India's where I belong."

"Well, I belong with Edward!"

"Oh, come, that's rubbish and you know it. You left the ballroom last night to get away from him, didn't you? That's why I found you out in the garden."

"Look, I'm not going to discuss this with you. I just want the truth. Are you going to tell Edward what happened last night or not?"

"You think I'd do that?" he asked softly, gazing into her eyes. "Do you distrust all men, or is it just me?"

When he saw how she faltered, he realized he might have pushed her too hard. "You have nothing to fear from me," he murmured. "I'd just hate to see you make a massive mistake."

"What mistake?" she asked warily. "What do you mean?"

"Your choice of husbands," he exclaimed. "The girl who charmed the hell out of me last night was no callous fortune hunter. Is your family forcing you to do this? For I cannot bring myself to believe that such a sordid scheme could ever come from you."

"Sordid?"

"Miss Balfour, I know your family's bankrupt. Lundy himself told me so just this morning. I gather that's partly why this diamond of yours means so much. But you had better know he's onto you. You're not fooling him a whit. He knows you're only after him for his gold, and frankly, he did not appear overly sympathetic to your plight. He is using you for his own advantage."

She was silent for a long moment, staring at the lake; then she looked at him. "You think I don't know that?"

"I see. But that's all right with you because you're also taking advantage of him."

"There is no cause to cast it all in such an unsavory light, Major. Surely you understand the way of the world."

He shook his head at her—a mere chit of a girl telling him about the way of the world.

She furrowed her brow when she noted his cynical stare. "For your information, Mr. Lundy happens to be a—a very agreeable man!" she burst out. Her frustration was rising visibly, probably because she was not convincing herself any more than she was convincing Derek. "He's a good man! A solid man. He has cause to be proud of himself. Look at all he's accomplished in life, and he's barely forty. Edward is a survivor, and that is a quality that I greatly admire."

"Well, that much may be true." Derek looked her over. "But I doubt you've ever kissed him the way you did me."

She let out an unladylike curse under her breath and turned away.

"Have I unmasked you again?" he whispered, studying her delicate profile. "Last night, you know, I enjoyed it. A great deal, actually. You left me wanting more."

"Why are you torturing me?"

"I want to know what we're going to do about this."

"About *what*?"

"This," he whispered, and when he ran the back of one finger along a section of her arm, she quivered violently, then looked at him in fear and backed away, as if she knew that her response to him only underscored the fact that she wanted Lundy as much as she wanted a hole in her head.

She could not hide the fact that she wanted Derek.

And he wanted her.

"You don't care about Lundy and he doesn't care about you," Derek told her. "That's not a situation that a smart girl like you ought to put herself in. I am sorry for your family's hardships, but can it really be so bad that you must sell yourself to the likes of him?"

"I beg your pardon," she forced out bitterly to put him in his place, but he was not so easily deterred.

"You're better than this, Lily Balfour. Don't sell yourself for gold. Someone as lovely as you should never join the ugly ranks of cutthroat fortune hunters."

"*How dare you?*" she uttered, taking a step back and glaring at him. She looked truly shaken by his words. Her face was white. "Who do you think you are, to judge me?

You, of all people! A—a militaristic adventurer!" she flung out. "As if you can talk! Perhaps I am willing to *marry* to secure my future, but at least I don't make my living *killing* people!"

Derek's jaw dropped at her counterattack. He stared at her in astonishment.

"You think you're better than me?" she charged on. I know why men join up to go and fight in India! Believe me, I know it better than most, so you can get off your moral high horse, Major. Greed, that's why! Fortune and glory! No doubt you'll claim it's for King and country, but the real reason all you foolish males go storming around that horrid place is to try to get your hands on Hindu gold and plunder!"

The moment she said it, Lily realized she had pushed him too far, but so be it! It was true.

Besides, he had overstepped his bounds, too, calling her a fortune hunter, making her feel like an out-and-out harlot for sale at some brothel. The nerve he'd touched was more raw than even she had realized. She had spent too many years submerged in shame to endure this chiding, this load of guilt from him.

But he was not happy with her, that much was plain, and when he spoke, his tone was ice. "Would you prefer that England go bankrupt? Become easy prey for her enemies? In the grand scheme of things, darling, if I kill, it is for England—and for you."

"I don't believe you."

"You don't *want* to believe me, no doubt, for then all that blood would be on your hands, too, instead of just mine and my men's. Civilians," he said in disgust, shaking his head at her as though it were a name for some loathsome, useless thing.

His eyes had hardened, their expression as closed as silvery-blue mirrors to her now. "Before you accuse me of being some sort of hired mercenary, keep in mind it was the wealth of India that sustained our country through the war against Napoleon. Our nation has a right, indeed, a duty, to do what it must to survive."

"And so do I," she answered fiercely.

"Miss Balfour," he said in a strangled tone, his face taut with rage, "you are very lucky that I am a gentleman."

He grasped her hand, thrust her earring into her palm, and swung up onto his horse without further ado.

The look he shot her as he gathered the reins could have ground her down into the dust.

Her heart pounding, Lily watched him wheel his horse around with smooth expertise, urging the animal into motion with a click of his tongue and a light squeeze of his legs.

He rode off at a restless canter, leaving her alone.

Lily clutched her earring with such a hard grip that the sharp post on the back of it pricked her palm. The little jab of pain brought her back to the here-and-now, and the grim reality that they had laid bare for each other chased away the idle fantasies that had danced like wisps of smoke at the back of her mind ever since their brief encounter at the garden folly.

The whisper of a happiness that she had just barely glimpsed dissipated like dreams as she stood there. Her body trembled, but she refused to regret this angry break with Derek Knight. They had no business, really, even speaking to each other.

Well, then, she thought, steadying herself with a lift of her chin until she had forced the bewildering threat of tears into retreat. *That's that, then.*

Good riddance.

At least she had got what she came for.

I have never been so insulted in my life.

Derek was still seething when he walked into his apartment at the Althorpe and slammed the door behind him.

Gabriel looked over in surprise. "What's the matter with you?" he panted, hard at work on his punishing regimen to rebuild his strength.

Derek merely growled in answer as he threw his coat at the coat tree.

Gabriel put down his iron dumbbells and dabbed the sweat off his face. He frowned as he watched Derek pace to the window and back again, restless in silent tumult and obvious fury.

"Damn her!" Derek burst out with sudden vehemence. He would have punched the wall but stopped himself, not wanting to pay for the repairs he'd have been charged for it. He was not rich, after all.

"Damn who?" Gabriel asked in a quizzical tone.

Derek looked at him, paced some more, then turned when he reached the fireplace. "Lily Balfour, that's who. Only the most infuriating woman I have ever met."

"Why? What did she do?"

"She," he ground out, "insulted my honor."

"Oh, I see. Are you going to challenge her to a duel?"

If his brother were not injured, Derek would have charged him for that remark as if they were still schoolboys on the rugby field. He narrowed his eyes.

Gabriel laughed at him; Derek glowered at his brother and kicked the ottoman out of his way as he left the room, stomping off to his own chamber to try to bring his fury under control.

Ungrateful wench!

He spotted a farewell note from Lady Amherst on his pillow but did not give a damn about reading it just now. At the moment, he wanted nothing to do with any one of their species.

He planted his hands on the edge of the dressing table and glared fiercely into the mirror.

It was one thing to be so disrespected by the politicians that they would steal funds earmarked for the troops. But this was more painful, more personal. She was not just anyone to him, devil take her. She had gotten under his skin, and her words had just negated all he held most dear.

She had made him feel like he was nothing, he and all his men, useless cannon fodder, as if all their sacrifice were meaningless.

Well, he thought after a long moment, what did it matter

to him whom she married? Lundy would probably beat her, but that was not *his* problem, was it? She seemed hell-bent on making her miserable bed, so let her lie in it. It wasn't as though he had any desire to offer for the little fortune hunter himself. Not that she or any of her kind would have accepted an offer from a mere younger son.

Gabriel, now, *he* might have had a chance with the fine and frosty Lily Balfour, but for his part, Derek knew the score. He'd been dealing with this all his life—and his brother wondered why he was ambitious! Ah, it was the same old story, the age-old quandary of the younger son.

He had learned the way of the world at his mother's knee. As firstborn, Gabriel could afford to lounge on his arse if he wanted, but there would be no such luxury for Derek. No one was going to help him, and since, by necessity, a younger son would always seem the lesser choice, he had been brought up shrewdly doubtful that any woman was ever going to love him unless he could give her several very good reasons to choose him, advantages like fortune and glory to make up for his lower status by birth.

In truth, there was a time when he would have done much more than that for true love, a figment in which his foolish heart had insisted on believing. Even as a boy, Derek could imagine no worse fate than never being loved by some wonderful girl. He had always been completely fascinated by girls, even when other lads his age had scoffed at them. He'd had no trouble talking to the magical creatures when other boys had stuttered, thrown rocks, and run away, and the only thing better in his youthful view than riding a very fast horse had been making a pretty girl laugh. Oh, yes, he intended to be loved one day—well and often. It was the very motive that, years ago, had set him on the path of his present career.

If he had to risk life and limb to gain the riches that would bring love to him, if he had to face death undertaking magnificent deeds to get himself hailed as a hero, he had told himself it would be worth it.

Otherwise, he might just as well be invisible.

Well, the job was habit now, and as for his faith in true love, it had long been fading. It dissolved a little further with each married woman he seduced.

Then last night he had met "Mary Nonesuch," and for a few hours he had dared to hope she might really be different from the rest. But he saw now he had been deluding himself. She was like all the others, a common schemer with a pretty face. Her kiss had been sublime, but, Derek thought with a snort, no young lady who went around kissing strangers in garden gazebos was marital material for him.

Ah, well. At this late date, he did not really expect to marry for love any more than Lily Balfour or her vulgar nabob Lundy did. There was none of that romantic boy left in him. He was older now, wiser, hardened by life, and he understood better what love meant.

After all, if he still believed in true love, he would have hoped for someone who would love him *now,* when he had only a small fortune and the fuel of large ambitions, large capabilities. Women sometimes claimed to love him, but his mental answer was, *Then bloody prove it.* Let any woman steel herself to share in his burden now, before he was rich. Let her follow the drum and come to the edge of the war, like some officers' wives would do. That was love.

Let her see for herself the daily hell he knew. Let her help him tend his mangled men and shoot a broken-legged cavalry horse or two to spare it from its agony. Let her watch him behead a few fellows in battle and slash the enemy to bits with his razor-sharp saber, and then they'd see if any lady had the stomach to be wed to a bloodstained killer . . . just like Lily Balfour had accused him of being.

No, Derek did not even bother trying to find that kind of love. It was never going to happen. He simply did not believe it could exist.

Besides, he would not have asked for such sacrifice from any gentle female. He was too protective to have allowed it. He knew too well that even to see a war was a kind of violation of the soul.

He had learned that it was better on the whole just to let the girls admire the uniform. The uniform was mask enough for him.

Besides, he had already devised a more realistic plan for his future marriage. One day, when he had made his fortune of Indian treasure, why then, he would buy the best bride that he could afford—the haughtiest, the highest born, the purest.

Until then, it was merry widows and other chaps' wives for him, and if Lily Balfour didn't like it, she could go to Hades.

Unfortunately, their mutual acquaintance with Edward made it inevitable that they would have to endure each other's company again before long.

By the night of Lord and Lady Fallow's musical soiree, Lily had nearly managed to convince herself that she had forgotten all about Major Derek Knight.

This was no small feat, given the fact that he had begun associating with Edward on a regular basis, to say nothing of the frequency with which her chaperone saw fit to mention the blackguard.

While Edward mentioned meeting with him on committee business, Mrs. Clearwell seemed to have decided that Major Derek Knight had hung the moon. And much to Lily's horror, her chaperone had opined on more than one occasion that that cad, that "stud of the Season," was the man she ought to chase, snare, and wed.

Over my dead body, was Lily's mental reply. But such a vehement response would only have intrigued her shrewd sponsor, so rather than run screaming from the room whenever his name came up, as she would have preferred, Lily merely smiled at her godmother in a superior fashion and made no comment on the topic. Anything she said was certain to incriminate her. Once, however, in a moment's weakness, she *had* pertly suggested that Mrs. Clearwell chase, snare, and wed the rogue herself. He seemed to fancy rich widows.

But for her part, Lily was done with the man. Having

rescued her earring from his evil clutches, she really had no reason ever to think of Derek Knight again, nor did she care to.

Unfortunately, she still did.

She was still stung by his words that day at Hyde Park. Who was he to make her feel ashamed of herself for her plan to marry Edward? He had called her a fortune hunter, a species he seemed to equate with the ranks of soiled doves! If others had seen her in this light since she had arrived in London—an impoverished aristocrat in search of a wealthy husband—Major Knight had been the only one rude enough to say it to her face, and as far as she was concerned, he could go hang.

It was all very easy for him to sit back and judge her. Men had a hundred courses open to them in life. They could go to school, receive an advanced education, or learn a respectable trade, but not women, and certainly not ladies. As her mother had said, there was only one acceptable route open to ladies of quality, and that was the path of an advantageous marriage.

So let Derek Knight mock her, then, if he was cad enough to be so ungallant. He with his countless advantages, his wealthy family and powerful connections, his training, his talents, the whole male-ruled world at his feet. Fortune and glory, indeed.

But—if he *dared* utter one uncivil word to her again, Lily vowed, she would give him a tongue-lashing he would never forget, and she didn't care who heard.

With that, she banished Derek Knight from her mind and focused her efforts on Edward.

She was quite impressed with her beau so far tonight. Edward was on his best behavior since their host of the evening was Lord Fallow, his longtime patron.

Edward was looking smart in a luxurious plum tailcoat and cream-colored breeches. He was as elegant as Lily had ever seen him. He fidgeted uncomfortably—perhaps his valet had put too much starch in his cravat—but all in all, Lily was pleased and could not help patting herself on the back for the visible improvement in his demeanor. Clearly, she had been a good influence on him.

A courting couple, they promenaded through the statuary hall, where the checkerboard marble floor stretched on for miles beneath the soaring arches above the white colonnade. The architectural lines of the grand hall were crisp and clean, the walls a soft gray-blue, a quiet background for the dark, heroic bronzes that posed dramatically among the guests while ancient alabaster busts of Greek philosophers peered out from their niches in the walls.

The statuary hall opened onto the formal garden in a large, square courtyard around which the house was built. Knee-high parterres were sculpted into intricate designs with abundant flowers and topiaries. Twilight had come, but delicate lanterns strung across the garden illuminated the place where the pianist and his accompanists would soon perform beneath the stars. The grand pianoforte had been stationed in the center of the garden, the paper lanterns reflecting on its shiny angled top.

For now, a harpist played in the statuary hall, creating a serene and elegant mood for the evening. The guests mingled quietly, taking wine and light refreshments ahead of the private concert.

Lily pulled Edward aside to admire a mosaic table by the wall. Under glass, the tabletop was inlaid with the fading but still colorful fragments of ancient Roman tiles. Lily gasped when Edward started to set his wineglass on it, but he stopped and looked at her with a twinkle in his hazel eyes that confessed he was only teasing.

"Don't scare me like that!" she whispered with a chiding smile, pressing her hand to her heart.

He turned away with a chuckle. "Ah, finally, there's someone I know!" he said, squinting toward the ballroom's distant entrance.

Lily followed his glance, but when she saw the person Edward was referring to, her whole body tensed.

It was Derek Knight . . . with yet another woman.

He was not in uniform, but had donned sleek finery of formal black and white. She stared at his wild, black mane, which he had worn unbound tonight, all at odds with his evening attire, a clash of elegance and savagery.

His long hair, shiny and thick, spilled to his massive shoulders. It made him look completely uncivilized, and for the life of her, Lily could not tear her gaze off the man.

Oblivious to her agitation, Edward waved the handsome scoundrel over with a hearty laugh.

Lily glanced at Edward in dismay, but she supposed she shouldn't object too much. Derek Knight was one of the few men connected to London's best families who seemed genuinely to accept Edward. Their affinity was no doubt based on their common ties to the army in India.

For her part, she could only wonder whether the major would acknowledge her or snub her with a cut after their private tiff at Hyde Park. Then Lily's gaze wandered to the formidable beauty he escorted this evening, a sultry brunette garbed in deep purple satin trimmed with black lace—half mourning. Another well-heeled widow, it would seem. But, of course. How convenient for him that so many beautiful brides of the ton had been married off to gouty old men.

An elaborate amethyst necklace dripped across her white chest. The lady, too, had loosed her mahogany hair, apparently joining the major in setting this new, uncivilized trend. The beautiful pair seemed to savor their shared rebellion.

Lily looked away, wishing she hadn't noticed the glow of recent sex in the woman's cheeks. For all she knew, that beast might have ravished her in the carriage on the way over here. *Humph.* When a twinge of envy struck, she dropped her gaze, cursing all men and Derek Knight and herself most of all, for her distressing failure to remain indifferent to him.

Walking into the earl's home with his latest companion, Derek saw Ed Lundy wave to him and returned the distant salutation, but he tensed when he spotted Miss Balfour standing by him, trying to look nonchalant.

He would not have admitted it for a maharajah's ransom, but after several days away from her, the sight of Lily Balfour roused the most curious reaction in the region of his solar plexus. It constricted his lungs and set his idiotic heart to pounding, much to his annoyance. *What is this?* he thought impatiently, confused and a bit disgusted with himself. *I don't even like her, the little hussy.*

Of course, for a man of such vaunted honesty, this was a bold-faced lie, but then again, he had some skill in ignoring facts regarding his own emotions. All he would admit to was a begrudging admiration of her beauty.

The girl looked good.

Good enough to eat.

A wistful ache of longing pulsed through him at the sight of her simple loveliness, so different from that of the dangerous seductress on his arm.

Miss Balfour was dressed in light blue silk, a jaunty toque with a white ostrich plume curling over her head. Flaxen spiral curls peeked out from beneath her little hat. Her pale satin gloves gapped beneath her elbow, a tempting spot for a man to slip his finger.

Derek routed a fleeting mental image of the girl wearing nothing but her dashed diamond earrings and reminded himself briskly that the little harpy had impugned his honor, not to mention insulted his military service.

Mercenary, indeed, he thought with a low snort, the memory of their verbal duel in Hyde Park still fresh in his mind. Unfortunately, their mutual business with her suitor meant their paths were bound to cross again.

It seemed they would be forced to play nice together—at least in front of Society. Unlike her suitor, after all, they were two people of excellent breeding.

For his part, Derek was sure he could be civil to her, at least on the surface. In truth, he had been looking forward to this for the past several days, a new chance to taunt her, albeit politely—an amusing opportunity to make her squirm a bit, the little liar.

No doubt she was still scared to death that he might tell her precious Edward about their wild kiss on the night of the masked ball.

Alas, Derek thought of it often. Even now, desire whispered through his senses, but he refused to admit to any low impulse of envy toward her clod of a beau.

If, by contrast, Miss Balfour betrayed signs of jealousy toward the curvaceous goddess on his arm, well, Derek thought with a bland smile, he believed he'd quite enjoy that.

Masking his eagerness to spar with her again, he gave his new paramour an artificial smile as he tucked her hand into the crook of his elbow and escorted her toward the happy couple.

CHAPTER
◌ EIGHT ◌

*L*ily studied the ceiling medallions and waved her fan, affecting boredom, as the stud of the Season joined them with his latest plaything hanging on his side.

He nodded when he saw her and his eyes, pale steel blue, locked on hers in chilly recognition. Cynical amusement glinted in their depths. "Miss Balfour," he said ever so politely.

She held her breath and forced out, "Major."

He did the introductions then, presenting his lady friend to her and Edward as one Mrs. Frances Coates.

Edward did his best not to gawk and stammer in the gorgeous creature's presence. Meanwhile, Lily noticed several women around the marble hall glaring at the new arrivals, including the patrician blonde who had been by the major's side at the masked ball and had interrupted their tryst at the garden folly.

Poor woman, Lily thought. Just another unfortunate thrall he had left in his wake. *I am so glad I have more sense than these women.* Mother was right. Rich and stupid was the way to go, and her Edward was the best of both worlds. He wasn't stupid in business, otherwise he would not have grown so rich, but in truth, he was really rather dense when it came to women, and far from being jealous of his dazed staring at Mrs. Frances Coates, Lily was beginning to see how his awkwardness with females could work to her advantage.

In any case, she could not have borne it if he were as

suave and sly as his new friend. For that matter, she sincerely hoped Derek Knight did not become a bad influence on her beau.

Mrs. Clearwell had now noted the arrival of her favorite and flew over from where she had been conversing with some of her acquaintances, exclaiming over the exotic major and making much of him, like a dashed mother hen.

"My dear boy! How charming to see you again!"

"Mrs. Clearwell." He bent and gave her a quick, filial kiss on her offered cheek. "I see you are in need of more wine, madam. Red or white?"

"Champagne punch, if you are offering!"

He asked his companion, too, what she would like to drink, but when he took leave of them to fetch their beverages, Mrs. Clearwell invited herself to go along with him.

Lily tensed in private alarm as she watched her chaperone go bustling off into the crowd with the major. *Oh, dear.* Heaven only knew what her godmother might say to him about her. Meanwhile, the gorgeous Mrs. Coates remained with Edward and Lily. She watched her lover walk away with a savoring stare.

Enjoy it while it lasts, Lily thought irreverently, looking askance at the woman. *After you, he'll be on to the next.*

"So." The sophisticated widow turned to them with a dazed smile. "How do you all know *Derek*?"

Lily flinched slightly at the lascivious way his name dripped off the woman's tongue, but Edward quickly explained their acquaintance through his important committee post. It seemed he could not resist adding that, like the glamorous major, he, too, had served in India.

"Really?" Mrs. Coates echoed, looking at him with new interest.

"Yes, ma'am," he answered gravely.

Lily could tell her suitor was thrilled by the elegant beauty's attention, a fact that, strangely, amused more than irritated her.

"I imagine it's very exotic," Mrs. Coates said breathlessly.

"Mainly, ma'am, it's hot," Edward said in his blunt way. "At least the part where I was."

"Hm." Mrs. Coates twirled a lock of her dark hair around her finger and tilted her head with a curious frown. "You know, I never understood how the whole thing works—how it is that you brave fellows manage to come back from India with such kingly fortunes."

Edward laughed. "Well, I can explain it to you, Mrs. Coates! It's the same idea as how the Royal Navy compensates its men in addition to their wages, which the whole world knows are very small."

"Yes?"

"When an enemy ship is taken, you see, both officers and men are rewarded with a set percentage of the value of the prize ship taken—the spoils of war. Likewise in India; for every victory attained, the booty is doled out from the treasure of our vanquished foes."

"Quite right," Derek Knight agreed as he rejoined them and handed Mrs. Coates her sparkling goblet of champagne punch.

The woman beamed at him.

Lily looked away.

"The reward system attracts talent and keeps morale high," the major explained, continuing where Edward left off.

"Sounds to me like it merely creates an incentive to engage in bloodshed," Lily said under her breath.

The others turned and stared at her in surprise, but Derek Knight smiled uncomfortably. "There's more to it than that, Miss Balfour."

Realizing her unguarded comment had been overheard, Lily shrugged. Though coloring a bit, she held her ground. "If you look at it logically, this reward system you describe encourages violence, even in cases where perhaps it is not warranted. All I mean to say is that there must be better ways to make a living."

"To be sure," Derek replied with a smooth laugh. "It would certainly make my life easier simply to snare a rich wife to keep me in the style that I'm accustomed to." He snaked his arm around Mrs. Coates's slim waist and gave her a squeeze. "What do you say, my little honeycomb?" he drawled. "Why don't you sign your fortune over to me in holy matrimony?"

"Fat chance," she replied in worldly amusement. "You have no idea what I had to go through to get it."

The woman's droll riposte broke the awkward tension that Lily's stern opinions had created, but the sharp light in Derek's eyes when he glanced over at her made it clear to her alone that of course she was the intended target of his jest. And then, to make matters even more unpleasant, Bess Kingsley intruded, as usual. "Eddie! Look at you, lookin' all handsome! Where's your mother tonight?"

"Er, she weren't invited."

Bess let out a thunderous gasp. "You're funning me!"

"No."

"And who is this fine young lady?" the major inquired, passing a quizzical glance over the boisterous, chunky hoyden.

Oh, Lord, Lily thought. Not her, too! Surely even a prowling tomcat like Derek Knight had better taste than that.

Edward hastened to make the major and the loud heiress known to each other while Lily looked on, privately aghast.

After all, if Derek's words of a moment ago were no jest, if he really was looking for a rich female to wed to obtain a life of ease, then he could hope for no more convenient a find than the wealthy she-barbarian, Miss Kingsley. A charming, smooth-talking scoundrel like him could have twisted a simple-minded hoyden like Bess Kingsley easily around his little finger.

"We were just talking about how things work in India," Edward informed her.

"No!" Bess declared.

"What?"

"Surely you couldn't be so cruel, Eddie, you stupid oaf!"

"Uh, pardon?"

"You *wouldn't* speak of such things in front of Miss Balfour! You couldn't!"

"Why not?" Derek asked.

"Because her father died there," Bess announced before Lily could stop her, "trying to restore the family fortunes."

The girl's bald declaration of her family's circumstances rendered Lily speechless, breathless, and more than slightly humiliated.

"Poor dear," Bess added, with a pitying smile on her lips and cruelty in her eyes. "Everyone knows Langdon Balfour died penniless in that godforsaken place. Tsk, tsk. Eddie, you were awfully mean to talk about it here."

With an awkward mumble, Edward stammered a belated and quite needless apology for his insensitive choice of conversational topics, but Derek Knight said nothing, holding Lily in a steady gaze. Then he glanced at Bess.

"How thoughtful of you to bring all this to our attention, Miss Kingsley," he said in a low, velvet tone edged with menace.

"I am sorry for your loss," Mrs. Coates offered with an elegant nod, which Lily returned.

"Thank you. It was a long time ago." She cast about for an excuse to flee, could not find one. "Would you all excuse me? I have to . . ." Her voice trailed off, but she did not stay to try to find an explanation.

"Lily?" Mrs. Clearwell asked softly as she began walking away.

"I'm going to fetch a glass of punch before the—concert starts."

"Shall I—" Edward started.

"No," she said brightly. "I'll be right back."

Derek Knight's stare intensified, still fixed on her, unnoticed by the others. But Lily could not bear to meet his searching gaze. She turned and walked away.

Her misfortune was none of his business. Her great Balfour pride would not tolerate one iota of pity from him or from anyone else. She kept her shoulders squared and her chin high as she went toward the refreshment table, but in truth, she could have wept.

It was all such a waste.

The most wonderful man she'd ever known had died on a distant continent, all for naught. And though the charming major might believe that he, too, was invincible, someday he'd probably share her father's fate.

Soon the music started.

Derek was confused. He had come here tonight still irked at Lily Balfour, prepared to be offended by nearly anything the woman said.

He had not anticipated this tug on his heartstrings.

Of course, he had had no idea that she had lost her father to the vagaries of India, but it wasn't hard to guess that his death was what had led to her family's hard times and precipitated her scheme, in turn, to marry a rich man. Certainly, it accounted for her harsh opinions of Englishmen who went to India to seek their fortune.

It's not me you're angry at, is it, Lily? he mused, watching her as the concert unfolded. *It's your father.*

Going off to India, leaving you behind. Leaving you to fix the problems he failed to solve.

Now that he had a clearer picture of her situation, he felt like a damned heel for chiding her about her fortune-hunting quest. He still didn't like her plan about marrying Ed Lundy, but she was right—he'd had no right to judge her before he knew the facts.

He couldn't stop staring at her during the concert, studying her delicate profile while the tender music played. He ached as he gazed at her gloved hands, so sweetly folded on her lap. The diamond in her earlobe winked like a star in the candlelight, reminding him of the secret they shared. God help him, he wanted more.

He would handle it much differently if only he could be alone with her again. He would be gentler with her, for as he watched her, he realized she really was a very gentle person. Even with Lundy, she was kinder than she had to be.

In between the movements of the piano sonata, when the audience shuffled a little and shifted about, Derek observed the pair together and noted that she never flinched, even when her suitor was at his coarsest. She was all patience and tranquil tact. Derek quite admired her unflappable grace.

Maybe she did really care about Lundy, he mused, but she deserved better. By God, she did.

At the very least, she deserved better treatment from *him*.

When the pianist and his accompaniment finished the sonata, Derek joined the rest of the audience in polite applause for the musicians. The guests were then allowed an intermission. His gaze sharpened when Lundy got up from his seat beside Miss Balfour and trudged off to attend Lord Fallow. Seeing Miss Balfour left alone with her amiable chaperone, Derek turned to Mrs. Coates.

"Would you excuse me, dear?"

"Are you deserting me already?" she murmured.

He kissed her hand. "On the contrary. But . . . I am afraid my words earlier may have offended young Miss Balfour."

"Really?"

He nodded sagely. "I wouldn't want any ill feeling between us, since I have to associate with her future husband in my work. I'm going to go and have a word with her and Mrs. Clearwell. Smooth any ruffled feathers and all that."

"Shall I join you?"

"Er, no. That won't be necessary," he said with a quick smile. "I'll be right back. If you'll excuse me."

"Of course," she replied, giving him a knowing look.

Derek rose, gave her a gentlemanly bow, and then left her without a backward glance to return to Lily Balfour.

When he made his way through the crowd to the row of garden seats where she had been sitting, however, he found her chaperone alone.

Mrs. Clearwell directed him toward the tall, white trellis mounded with creamy pink roses, where he saw Miss Balfour standing by herself, admiring the lush cascade of flowers. Derek thanked her with a nod, then strolled toward the girl just as Miss Balfour leaned in to inhale the blooms' exquisite fragrance.

"A lily among the roses," Derek teased in soft greeting as he intruded upon her solitude.

She turned in surprise, and then smiled uncertainly when she saw him. "They're beautiful. Smell." She cupped her hand beneath a flower and lifted it gently toward him, as far as its green tether of vine would allow.

Holding her gaze, mesmerized by her grace, he leaned down obediently and inhaled its sweet perfume, then smiled at her with a low sound of pleasure.

He straightened up again, unsure how to begin. Lord, was he tongue-tied with this girl?

Extraordinary.

"I see you have your earrings on," he offered in guarded warmth. "Both of them."

"Yes." She quickly touched both of her diamonds, making sure they were both still safely clasped. "I brought them to a jeweler to have the backs tightened. I—wouldn't want to lose one again."

"If you did, I'd help you find it," he said with a rueful half-smile. "Look, I'm not very good at apologies, but I know when I was wrong. The other day at Hyde Park, I was a little free with my opinions. I had no right to judge you. I did not know about your father. Will you . . . accept my apology?"

"If you'll accept mine," she answered softly.

He looked at her in question.

She lowered her gaze with a tentative shrug. "I don't really see you as a mercenary, Major. Your military service is entirely honorable, of course, and you had every right to point out the facts about how operations in India helped to keep us safe here throughout the conflict with Napoleon. I guess I got angry for fear that you'd end up like my father. And," she admitted in chagrin, "I was insulted. I wanted to insult you back."

"Well, it worked," he murmured with an amiable lift of one eyebrow.

She looked at him and covered her lips with her hand as they both started laughing—both at each other and themselves.

"Truce, then?" he asked, smiling. "Are we all done trading insults, or should I summon my diplomat brother-in-law to negotiate a treaty between us?"

"Truce," she answered firmly, holding out her hand.

Derek accepted it and shook her hand in amusement.

Under normal circumstances, he would have kissed a lady's knuckles rather than shaken her hand, but somehow with Lily Balfour, the smooth gallantry he exercised in his usual dealings with females did not seem to apply.

When she released his hand, he gestured toward the garden path. "Shall we go exploring, Miss Balfour?"

Her eyes widened. "Pardon?"

"I meant the garden," he chided. "Someone told me this path goes down to the river."

"The Thames?" she asked with a nervous glance.

"No, the Blue Nile," he said dryly. "I am no longer trying to seduce you, believe me. I merely thought I'd go and have a look. You are welcome to join me."

"Oh. Right. Very well, then." She nodded, clearing her throat a little. "That sounds very pleasant, but I don't know if my chaperone will . . ." One glance in Mrs. Clearwell's direction answered that question before she could utter it.

When they looked over, Mrs. Clearwell was engaged in conversation with another matron while simultaneously keeping a watchful eye on the two of them. Noting her charge's questioning glance, the matron waggled her fingers cheerfully at them, showing no signs of concern for her charge's virtue while under his care.

"Mrs. Clearwell, um, doesn't seem to mind," she mumbled shyly. "I don't suppose a few minutes can do too much harm."

"No."

With this matter decided, she relaxed considerably, gave him a nod, and then set out on the garden path.

As he fell into step alongside her, he almost offered his arm to escort her, but then he decided against it. She was so very tentative with him, so unsure; he did not want to do anything to scare her away or to make her nervous again. He wanted her to know she was safe beside him.

Oddly enough, he discovered that he wanted her to trust him.

They strolled under the stone arch that led out of the courtyard and into the sculpted grounds. Other guests clustered here and there, waiting for the next portion of the concert to begin. Ahead, the graveled walk snaked through the stands of windy trees down to the dark river, silver-spangled with moonlight.

"Mrs. Coates won't mind your absence?" she asked, glancing at him in amusement.

"I told her I would rather talk to you."

"I'm flattered," she drawled, then paused. "She's very beautiful. But they always are, aren't they?"

Derek shrugged with a low, cynical laugh and kept his gaze fixed on the path ahead. "Did your Mr. Lundy enjoy the sonata?" he teased in a grave tone as he slid his hands into his pockets.

"Please." She succumbed to a wry chuckle. "I'm afraid my Mr. Lundy is not a great appreciator of the musical arts as of yet. We're working on it," she added. "I'm fairly sure he was bored senseless. For my part, I thought it was beautiful."

"Yes." Derek pushed his blowing hair out of his face and considered his next move. "I . . . wonder if I might ask you a question of a personal nature, Miss Balfour."

"As if I could stop you?" She sent him a look of amusement. "Very well, Major. You may ask, though I may not answer."

"Why him?"

"Pardon?"

"Why Lundy? And don't give me all that rot that you spouted in the park about all his fine qualities. There are highborn, cultured men of wealth who've been eyeing you all night. Surely you have noticed."

She snorted.

"Why not some young lordling instead of the self-made man?"

She walked along beside him, silent for a moment as she debated, it seemed, on how much to say. "The men you speak of, yes, I've noticed them. The rakes, the fribbles, the frequenters of White's. Frankly, Major, I find them loathsome as a breed."

"Loathsome?" he exclaimed with a laugh, puzzled by her vehemence. "Why?"

"I just do."

"Very well. So, what about you and Lundy, then? I see you are openly courting, but is it true you are not yet engaged?"

"Yes. That is true." She eyed him skeptically. "Why do you ask?"

Derek shrugged in cool nonchalance. "I only wonder why he hasn't yet proposed."

"He will, when he is ready," she assured him.

"Are *you* ready?" he countered, turning to her.

She squared her shoulders and lifted her head. "Of course I am."

He frowned down at her. Unable to resist just one small touch, he captured her chin with his fingertips. "Such determination," he remarked in a low murmur. "I've seen that look before. On my young soldiers heading into battle."

She furrowed her brow, but he dropped his hand before she could rebuke him for the light contact.

They walked on.

"When did you lose your father?" he asked.

"Fifteen years ago."

"You were a child."

"Yes."

"Truly, I am sorry for your loss. India's a . . . hard place."

"You would know."

"He fell in battle?"

"No. No." She let out a sigh. "Nothing so glorious as that. He died of monsoon fever."

He looked askance at her. "Death in battle is not always as glorious as you may have heard," he remarked, then he paused, hesitating. "Still, it's rather odd that the same phenomenon orphaned us both."

She glanced at him in surprise.

"My mother died in a monsoon flood. Floods, fevers. They always go hand in hand, I'm afraid. Fever season always follows on the heels of the annual monsoon floods," he explained in answer to her inquiring look. "All that stagnant water left behind after the rains have moved on. The doctors say it breeds disease."

She shuddered. "And this happens every year?"

"Without fail."

"My word, that sounds terribly unpleasant."

"It is," he agreed with a low laugh. "Insects the size of rabbits. Man-eating tigers. Maharajahs firing a rain of swords down on us from their cannons. A nonstop festival of fun."

She shot him a wry smile. "Well, you must have a death wish, Major, because the other day at Hyde Park, you seemed awfully eager to get back there."

"It's home," he replied. "Besides, there's a war on. My men need me."

"And opportunity awaits," she reminded him with a cheeky little smile.

Derek did not take offense. "Oh, I think you understand about ambition, Lily Balfour." He deemed it a reasonable time to offer his arm, and when he did so, she warily accepted. "In fact," he continued, pleased to find her warming up to him, "I think we have more in common than either of us cares to admit."

"How so?"

"We are in the same boat. Money-grubbing in London, for a cause larger than ourselves. You to save your family, I, to get the military funds released. Still it is a rather galling duty, is it not?"

She just looked at him.

"Ah, well." He did not see fit to press the issue overmuch. "At least now that I know about your sire, I can understand why you would hate all things Indian, but I assure you, in spite of its many dangers, it is a land of astounding beauty."

"That's partly why my father was obsessed with it. He promised to bring back a sack full of rubies for Mother and one full of diamonds for me," she said wryly.

"Ah, one of those, was he? Well, I think I have the picture now." Derek shook his head. "If I had a shilling for every new recruit I've had to educate about the realities versus the myths concerning the treasures of the East . . ."

"Yes, well, Papa didn't have much use for stark realities, Major. That was the heart of the problem. He was a dreamer—which is why my family should've never let him go. My mother, my grandfather. They both should have known perfectly well that he was not the sort of man who could survive it. Papa was not—like you," she added haltingly. "He did not have—your qualities."

"What qualities?" he demanded when she immediately protested with a mumbled, "Never mind." "No, I am altogether intrigued now," he said in amusement. "What *qualities* do you mean, Miss Balfour?"

"Well—ruthlessness, for one thing."

Not exactly a compliment, then. "Me? Ruthless?" he exclaimed, all innocence.

They both started laughing.

"Perhaps not entirely, but you must admit you do have a ruthless side, at least."

"Never!"

"Don't lie. Oh, yes, it shows," she assured him. "Somehow I can easily picture you in battle."

"I'd rather you didn't try. It might give you nightmares."

"Well, I certainly can't picture Papa fighting a war. It's funny, though. I was thinking about him that night at the garden folly before I met you. He built me a garden folly to play in when I was a little girl—or half built it, I should say. Papa never quite finished anything."

Abruptly, she fell silent—at which moment Derek leaned down and kissed her head.

"It'll be all right," he whispered, based on absolutely nothing. He didn't even believe it himself half the time, but somehow, those few words always seemed to work. She gave him a strange, grateful little half-smile.

Releasing his arm, she stood beside him as they came to the river's edge and watched its relentless current.

"Life, Miss Balfour," Derek said after a long pause, "is not for the faint of heart, is it?"

"No," she whispered, turning to hold his grave glance.

Emotion came from nowhere as he stared at her. Unshed tears that could have strangled him; the echo of a thousand screams that he had never given voice; the profound despair left behind after unfathomable violence. Sometimes he wondered how he was still standing. The night sky spun like the darkness that enveloped him. He just stood there beside her, completely at a loss.

After a moment, she slowly reached out and took his hand.

Her light eyes were locked on his face, searching his very soul, it seemed, with her exquisite gentleness.

"Come," she murmured, taking a firmer hold on his arm, turning him around to face the house, its distant lanterns and music.

Derek gazed at her.

He did not say another word throughout their slow, somber march back to the realm of light.

She did, however.

She chatted away as blithely as a canary, as if she knew her voice was the only thread he had left to follow to keep him from getting lost in the darkness. She made casual remarks about the flower beds here, the ornate birdbath over there, the hors d'oeuvres that awaited them back at the house. He didn't pay much attention to the words, but somehow her reassuring tone brought him back safely from the savage deserts that had formed inside him over the years.

When they approached the stone arch that would take them back into the courtyard, back into the hustle and bustle of ton civility, he finally managed a smile.

And back we go to our appointed partners.

She stopped and turned to him, searching his face with a probing stare that could not hide her obvious distress for him. Her concern made it hurt a little less. Why it hurt tonight, that was the question. He had gotten so good at ignoring his feelings, but that was harder to do in her presence.

"You know, Major," she said with a bolstering smile, "I never did get to say thank you for rescuing my earring. Thanks."

He bowed to her, all the more captivated. "If anything else needs rescuing, Miss Balfour, you let me know."

"I will. And Major—" she added as he turned to go.

Derek paused and looked at her in question.

She bit her lip and smiled. "I think now you can call me Lily."

He raised his eyebrows. "May I, indeed?"

"Well—only when no one else is present, of course."

"Of course . . . Lily," he echoed, savoring her little gift. He did not want to leave her, but it couldn't be helped. He contented himself with a discreet, appreciative glance over the alluring length of her. Then he smiled wryly. "Give Edward my best."

"Have fun with Mrs. Coates," she answered.

He snapped his fingers. "Right! I could not remember her name for the life of me."

She shook her head at him but made no effort to detain him any longer.

He nodded and took leave of her, confident that his mask of insouciance was firmly back in place as he returned to his proper station.

Lily watched him in troubled tenderness as he strode back gracefully into the courtyard.

Before long, she was in Edward's company again, Mrs. Clearwell nearby, minding her with palpable curiosity. She knew her chaperone was dying to ask her what they had talked about on their stroll down to the river, but Lily wasn't sure what she would say.

She had gained more of an insight into what drove this man than she had ever expected to, and what she had glimpsed in him . . . was pain. Her heart hurt for him.

She knew from firsthand experience how much it hurt to lose a parent at a young age, but on top of that, Derek had also lived through the horrors of war. Clearly, his brave service had cost him just as much, if not more than, it had gained him. She felt awful for her previous accusation that he had only joined the military for self-interest's sake.

But dash it, relatively speaking, it had been easier for her peace of mind when she could dismiss Derek Knight as a hedonistic rakehell, or at the very least, a mercenary adventurer.

Now that she had witnessed the shadowed depths behind his breezy exterior, there was no escaping the realization that all of his amorous conquests were driven by more than mere sensual indulgence. She saw now that he used these women to escape his demons, as though love-making were some sort of anesthesia, as if he could numb his mind with the pleasures of the flesh.

Knowing this, however, did not make it any easier to see the major leave at the end of the night with the eagerly smiling Mrs. Coates hanging on to him as before.

Lily flinched as the glamorous pair went out the door together. But then she lowered her gaze. For the worst of it was, she was all too familiar with that impulse, seeking comfort in the arms of someone who didn't really care about you. Though it numbed the pain for the moment, in the end, it only left you feeling worse.

Derek . . .

And all the way home with her chatty godmother, Lily had very little to say.

For reasons unknown to himself—reasons he did not care to question—Derek dropped the ravishing Mrs. Coates at her fashionable townhouse after the soiree and declined her silken invitation to her bed. He knew his refusal had shocked her. Truth be told, he had shocked himself, but bloody hell, he did not particularly feel like servicing anyone tonight. Was that so wrong?

He refused to acknowledge that his sudden distaste for the prospect of a night of debauchery with Fanny Coates could have anything to do with Lily Balfour.

Instead, he stubbornly turned his attention to practical matters. He had things to do. His mood was restless and still decidedly dark, but all that he would admit to in his own mind was the handy rationale that it was the perfect time to press on with his investigation.

The dead of night was an ideal hour for covert snooping, a perfect chance to survey the various committee members' houses. Under cover of darkness, he could spy on them freely with little danger of being seen.

With that, he went back to the Althorpe, changed into all black clothes, and saddled his horse. Before long, he was riding out to the northwest fringe of London, where the committee's top-ranked East India Company magnate resided in a fine villa.

Along the way, his magnificent Tattersall's beast sweeping through the darkness at a fluid canter, Derek mused on the events of the evening. It had been a fruitful night, even apart from the new developments between him and Lily.

He had run across Lord Sinclair at the concert and furthered the chairman's skewed but useful misapprehension of his character by the simple presence of the hot-blooded beauty on his arm. At first, Derek had been insulted by the earl's impression of him as a typical swaggering cavalry man, but he had since shrugged it off.

Hell, it never hurt to let the enemy underestimate you. Showing up at Society events with the Mrs. Coateses of the world nibbling on one's earlobe maintained a useful illusion. If Sinclair judged him some sort of dull-witted savage, awash in sensuality and therefore easily manipulated, then he might let his guard down long enough for Derek to get to the truth about what had happened to that 300,000 pounds sterling.

So far, both the money and answers proved elusive. But

while Lord Sinclair might not be the actual embezzler, given that any shortage in the fund was ultimately his responsibility as chairman, Derek still did not trust the old fellow.

Meanwhile all week, Lundy had been keeping him abreast of what was happening in the committee behind closed doors. According to Lundy, Sinclair was still determined to keep the whole thing quiet and solve the matter internally without involving the Home Office, which would no doubt demand a formal investigation—a slow and tedious process.

There wasn't time for that nonsense. The men needed their resources now.

In any case, Lundy said they'd had another private meeting. Once more, Sinclair had called the committee members together and expressed his disgust, demanding that whoever was responsible come forward and replace the "borrowed" money at once, no questions asked.

At the moment, they were waiting to give the as-yet-unknown embezzler one week to gather the stolen sum and return it to the fund. Then the army's treasure trove could be released in total, avoiding the disgrace of any shortage being found out.

Sinclair's directive might bring swift results, but Derek had begun preparing in case it did not. If no one came forward, then his task would be to investigate the financial picture of each committee member.

How exactly he was going to do that, he had no idea. He was used to much more forthright conflicts, the kind you could solve with a sword. This called for a subtler set of talents.

All the men on the committee *appeared* wealthy, but appearances could be deceiving. Somehow, he would have to find a way to see through the mask of wealth and find out which of the men might recently have been in enough financial trouble to be desperate enough to embezzle government funds placed in their trust.

As best he could figure, the first step would be to take a

cursory look at each of the men's houses and holdings, the number of servants they employed, recent large purchases, debts held, investments, and so forth—any major expenses.

Meanwhile, Lundy was working on putting together a list for him of the names of those who helped the committee members handle their own financial affairs: solicitors, secretaries, land agents, bankers. Derek intended to question these employees if necessary. Getting them to talk would not be easy, but if he impressed upon them the seriousness of this matter and their own culpability in a possible hanging offense, they could likely prove excellent sources of information.

Oh, yes, he intended to study each man on the committee, check them out one by one until he could clear those who were probably not involved and narrow down his list of likely culprits through a logical process of elimination.

He still wasn't sure where to place Ed Lundy on that list. Whether he could really trust his supposed ally was another whole question unto itself. The man was being helpful, but, obviously, that could be a ruse meant to throw him off the trail.

For Lily Balfour's sake, Derek prayed to God that Lundy was not involved. He did not want her anywhere near that kind of danger.

Meeting their host Lord Fallow earlier tonight, though briefly, had been somewhat reassuring. Recently retired from a long career in public life, the slim, gray-haired earl was renowned for his integrity, and if a man like Fallow gave Ed Lundy his seal of approval, then that counted for something, as did Lundy's military service.

Perhaps his sympathy for a fellow soldier was a blind bias on Derek's part, but he sure as hell didn't trust the rest of them, and he had to start somewhere. He had to trust someone, at least a little bit.

If life in the army had taught him one thing, it was that you weren't going to get very far all by yourself. It was common sense. Only by working together could anyone hope to accomplish such ominous tasks.

Cautiously, therefore, he had placed Lundy down at the bottom of his list.

Perhaps tonight would yield another suspect he could blame.

He hoped so, for Lily's sake.

After all, he could not let her marry an embezzler bound for the gallows. Her good name would never survive the scandal of being associated with—let alone marrying—a ruined thief. Her reputation would be destroyed, and then who would marry her and help her save her family?

Derek could not possibly let such a calamity happen to her. Hell, no. He'd be watching out for her every step of the way, whether she knew it or not.

And if Lundy turned out to be guilty, well, then, Derek mused, he might just have to take his big brother's advice and wed the lovely little gold digger himself.

With that, Derek spotted the villa in the distance. Maneuvering his horse into a grove of trees, he sprang down from the saddle and stationed his animal in a safe place.

Relishing the chance to have some proper action after so long away from the front, he touched the various weapons he had girded himself with out of habit, and then stole through the darkness toward the committee man's sprawling residence.

All was quiet.

Moments later, he scaled the walls around the manor with a stealth gained in countless raids with his men in the cool of the black Deccan night. But although he worked alone tonight, the isolation that had plagued him of late seemed to have gone into retreat.

For it was not terror haunting him this time, but the memory of a wary smile, and shining eyes the soft lavender shade of English bluebells . . .

CHAPTER
∞ NINE ∞

*D*erek Knight was becoming a problem.

The instant Lily awoke the next morning, the image of his wry smile flooded into her mind. She let out a small sigh and merely stared at the ceiling.

This would not do.

She refused to want what she could not have. She thought of Edward, took a deep breath, and arose, refusing to waver in her decision.

As soon as she was dressed, she went downstairs to take breakfast with her doting chaperone. All of a sudden, over eggs and toast, Lily surprised them both by abruptly proposing a shopping excursion.

Indeed, browsing through the luxurious shops on Bond Street later that day helped her keep things in perspective. One day the great Balfour clan would be restored to wealth and dignity, thanks to her sacrifice; her conscience would finally be cleared, the record of her blame expunged, and when she married Edward, all these fancy trifles that loaded the shops' shelves would be in easy reach instead of unattainable, and then surely Mother would think well of her again.

Lily made a point of idling at length in the busy shops of London's top modistes who specialized in designing bridal gowns for Society's loftiest weddings.

What *was* Edward waiting for? she wondered, recalling with a twinge of uneasiness Derek's impertinent question last night about why her suitor had not yet seen fit to propose. Fingering a bolt of glorious ivory silk, Lily shrugged off her doubts and went to sit at the low table in the center of the luxurious shop, where she indulged herself in perusing the dressmaker's sketchbook showing off her beautiful designs.

No doubt Edward would soon come up to scratch, she assured herself. In the meantime, she always liked to have a plan, and what young lady did not enjoy a bit of daydreaming about her wedding day?

There were veils and jeweled hair ornaments to be considered, the perfect satin slippers to be found, beautiful white silk stockings, lace garters and satin stays, and fluffy petticoats to give the skirts just the right shape.

It was so much easier to consider these details than to ponder the dreary bulk of her married years ahead.

As she slowly turned the pages of the modiste's sketchbook, the words of Derek's latest fashionable widow kept echoing through her mind. When he had tendered that irreverent marriage proposal to Mrs. Coates last night at the concert, teasing her to sign over her fortune to him, she had answered, "Darling, you have no idea what I went through to get it."

Lily didn't want to think about what Mrs. Coates might have had to go through in order to inherit her late husband's wealth.

Meanwhile, Mrs. Clearwell had charmed the modiste into inviting the two of them to have a peek at some of the gowns in progress, which the woman told them could take weeks to create, what with all their exquisite beading and row upon scalloped row of intricate rosettes, airy layers of fine net, and ribbon trim.

Yet somehow the haughty modiste's finest samples left Lily uninspired. Disastrously, it was not Edward's face her heart conjured when she gazed at one of the lavish bridal gowns, imagined herself in it, and then saw in her mind's eye the man standing by her at the altar.

Oh, for heaven's sake!

She didn't bloody deserve to wear white, anyway.

"All this is a bit too ostentatious for my taste," she murmured to her godmother when the modiste had hurried off to tend to other ladies. Mrs. Clearwell was ogling a sumptuous rose-colored gown that the seamstresses were making for some highborn mother of a bride. "I need more choices," Lily said restlessly.

Her chaperone gave her an arch look. "Indeed, you do."

"Why don't we go over to the bookstore? The ladies' magazines they have might give me more ideas."

"Capital notion, dear. Onward."

They thanked the women and left the shop. Lily took her godmother's arm, helping to steer the older lady along as they crossed the busy street.

Marry Derek Knight! she thought, mentally scoffing at the purely devilish notion that had popped into her head back in the bridal shop.

What an excellent way to ruin her life!

No doubt he could make it worth her while in their marriage bed, but that would be the only compensation.

Besides, he was already married—to the army. The wild major showed not the slightest interest in becoming domesticated, despite his cheeky proposal to the rich Mrs. Coates.

If he *could* be lured into captivity, and if Lily were mad enough to marry such a barbarian, it would not only mean that she'd have to stay poor and fail her family, but worse, she'd have to follow the blackguard to that horrible land of monsoons and man-eating tigers—make a home for them in the midst of an army camp, and patch him up after every bloody battle!

Good Lord, what if she went with him and he was killed in the war? She'd be stranded in India without another soul she knew.

It was the worst idea in the world. Indeed, if she ever showed the slightest willingness to do all that, they should lock her up at once in a lunatic asylum.

She was a *lady,* and ladies did not live in tents.

Ahead, the door of the bookshop stood invitingly open beneath a dark-green façade with gilt lettering. A knot of idlers crowded around the bay window, laughing at the newest satirical cartoons, which the bookseller posted daily to help lure customers inside.

Mrs. Clearwell and she walked into the bustling establishment and set out to find the ladies' magazines, along with any new pattern books with more gowns to consider or other publications featuring the latest bridal fashions.

But as they began to meander through the dim, cozy aisles, squeezing around people here and there, Lily gnawed her lip, struck by yet another reason why the mere notion of marrying Derek Knight was entirely preposterous.

The whole point of marrying a rich but stupid man was to gain access to a husband's fortune without having to explain her lack of virginity. Since Derek Knight, the cunning warrior, was no more stupid than he was rich, she knew he would require a detailed explanation if he was her husband, and there was no way on earth she could ever confess her stupidity to him.

She shuddered at the thought of the whole sordid matter being broken open and dragged out into the light again after all this time. The prospect nearly made her nauseous.

Still, she couldn't help wondering in one corner of her mind how he would react to the story of her deception at the hands of a handsome but conscienceless roué. It was all too easy to imagine how a wild man like the major would respond. To be sure, he would probably hunt Lord Owen Masters down without any further questions and proceed to tear him limb from limb.

Ah, well. Though there was a certain satisfaction in contemplating it, Lily knew this was nothing but a dark, fleeting fantasy. She was a Christian woman and had heard enough sermons to mind the warning that vengeance belonged to the Lord.

Besides, she thought with grim stoicism, she had survived. She had learned her lesson and was never trusting anyone again.

Not really.

"Ah, here is what you're looking for." Mrs. Clearwell halted, plucked a slim booklet off the shelf, and handed

Lily a copy of *La Belle Assemblée.* "Their 'Mirror of Fashion' column might have something for you. Here's another." Mrs. Clearwell also discovered a stack of the newest *Lady's Monthly Museum.* "Are you at all hungry, dear? I'm a bit peckish. There was a little coffeehouse on the corner we passed—"

All of a sudden, her words were cut off and she nearly fell forward as a little boy knocked into her, having just come barreling around the corner in the blink of an eye and running down the narrow aisle between the bookshelves.

"Oh!" Mrs. Clearwell exclaimed as Lily quickly steadied her.

The boy, barely waist-high, darted past them, but they could already hear his minder coming.

"Matthew! Come back here! Excuse me, ladies. I'm so sorry. My nephew's a little rambunctious."

Still holding onto Mrs. Clearwell, Lily turned to give the offending party an indignant look, but her eyes widened.

"Miss Balfour! M-Mrs. Clearwell," Derek Knight stammered in surprise. He hesitated. "One moment, please—I have to catch my nephew. If he runs off, my sister will have my head. Don't go anywhere! I'll be right back."

"Do you need any help with him?" Lily offered, but Derek was already gone.

Mrs. Clearwell and she exchanged a startled and rather uncertain smile.

"His sister's child?" Lily whispered.

"That little hellion's a future marquess?" her chaperone answered.

They laughed and followed in the direction the seemingly overwhelmed Uncle Derek had gone, but soon found the pair again. This time, the major had the five-year-old firmly by the hand.

He presented Matthew Prescott, Lord Aylesworth, to the ladies. "Matthew," he added sternly, "apologize to the nice ladies for running into them like a ruffian."

Matthew turned his great, brown eyes imploringly at his uncle; Derek gave him a no-nonsense stare.

Lily fought not to smile as Matthew heaved a sigh. "I'm sorry."

Lily gave him a sage nod of forgiveness, but Mrs. Clearwell couldn't help smiling.

"No harm done, my young sir, but do have a care if you intend to run amok. A boy could fall and break his head."

Lily and Derek exchanged a private smile, their gazes mingling perhaps longer than they should have.

Her heart was racing. She couldn't believe how delighted she was to see him. She feared she was blushing.

Meanwhile, her chaperone befriended Matthew. "You must be a very clever boy if you had your uncle bring you here to buy you books."

"We were looking for, er, quieter pursuits," Derek interjected. "My sister wasn't feeling very well, so I said I'd take him out so she could rest. Otherwise, he'd never leave her side."

Lily gazed at him, warmed by his attentiveness to his family.

"Did you find anything to read, Matthew?" Mrs. Clearwell asked the boy.

Matthew turned to her matter-of-factly. "I can climb all the way to the top of these shelves!" he announced, not quite in answer to the question, but no matter. He pointed upward with an air of great urgency.

"No, Matthew," said Uncle Derek. "I told you, you are not to climb the shelves." He looked ruefully at the ladies. "We were trying to find a book on animals."

"I'm a tiger! *Roarrr!*"

Mrs. Clearwell feigned fright. "Oh, dear!"

Derek regarded the child dryly. "Yes, I know, it's hard to imagine he'll be a leading peer of the realm one day."

"We were all small once, Major," Lily answered, chuckling. "He is your sister's child, you say?"

"Lord Griffith was widowed before he married my sister. Matthew's mother was the marquess's first wife."

"Oh, the poor child's an orphan?" Mrs. Clearwell asked with great sympathy.

"Not anymore," Derek replied. "He's got a new mother now, and he adores her."

Matthew grinned.

Lily smiled, warmed by the pleasure that showed in Derek's eyes when he spoke of his family. He obviously loved them a great deal. She turned to the boy. "What will you do when you're a tiger, Matthew? If I may ask."

"I'll scare the bad people away from all the little children," he answered somberly. He brightened again. "Then I'll eat them!"

"I say!" Mrs. Clearwell exclaimed, pressing her hand to her heart.

"He's been through some hard things of late," Derek confided to the women in a softer tone. "He was nearly abducted less than a month ago."

Lily's eyes widened. "How horrible!" she breathed.

He nodded. "His father has made some unsavory enemies in the course of his diplomatic career. But all's well now. We're just hoping that Matthew understands he's safe now and life is back to normal. He's finally coming out of his shell—as you've probably noticed."

"I'm sure he feels safe with you, Major," Mrs. Clearwell murmured, beaming at him.

Not just feels safe, Lily thought. *Is safe.* There was a difference.

Derek gave Mrs. Clearwell a modest smile, then he noticed Lily's ardent gaze fixed on him. When his glance happened across her trusty diamond earrings, which she wore again today, he slipped her a knowing little half-smile, fraught with secretive intimacy. "I see you ladies found some books to purchase," he remarked, changing the subject.

Lily's blush deepened. "Just some silly fashion magazines." She tried to put them casually behind her back.

"Full of wedding gowns," Mrs. Clearwell added sweetly.

Lily winced.

"Ah." Derek looked at her intently.

"What about you, Major? Oh, no—is that what I think it is?" Happy to direct attention elsewhere, Lily beckoned to him to hand over the small, cheaply bound volume tucked under his arm.

"What, this?" he evaded. "Oh—nothing."

"*The Castle of Otranto*?" she read out in hilarity. "Surely not! Oh, Major, and I thought you were a man of sense."

"You're the one reading brainless fashion magazines!" he retorted as both ladies had a hearty chuckle at his less than intellectual selection—as if they could talk.

"For your information, I happen to enjoy these little dreadfuls," he defended. "Perhaps it's not the most challenging material, but it's a nice . . . bedtime story! It helps me fall asleep."

"Asleep? Who can sleep after reading one of these blood-thirsty tales?" Lily retorted, relishing this rare chance to tease him.

Clearly, the proud major was thoroughly chagrined at having been discovered in his propensity for Gothic horror novels.

Lily nudged Mrs. Clearwell. "Cousin Pamela would be so pleased."

"I know!"

"Who's Cousin Pamela?"

"Er, my cousin," Lily said sardonically. "Her name is Pamela."

He tilted his head at her with a warning look.

"She writes Gothic stories," she added in an ominous stage whisper. It was hard to resist teasing him.

"Really?" His interest was genuine, whatever his flimsy excuses about his choice of reading material. "Have her tales been published?"

"Heavens, no," Lily replied in an ironical tone. "Ladies don't write novels."

"But you just said—"

"Nevertheless."

His lips flattened and he arched a brow at her. "If your cousin sold her books under a pen name, wouldn't that help to relieve your family's predicament?"

Apparently, they had moved on to warm enough terms

with each other that they could now joke about the great Balfours' misfortune.

For some strange reason, Lily was not offended.

"My dear Major," she retorted in a flippant tone, "when family honor is all one's got left, it must be preserved with the utmost stringency."

"Yes, but don't deprive an eager audience of worthy entertainment. Are your cousin's stories any good?"

"They're horrifying. Terrible. *Macabre*."

"Excellent!"

"They're better than this one, at any rate." Lily gave him a jaunty grin full of pride in her oddball cousin as she handed his chosen book back to him. " 'And if you should have nightmares, Gentle Reader,' " she intoned, " 'I suggest you try a cup of warm milk!' "

"You're mad." He laughed, but there was something slightly uncomfortable behind his eyes.

Lily had almost failed to notice it. "Just a little," she conceded.

"Er, Matthew!" Mrs. Clearwell called, directing the major's attention to his errant nephew.

Derek hastily plucked the climbing boy off the bookshelves, then set Matthew up on his shoulders, where he could not escape again.

Lily looked up at the child, smiling.

Hazy memories shimmered of the years gone by when her father used to carry her on his shoulders like that.

Seeing Derek Knight in the unexpected role of family man did strange, quivery things to her insides.

"Oh, I'm famished from all this shopping!" Mrs. Clearwell suddenly declared. "Major, have you tried the famous Gunter's since you've come to Town?"

"No, but I've heard about it."

"Matthew, do tigers eat ice cream?"

The future marquess threw his small fist triumphantly into the air. "Gunter's, hooray!"

There in the heart of fashionable Mayfair, the sweet smells from London's most extravagant ice-cream parlor poured out onto Berkley Square as they approached the famed establishment a short while later. It was impossible to walk past Gunter's without being irresistibly lured inside, and woe to anyone intent upon "reducing."

Mouths watering, the four of them walked into the crowded shop and soon became intoxicated with the thick scents of vanilla and cinnamon that hung in the air. The bakery section, busily turning out fabulous cakes and confections, gave off heavenly odors, while the savory counter on the opposite wall added the flavor of smoked meats and cheeses—to say nothing of the dazzling fragrances of the dozens of teas and coffees for sale.

Merely to breathe the air inside Gunter's was sheer decadence. But most of those who mobbed the shop on this warm, sunny afternoon had come for the lavish selection of ice cream, sorbets, and velvety cream-fruit ices.

They wasted no time in joining the queue.

"Why, look, Miss Balfour." Derek pointed as they took their places in the line. "They have wedding cakes." He slid her a devilish look. "Pertinent to the topic of your day's research, I believe?"

"Oh, yes, Gunter's is famous for their wedding cakes," Mrs. Clearwell informed them while Lily shot Derek a defiant look.

Matthew dashed out of the line without warning and ran over to the glass case where a gorgeous multi-tiered wedding cake was on display.

"Whoa!" he cried, agog at the towering cake. He pressed his nose against the glass, ogling all of the goodies on offer—plum cakes, ratafia cakes, ever so many kinds of cakes, and a pastel profusion of bonbons, too.

"Duty calls," Derek said wryly, pardoning himself to go and retrieve his nephew.

While the ladies patiently held their place in line, Derek took his nephew on a brief tour around the thronged shop to keep the boy busy.

Lily watched them stop to admire another sparkling glass case, where a heated silver epergne offered up a cheese fondue with neat hunks of bread to dip into the soupy golden stuff. They moved on. Next to the fondue case was a counter displaying all the makings of Gunter's famous boxed meals for picnics and outdoor parties.

Matthew pointed, asking his uncle endless questions while the clerks bustled about, packing venison slices, hunks of cheese, grapes, and champagne into an artful arrangement in the box, which was then delivered to the waiting footman of some wealthy customer. Lily watched the footman hurry away.

The wide-open double doors of the shop saw an endless parade of hungry folk, along with a constant stream of harried waiters rushing in and out to deliver ice-cream orders to the people waiting in the park across the street. Others collected on their trays the dirtied spoons and emptied glass goblets of customers who had finished their sweet indulgences, and then sped back inside to clean the lot for the next round of ice-cream seekers.

Derek and his charge returned as their turn to order finally arrived.

"Look at all these flavors," he said in amazement, holding Matthew up to see the ice cream being scooped out of great, frozen tin boxes into the whimsical glass goblets in which the delicacy was served. "What'll we have?"

Mrs. Clearwell was ready. "I shall have the peach sorbet."

"Peppermint!" Matthew cheered.

"Miss Balfour?" Derek sent her a smile.

"Hm, I'm feeling adventurous. I'll try the white currant."

He made a face at her selection, then turned to the waiter. "One scoop of almond for me, and one of pistachio."

"You're getting two?" Matthew cried.

"Just in case Miss Balfour doesn't like her choice quite as much as she thought. How *is* Edward, anyway?" he added under his breath.

Lily shook her head, laughing at his wickedness. "On second thought, I'll just take vanilla," she told the waiter.

"Vanilla?" Derek scoffed. "Talk about boring."

"Vanilla's a perfectly lovely flavor, for your information."

"I don't think she knows at all what she wants, Mrs. Clearwell."

"No, indeed, Major. No, indeed." Her chaperone was chuckling merrily at the entertainment they were providing her.

"If you two would stop talking, perhaps I could think!" Lily ignored the pair laughing at her and searched her taste buds with all earnestness.

Every flavor on the menu sounded so delicious.

"Pineapple!" she declared all of a sudden.

"Ah, the noble pineapple," Derek said in approval.

"Symbol of hospitality," Mrs. Clearwell agreed with a sage nod.

"Would you two stop it?" Lily scolded them.

"We'll bring it out straightaway," the annoyed waiter said briskly, apparently eager to be rid of them and on to more serious customers.

Derek waved off Mrs. Clearwell with a dismissive frown when she reached for her reticule. He refused to let her pay, and treated them all. They thanked him as they left the shop, sauntering back out to sit in Mrs. Clearwell's open-top barouche while they waited for their order to arrive. Her coachman had parked the barouche alongside the garden square in the shade of the flourishing plane trees.

This, Mrs. Clearwell informed them, was the proper London way to eat ice cream from Gunter's.

Lily was aware of the curious glances her party received from certain denizens of Society, who were also taking ice cream in the park. No doubt it startled the gossips to spot the notorious Major Derek Knight escorting a little boy, a genteel young lady, and her chaperone, rather than one of his usual fast women.

Oh, dear, Lily thought. There might be talk.

But there was nothing improper going on here, she reminded herself. Of course, if Mrs. Clearwell were not present, her reputation would have been destroyed before the frost was melted off the ice cream—which presently was delivered.

Derek jumped down easily over the side of the barouche as the waiter approached.

"Going somewhere, Major?" Lily inquired.

He flashed a smile as he took the ladies' treats off the waiter's tray and handed their dainty glasses up to them. "Here, Matthew," he summoned his nephew, holding out his arms to the boy. "We're going to eat ours standing right here. Otherwise, believe me, there will be peppermint ice cream all over that pretty carriage." With an easy swing down, he set Matthew firmly on his feet on the pavement, then handed the boy his ice cream.

Matthew rejoiced over his prize, but within a few bites, his attention wandered until he took a fascinated interest in a shiny beetle crawling on the ground.

He leaned down for a closer look, whereupon his single scoop of ice cream rolled right out of the bowl and landed at his feet.

Matthew looked up at his uncle in panic, while the beetle after that near miss wisely took wing and flew away.

"Oh, no," Mrs. Clearwell said sympathetically.

The boy looked from Derek to the ladies, his lower lip trembling as if he might cry.

"Here, Matthew, you can have mine," Lily said softly, offering it to him at once, but Derek countered: "Nonsense."

Without the slightest hesitation, he reached down with his bare hand, picked up the softened glob of ice cream, and plopped it right back into Matthew's bowl.

Matthew looked at him in alarm.

Lily's eyes widened.

Mother would have fainted on the spot if she had seen him do that, but Derek merely took a handkerchief out of his pocket and wiped off his hand. "What? It's still good," he said to his flabbergasted nephew in a most reasonable tone. "You don't believe me?"

Matthew watched his every move, open-mouthed.

"Here," Derek ordered. "I promise you, I've eaten much

worse than that at the war." He scooped a spoonful out of Matthew's dish and put it in his mouth.

Lily and Mrs. Clearwell both grimaced.

Derek slapped his nephew fondly on the back. "Eat up, lad. You'll live."

"Are you sure about that?" Lily murmured, eyeing the child in doubt as Matthew visibly decided to shrug off his fears and dove back into his ice cream as happily as before. "I hope he doesn't catch a disease."

"Eh, he'll be fine. A little dirt's good for him."

Men. Lily looked at the major. "You are a character, aren't you?"

"A little ice cream off a London pavement never hurt anyone. Too much precious coddling, now, that could be the death of any self-respecting boy. Isn't that right, Matt?"

"Yes, sir!" He looked up and gave him a sticky grin, apparently thrilled by this uncle who dared to break the rules, but Lily doubted the child knew what they were talking about.

She turned back to Derek and had the pleasure of watching him savor a bite of ice cream as he leaned against the carriage in a casual pose. "So, you've worked out your whole philosophy on raising children, then, have you?"

His eyes danced. "It's not that much different than training troops, really." He gave an idle shrug. "Turning aimless, untried youths into hardened soldiers is what I do, Miss Balfour. Of course, he's a little younger than the ones they usually send me. Look at him." He shook his head in obvious pride. "Tiger in training."

"He's lucky to have you," Lily said softly.

Derek looked up at her, silent for a moment. "I have to get him back to my sister soon. Actually, I was thinking, why don't you ladies come with me and let me introduce you?"

"I thought you said Her Ladyship wasn't feeling well."

"Her Ladyship?" He snorted. "Right. I forgot. Still can't get used to her having a title. At home among ourselves, we just call her Georgie. Lady Griffith. Very grand, indeed."

Lily laughed. "Are you two very close?"

"Frankly, my sister and I have always been the bane of each other's existence, but *you* may like her." He was teasing again. That dancing light in his pale blue eyes beckoned her with a magical attraction.

She shook her head. "I don't wish to disturb your sister if she's ill."

"She isn't ill, Miss Balfour." He lowered his voice and leaned closer. "She is breeding."

Lily turned red, captured in his potent stare. "Oh," she said faintly.

His worldly smile betrayed his amusement at her discomfiture. "At any rate, it's not morning anymore, so she should be fine by now. Shouldn't she, Mrs. Clearwell?"

"Hard to say." The matron shrugged. "Every woman's different."

"At least come along when I return Matthew and we'll find out if 'Her Ladyship' is receiving visitors today." He glanced at Lily and must have seen that she was still unconvinced.

"Miss Balfour, have you ever been inside a marquess's London house before?"

"No."

He nodded. "You have to see this. At least it might inspire you to aim a little higher." He gave her a devilish wink and took another big bite of ice cream, while Lily in turn smacked him on the shoulder.

"You great lout."

Mrs. Clearwell laughed gaily.

"I'm only jesting," he insisted, but his laughter faded. "No, the truth of it is, it would mean a lot to me if you would come and meet her."

"Why? So she can join you in mocking me, hm?"

"No, of course not." He paused and lowered his head, poking at a chunk of pistachio in his ice cream. "Because Georgie knows even more about India than I do. And I thought it might comfort you in the loss of your father to learn more about the place that took him from you. The good as well as the bad. Maybe if you speak to her—and meet our Indian servants, who are practically like family members to us—then you might glimpse the beauty that made your father want to go. And," he added with another smile full of easy charm, "if you're feeling *very* brave, I'll have Purnima cook you ladies one of her spiciest curries for supper some night. You'll need your vanilla after that."

Lily stared at him, not knowing what to say. Indeed, she could not even speak, taken off guard by the thoughtfulness of his desire to help her find out more about the land that had claimed her father.

It was such a kind-hearted gesture that she could not answer, startled into silence by the realization that he genuinely cared about her feelings.

She cast her chaperone a lost look.

Mrs. Clearwell took charge with a queenly nod. "We'd be honored to meet Lady Griffith, Major, if she is well enough to see us."

"Excellent news. Matthew, are you done with your ice cream? Are you ready to go home to your mother?"

Matthew nodded eagerly, thrust his empty cup and spoon into Derek's hands, and climbed up into the carriage.

"Someone needs a nap," Mrs. Clearwell sagely observed.

Lily kept her head down, her hands folded in her lap. Seeing the inside of Lord and Lady Griffith's Town mansion or even meeting Derek's sister at the moment was entirely secondary.

He cared about her.

She had never felt like this before.

As Derek finally took his seat across from her in the carriage, Lily's heart raced; her very soul seemed to tremble.

Heaven help me, she thought, barely daring to breathe.

She was actually starting to trust him.

In another moment, Mrs. Clearwell's driver maneuvered the barouche out of busy Berkley Square and headed toward the opulent environs of Green Park, where the Marquess of Griffith lived in splendor.

The carriage traveled several blocks, and all the while Mrs. Clearwell engaged the young lordling in amused conversation.

Meanwhile, for as long as she could, Lily kept her gaze shyly downcast, trying to mask her powerful reaction to Derek's generosity.

But when she finally dared to peek in his direction, she found him watching her, his cheek resting on his fist, one elbow propped on the edge of the carriage.

She felt the force, the thrill, the heat of his gaze all the way down to her toes.

Edward never looked at her like that.

She was routed: blushing, blanching, maybe both. She was flustered, to be sure. She tried to look away but couldn't do it.

Derek sent her an unthreatening smile.

The smolder in his eyes turned soothing, and Lily remembered to inhale.

This is foolishness, she thought.

I'm not going to hurt you, his gaze reassured her.

The unspoken promise of his gentle, undemanding approach shook her.

And yet, by slow, wary degrees, the clenched muscles of her chest and shoulders began to relax.

Dear Lord, if he could have such effects on her body without even touching her . . .

Lily swallowed hard and thrust her attention toward the fine view of Green Park as they went rolling past.

CHAPTER
❧ TEN ❧

"*T*here's my house!" Matthew cried, pointing to a tall, stately townhouse faced in light Portland stone, its front door and shutters painted striking burgundy.

Lily sat up with renewed interest.

They turned the corner ahead, rounding the park, and in another moment, Derek bade Mrs. Clearwell's driver to stop at the front door. He got out first, helped Matthew jump down, then smiled, assisting the ladies as his nephew went barreling homeward.

The door opened before the young master even had to knock and there stood a short, balding, portly butler who beamed at the boy like a kindly old elf.

"Mr. Tooke!" Matthew cried, running toward him.

"Good day, Lord Aylesworth. Major." Mr. Tooke opened the door wider in welcome as Derek ushered Lily and Mrs. Clearwell toward the entrance.

"Matthew and I found some strays on our adventures today," he greeted the butler with a roguish twinkle in his eyes. "These are my friends, Mrs. Clearwell and Miss Balfour. Is my sister receiving? I should so love to introduce everyone."

"I believe she may be, sir, though I am not certain. Ladies, won't you come in, and I will inquire?" His face wreathed in smiles, he gestured them into a soaring marble entrance hall, and at once, Lily's eyes widened as she stepped inside.

The restrained elegance of the exterior had not prepared her for the sheer opulence within.

It was a palace.

Twin colonnades flanked the entrance hall in Corinthian splendor, striding down to the spectacular double staircase that swept up to the main floor seemingly miles ahead. She recalled the holes in the roof at Balfour Manor with a sinking feeling while Mr. Tooke closed the door behind them.

Mother would have been drooling if she could see this place, Lily thought, and yet, amid all this grandeur, incongruously, an ice-cream-covered little boy was pounding through the pristine hall, running to meet the spotted puppy that came bounding out to greet him. The dog's yips and Matthew's shouts of joy reverberated through the great space.

"Who's making all that ruckus down there?" a deep, mellifluous voice boomed from the top of the great staircase.

Lily looked up in surprise; Matthew did the same.

"Grandpapa!" the boy cried.

Marching down the stairs came a tall, robust, indeed, a kingly gentleman in his sixties, gray-haired but still quite fit, all handsome dignity and twinkling blue eyes. "Come here to me, you little scamp!"

Matthew ran to him and was swept up in his arms.

Derek shepherded the ladies toward the gentleman.

"Father," he greeted him in an easy tone.

Derek's father?

The older man looked over absently, holding Matthew in his arms. "Hullo, son."

"I did not expect to find you still here."

"I didn't think I would still be here, either, but you know how we all get to talking."

Lily did not know why she was so astonished to learn that this impressive personage was Derek's sire, but what had she expected? He might look like a demigod, but he had hardly sprung full-blown from the head of Zeus.

Equal surprise registered in the elder Knight's blue eyes

when he turned his attention to the ladies who had arrived with his second son.

Derek quickly introduced them to his father, Lord Arthur Knight, the younger brother to the previous Duke of Hawkscliffe. Setting Matthew down and sending him back to his dog with a fond pat on the head, Lord Arthur bowed to the ladies.

"Where's Mama?" Matthew asked Lord Arthur, tugging on his billowy white sleeve, for he had removed his jacket and was in his casual at-home attire.

"In the blue parlor," he informed the boy.

"Do you think she'd be up to a visit?" Derek inquired.

His father looked at him intently. "Why don't you go and ask her?"

"I will. Come on, Matt. Let's go see your mama. Back in a moment," he said with a smile to the ladies.

"I beg your pardon, Miss Balfour," Lord Arthur addressed her after the pair had gone. "You wouldn't happen to be any relation to Viscount Balfour, I suppose? He was an old friend of mine ages ago."

She stared at him. "Do you mean Noah Balfour, my lord?"

"Yes, Noah! Are you his kin?"

"He was my grandfather!" she cried in amazement.

"Your grandfather?" he exclaimed. "By Jove, it has been years since I have seen him! Good old Balfy! We used to play cards together at White's before I moved away from England and sailed off to seek my fortune in India."

She could only stare at him incredulously.

Balfy?

They all laughed over this most unexpected discovery of their common acquaintance, but then Lord Arthur asked the obvious question.

"So, how is the old devil these days, anyway?"

Sadness crept across Lily's face. "Oh, Lord Arthur." She faltered, barely able to imagine her gruff old grandsire in his youth playing cards at White's with rakish cronies who called him Balfy. "I am sorry to say he passed away these two months ago."

"No." His face fell. "Oh, dear. I am so sorry to hear it. What a loss."

She nodded. Mrs. Clearwell patted her shoulder, but Derek's return to the entrance hall chased away the lump that had risen in her throat.

"Good news!" he announced as he came striding back, full of vigor. Lily could not help letting her gaze sweep over his magnificent form in admiration as he approached. "Georgie's well enough at least for a quick visit."

"Are you sure, Major? We do not wish to disturb Lady Griffith—"

"No, she really wants to meet you! Believe me, Mrs. Clearwell, if my sister wasn't feeling up to it, she'd say so."

"That is true," Lord Arthur agreed with a sigh. "That daughter of mine was never one to shrink from speaking her mind."

"Except for when she fell in love with Griff," Derek drawled. "They'd have never got together if it wasn't for me."

"Is that true?" Lily asked, unsure if he was jesting as they all followed Derek toward the "blue parlor," where the young marchioness was waiting.

"Of course, it's true!" he exclaimed. "I gave him the idea to marry her."

"Now he's exaggerating," Lord Arthur said. "You have to watch this one, ladies."

Derek laughed. "You wait, Father. One of these days I might just summon my matchmaking skills again to locate a lady for *you*."

Recalling what Derek had said about his mother dying when he was a child, she was nonetheless startled by the sly look the major cast Mrs. Clearwell. To Lily's extreme amusement, her chaperone looked at him in amazement and then turned bright red.

Lord Arthur hadn't noticed, bringing up the rear of their small party. "Well, that's very thoughtful of you, son," he answered sardonically. "But first you might consider finding some nice young lady for yourself. Ahem!"

Now it was Lily's turn to blush. Obviously, Lord Arthur did not know she was nearly engaged to someone else.

Derek made no comment. He walked through a door ahead and waited as the rest of them filed in.

Lady Griffith's choice of the blue parlor in which to receive them spoke volumes about the woman, Lily mused when they arrived at the simple, cozy salon at the back of the first floor, bypassing all those glittering staterooms.

Her first glimpse of Derek's sister was of a black-haired beauty with porcelain skin. She was holding Matthew on her lap. "You're all sticky," she chided affectionately as Matthew rubbed noses with her. The boy's arms were draped around her, and behind Lady Griffith, her handsome husband stood in a casual pose, his elbows resting on the back of her chair.

He was watching her with his son with a besotted look on his patrician face, but he glanced over with a cordial smile when they walked in.

Their easy introductions were soon made, but when Derek presented Lily to his sister, she could not fail to notice the mystified look that Georgiana gave her brother. It seemed that his bringing a female to meet the family was no ordinary event.

Lily couldn't help but feel pleased.

"We shan't stay long," Mrs. Clearwell was saying. "We just wanted to express our compliments at what a fine boy you have. We so enjoyed Lord Aylesworth's company today."

"Did you?" Lady Griffith was visibly pleased by the praise as she petted Matthew's head. "I wished I could've gone out with them today, myself. Oh, I am not usually so tired. It's just, well," she said, blushing, "we are expecting a blessed event." She reached up to touch her husband's hand where it rested on her shoulder.

As they congratulated the beaming couple, Lily saw the private squeeze that Lord Griffith gave his wife's hand and felt her heart clench.

A true marriage.

Not a sham like she would have with Edward.

"Has it been difficult for you, my lady?" Mrs. Clearwell asked in her comforting way.

"Oh, I've been perfectly miserable!" she admitted with a rueful laugh. "My physician vows it will pass within a few more weeks." She shook her head. "Not soon enough for me."

Indeed, now that she mentioned it, Lily thought, the woman did look a bit green around the gills, though her blue, high-waisted gown hid any signs of her early pregnancy. Her form was still slender, full of a lithe, willowy strength. But on the little drum-table beside her sat the telltale cup of peppermint-and-ginger tea, along with some half-eaten dry toast.

The poor woman.

At least she had her husband looking after her. Lord Griffith was practically hovering, clearly attentive to her every need with the utmost solicitude.

"But no matter," Georgiana said stoutly. "It'll be worth all my suffering to get our prize at the end, won't it, darling?"

"Hear, hear," he agreed with quiet intensity, and pressed a heartfelt kiss to her hand.

Moved by the beauty of their devotion to each other, Lily's gaze was drawn inexplicably to Derek.

She found him watching her once again. This time, the magnetic force of his stare took her breath away.

As they held each other's gaze, she was fairly sure that the same wild thoughts that were going through her head were also running through his. For one fleeting moment, it seemed possible to dream that they, too, might find that kind of bond—with each other.

He looked away.

Lily lowered her head, unsettled by the glimpse of a happiness she had never seen before, let alone aspired to.

But obviously this was naught but a foolish fantasy. How could she possibly share a bond like that with Derek Knight when the only way they could be together was if they both gave up what they held most dear?

If she married a handsome half-pay officer, she would

probably have to abandon her hope of keeping Balfour Manor. Yes, the Knight clan possessed a great fortune, but she had not failed to notice that Lord Arthur's statement downstairs had summed up the family's ethic for younger sons. As a young man, the second-born Arthur Knight had had to go to India to seek his own fortune, and no doubt Derek would be expected to do the same.

Lily had no intention of going there with him. In order for him to be with her, Derek would have to be willing to stay in England, and clearly, he was not.

Give up his role as the glorious cavalry hero? Become a civilian, just a regular chap? She seriously doubted he would be willing to make the sacrifice.

"Derek," Lord Griffith spoke up. "Have you given any thought to that new post we talked about last week?" he inquired in a casual tone.

"Griff, my mind's made," Derek said. "It's a good offer, but I am not prepared to take a bullet for any hen-witted politician. On the whole, they aren't worth it—present company excepted, of course."

"We're doing all we can to try to keep my brother in England," Georgiana said archly to the ladies. "Ian's been trying to lure him into accepting a plum post connected to the Foreign Office. He would be providing diplomatic security for visiting dignitaries to the Court of St. James."

"I see," Mrs. Clearwell murmured, nodding, but Derek snorted.

"They'd have me lounging 'round the palace like some sort of overfed poodle. Hardly."

"Maybe you can help us persuade him, Miss Balfour."

"She's certainly welcome to try," he drawled, sliding Lily a grin.

"Derek!" his sister exclaimed, covering Matthew's ears with her hands. "Not in front of the boy, with your roguery! For shame, I apologize for my brother, Miss Balfour. He has always fancied himself the jester of the family. Maybe the Court of St. James could use a new fool, hm?"

"I beg your pardon," he protested, scowling, but Lily

smiled sweetly, not about to be embarrassed by the rogue in front of his kin.

"Actually, my lady, I think you're onto something. He would look perfect in a harlequin cap." She sent a pointed smile in his direction, while his father and sister laughed heartily.

"You see what I have to put up with?" he exclaimed, feigning outrage. "And they wonder why I'm going back to India."

Lily chuckled, shaking her head at him.

"Well," Mrs. Clearwell concluded at length, "we really should be going."

Lily nodded, for they did not wish to tire out their hostess.

"I'm leaving, too," Derek announced. "I'll walk down with you, ladies." He bent and kissed his sister on the cheek, rumpled his nephew's hair, took leave of his father and brother-in-law, then escorted Lily and her chaperone back downstairs. Once more passing through the vast, columned hall, they were soon back outside, where he went toward the street to hail a hackney.

When they asked why, he explained that he had come on foot, but Mrs. Clearwell insisted on giving him a lift.

"Where are you headed, Major?"

"Home. I live at the Althorpe."

"Then you must let us drop you there."

"I don't wish to impose—"

"Not at all—Piccadilly, isn't it? Just as I thought. It's right on our way."

"Oh! Well, then." He agreed to the offer with cheerful thanks, and soon the barouche was under way again.

He pointed out Knight House on the far end of Green Park, a magnificent Town palace that nearly dwarfed Lord Griffith's elegant home.

That, Derek said, was the official Knight family headquarters, where his cousin, the head of their clan, Robert Knight, the Duke of Hawkscliffe, resided, as had his father before him, and his father's father, and so on for several generations.

Listening to his amiable discourse, Lily reflected on all the fun they'd had today and wondered when she might get to spend time with him again. For that matter, she wondered what she would tell Edward if word traveled back to him about her being seen around London today with his handsome new friend.

Nothing even close to improper had happened, but still, she didn't think Edward would like it. Strangely, however, she felt not the slightest bit guilty.

Noticing that the barouche had begun to slow, Lily glanced down the road and saw that the intersection some fifty yards ahead was jammed with a row of carriages that had been forced to a halt.

The flow of traffic had come to a standstill. They tried to see what was happening.

"Someone's carriage has probably broken down," Derek murmured.

Lily shook her head in worry. "I hope there has not been an accident."

"Well, it would be no surprise, the way some of these young rakehells drive their high-flyers through the streets," Mrs. Clearwell said in disapproval. "Galloping around like madmen. One of them probably ran someone over, poor soul."

Derek noted her words with a dark glance in her direction. His face hardened.

He stood up all of a sudden. "I'll go and see if anyone's been hurt. They may need help."

"Help?" Lily echoed, startled.

"My dear ladies, if you knew how many hasty battlefield surgeries I've performed," he muttered, but his words trailed off as he vaulted over the side of the barouche.

Striding swiftly toward the intersection, he disappeared into the crowd.

Lily turned to Mrs. Clearwell in astonishment. "*Surgeries?*"

Her chaperone shrugged, looking equally amazed at the major's hidden talents.

Of course, in hindsight, it made sense that he would have a certain amount of doctoring skills. No doubt there were more wounded men than army doctors after a battle.

This man has saved people's lives, she thought in dawning awe. Until now, she had only thought of him as taking them in his warrior role.

Her heart beat faster as the barouche began to move again in the next moment, for busy Londoners were not about to be detained by a traffic mishap.

If someone had been run over by a carriage, Lily was not sure she wanted to see it. The sight of blood usually made her queasy. On the other hand, she couldn't wait to see Derek in action.

Making progress again, though at a snail's pace, the carriages ahead of theirs were simply snaking around the stopped vehicle. The cause of the commotion now became apparent: an overloaded stagecoach with red wheels on bottom and a mountain of luggage and yelling passengers on top. Angry heads craned out of the stage windows as impatient passengers complained to the driver.

"Come on! Let's go!"

"Get your nag to move!"

Lily's eyes widened as she spotted Derek standing next to one of the stagecoach horses. The thin, broken-down sorrel was in a pitiful state; either hurt or sick, it was in no condition for its normal duties. Trapped helplessly in the harness, the horse was trembling and wild-eyed with fear, cowering next to Derek as though it could sense that, at last, one kind soul had finally come to its rescue.

The horse's red coat was darkened with sweat, and its back was bleeding from the brutal lashes it had taken from the coachman's whip.

"Get out of the way!" the burly driver was shouting at Derek from up on his box.

Something about the thick-featured bruiser reminded Lily instantly of Edward, but the man obviously had no idea whom he was dealing with. When Derek looked over, his face was livid.

He pinned the man in a menacing stare and pointed at him. "So help me, if you strike this animal one more time, I'm going to show you what it's like to take a beating."

"Don't you threaten me! Get away from my horse!"

"I'm taking her out of the harness. This horse can't pull today."

"The hell you are! You think you're going to steal my property? I'll see you hanged for a horse thief!"

Traffic slowed once more as onlookers took interest in the altercation brewing. Pedestrians had wandered into the intersection to gawk at the goings-on. Mrs. Clearwell's driver, Gerald, pulled the barouche over to the opposite side of the street to let the few carriages behind them squeeze past.

"I'll buy her from you, then," Derek told the coachman. His voice had taken on an ominous tone that Lily had never before heard him use.

"She ain't for sale! I'm warning you, mister, get the hell out of my way!" The driver hooked an angry thumb over his shoulder at his clamoring passengers. "I've got a schedule to keep!"

"Well, you're going to be late," Derek bit back, calmly reaching for the buckles on the leather traces in order to free the animal.

"Damn you!" the coachman bellowed.

Lily gasped as he brought up his whip to strike again, but Derek reached up one leather-gauntleted hand and grabbed the whip out of the air. Yanking it with a mighty heave, he brought the coachman tumbling out of the driver's box.

He marched toward him as the man fell in a heap beside the stationary front wheel.

At once, the stage's groom and mail-guard both jumped down from their seats atop the vehicle and ran toward Derek, cursing.

The whole intersection broke out in chaos like a crowd at a prizefight, watching as the major looked at them with an air of cool unconcern.

Armed guards were assigned to protect the mails aboard each stagecoach, but this one, thank God, had the sense not to fire his musket into a crowded street. Instead, he used his gun as a club and swung it at Derek's head.

Derek blocked the blow with his left arm, flattened the hefty guard with one explosive punch from his right, and moved on to the groom. Backing away slowly, but seemingly loath to run like a coward in front of such a large audience, the wiry young man tried to kick out Derek's knee.

Derek scoffed, grabbed the man's heel, and yanked him off his feet.

The groom yelped as he fell flat on his back on the cobblestones, much to the crowd's hilarity; he opted not to get up, even if he could.

Lily didn't blame him. If this were a real battle, that clever trick would probably have been followed by impalement on Derek's sword, she thought worriedly, but the major's manner was so relaxed against these foes that he reminded her of a cat that toyed with its captive mouse before casually biting its head off.

The crowd was enjoying the spectacle lustily, cheering Derek on, but he spared his second victim further punishment and turned his attention back to the coachman, who had recovered from his spill.

He's really going to do it, Lily thought, furrowing her brow, her pulse pounding. *He's going to thrash him.*

The cruel driver was slowly climbing to his feet with the look of a wrathful bull.

"Go on, get up!" Derek taunted as he sauntered toward the man. "On your feet! Faster!"

Her eyes widened as he pulled back his wrist and struck the burly coachman with his own whip.

The man bellowed at the sting, dropping back against the wheel again, though Derek had not hit the ogre hard enough to tear his clothes.

"What, you don't like that?" he mocked him with increasing savagery. "Maybe I didn't do it properly!" He struck him again, harder. "Get up, puff-guts! Let's see how you fare against somebody who can fight back!"

"Derek!" Lily cried.

Her shocked call seemed to draw him back from a dark place within where he was all too much at home. When he glanced over at her, his face was flush with violence, and his pale, wolflike eyes flickered with cold rage.

They were the eyes of a stranger.

The look on his face reminded her of that hard, bleak darkness she had glimpsed in him last night when they had stood beside the river.

It had unsettled her then; it bewildered her now.

Perhaps he saw his own savagery reflected in her appalled stare, for he seemed to regain control of his fury in the next heartbeat. Veiling his gaze to mask his true feelings, he passed a contemptuous look over the driver. "He deserves it."

He left off terrifying the coachman then, but he coiled up the horsewhip, stepped back, and threw it skyward, hard. It unfurled like a snake in midair as it flew upward, high over the row of buildings, and landed on one of the roofs.

Derek dusted off his hands, gave the driver another scornful glance, and then calmly returned to his task of freeing the sorrel mare.

This was quickly accomplished. Leaving her place in the harness empty, he laid a gentle hand on the mare's neck, talking softly to her. Taking hold of her grubby leather bridle, he began to lead the limping animal away.

The crowd's mood had turned strangely somber now that their attention was drawn back to the horse's suffering.

Quietly, they parted to let the pair pass.

But before Derek left the scene, he faltered almost imperceptibly. He paused just long enough to send Lily a look of apology over his shoulder.

She shook her head at him tenderly.

He lowered his chin and then walked on.

Within moments, the sea of people had closed up behind him once more; the cavalry hero and his equine damsel in distress disappeared into the crowd.

It was only then that three constables came charging somewhat belatedly into the crowd, but the coachman wasted no time in setting them after Derek.

"Stop, thief! Stop him! Murderer!" Scrambling to his feet from where Derek had left him cowering beside the wagon wheel, the driver began hollering for all he was worth, pointing eagerly in the direction that Derek had gone. "Officers, he went that way! Some maniac just attacked us and walked off with one of my horses! Big fellow, long black hair. What are you waiting for? He's getting away—and he's taken my horse with him! See?" He held up the empty leather straps where the mare had been.

"Is this true?" the first constable demanded, glancing around at the scene of the fray.

"Yes, sir!" the groom seconded his master. The wiry lad was still on the ground. He lay on his side, gingerly rubbing his rear end. "He threw me down and now I've broke me bum!"

A few feet away from him, the mail-guard was not in much better shape, shaking his head dazedly as he struggled back to full consciousness. He wiped off a trickle of blood from one of his nostrils.

The policeman's face hardened. "Right." He looked at his men. "Boys, you know what to do. After him!"

Lily's eyes widened as they dashed off to arrest Derek, gripping their nightsticks.

She and Mrs. Clearwell exchanged a fearful look, knowing that he and his "stolen" horse could not have gotten far, given the animal's limping gait. She could only pray that Derek's basic respect for authority would hold him back from giving the constables the kind of beating he'd have liked to have given the coachman.

Perhaps with his charm, he could talk his way out of it— but her hopes were dashed in the next moment when someone in the crowd hollered, "They're putting him under arrest!"

That does it.

Unable to contain herself, Lily jumped out of the

barouche, lifted the hem of her skirts in both hands to avoid tripping on them, and ran toward the constable.

"Officer, wait!"

The policeman turned to her. "Miss? What is the matter?"

"This man's claims are rubbish!"

"Oh? It would appear that *someone* assaulted these men."

"I assure you, they deserved it—especially him!" she flung out, pointing at the coachman.

The crowd seconded her defense with numerous "ayes" and "hear, hears."

"The man they accuse is a noted cavalry officer. He wasn't trying to steal this fool's horse—that's a ridiculous charge, and he knows it! Why would anyone want to steal that poor, pathetic bag of bones? The major only did it to *save* the animal from this man's cruelty."

"*My* cruelty?" the coachman barked. "He's the one who tried to kill us all! That man's dangerous! He ought to be locked up!"

"You fool, if he had wanted you dead, you'd *be* dead. You should be thankful that he let you live."

"The chap in question, ma'am." The constable turned to Lily. "I take it he is your husband?"

"No!" The question threw her. "He is my—friend."

The coachman scoffed. "Your 'friend,' eh? Well, my fine ladybird, you better start looking for a new *friend,* because your fancy man's going to Newgate where he belongs."

"I beg your pardon! Constable, I am a decent woman. My chaperone is sitting over there!" She pointed to Mrs. Clearwell and then gave the constable an imploring look. "The major offered to buy the horse from him, but for sheer obstinacy this man refused to take payment!"

"Ha!" the coachman cried triumphantly. "So, you admit the blackguard walked off with my property! Stealing is stealing."

"Th-that's not what I meant—" Lily stammered, fearing she had just said exactly the wrong thing.

The constable glanced shrewdly from her to the coachman. "You'll be pressing charges, then, sir?"

"You're damned right I will."

Lily turned to him in fury, but seeing the two men start to walk away to view the prisoner, she somehow managed to keep a civil tongue in her head. "Wait."

They both looked at her in question.

She was not going to let them do this to Derek, jail him—hang him? It was madness! This was completely unfair. He was no horse thief, but even if a jury cleared him of the trumped-up charges, at the very least, the arrest would be a blot on his military record that could permanently damage his career.

She did not want Derek to go back to India, but she would not allow this petty ogre to deprive him of the choice.

"What do you want?" the coachman grunted, waiting for her to speak.

"Before you take this matter any further," she replied, "may I have a private word with you, Mr.—?"

"Jones," he growled. "Fine, if you'll be quick about it."

The constable nodded as the two of them stepped aside to confer.

Coachman Jones was an awfully large man—and he smelled bad, to boot—but Lily looked him straight in the eyes. "What is it going to take to make you drop this foolishness?"

"Foolishness? I'm within my rights! Stealing is stealing, like I said!"

"Be reasonable! You know your treatment of that horse was wrong. You're just doing this for spite, because he thrashed you in front of this crowd."

"I deserve compensation for my property—and my pains!—or I'm pressing charges."

The man was loathsome, but she was encouraged by his admission. "Good, then! Compensation you shall have! I will pay you right now and we can put this whole unpleasant business behind us. What's the horse worth?" she persisted. "A few sovereigns at most, considering it's already half dead. Here!" She thrust her hand into her reticule and took out what little pin money she had left.

He looked at the few silver coins in her outstretched palm and slowly began laughing. "Is that all your fine major's freedom is worth to you, poppet?"

Lily looked at him in shock as he folded his bulky arms across his chest.

Then she glanced at her money again. "It's all I have."

His eyes narrowed. "What about them earrings you got on?"

CHAPTER
∞ ELEVEN ∞

*T*he charges had been dropped.

Lily was still numb by the time the barouche turned into Mrs. Clearwell's street a short while later. She could not believe she had given away her great-great-grandmother's earrings to save Derek Knight.

But at least it had worked.

The coachman had walked away satisfied and Derek had been freed, unaware of what she had done. She didn't mind if he never found out. Watching him from a distance as he led the injured horse away, she had been filled with a deeper satisfaction than she had ever experienced before, knowing that she had helped him.

He was worth it.

That was the scariest part . . . how much she was starting to care about him.

Still, giving up her earrings had left her with one less asset to her name, one more reason why she'd have to marry Edward.

At least she had taken measures to protect her reputation. She had made her bargain with the coachman on the one condition that he keep quiet about receiving her diamonds in exchange for dropping the charges against Derek. Greed made him more than willing to be discreet; indeed, he had not even bothered asking her name, but that suited Lily quite well.

She did not need news of her sacrifice getting back to

Edward, and as for Derek, if he heard nothing about her reckless gift, it would spare his pride . . . and keep him from realizing how foolishly infatuated with him she was becoming.

Still, she did not regret what she had done, for it was impossible to imagine his fierce, free spirit locked up in some horrid cage in the bowels of Newgate.

Across from her, Mrs. Clearwell was still looking at Lily as if she had sprouted two heads. "When we get home, my dear, I believe I shall brew a pot of tea and you and I are going to have a little talk."

Oh, dear. "Yes, ma'am," she mumbled, abashed by the rare disapproval in her godmother's voice—not that she blamed her after that spectacle.

But unfortunately, as the barouche glided to a halt in front of her chaperone's cozy house, Lily saw that her troubles were not over yet.

Edward was already there. Waiting for her.

Oh, God! She had been out with Derek all day—and then that debacle at the intersection! Was she found out already? But how?

What was she going to say?

All she knew was that the sight of his big, black carriage parked outside Mrs. Clearwell's little house made her stomach plunge with a sickening drop.

Panic flooded her veins at the thought of her burly suitor's certain jealous wrath. She cast her sponsor a terrified look; Mrs. Clearwell returned it with a firm, bolstering nod. Her look checked Lily's panic, but nevertheless, a sense of doom came over her—and guilt.

Familiar guilt. It was back. Edward was going to jilt her now, she was sure of it—and what would she tell Mother then? She wasn't sure who she was more afraid of in that moment: towering Edward or the dagger-eyed Lady Clarissa.

But it was too late now. No, damn the man, she had known from the second she saw him that Derek Knight was going to wreck her life. Oh, how had she ever dreamed she could have succeeded in this miserable mission when she had proved her shameful inability to control herself years ago?

When Gerald came to get the carriage door for them and put the metal step down, Lily closed her eyes briefly, envisioning the ton's laughter when they heard how the "haughty" Balfour girl had been hilariously dumped by an encroaching toadstool like Edward Lundy.

That's what you get for grasping after fortune, they would say. And how Bess Kingsley would squeal with glee to hear the news of her misfortune!

But so be it.

Climbing down slowly from the carriage, Lily walked, heart pounding, toward the house. There was nothing she could do now but brace herself and resolve to meet her fate with dignity.

The butler had shown Edward into the dainty drawing room, where his large bulk dwarfed the satin sofa.

Lily forced a brave smile as she went in to greet him. He rose, hat in hand. From the corner of her eye, she glimpsed her pale reflection in the mantel-glass, the artificial smile frozen in place.

She was shocked by how much she looked like her mother.

And by the glaring absence of her earrings.

Her naked earlobes peeked out for all to see.

I'm doomed, she thought.

Edward bowed to her. "Miss Balfour."

"Mr. Lundy." She started to offer her hand, then realized that, stupidly, she was still holding onto the ladies' fashion magazines.

The ones with the bridal gowns.

Instead, she limited herself to a polite nod. "How are you today?" she inquired with probing caution as she sat down across from him with a deliberate show of grace.

Mrs. Clearwell lingered in the doorway of the drawing room, eyeing them both with a questioning look that asked if Lily wished her to stay to lend moral support.

Normally, respectable courting couples could be permitted fifteen minutes or so alone. Lily sent her a discreet nod, signaling to her to go. She did not want her dear godmother to witness her humiliation.

Besides, if Edward's anger climbed to frightening heights, then Mrs. Clearwell would not be far away with her footmen and butler to throw him out.

"I'll just, er, go and make the tea," Mrs. Clearwell said hesitantly. With a worried smile, she withdrew. But she left the door open.

As they labored through their usual, meaningless, stilted pleasantries, Lily discerned the same dark agitation in Edward that she had sensed the night of the masked ball, though he seemed to be trying to hide it. Something was definitely bothering him, but when he inquired about their outing, she gave only the sketchiest answer, unsure of how much he knew. No need to rush her doom.

Then Edward cleared his throat. "Miss Balfour, I have a particular question to ask you today. That's why I'm here."

"Yes?" she replied in attentive gravity, folding her hands on her lap. Her heart pounded faster.

Edward rubbed his mouth. "I noticed at the concert last night that you disappeared for a while with Derek Knight."

The air vanished from her lungs. He stared at her.

Hanging onto her wits for dear life, she managed a poised nod. "He was afraid he had given offense when the conversation turned to the subject of my father's death in India. The major approached me to apologize." *Which is more than I can say for you,* she thought.

"I see," Edward rumbled.

"You were attending Lord Fallow. So I joined the major on a walk down to view the prospect of the river."

While he considered this, a most unexpected reaction began to take shape inside Lily.

Anger.

Perhaps the terror she had felt walking in here had pushed her too far, or maybe the thought of the fearless Derek Knight inspired her courage and made her own fear start to fade. But it was more than that, for the guilt that had squeezed her nigh constantly for years like a too-tightly laced corset began dissolving as she sat there, faced with her suitor's suspicious and judgmental stare.

For the first time in ages, Lily felt like a woman prepared to fight to defend her own honor.

"What are you implying, Edward?" she asked in an icicle tone. "Do you mean to tell me you are jealous?"

"No," he said with a dismissive scoff, startling her anew. "It's not that at all. I know you're too sensible to let a penniless coxcomb like him turn your head."

His answer routed her. She stared at him. If he was not jealous, then why did he look so disgruntled? No longer sure of the purpose behind his line of questioning, Lily waited, motionless—on guard and a bit bewildered.

"I want to know if he asked you any questions about me."

Lily tilted her head as the conversation pivoted in this mysterious new direction.

"My business, my holdings," Edward said urgently. "My work with the committee. Anything like that. I need to know whatever you might've told him about me."

Why? she wondered at once, but the perfectly genteel young lady that she had always portrayed herself to be with Edward would never have asked such an impertinent question.

Half reeling with confusion, Lily opted for her usual answer to Edward—unquestioned obedience. Within reason.

No wonder he wanted to marry her.

"Major Knight did not ask me anything like that," she answered quietly. There was no way in Hades she was telling him that Derek had also inquired why Edward had not proposed to her yet.

"Think, Lily. Are you sure?"

She gave him a cool nod. "The only thing he asked about you was if I thought you had enjoyed the concert."

Edward studied her. "Really?"

"Yes, I'm quite certain." She paused, and then crept out on a limb. "Why?"

"Because I don't trust him, that's why," Edward growled. He rose and paced over toward the fireplace.

Lily looked at him in wonder. "But—Edward, I thought he was your friend."

"Maybe he is and maybe he ain't. That remains to be seen," he said gruffly and rested his hand on the mantel for a moment, brooding. "You must be on your guard with him, Miss Balfour."

This conversation was becoming entirely strange! "You know me, I am on my guard with everyone. But," she continued with the greatest delicacy, "may I ask why you advise me thus?"

"I don't want him using you to try to get to me." He turned around with a matter-of-fact expression as Lily felt her heart lurch.

Derek . . . using her?

She thought she might be sick. But, no! That made no sense, she assured herself, trying not to think about the time before when she was duped, or the diamond earrings she had parted with so easily for his sake.

"Get to you?" she echoed his words in a strangled tone. "Whatever do you mean?"

Something strange and dark and covert flickered behind Edward's eyes as he turned away with a vague, impatient wave of his hand. "Ah, you know these younger sons of the aristocracy. They're sharpers and swindlers, the lot of 'em. All arrogance and no blunt! Especially his kind, bloody Regulars," he muttered. "You should see the way they strut around Calcutta, thinking they're better than everyone else. The only reason he's been so chummy with me is probably because he thinks I'll be good for an advance if he gets in over his head at the gaming tables."

No, but that's impossible, Lily wanted to tell him.

Having just been inside the opulent home of his brother-in-law, the marquess, and having seen from a distance his cousin the duke's mansion on Green Park, Lily knew that Edward's suspicion against Derek on this point was pure foolishness.

She pushed away another thought of her earrings as she realized in sickening hindsight that maybe she needn't have parted with them at all. His rich family could have easily bailed him out of Newgate and hired the best legal experts for his defense.

But the arrest would have gone on his record and tarnished his brilliant military career, she reminded herself with a pang. At least she had saved him from that.

As for Edward's claims, she quickly concluded that this was no more than the self-made man's usual acute distrust of people he still perceived as his "betters." It had long puzzled her how Edward alternated between slavishly seeking the approval of the highborn folk he now brushed shoulders with in Society and hating them. Both impulses seemed to have come together in his dealings with the major.

Lily dared not tell Edward about the earrings or any other aspect of the . . . friendship? . . . that she had been developing with Derek Knight independently of him. As it was, Edward's angry intensity concerning the major could prove dangerous all around.

Seeking with great care to defuse Edward's fears, Lily gave him a winning smile. "Edward, I'm sure that if the major runs into trouble at the tables, he would not dream of bothering you, but would turn to his family for an advance. You always think that everyone is out to get you! Come, I am sure he genuinely likes you. How could he not? You were both soldiers, both served in India—"

"Oh, he's likable enough on the face of it, I suppose," Edward grumbled, calming down a bit. "But I'm keeping my eye on that blackguard, and I suggest you do the same."

"Very well—"

"And if he starts asking you any questions about how much money I have, I want you to tell me so!"

"Without hesitation," she soothed.

He heaved a rueful sigh and dropped his head. "It's good to know I have you on my side, anyway."

She smiled at him, but in the back of her mind, she felt the first stirrings of wonder that it did not even cross Edward's mind to be jealous of her where "the stud of the Season" was concerned. Derek had warned her that Edward knew she was mainly after his fortune, but was her suitor so very confident of her financial desperation that he believed that nothing would make her jeopardize his favor? His certainty that he had her in the palm of his hand rankled her old Balfour pride.

Edward glanced at the door to make sure her chaperone was still absent as he stole over to her and sat on the couch by her side. "My dear Miss Balfour." Boldly, he took her hand. "All these questions, you know, aren't the only reason I came."

She gave him a dubious look. "There's more?"

"Of course! I wanted to see you. But that can't come as a surprise. You are well aware, I think, that you are my favorite lady."

"Am I?"

"Of course you are! Next only to my mother. Favorite and only."

"Let's not forget Miss Kingsley."

"Her?" He snorted, but to Lily's arch amazement, the great brute blushed a bit.

"And what about your new acquaintance, Mrs. Coates?" she persisted, acting as if she were jealous. "Last night you seemed quite awestruck by her beauty."

He laughed uncomfortably. "Well, none of them have captured my interest like you, dear. Lily—" Bravely, he tested the use of her first name and pressed her hand more tightly. "Let me prove my sincere admiration. May I . . ." His husky words faded as he shrugged off seeking permission and suddenly kissed her.

Lily's eyes shot open in shock, but Edward's were closed as he squashed his cold lips against hers.

She held motionless, praying that Mrs. Clearwell would not walk in on this. It was too embarrassing! Oh, Lord, she thought, waiting with heroic patience for him to finish up.

For a heartbeat, she struggled to muster up some shade of the wild thrill she had experienced in answer to Derek's kiss at the garden folly, but the experiment proved in vain. Nothing.

The same could not be said for Edward. Unable to take any more of his attentions, she managed to pry him off her at last. His eyes were glazed.

"My darling," he rasped. "Forgive me."

"No matter," she said briskly, wiping off her lips as she turned away in discreet distaste.

Edward rose at the sound of Mrs. Clearwell's loud "ahem!" from outside the parlor door. "Good day—Miss Balfour," he said hesitantly.

Lily folded her hands in her lap once more. "Good day, Mr. Lundy."

She answered his bow with a graceful nod, then watched him guardedly as he walked out of the drawing room, bade Mrs. Clearwell a polite good afternoon, and showed himself the door.

The moment she heard the door close, Lily collapsed into the cushions behind her and pressed a hand vaguely to her thumping heart. Her whole body felt limp with relief at that narrow escape.

"He didn't mention the earrings—thank God!" she reported as Mrs. Clearwell glided in with the tea.

"I heard," her sponsor said sternly.

"You did?" Lily glanced up at her in surprise.

"I am your chaperone, darling. It is my God-given right, nay, my duty to eavesdrop. Now, then." Mrs. Clearwell set a cup of tea on its saucer before her and sat down to perch on the low table across from the couch. "You let him kiss you?"

"Yes," she admitted ruefully. "It was horrid."

"I am glad," she shot back. "Drink your tea, dear. You're as pale as a sheet."

"That was fast," Lily mumbled as she accepted her cup.

"Eliza knows us well. She had already put the water on to boil."

Indeed, the sip of soothing tea with sugar and milk helped restore a modicum of calm, which was fortunate, for in the next moment, Lily was going to need it.

Mrs. Clearwell shook her head ominously. "Any day now, you are going to have to make a momentous decision, my girl. First a kiss, next a proposal of marriage. You'll need to be sure."

But I am sure, my decision is already made, Lily wanted to say. Instead, she found that she faltered.

Was it?

"Lily, darling." Mrs. Clearwell cupped Lily's cheek in maternal tenderness for a moment. "You know I adore you, but you cannot marry one man when your heart is fixed upon another. It would be wrong."

Lily could only gaze at her, at a loss.

"Well, you've already been through enough for one day, so I will say no more. I have faith in you to do the right thing."

"Ma'am, I am sorry if I embarrassed you with my behavior in the midst of that whole—debacle."

She rose. "Yes, well, love makes people do foolish things."

"Love!"

"You heard me." Taking her cup of tea with her, Mrs. Clearwell wafted back toward the door. "I'm worn out from all our shopping. I'm off to take my nap."

"But Mrs. Clearwell, he's going back to India!" Lily burst out before her sponsor disappeared.

"La, child! Plans change," her godmother assured her with a mischievous twinkle in her eyes.

Lily's shoulders drooped as she considered this uncertainty. "You mustn't tell him about the earrings, in any case. He'd be mortified, proud as he is."

Mrs. Clearwell pretended to button her lips. Then she paused. "I could attempt to get them back for you, you know."

"No, ma'am." Lily shook her head. "I would never put that debt on you. It was my choice and my responsibility to trade them away. I do not regret it."

"Aha, I see. But you are not in love with him?"

"No!"

Mrs. Clearwell turned away with a knowing chuckle. "I will see you at supper, then. That Lord Arthur, my, what a handsome fellow. I can see where the major gets his looks . . ."

Lily smiled ruefully as her chaperone sailed off to take her daily rest.

For a long moment she remained on the couch, staring at nothing, still dazed by all that had happened. She let out a sigh, took a sip of tea, and leaned her head back on the cushions. So, she thought dully. She still had Edward on her fishhook. Some cynical part of her asked, *Did you think you could get out of it that easily?*

God, it was impossible to consider Derek Knight side by side with Edward Lundy and pine for the latter. *What shall I do?* Her emotions were all a-tangle. Heartbreak from the loss of her earrings. Amazement to find how much she really cared about Derek. Awe after having witnessed a glimpse of his warrior ferocity. Uneasiness after all Edward's paranoid questions about him. And dismay at the thought of having to spend the rest of her life with those clammy lips squashed against hers.

Maybe she really *should* put an end to this match.

Alas, she was not brave enough to jump off that particular cliff unless she was sure there was someone with very strong arms waiting to catch her below.

But that *someone* had other priorities, contrary to what her chaperone might believe. That someone did not feel toward her what she was beginning to feel all too strongly toward him.

With a wince of angry frustration, Lily shut her eyes again, feeling trapped. *Derek! I want to see Derek.*

Yes . . .

As inspiration dawned, new energy suddenly spurted into her veins.

She should go and see how that poor horse was doing!

* * *

The sorrel mare was in sorry shape, but he had nursed far worse-off creatures back to health.

In the stable that served the Althorpe, the rescued horse now stood safely tethered in the cross-ties with her injured front hoof soaking in a bucket of warm water with Epsom salts. His shirtsleeves rolled up, Derek sat on a low stool beside the problem leg, keeping the mare calm and making sure she did not try to kick away the bucket.

They were housing her in the large box stall at the far end of the aisle, away from the other horses, until they could be sure she was not sick as well as maltreated. In the short couple of hours that had passed, she was doing remarkably well. Cleaned and dried, groomed and fed, the coachman's lashes on her back lightly dressed with a warm bran-and-herbal poultice that Derek had made himself to draw off any risk of infection, her overall condition was vastly improved.

He, too, had calmed down from his earlier anger. The stable had always been his favorite place to escape to, and being here with useful work to do had relaxed him considerably after that irksome altercation.

Still, he remained in a troubled, dark, brooding frame of mind.

The charges against him had been dropped, he guessed, due to their inherent absurdity. Still, the coachman's attempt to have him arrested had left him fuming.

A hundred witnesses in the crowd had seen that bastard's cruelty to his animals. All *he* had done was give the man back a bit of his own medicine.

It had felt good, actually.

Until the moment he had remembered that Lily was watching.

Now he couldn't stop wondering how badly he might have had alienated her with his actions . . . and he was a little uneasy about why he cared quite so much.

Once more, the restlessness had come back to plague him with all those unsettling questions that he tried his best to ignore. Questions about what his chosen career just might be doing to his soul.

The shocked look on Lily's face when she had seen him whip the coachman had brought them all rushing back. But if she thought that was bad, why, that was nothing compared to the average battle.

Damn it, what was he doing with this girl, anyway? He was only putting his fragile alliance with Lundy at risk.

And yet he could not seem to stay away from her. He felt so strangely drawn to her.

Ah, hell, he was being absurd even thinking about it. Even if he weren't going back to India, her family needed money and he wasn't rich. Not like Lundy. His own clan was prosperous, of course, but he'd rather swallow his sword than go begging his father for an allowance like some callow boy.

When a warm puff of air from a soft muzzle reached his cheek, he looked up with a wry smile as the mare nuzzled him. "I know, sweetheart. You're welcome."

He stroked the mare's shoulder and then felt to see if the water in the soaking pail was still warm.

It turned out his blond-maned foundling had a lovely temperament. While applying the medicinal dressing, he had been pleasantly surprised by the horse's sweet and trusting disposition despite the abuse. In his experience, most animals did not enjoy humans poking around at their wounds, especially if they had been cruelly treated, but the mare had let him put the poultice on her back without too much protest. Her docility led him to suspect she had been someone's beloved pet before fate had cast her into the role of beast of burden, probably by way of the auction block.

That was when it had dawned on him why she had not fared well on the driver's team. She was a saddle horse! He could not determine with certainty the exact makeup of her mixed breed, but the lighter, more even development of her musculature hinted at her prior usage. She needed more meat on her bones, true, but she had a nice, clean confirmation.

Certainly, Derek's own excellent riding horse deemed the mare worthy of his attentions. The black stallion from Tattersall's had been sending his compliments with amorous whinnies since they had arrived, sticking his head out of his stall and tossing his mane to gain her notice.

The mare seemed to think her admirer a bit too forward.

For his part, Derek had a strong notion of who ought to be her future owner. The horse would make a useful gift for Lily. If she had her own mount, it would be one less way in which she'd have to depend on the goodwill of others—that of her chaperone or her suitor. He knew that it bothered her pride to have to rely on others for everything. He decided that this was a capital plan. He'd fix the mare up and give her to someone he knew would never abuse her.

Satisfied that the hoof had had a good soaking, Derek made the mare lift her leg out of the bucket, moved it aside, and proceeded to rub the leg and hoof dry with soft, clean towels. Bending over, he took another look at the soft underside of the hoof, the injured frog, and shrugged to himself. Time would tell.

Then he let the mare put her foot down and straightened up, giving her a pat on the neck.

"How is your patient, Major?" a soft voice asked from behind him.

Derek turned in surprise. "Lily!"

Hoping the jolt to his heart at the sight of her did not entirely show on his face, he reined in his reaction, wiping his hands on a towel. "What are you doing here?" he asked in a warm and easy tone.

"Visiting the sick," she said. "It's what we genteel ladies do."

With her slender hourglass shape silhouetted against the bright daylight beyond the wide-open barn doors, she sauntered closer, pushing her straw bonnet back and letting it hang behind from the ribbons tied around her neck. Drawing off her tan kid gloves, she reached into the basket hooked over her arm and pulled out a carrot. "I come bearing gifts. May I?"

"Please." Unable to take his eyes off her, Derek gestured toward the horse. "You are alone?" he asked in surprise when no maid appeared behind her and no Mrs. Clearwell.

"Only for a brief visit."

"How venturesome of you, Miss Balfour."

She flicked a wary glance over the bare part of his chest where his white shirt fell open. "I hope you don't mind."

"Not at all," he murmured heartily.

She made a show of turning her attention back to the sorrel. "So, how is she?"

"On the whole, I'd say she's glad to be rid of this." He picked up the sharp, nasty, little stone that had been lodged in the mare's right front shoe. "That's what was making her limp."

"Look at that, Lord! It would make me limp, too. Poor girl. Is she going to be all right?"

He had to jerk himself out of the spell of watching her hand stroking the animal's soft hide. He would have liked to know how that gentle caress would have felt on his skin. "Hard to say." He looked away, hands on his hips, hoping his hunger for her wasn't too terribly obvious. "Any wound to the soft parts under the hoof can turn serious, but I'm optimistic we caught it in time."

"She looks happy."

He smiled at her, charmed by the pink in her cheeks from her walk here as she set the basket aside, then untied her bonnet strings and put her hat with it.

As Lily began making friends with the mare, feeding her a couple of carrots and one of the apples from her basket, Derek's gaze traveled over her slim figure in lush admiration. She had changed into simpler attire, a plain blue walking dress with a light, open, beige pelisse that skimmed her curves down to her knees. He had seen her dressed in ball gowns, but he decided that he liked her best of all just like this.

Warm. Accessible. Even her smile seemed easier.

Her mask and sparkly costume were far behind them now. He got the feeling he was finally seeing the real Lily.

Before he knew it, he was caught up in staring at the flowing tendrils of golden hair that had escaped from the loose and pleasantly dishabille chignon at her nape.

"What?" Lily murmured, smiling back.

He shook his head, mystified. "I'm just surprised to see you, that's all. I mean, it's a bit of a risk to your reputation, is it not?"

"I had to come and check on her. And on you," she added with a probing glance at him. Then she let the mare nibble another apple from her hand, leaving him to wonder what she intended as far as he was concerned. "I can't believe how much better she's doing. She's precious. Are you sure this is the same horse?"

"That's her," he replied as he turned away and emptied the bucket of used water out the stall window.

"I'm impressed with you, Major. Veterinarian, surgeon, child-minder, lobbyist . . . warrior."

"Er, yes, about that," he said in chagrin, putting the empty pail aside. "I really am sorry—"

"Don't be." With a small, knowing chuckle, she reached out and gave his arm a swift, reassuring touch. "It's all right. That's why I came, actually. I had a feeling you'd think I was cross."

"You should be cross." He furrowed his brow, puzzled. "I acted like a barbarian."

"Maybe, but it would be hypocritical of me to judge you, wouldn't it, when I was so adamant that you not judge me—as a fortune hunter, remember?"

Derek remembered.

"Anyway, when I got back to Mrs. Clearwell's today, guess who was waiting for me?"

Derek halted. "Lundy?" The air seemed to evaporate out of his lungs. "Did he finally propose, then?"

"No." She sent him a rueful smile, still petting the horse. "He was acting strange. Asking questions. Saying odd things."

His stare homed in on her. "What sorts of things?"

"He heard about our walk last night."

"Are you sure that's all he heard about?"

"I think so." Lily paused. "He made a point of telling me he wasn't jealous, actually. Why should he be?" she added wryly. "He knows my situation."

Hands on hips, Derek clenched his jaw and looked at the ground. "So, what did he want?"

"He wanted to know if you had been plying me with questions about his holdings and possessions." She shrugged. "I think he's afraid you're only pretending friendship with him because he's rich and you're a younger son. I guess he's grown accustomed to people trying to use him for his wealth. But you and I both know that you would never do that." She glanced at him with guilt reflected in her big, blue eyes for her own motives in pursuing the nabob. "Can you . . . think of any other reason why Edward might not trust you, Derek?"

Of course he could. The investigation. Though he couldn't tell her that.

So, Derek mused, his supposed ally Lundy did not trust him, after all. No more, it seemed, than Derek trusted *him*. Lundy must have realized that Derek had not yet cleared him from the list of suspects.

But, bloody hell, bringing the girl into the middle of their chess game was a boundary Derek refused to cross.

She was waiting for his answer, but he side-stepped the question.

"Did he say anything else of note?"

"Only that he wanted me to tell him if you ever asked how much he's worth. I agreed," she added with an earnest glance.

"Well, then, it seems I have been warned," he said dryly.

"I didn't mean it like that."

"How did you mean it, then?" He unhooked the sorrel from the cross-ties.

At once, the mare ambled over to the far corner of her new stall and lowered her head to investigate the pile of fresh hay that Derek had thrown down.

Lily's cheeks had turned red. "I don't know. In any case,

you do not need to worry. I managed to put Edward's fears at ease."

"I wasn't worried—and how did you do that?"

She ignored his jealous question with an impatient shake of her head. "I just wanted to let you know he's not really being as open with you as he's probably pretending to be."

"Well," Derek said philosophically, his pulse pounding out an angry beat, "that's mutual, isn't it?"

"What do you mean?"

"I mean I'm standing in a box stall with his future wife, and all I can think about is how much I want to kiss her. He'd be a fool to trust me." Derek paused, slowly curling one of the cross-tie ropes around his hand, looping the circle of rope on its peg. "And so would you."

The pink in her cheeks had darkened at his bold words. She glanced at him longingly, then dropped her gaze.

Derek closed his eyes, throbbing.

Think.

"You should go," he murmured hoarsely.

"I don't want to," she whispered, moving closer to him. "Derek—I'm confused."

"So am I."

He was practically panting, wanted to lay her down in the hay right now, but he held back, recalling her shocked look in the midst of his brawl. And now here she stood, offering herself. God, he did not know what to make of her.

"Lily, you don't want a man like me," he informed her brusquely, running his hand through his hair. "I saw how you looked at me back in that street, but you have no idea."

"I'm not afraid," she breathed, taking another step closer to him. "Derek—I want to help you."

At once, he went on his guard. "Help me?"

Her soft words brought back the aftertaste of despair that he had come to know in his nightmares, that hellish world of smoke and death where he was so alone.

"Last night when we stood by the river, you grew distant all of a sudden—as if something in your thoughts had disturbed your peace of mind. And then today, I saw that same look in your eyes, that same wild, ferocious look. You are—in pain, I think."

He felt unmasked. Naked. He did not know how to answer.

He was so unnerved by her perceptiveness that all he could manage to do in this moment was lie. "I'm fine, really."

"No," she implored him. "You're not. You told me you are an honest man, so prove it. Tell me what is wrong."

"What do you want me to say?" he exclaimed, backing away until he reached the interior wall of the box stall. He leaned against it, struggling for words. "Obviously, I am out of my element here."

"Where?"

"This city, this country, this continent! I don't belong here. I'm glad I met *you*, of course, but frankly it was never my desire to come to England. These were my orders, and what my family wanted me to do."

"You're homesick? Is that it? Because, Derek, believe me, I certainly know how that feels—"

"No, it's not that."

"What is it, then?"

"There's a war on! Why can't anyone here seem to get that through their heads? I should be in India with my men! I'm sick with worry for them. I can't even think about it. Without me there to lead them . . ." He shook his head and looked away with a low growl of frustration. "This mission of mine to secure the Army funds—it was more of a punishment than a promotion, if you must know."

"Really?"

He nodded in disdain. "My lofty family ties were deemed useful for the task, but the real reason I was chosen for this assignment was to teach me a lesson. My command was temporarily suspended, my post reassigned to another officer. I have no way of knowing if he's any good, and the only way they're going to put me back where I belong is if I bring them back their damned Army funds."

"Why? What did you do?"

"What did I do?" He snorted, eyeing her with no idea of how she might react. Then he shrugged. "I killed a few palace guards inside the fortress of a maharajah."

Her eyes widened.

"I had no choice. Their prince went after my sister. We had to protect her—Gabriel and I. Unfortunately, this was not well received. Our colonel nearly had to hand us over to the maharajah to be beheaded for breaking local Hindu law."

Her jaw dropped, and he supposed he'd better explain.

"You met my sister's husband, Lord Griffith. He came to India on a diplomatic mission to negotiate a treaty with the Maharajah of Janpur. Gabriel and I were chosen to head up his security detail, providing armed escort into hostile territory. Well, Georgie managed to invite herself along, and let's just say chaos tends to follow in my sister's wake. So, Gabriel and I, we did what we had to do, and people died," he said grimly. "Including the prince, by Gabriel's sword, and most of his bodyguards, by mine. Their deaths cost me my command, while Gabriel very nearly lost his life. We were both removed from our posts to appease the maharajah. If Georgie's snooping had not uncovered the fact that the prince had been plotting against his father, my brother and I would've been headless months ago."

She winced at his graveyard humor.

He shrugged. "What else could we do? Let that royal bastard harm our sister? We had no choice. It was us or them."

"Well, goodness," she said faintly. "After all of that, does your brother want to go back to India, too?"

"No." Derek fell silent. "He was nearly killed right at the end of our battle. He's still not quite himself. So far, he has no interest in getting his old post back. He said the brush with death has made him rethink how he lives his life."

"I see." Lily tilted her head, studying him. "And it didn't have that effect on you at all?"

"No!" he replied with great, stubborn vehemence, refusing to acknowledge these exact doubts that had plagued his mind for months now.

"Oh—I see." She gave him a dubious look.

"War is what I know, Lily. I don't want to start over. I'm a soldier. This is what I'm trained to do, and I'm good at it. That's what I'm trying to tell you. I know you think I acted like a barbarian today—and you're right. But the truth is, what you saw was only the barest glimpse of what I'm capable of, the kinds of things I've done many times over. That's why I got so angry in Hyde Park when you called me a killer. Because, unfortunately—" He took a deep breath. "There's a grain of truth to that. How am I supposed to forget it all and suddenly become a civilian? I don't even think it's possible for me."

"Of course it's possible, Derek." She gazed at him in compassion and slowly shook her head. "All these things you've done, it must be such a burden to carry. How do you manage to live with it all?"

"You just don't think about it," he said.

She veiled her gaze behind her lowered lashes. "Don't you think it's taken enough of a toll on you already? Maybe your family's right. Going back for more cannot be good for you."

"My men are still there. It isn't good for *them*. Why should I have it easy?"

"Derek."

He swallowed hard. "I don't belong here, Lily. Today made that abundantly clear. Maybe I'm too far gone to fit in with civilization anymore. At least on the battlefront, I fit right in with . . . all the other savages."

"Derek, that coachman today was the real savage," she countered with a firm stare, gesturing toward the sorrel mare. "And so were all the other people who drove right on by without even stopping to help. They didn't care. You call yourself a barbarian, but you were the only one who even noticed this poor horse's hell."

"And now you've noticed mine," he answered quietly, looking into her eyes. *What am I supposed to do?*

Going back meant returning to Hell. Staying here was making him lunatic. He was damned either way.

"How can I help you?" she whispered as she slowly closed the space between them.

"Have you got a gun?" he drawled with a grim smile as he opened his shirt and showed her his heart.

"That's not funny!" she scolded in answer to his mordant jest. But she pressed her hand and then her lips softly to his chest, and the tenderness she gave him shook him to the core.

Derek closed his eyes and tilted his head back. Words failed him as her lips caressed his chest as if to kiss the broken heart inside him. The lure of her beauty was too much to bear.

He reached out, hazy-eyed, slid his hand beneath her hair, and drew her to him by her nape, claiming her mouth in a fevered kiss.

Then she was in his arms, pressing her body close against the length of his. She clutched his shoulders and stroked his face, feeding on his kiss in a ravenous desire that matched his own. Derek's palms molded her waist; she inched her hands down his bare chest until he was quivering, and then he eased her down into the soft bed of hay and moved atop her.

She kissed him, on and on, holding nothing back. He was completely wrapped up in the taste of her tongue, the hungry rhythm of her mouth stroking his. His body burned.

His fingertips skimmed up and down the curve of her silken neck; she ran her hands through his hair, and then moaned gently when he cupped her breast.

"Oh, Derek—"

"I want you so much." His whispered confession slipped out before he could stop it.

He kissed her again.

"Maybe you should stay here," she breathed, pausing to gaze into his eyes. She caressed his cheek, with the most exquisite yearning etched across her beautiful face. "Maybe you should stay with me."

"Maybe you should come with me to India," he answered.

Passion ebbed from her eyes as shock at his words registered in their depths. He felt her melting body stiffen suddenly beneath him. "You know I can't do that."

"Can't or won't?"

She shook her head with a stricken look, her voice a strangled whisper. *"No."*

Her answer brought Derek back to his senses. He lowered his head and looked away. "This is not a good idea. Somebody could see us. You should go."

He could tell that she was suddenly embarrassed. "I-I suppose you're right."

Without a word, he offered a hand to help her rise, but she didn't take it.

"Derek, I'm sorry—"

"Never mind. It was just an idea." These were his words, but he avoided her gaze, feeling as if he'd been punched in the gut.

Why was he surprised at her refusal? It was an unreasonable request.

But another part of him, the secret, wild, romantic part that would have done absolutely anything for the woman he loved once he found her, could not understand her denial.

He knew she needed money, but if love was real, the money shouldn't matter.

He was beginning to think he would always be alone.

He could feel Lily staring at him, but he could not bring himself to look at her. Instead, he shut her out. A cold, knee-jerk reaction to protect himself. "You should go," he repeated, trying but failing to keep the bite of hurt irony out of his voice. "I don't need Edward calling me out."

For a moment longer, she hesitated, as though confused by the sudden chill in his attitude, then she seemed to conclude mentally, *The hell with you.*

She climbed to her feet without the help of his offered hand and stepped past him with a show of dignity, brushing little bits of hay off her dress. Then she gave a quick tug to pull her bodice back into place.

She picked up her bonnet but left the basket of treats behind for the horse. On her way out, she paused, glancing back at him with tears in her eyes. "Good-bye, Derek. Please try to be careful—in India."

"Careful?" he drawled with a desolate twist of a smile. "Little glory in that."

When she flinched at the thought of danger to him, he instantly regretted his empty words and paused. "Good-bye, Lily," he said finally in a low tone. He might run into her again in Town, but he knew that it would never be like this between them again. This was farewell. "I hope your family appreciates what you're doing for them, you know, because you really are—" he faltered, lowering his head— "the most enchanting person I have ever met. And I'm just damned sorry I'm not richer."

She stared at him with a stricken look for a moment more, then she was gone.

Derek squeezed his eyes shut and spat the filthiest curse under his breath that he could think of in any Indian dialect.

"Good God, who died?" Gabriel exclaimed the second he saw Derek's face when he entered into their apartments a few minutes later.

Derek just looked at him. "You're coming with me next week to the Lundys' garden party," he informed him in a deadened tone.

"I am?" Gabriel leaned forward with a look of concern as Derek stalked past, stony-faced. "Why?"

"You're to provide the distraction so I can slip away from the party and break into Lundy's files. He keeps them in his home."

"You're going to do that in the middle of their barbecue? Why?"

"Because this is the best chance I'm going to get," Derek ground out. "I'll be *damned* if I'm letting her marry him until I can verify he's not a thief."

If he could not have her for himself, at least he could protect her.

CHAPTER
∽ TWELVE ∽

She hadn't wanted to admit it to herself at the time, but the real reason Lily had gone to the stable was to see if there was any chance at all that she and Derek could be together, that he might reciprocate her feelings.

Well, she had her answer now.

It wasn't the one she had wanted to hear, but falling in love had never been part of her plan.

And so she had made up her mind to forget about Derek Knight for once and for all—to stick with her original design and marry Edward.

If only he would ask her!

What the blazes was he waiting for? She was really beginning to resent being dangled on his line like this. He knew full well his hook was buried in her gills, but for some reason, he was letting her suffer, taking his time about reeling her in. She wished he would finally put her out of her misery.

When the day of the garden party rolled around, the brass band played cheerfully in the shade. Beneath the large striped tent, the drink flowed, sparkling bowls of fruit punch, barrels of amber ale. The food for the picnic feast, delicious and abundant, sprawled over the long tables.

Even the moody English weather proved agreeable.

All around Edward's estate, the games and athletics were in progress as summer swelled to its verdant crescendo. Cricket and archery, tennis and lawn bowls, rowing on the little lake, and, of course, gambling on all of the above, along with much flirting and lively conversation. Those denizens of Society who had arrived with uneasy looks about whether this host really was too far beneath them had warmed up in time amid all the fun and frolic.

Lily was relieved for the Lundys' sake—and for her own, as his future spouse. She prayed that neither Edward nor his mother would disgrace themselves, and so far, their first attempt at hosting a Society event was running smoothly.

For her part, however, she was tied up in knots over the prospect of seeing Derek again. It had been nearly a week . . . and his refusal to stay in England with her still hurt.

It hurt terribly.

But she could not possibly go with him to India! Surely he knew that. She wasn't even sure if he had been serious in asking. Maybe this shocking demand was merely his way of getting rid of young ladies who became overly attached to him. She wouldn't put it past the rogue.

All she knew was that even though he hadn't left yet, it felt as if she were being abandoned all over again, painfully similar to when her father had sailed off smiling and never came back. In all fairness to Derek, truthfully, she was unsure how much of her brooding anger all week was directed at him and how much was left over from her sire's absence from her life, but it hardly mattered now.

The plain fact was his military career was more important to him than the possibility of a life and a love and a future with her, and it left her feeling like she simply didn't matter.

At least she mattered to Edward.

Well, it was Derek's loss if he wasn't smart enough to know what he was missing out on, she thought morosely as she stood in the day's brilliant sun, half craving, half dreading his arrival. Her great-great-grandmother's earrings were the least of what she'd have given for her true love, but the swaggering cavalryman was blinded by fortune and glory and did not care to fill that role.

Of course, now she hoped desperately that he *never* found out about the sacrifice of her earrings, for she would be mortified if he realized how crazed over him she had allowed herself to become.

And still one other thing about their liaison at the stable kept preying upon Lily's mind.

While it was easy to compare Derek's plans to leave England with those of her father, it was equally easy to *contrast* his behavior with that of Lord Owen Masters in her past.

Last week in that dashed box stall, they had been going mad in each other's arms; but unlike her seducer of years ago, Derek had in no way pressured her for more. Indeed, he was the one who had brought their explorations to a halt. For her part, Lily would have been quite happy to continue, but Derek had forced himself to stop.

That had surprised her.

Owen, amid much pleading, had instructed her that if she didn't lie back and let him slake his body's needs, he would suffer pain in his anatomy that no female could ever understand.

Fifteen and all too trusting, Lily had believed him completely and could not bear for her "beloved" to suffer for her sake. So she had borne it—even though what he'd done to her, in turn, had certainly hurt *her* anatomy. She was the one who had ended up bleeding.

Now Derek's restraint, by contrast, had her wondering, sickeningly, if all that had been just one more of Owen's many lies. It was not the sort of thing that she could ever have asked her mother.

Just then, she spotted Derek arriving at the party and tensed from head to toe. At first she thought in shock that he had *two* women with him, but then she realized one was with his brother.

Gracious, she thought, studying the other tall, black-haired man. Gabriel Knight was making his long-anticipated entrance into Society at Edward's barbecue. Wouldn't that be a feather in the Lundys' cap?

As they came nearer, she was startled to see that the two

brothers looked almost exactly alike, only Gabriel's hair was cropped short. His guarded gait and just the hint of gaunt strain in his form and face reminded her of Derek's story about how Gabriel had nearly lost his life in their last battle. He had a gloomy look about him, dressed all in black.

Lily recognized the elegant blonde with Gabriel as the same woman who had come hunting for Derek that night at the garden folly. It seemed he had passed her on to his brother.

As for the second-born Knight, he had the glamorous Mrs. Coates on his arm once again.

Lily watched Derek bleakly with his carefree paramour, barely listening to Edward next to her, bragging to one of his male guests. It was hard to see Derek laughing and being his usual charming self with not one, but two of his former conquests.

After ending up in the hay with him herself last week, she had already decided on what her policy must be toward him today: She'd be keeping her distance, thank you very much.

Kicking herself for letting him take such liberties with her—especially when she knew *she* was the one who had provoked it—Lily was all the more determined to control herself around him.

Derek, for his part, appeared all the more intent on focusing his desire elsewhere. No doubt he should find Mrs. Coates quite obliging, Lily thought with jealousy.

Oh, marvelous, she mused, watching the four. *They're coming this way.* Her stupid heart beat faster, curse it.

Their progress, however, was delayed. They seemed to be having trouble getting through the crowd of people who swirled around them. The arrival of this notorious quartet had caused a stir all over Edward's sculpted grounds. If one of the Knight brothers alone created a sensation, the pair together nearly touched off a riot.

Lily knew, however, it was only a matter of time before she'd have to face Derek, for, of course, it was de rigueur for guests to come and greet their hosts.

The Lundys, along with Lily and Mrs. Clearwell, who were serving as co-hostesses of the day, had positioned themselves in an informal reception line in the shade of a massive oak tree, where it was convenient for them to welcome each newly arriving guest.

Although Lily tried to keep her attention on whatever inconsequential thing Edward was saying, she couldn't help but watch Derek—though only from the corner of her eye.

The brothers had their hands full trying to bring their troop of lady admirers under control, but at last they succeeded, thankfully without having to resort to barking orders military-style.

Having fought their way free of their doting entourage, the majors and their sophisticated companions now joined Lily and the others under the oak tree.

Lily did not know where to look as the handsome pair came sauntering into the breezy shade. Her pulse sped up as greetings were exchanged.

With Edward standing right there, she knew she was in danger of betraying herself by her reaction to Derek. Could she hold her polite mask in place?

Her nerves stretched thin as the man she meant to marry shook hands in amiable fashion with the man she had thrown herself at in a box stall last week.

Then Derek introduced his brother, and when he came around to her, Lily sketched an automatic curtsy to the elder Knight.

"Miss Balfour, I have heard so much about you," Gabriel Knight said, giving her a noble bow.

You have? Her eyes widened in pleasure and uncertainty and then sudden dread that Gabriel might say something wrong in front of Edward—good Lord, what all had Derek told his brother about her, anyway? Scandalous things?

Her reaction went unnoticed thanks to Mrs. Clearwell's swift intervention, directing everyone's attention to the antics of the entertainers over by the tent. Lily's relief at her sponsor's quick thinking was short-lived, however, for in the next moment, she felt someone watching her.

She glanced over cautiously and found Derek's brother studying her. There was a strange, otherworldly intensity in Gabriel Knight's deep, ocean-blue eyes. He looked like he could see right inside a person's soul, she thought with a small gulp. The mysterious firstborn's brief scrutiny rattled her, but she got the feeling that Gabriel was sizing her up, as if to determine whether or not she was worthy of his little brother.

She did not appreciate being judged.

When she glanced at Derek to send a silent protest his way, she found him also watching her, his eyes, by contrast, wolflike and silvery-pale, with a different sort of intensity in their depths.

An unwilling hunger.

Her blush crept in of its own accord as she held his gaze in spite of herself. Edward was preoccupied with telling Gabriel all the kinds of beer they had on tap beneath the tent. Meanwhile, Derek's stare smoldered with equal parts hostility and lust.

Lily dropped her gaze, shaken. Lord, this double life of hers was getting complicated.

Well, there she stood in all her glory, the little fortune hunter, her choice made, Derek thought, and so be it. He had washed his hands of Lily Balfour.

At least that's what he had been telling himself all week.

Seeing her now, in her pale green gown with a pink rose tucked in her silky blond hair, turned him inside out like some sort of hideous Eastern torture. But it did not signify. There was no point wanting what a man could not have. She was standing next to Lundy for a reason.

Derek reminded himself he had other entertainments in store for later, anyway. With that, he slipped his arm around Fanny's waist and met her sideward glance with an easy half-smile. Women like this were so much less trouble.

Fortunately, the investigation had kept him too busy—by day, at least—to think about the whole vexing female species much.

He had made huge progress over the past few days. He had just completed his stealthy survey of what each committee member owned, constructing detailed lists of what he observed. He had also decided to press his luck and have a few private conversations with four of the men who struck him as completely innocent of any wrongdoing.

All three gents from the House of Commons and the lowliest of the Lords he had struck off his list of suspects. That left five: the Chairman Lord Sinclair and the second-ranked lord, as well as all three from the East India Company hierarchy.

Lundy was still on the list.

In fact, he had moved up a few notches now that he had proved himself to be such a very good actor.

Thanks to Lily, Derek now knew Lundy didn't trust him. Her suitor had told her so flat-out, and Lily had relayed that fact to him.

But in Derek's presence, why, one would have thought that they were blood brothers, bosom mates. Lundy's unexpected skill at playacting set off all sorts of alarms in Derek's head.

Today he intended to get some solid answers when the time came to slip away from the party and break into Lundy's files. He and his brother had planned it all out. Gabriel would ask their host for a tour of his magnificent stables. Derek had already seen them and well remembered Lundy's gloating pleasure in showing off his bloodstock; he would skip the tour.

In the meantime, Derek had quietly recruited specialized help to assist in the next step of the investigation. He was shrewd enough to know his own limits, and outside of today's upcoming adventure sleuthing inside Lundy's castle-house, his inquiry was now moving out of the field of action and into an area Derek did not at all relish, one where he could claim no expertise, nor desired to gain any.

Bloody paperwork.

He did not know the details, but he figured there were ways that crooked men could hide their windfalls, bury the truth in all those blinding little columns of numbers. The next step, therefore, was to look for discrepancies between the lists of their holdings that he had carefully constructed based on observation and what was on the books.

By God, he was a patriot and would stop at nothing to send the Army its promised funds, but poring over old bank records, tax forms and receipts, stockholding certificates, deeds and trusts, a veritable wasteland of paperwork—this was enough to make a man of action lose his mind.

And so he had paid a call at Knight House and asked his London cousins to recommend a good accountant.

They had presented him with Charles Beecham, Esquire, their tidy little solicitor and all-purpose man-of-business, who had come to earn the supreme trust of the entire Knight clan. The Duke of Hawkscliffe himself had asked Beecham to add Baby Kate to his will when Her Ladyship had done them the honor of being born—and if anything untoward happened to His Grace, the ducal daughter would be one very wealthy infant.

At any rate, the brisk, balding, and meticulous Charles had joined Derek's mission with a numerical zest that belied his pasty face and slight stature.

The little fellow looked like he might faint at the sight of blood, but so far, Charles had proved to be a godsend. In his years of service for assorted men of wealth before devoting himself exclusively to the Knight clan, he had seen all the dirty tricks dishonest men could try.

Instinctively confident in the integrity he sensed in the man within minutes of meeting him, Derek had sworn Charles to secrecy and then explained the whole unpleasant matter about the suspected embezzlement.

Charles had quickly grasped the scope and consequence of the problem, whereupon he had rolled up his sleeves and put his spectacles on like a man arming for battle. "Fear not, Major. If there is wickedness afoot here, we will find it," he had vowed, and then, before Derek's eyes, Charles had begun to attack that paper mountain with a singleminded fury, determined to ferret out whatever corruption might be hiding inside all those blinding little columns.

Derek had watched him, bemused.

Charles had high-placed patrons in Derek's kinsmen, true, but it struck him as somewhat extraordinary that this small, harmless man—who looked like he wouldn't stand a chance defending himself in a milling match against even the youngest water boy back at the regiment—this unlikely little hero showed not the slightest fear about crossing the supremely powerful Gentlemen of the Sub-Committee.

This was a new kind of courage to Derek. He found it rather impressive for a civilian. Who'd have guessed it? Behind the accountant's unassuming face and paunchy form beat the heart of a lion.

For the past few days now, Charles had waged his holy war on the ledger books. He had even agreed to bend the rules a bit and use the influence he wielded through his patrons with the chaps in the back offices at the Bank of England. Thanks to Charles's role as the man-of-affairs for one of the richest families to store their millions there, he managed to persuade certain clerks of his acquaintance at the Bank of England to let him have a brief glance at the banking records of the committee members under suspicion.

Derek knew they could all get into deep trouble for this, but there wasn't time to fool with chasing after all the correct permissions in London's dizzying bureaucracy. The bloody good of the nation was at stake. If the troops didn't have their gold, they might lose the war; the colonies in India could then begin to fall like dominoes, and who could say what advantage that would give the French or some other rival power?

In any case, that bit of illicit snooping helped him clear another pair of names off his list.

Since most of this lay within Charles's expertise, Derek floundered, finding that he wasn't much use in this particular stage of the investigation.

Given his restless state of mind after his falling-out with Lily, any hour of idleness was an unwelcome plague. He resorted to cleaning his horses' tack and repacking his things an eighteenth time for his journey home. There was still no word, no letter from Colonel Montrose. He worried about his lads, wondered where his men had been dispatched to, how they were faring under the new major, whether they had seen any action yet, and if there had been casualties.

Lundy had no news to report about what was happening with the Chairman Lord Sinclair's efforts to find the embezzler within the committee. Derek had not told Lundy about bringing Charles into the fray, of course. He finished up the last few spying sessions needed and did what he could to help Charles. That, at any rate, was how he spent his days. The nights were another matter.

Nights were hard.

He lay awake thinking nonstop about Lily and even when he slept, she invaded his dreams. In his same battle-field nightmares now, he could hear her calling to him through the barrage of cannon-fire and black smoke. In his dreams, they were desperately trying to find each other, so somehow they could both escape that hellish place and survive.

Indeed, his stark nightmares about his past battles had led him to a change of heart about having invited her to come with him to India. Thank God she had said no. For when he thought in cold, hard, realistic terms about her actually being there, he knew he didn't want her anywhere near his army life.

Death was everywhere. If she were killed, he would never forgive himself. Then there was the threat of capture, arguably worse for a woman. A golden-haired English girl would be considered a most exotic addition to any of the local nizams' private harems. Her very beauty would make her a target—and that would only increase the danger for his whole squadron.

He could protect Lily and he could fight a war—but he wasn't sure any man could do both, every day, around the clock. Even "strong-arm'd Achilles" had to rest sometime.

For now, he counted himself lucky for this chance to

stand here near her, in earshot of her soft, melodious voice; he wondered if she knew that he was watching her in fascination.

Earlier, he had tried to read her reaction when he had arrived, but all he could glean was that she was not happy to see him with Fanny again.

Well, good. Let her take a dose of her own medicine.

She seemed resolved to treat him just the same as anybody else, but privately, Derek amused himself by watching Lily deal with each new trial that came her way.

When Mrs. Lundy started gushing again about her upcoming trip to Jamaica, Derek observed Lily's fleeting exasperation when she thought no one was looking. It was barely there, a subtle glance to heaven, as though praying for the strength not to scream upon having to hear it all again.

He lowered his gaze with a private smile. The first time he'd met her, she had been masked, but somehow she had become an open book to him by now, one he knew he could never get tired of reading. He looked at her again, engrossed.

Her gaze was fixed across the green and now he watched her delicate face harden. She was battening down for a siege, and quickly, Derek saw why. Bess Kingsley was making her way over to them, skirts and petticoats flouncing with her big, pounding strides.

This should be interesting, Derek mused.

Oh, not her again!

Certain that within moments her nemesis would search out some new way to humiliate her in front of everyone, Lily barely had time to brace herself before Bess flung herself as usual into the center of their party, monopolized Mrs. Lundy, and began talking loudly. At once, she began hurling her opinions about, critiquing the food, the drink, the tent, and the musicians, as if anyone cared about what details had displeased her.

Gabriel looked at the girl in surprise.

I think I feel a headache coming on, Lily mused, but then

she noticed the hint of a sympathetic smile coming from Derek, and that soft curve of his lips becalmed her soul so that the sun came out again and her floating heart ignored Miss Kingsley's bellowing verbiage, and all she heard was the lilting song of a little bluebird perched high up on the mighty oak's branch above her.

Then the bird flicked its tail and deposited its droppings right in Lily's cup of champagne punch.

Mrs. Clearwell gasped.

The bird flew away without a care, and Lily just sighed, somehow not surprised, while Edward and Bess roared with laughter.

"Oh, Eddie, look! The curse of the Balfours has struck again!"

"What excellent aim the creature had," Lily drawled as she handed off the goblet to the nearest servant and received a wet washcloth in return, quickly wiping her hands, though thank heavens, there was no direct hit.

"Actually, they say it's good luck, you know," Mrs. Clearwell offered, with a pitying look for her humiliation.

"I've heard that," Derek seconded, while Mrs. Coates cringed and Lady Amherst murmured, "How disgusting!"

The men had stronger stomachs. Derek and Gabriel stifled their smiles, simultaneously stepping forward to offer their handkerchiefs.

"It's all right, Majors," Lily said dryly. "The little dickens missed me."

"Barely!" Bess burst out, red-faced with hilarity at the mishap. She elbowed Edward. "I told you you'd best stay away from her or something horrid would befall you! She's bad luck! Poor Miss Balfour! It must be such a trial, being cursed."

Lily came abruptly to the end of her patience and gave Bess a bright smile. "Actually, Miss Kingsley, all the *best* families have curses. Maybe your father can buy one after he's finished paying off the title."

"Hullo," Derek said mildly.

Bess's eyes had widened. "How *rude*!"

Mrs. Coates and Lady Amherst were snickering as only true Society ladies could do, but Mrs. Lundy looked like she might faint. "Oh—oh, my dear young ladies, do not—"

Her lower lip trembling, Bess whirled to Edward. "Did you hear what she said to me?"

"It was rather rude, Lily," he agreed in a low tone.

Lily glared at him in shock.

"No, no," Derek interjected, watching in amusement. "Our Miss Balfour has merely learned to parry. It's about damned time, too," he added under his breath.

"Oh, I always knew how, Major." Lily glanced at him, then at Bess again. "I was brought up on noblesse."

"You never had the guts before to say boo to me!"

"No, Miss Kingsley; you see, it's called manners."

"Well! Aren't you a fine one! Come on, Eddie. My father wants to talk to you." Bess grabbed Edward by the coat.

"Edward," Lily clipped out. She looked him in the eyes. *Don't you dare.*

"I'll be right back," he grunted. "Mr. Kingsley and I have been workin' on a deal."

Bess shot Lily a smiling gloat and yanked Edward along with her as she went flouncing off.

"I say," Gabriel murmured.

"Au revoir, Miss Kingsley!" Mrs. Coates gave her an elegant wave.

Lady Amherst joined in. "Do come visit us again."

"Oh! Oh, dear, I'm sure, well, that is—" Babbling incoherently, Mrs. Lundy lasted another ten seconds or so before hurrying after them.

"Darling, your mother would be so proud," Mrs. Clearwell murmured with a twinkling glance.

Lily gave her a wry look.

Her triumph over Bess was short-lived, considering *she* was the one left standing here, suitorless, in front of Derek and his gorgeous paramour. It was dashed uncomfortable, being the odd woman out—and really, it was too vexing how that spoiled girl always seemed to get her way!

"Charming girl," Mrs. Coates remarked in her sophisticated manner, breaking the awkward silence.

"Forgive me," Lily apologized. "We don't get along very
well."

"I can hardly imagine why," Lady Amherst drawled.

Lily did not desire any sympathy from Derek's worldly
bedmates, but she supposed she appreciated their senti-
ments.

"Miss Balfour, you never mentioned your family had a
curse. How exotic," Derek remarked, unaware that this
was a sensitive topic.

"Do you believe in curses, Major?" Lily shot back.

"No."

"Neither do I. The only 'curse' upon our family is that of
reckless Balfour men who make bad decisions, leading
straight to their own demise!"

"I see," he murmured, his sharp look affirming her point
was well taken. "But your grandfather lived into old age,
did he not?"

"He had sense," she replied. *Which is more than I can
say for you.*

"Er, Major—" Mrs. Clearwell had been casting worried
glances from Derek to Lily and back again, no doubt fearful that her matchmaking efforts had gone permanently
awry. Fortunately, she was a grand mistress of the art of
smoothing things over. "How is that adorable nephew of
yours? And the rest of your family?"

"Very well, ma'am. They are all doing fine. My father in
particular wished me to send his regards."

"Oh! Did he?" she asked in surprise. "How kind!"

Lily smiled at the beaming pleasure that broke out across
her godmother's face.

"Likewise, Major. Do give my best to Lord Arthur."

"I shall. And how is your family, ma'am?"

"Oh, I haven't any family but this one." Mrs. Clearwell
put a fond arm around Lily's shoulders.

Her answering smile was taut, because from where she
stood, she could see Edward talking to the Kingsleys.

Things were looking awfully cozy over there.

"Actually, now that you mention it, Lily had a letter from her cousin just the other day, didn't you, dear?" Mrs. Clearwell gave her an encouraging nod, trying to get her to talk to Derek.

"Cousin Pamela?" he asked, tilting his head in curious amusement. "And how is the family scribe?"

"Go on. Tell him about her letter. Pamela writes the most amusing letters!"

"Are they frightful?" Derek asked with a mock shudder.

"Only a little macabre," Lily conceded, reluctantly succumbing to a smile.

"Do tell."

The others looked at the two of them without the slightest inkling of what they were talking about.

Ridiculously pleased that Derek had remembered about her Gothic-writing cousin, Lily indulged his curiosity. "Cousin Pamela is in ecstasies over the uninvited guests who have taken up residence in the attic of the north wing of Balfour Manor."

"Balfour Manor?"

"My home."

"Her grandfather, the previous Lord Balfour, left it to her in his will," Mrs. Clearwell boasted, nodding at Lily.

"Oh?" When Derek's glance swung to her again, a strange look dawned slowly in his eyes.

"It's the home I grew up in. We're very lucky it wasn't entailed. At any rate, we haven't used that wing of the house in years," Lily explained, barely noticing the change coming over him. "Unfortunately, there must be a few holes in the roof, for our visitors were spotted swooping in and out from under the eaves after nightfall."

"Swallows?" Mrs. Coates inquired.

"Bats," Derek said, guessing correctly, since he was privy to Pamela's quirky turn of mind.

"You have a colony of bats in your attic, and your cousin is happy about this?" Gabriel asked in confusion.

"It's atmospheric, Major." Lily shrugged. "Our Pam's a little strange. But we love her. The difficult part is that nobody knows what to do about these bats."

"I do."

Lily arched a brow at Derek. "Why am I not surprised, with all your hidden talents?"

Mrs. Coates and Lady Amherst did not appear to like her cheeky comment one bit.

Lily pressed her lips shut, supposing her words could be taken as more risqué than she had meant them.

"What is the correct method, Major?" Mrs. Clearwell asked, sticking to the subject before her charge got into another verbal altercation, this time to be outnumbered. "Smoke them out with burning peat?"

"No, in fact. It's much simpler than that." Derek was eyeing Lily darkly.

He did not look happy and she couldn't figure out why. She thought the story about the bats would have amused him. Instead, that tension around the outer corners of his pale blue eyes and the firm line of his jaw hinted that he was annoyed about something. Maybe even angry.

Baffling man!

When he turned to Mrs. Clearwell, his tone was still polite. "The first thing you've got to do is close up those holes in the roof."

"Easier said than done." Lily shook her head, jumping in again. "The last fellow who came to appraise our roof situation said the whole thing needed to be replaced. It's nearly half an acre of roofing, and the house is of Tudor vintage. The repairs have to be done properly in a manner that's true to the period."

He stared at her in shock. "Good God, that'll cost a fortune. Have you told Edward this?"

"Derek!" Gabriel exclaimed at his brother's blunt nosiness.

Lily was used to it. She did not take offense. "Is there something wrong?" she asked him quietly.

"No!" he exclaimed, obviously lying. "I'm just surprised. This is the first that I've heard about Balfour Manor. I mean, really, Miss Balfour, I had no idea you were the owner of a huge Tudor mansion!"

Lily looked at him in confusion. "So?"

"Never mind. I'm going to play cricket." But as he marched off to join the trio of young men beckoning him over to join their team, he passed Lily with a cold glower like midnight in December.

"What?" she cried.

"You could sell the damned thing," he snarled, then strode away.

Her jaw dropped.

"Major, darling, I'm parched!" Lady Amherst announced, dimpling at Gabriel. "Shall we get something to drink?"

"I'll come along." Mrs. Coates seemed to have had enough of Lily's company, too.

"Er, yes, of course," Gabriel obliged them. "Miss Balfour, Mrs. Clearwell, if you will excuse us."

"Certainly. Major. Ladies," her chaperone said ever so pleasantly. "Enjoy the picnic."

Gabriel sent Lily an awkward and somewhat apologetic nod of farewell, then was whisked away by the worldly women he had on each arm.

As soon as they were out of earshot, Lily could no longer contain her exasperation. "He growled at me! Derek did."

"Yes, I heard."

"What a savage! He is *so* vexing!"

Mrs. Clearwell looked askance at her. "Especially when he's right."

"*What?*"

She shrugged. "If you sell the house, you don't need Edward's money, do you?"

"Sell the house? You must be joking."

"I have never been more serious in my life. It's time for you to wake up and face reality."

"But . . ."

"But, but. Of course! The Balfour family pride. Au revoir, my dear. Just remember, when you make your bed, you're the one who'll have to lie in it." With a nonchalant wave of her fan, Mrs. Clearwell drifted off to mingle with the other guests, leaving Lily alone.

She scowled, watching her chaperone fall in with a knot of lady friends.

Everyone had deserted her!

Sweeping her glance across the green, she spotted Edward still ensconced with Bess Kingsley and her rotund factory-owner father.

She'd have gone over to the tent to fetch a fresh goblet of punch, but poor Gabriel was over there with those two dreadful women.

Reluctantly, she looked toward the cricket field.

Derek had the cricket bat resting on his shoulder and was tossing the ball restlessly in one hand and catching it again, waiting for the game to begin. His teammates crowded around him seeking his counsel on the batting order, which she supposed made him their chosen captain—naturally.

Before long, the match was under way.

Lily shaded her eyes from the sun, watching the bowler take his hop and skip of a step as he made his throw; the ball flew down the pitch, then bounced once up to the striker, who stood with his bat at the ready. The wicket-keeper stood frozen, safely padded, in position behind him, and the umpire crouched nearby, watching all with an eagle-eyed stare.

Snick!

The hard brown ball glanced off the edge of the cricket bat and veered to where the fielders were least expecting it. With the growing crowd of spectators cheering them on, the two batsmen ran, tearing down the pitch, exchanging places, the striker still gripping his bat.

Derek's "select eleven" quickly began running up the score.

Lily did not want to admit her pleasure in watching him at play, but the easy movement of his tall, elegantly athletic frame radiated certainty and confidence. A lock of his sable hair worked its way loose from the queue and trailed down charmingly to frame his handsome face as he squinted against the sun. He brushed it behind his ear impatiently, but before long, it had slipped free again in the breeze.

He wore light tan-colored trousers and a loose white shirt, the sleeves of which he had rolled up to his elbows for the game. He had removed his jacket, but not the red neckerchief loosely knotted around the base of his tanned throat.

When Derek stepped up to the batting crease, he eyed up the delivery with a fierce look, and then promptly slammed the ball into an unguarded region of the outfield.

The fielding team scrambled to chase it. Before they got hold of it, the soaring ball had bounced and flown again, rolling past the chalked edge of the boundary, and thereby winning Derek's side four automatic runs.

Riveted, Lily watched him racing toward the bowling end. With the cricket bat in his grasp, it was suddenly easy to imagine him running at an enemy with a sword in his hand, charging into battle.

The sight left her breathless, but it also brought back to mind his determination to return to India and fight in the war, and, honestly, what if he died? She didn't think she could bear it. But he wouldn't listen to her.

Instead, he preferred growling at her. *Sell Balfour Manor?* She folded her arms indignantly across her chest. Three hundred years of noble family history auctioned off to the highest bidder?

I think not, Major.

He ought to understand about family pride.

As his fluttering admirers called out congratulations to him, he waved to his crowd of lady fans, and Lily decided it was time to amuse herself elsewhere.

Coxcomb!

She did not want to count herself among the crowd of infatuated females watching his every move.

With that, Lily stalked off to the archery field to distract herself and vent her frustration with the genteel bow and arrow.

A footman handed her a sleek ladies' bow from the table where the equipment was laid, and then presented her with an arrow and gestured politely toward the targets.

Other ladies were enjoying the sport down the row to Lily's right and left. She turned her attention to her target, refusing to look back at the cricket field where Derek's harem kept up their enthusiasms.

She lifted the slender bow and drew her elbow back, taking keen aim. The arrow flew, striking quite near the center as she watched it, shading her eyes from the sun with her hand. *Ah!* There was something so satisfying about the sound it made as it pierced the target and stood, shuddering, in the second circle out from the bull's-eye.

Not half bad.

Lily lowered the bow and accepted another arrow from the attendant, determined to put all males, Knight and otherwise, out of her mind, at least for a little while.

After loosing more than a dozen arrows, she was drawn into a polite conversation with some ladies who knew her mother. About half an hour had passed when she noticed from the corner of her eye that the cricketers had either quit or were taking a break. Stealing an oh-so-casual glance toward the oak tree, she spied Derek marching toward the house. She looked around for his brother and spotted Gabriel standing with Edward over by the stables.

Oh, of course, she thought. Edward was ever so proud of his pedigreed bloodstock. He wouldn't be able to resist the chance to show off his horses to the highborn cavalry men.

But then Edward paused with a gesture to Gabriel as if telling him to wait a moment.

Lily perked up when her brawny suitor lifted his arm and beckoned her over. *Hm.* "I think Mr. Lundy may require my assistance," she told the ladies as she pardoned herself.

"He certainly does," one of them commented under her breath.

Lily pretended not to hear and went hurrying toward Edward. He was walking toward her, leaving Gabriel up by the stable.

Derek had disappeared inside the house.

"Yes, Edward?" she clipped out as she strode toward her big, bluff beau. "Is there something you require?"

As Lily joined him, Edward took her elbow and leaned closer with a distracted nod. He smelled of too much beer.

"Would you do me a favor?"

She gave him an aloof nod. "What is your will?"

"Go into the house and keep an eye on Derek Knight for me."

She sucked in a low gasp at the request, because her first thought was that Edward suspected something . . .

"I can't leave m'guests," he mumbled, slurring his words with drink, "so you must do this for me. Watch that blackguard. Make certain he is not getting into anything he— shouldn't."

Guilt, she hoped, was not written all over her ashen face. A chill ran down her spine as she wondered if this was some sort of trick.

Had someone seen them together? Reported it to him?

But that was impossible. Edward would not be standing here staring into her eyes, waiting impatiently for an answer, if he knew how desperately she wanted Derek Knight.

"The staff won't question you," he said. "They know you have my trust. You remember what I spoke to you about the other day."

"Yes, but Edward, I'm sure Major Knight is not after your gold—"

"Lily, can I count on you or not?" he interrupted. "Will you do this for me? Now?"

Gazing at him, she realized he was asking her in no uncertain terms to prove her loyalty by doing as he asked.

She swallowed hard and set her panicked confusion aside. "Consider it done."

Edward gave a pleased nod at her speedy compliance.

Lily nodded back and walked away without another word, her heart pounding. *Oh, blast, I really don't want to do this. What if Derek sees me following him? What on earth will he think I'm after?*

But what choice did she have? This was her chance to remind the straying Edward of how valuable she could be to him. Besides, the sooner she could assuage her suitor's paranoia, the sooner she might have some peace.

Then an awful thought dawned on her.

Oh, God, she didn't want to have to find him in the arms of his latest amour! What if he had slipped away for another rendezvous with his beautiful companion, just like he had at the masked ball the night they met?

But maybe it was for the best. Seeing him in a torrid embrace with Mrs. Coates would certainly make it a great deal easier to eject Derek Knight from her heart for once and for all. Who could say? Maybe Edward *had* noticed her fascination with the major, and in his own crude way, was forcing her to face reality.

The reality that Derek had lots of women and probably always would.

But even as she thought these things, her heart refused to believe it. She had seen him with little Matthew. She had seen his kindness to that horse . . .

When she strode into the Lundys' giant castle-house, she found that on this fine day, only a few guests and servants tarried inside. A cluster of elders in the neo-Gothic great hall had had enough of the sun and were busy bemoaning the foibles of the younger generation. They paid no mind as Lily hurried past them, glancing into the various rooms for any sign of the major.

The dining room, red salon, library, and music room all were clear. The ballroom, too, was empty. She even went to glance in the great glass conservatory just to be certain. There was no sign of him until she passed the private lounge for the gentlemen and heard splashing water.

Aha, she thought, realizing he must have come inside to freshen up and tidy himself a bit after the rigors of the cricket match. When the splashing stopped, Lily realized he would emerge at any moment and rushed to hide.

Ducking into the salon across the hall, she whirled behind the white painted door and peered through the sliver-thin gap between its brass hinges. A brief melodic whistle heralded his approach a second before the door to the gentlemen's lounge swung open.

Derek strode out with a jaunty step, smoothing his jacket, which he had donned again, and straightening his cuffs. His long black hair was neatly bound once more in its queue, and so far, he was alone.

Holding her breath, Lily peered through the seam of the door and watched him pass.

He headed down the center hallway with a blithe air of unconcern. She waited until he was a safe distance ahead before slipping out of her hiding place and silently gliding after him.

Having made himself presentable once more, he marched toward the dining room—and it was then that the first glimmer of his true nefarious intentions surfaced.

Hiding behind a column, Lily furrowed her brow as Derek took a furtive look around, glancing over his shoulder to make sure he was unseen. Then he stole silently into the dining room, crossing it in the blink of an eye, and slipped out the other side.

Standing there, Lily couldn't believe her eyes. *Where is he going?* Could Edward have been right?

It certainly *looked* like Derek was up to no good.

Lily went after him without a sound, as instructed by her suitor.

At the far end of the dining hall, she peeked around the corner and spotted him doubling back deeper into the house. She narrowed her eyes and followed him surreptitiously. She hadn't the foggiest notion what the rogue thought he was doing, but his incursion into the private regions of the house was extraordinarily rude—and suspect.

When a footman appeared strolling down the corridor, the major took evasive action, disappearing into one of the side rooms ahead. Lily had no chance to escape detection and instead pretended to be engrossed in studying the nearest painting on the wall.

As the footman neared, he recognized her as the future lady of the house and offered a respectful nod. She smiled absently at him, but since she made no claim on his attendance, he moved on, going about his duties.

The moment his back was turned, she rushed out of sight before Derek chanced to see her. Whatever the major was doing, now more than ever, she did not want him to know that she was spying on him. Heart pounding, she pressed her back against the wall of the hallway's little alcove, waiting for him to go on about his sneaky business.

She had to admit, though, she was dashed relieved that so far there was no sign of any woman coming to meet him.

Some yards ahead, Derek glided out of his hiding place, emerging from the nearby library. He glanced around, then moved on.

I didn't know he could move like that. He swept through the house like a phantom, a ghost.

Lily trailed him down the hallway at a wary distance, watching, mystified, as he disappeared around another corner ahead.

She crept up to the corner, cocking her head to listen closely, trying to detect any sound that would betray his current whereabouts. Hearing nothing, she stepped around the corner.

At that precise moment, Derek whirled around the corner and ambushed her, pinning her against the wall, stifling her small shriek of fright with one hand clapped across her mouth; in a flash he used his other hand to manacle both of her wrists above her head.

It happened too fast for her to fight back, though feeling his iron strength, she doubted it would have done her any good.

She lifted her gaze to his in pure shock, but when Derek lowered his head, his eyes gleamed, fierce and pale.

"Something I can do for you, Miss Balfour?"

CHAPTER
∽ THIRTEEN ∽

She was the most damned inconvenient woman.

He was sure Lundy's office was right around here some-where, but leave it to Lily to jeopardize his one chance to get at the information he required.

Just get rid of her and get on with the task.

He hadn't seen any other servants wandering by, but just in case, he tugged her out of sight into a nearby curtained alcove off the hallway.

Turning to her once more, he barely knew how to begin.

He was still furious over the house, that in fact she *had* the means to provide for herself without marrying Lundy if she chose. For whatever devious reason, she had never vol-unteered that information.

There was so much he wanted to say to her—and it ap-peared the feeling was mutual. Wrathful sparks flew from her blue eyes while muffled protests sought to escape from under his hand. Derek could feel her plump, silky lips mov-ing angrily beneath his palm, but as he held her pinned against the alcove wall, every inch of her luscious body pressed against his, all the angry words in his brain fell away until all that remained was desire.

Raw, hot, burning need.

God, he wanted her. Well, he'd be damned if he let her know that. *Think, you idiot,* he ordered himself.

It was hard to focus when his pretty captive inspired in him such lust, but he refused to do anything that might let her guess his true intentions here.

He did not want her involved in his investigation in any way, and besides, after their falling-out last week, he had no certainty that if she realized what he was really up to, she would not turn around and tell her precious Edward that he had been snooping. His course was plain. Any progress on his mission would have to wait until he got rid of the vexing female.

Only, he so craved this rare chance to be alone with her at last.

He did not *want* to chase her away after she had obsessed his mind all week. Her mere presence was delicious. "I thought we weren't going to do this anymore," he murmured in a husky tone.

When two furious syllables sounded from under his hand in response, a rueful smile twisted his lips. He believed she had just called his parentage into question, but her buzzing, gnatlike fury amused him, wickedly, as she fought against his gentle but unyielding hold.

"Do *not* bite me," he warned when he felt the edge of her teeth start to nip at the flesh of his finger.

She stopped, probably realizing that ladies did not bite people. At least not in anger.

"That's better," he whispered. Relishing this fleeting departure into the joys of bondage probably more than he ought, he adjusted his grip on her wrists and held her in place. "Now, are we going to chat like civilized persons or would you rather wrestle about on the floor? I vote the latter."

She narrowed her eyes at him like a woman plotting murder. Death by her hands, he mused. It would be a good way to go. Gazing at her in deepening hunger, he was immensely annoyed that once again, he could not seem to tamp down his libido with this girl, even after she had hurt him. If anything, her rejection had only made him want her more. *Hmm, what to do.* He had Lily Balfour at his mercy, and he began to throb as he considered the prospect of covering her lips with his mouth instead of his palm. Of course, if he tried it, the little hellcat was likely to bite his tongue. And then he would have to spank her . . .

He quivered, but she still looked fighting mad over the way he had restrained her.

Carefully, Derek relented—gentleman that he was.

"Indecent creature!" she sputtered, plucking his hand off her mouth. "Don't flatter yourself! Whatever you're thinking—that is not what I came for!"

"Oh, really? Then why *are* you following me?"

"Why are you sneaking around Edward's house?" she retorted in a hurried whisper.

"I don't know," he said with an idle shrug, well versed in the art of talking his way out of scrapes with the fair sex. "Just thought I'd have a look 'round at your future cage, I suppose. Lily Lundy—it has rather an ill-sounding ring, don't you think? But I guess that's the least of your worries. Hard to imagine you living here in conjugal bliss with dear old Edward. You're really going to be the lady of this monstrosity, eh?"

She eyed him uneasily, but rose to the bait and seemed to accept his excuse. "It's not so bad."

"I for one think you'd be better off at home with the bats."

"Well, nobody asked your opinion."

Her impertinence drew him up short. Derek shook his head. "You know, you're really something else."

"What?"

"You're just too vexing! You and your *house*."

"Balfour Manor?"

"Oh, excuse me—a *manor,* not a mere house. How convenient that you never mentioned it to me. I wonder why!"

"What is the matter with you?"

"You own a Tudor mansion that's so large it has whole separate *wings* and half an acre of roofing, and yet you claim your family's in such dire straits that you 'have to' marry Lundy."

"Both happen to be true."

"Lily!" He tapped two fingertips irreverently on her cranium. "Think, girl! Use your head."

"I beg your pardon!"

"Sell the damned place rather than sacrifice yourself for Lundy's gold."

"I can't do that," she answered wearily.

"Of course you can."

"I am not going to be remembered as the Balfour who lost the ancestral estate. Besides—" She heaved a sigh. "The whole place is in such a state of disrepair, the truth is, I don't think anyone would even want to buy it."

"You don't know that. Someone might—and if they don't, then you can sell it to an architectural firm who'll dismantle it and use the materials in new buildings. The proceeds could set you and your family up very nicely."

"How's that?"

"There are companies that tear down old buildings to harvest the parts," he explained with a hurried glance past the gaudy red curtain veiling the alcove to make sure no one was coming. "They can re-use the brick or stone, tear out the chimneypieces to be installed in newer houses. They'll take the paneling, wood beams, the old glass from the windows. It can all be re-used, and they'll pay you quite handsomely for it—"

"Oh, how perfectly ghastly! Stop, please! No more." She waved his words away like objectionable flies. "Balfour Manor is my home! It's been in my family for three hundred years. I'd as soon hand over Grandfather's corpse to the medical college for a dissection lecture than hand over my poor old house to be dismembered."

"Well, when you put it that way, I suppose I can see your point," he muttered with a frown, folding his arms across his chest. "But we're talking about your survival here. The hell with your dead ancestors. The past is dead and gone—you're the one who's alive now. You're what matters. It's absurd to willfully ruin your life for the sake of mere ghosts."

She was shaking her head in exasperation. "Spoken like a true colonial. Burn the past. On with the future."

"Better to burn the past than try to live in it!"

"Oh, you're a fine one, aren't you? You expect me to turn my back on my family? Yet you're not exactly willing to walk away from what you hold dear. Maybe you should take your own advice. Let's see you turn your back on your troops."

"My men are human beings. Your house is an inanimate object. People are what matters, Lily. You're what matters. God, why must you be so stubborn? Did it never occur to you, anyway, that once you've married Lundy, your possessions revert to your husband by law?" he pursued. "What's to stop him from selling Balfour Manor out from under you once you're wed? What if he doesn't care to fund those roof repairs you mentioned? Did you ever think of that?"

"Of course I thought of that. Edward won't sell Balfour Manor because he knows full well that all his gold can't buy the prestige of an ancient family history like ours. What do you think he's marrying me for?"

Derek let his stare travel down, meaningfully, over her too-tempting curves. "I can hardly guess," he murmured.

"He's desperate to better his station in life," she explained, ignoring his lascivious perusal. "Besides, he has no reason to sell Balfour Manor. It's not as though he needs the money—and anyway, I shall have a solicitor draw up the papers to make sure Edward won't be able to sell my house even if he wanted to. Just in case."

"Aha! You see?" Derek pointed out at once, moving closer and seizing on her words. "You don't really trust him any more than I do! That is the heart of the problem, Lily. I don't trust this man. There—I've said it. I'm sorry, but it's the truth. I don't trust him with you, and it's driving me mad. I need to know that you'll be safe!"

"Oh, Derek." His low-toned outburst appeared to have surprised her. With a tender wince, she reached up and gently tucked a lock of his hair behind his ear. "What am I going to do with you?"

"I could think of a few things," he murmured, loving her touch. He captured her hand and pressed a light kiss to her wrist. "Has he asked you yet? Are you engaged?"

"No," she admitted with a look of chagrin. "What about you—any word from your commander?"

"No." He sighed and released her hand from his light hold. "It would seem that both our boats are becalmed," he said dryly, then gave her an ironic half-smile. "Perhaps the only way we shall ever escape our doldrums will be to chart a new course. Change the set of our sails."

"To what new port?" she murmured, smiling faintly as she played along.

"Lord only knows where the wind could take us." An idea suddenly dawned. "A storm of scandal might be just the thing! A good wild gale of gossip ought to blow us out of here." He lifted his eyebrow and sent her a devilish glance. "How many hundred guests are here today?"

"Don't you dare," she warned, backing up a bit.

"Oh, but it would be so easy, so efficient." He moved closer, caressing her arms. "I could ruin you right now, you know. Save you from yourself. I should do it, too, to stop you from this madness."

"Oh, yes, a capital idea," she replied, matching his sardonic tone with a wary gleam in her eyes. "Sorry, Major, but having met your brother and especially your sire, I'm very sure that if you stooped to ruin, they would force you to marry me—and then the joke would be on you."

"Maybe it isn't a joke." He looked at her suddenly. "Shall I do it? Shall I force you into marrying me?"

She lifted her eyebrows in astonishment. "Derek! You *didn't* just ask me to marry you—?"

"Well, no! Not like that. I mean—" *What do I mean?* He faltered, taken off guard by this sudden impulse. "I'm-I'm only trying to be helpful."

She tilted her head, studying him with a dubious look.

His heart was pounding. He glanced away with a one-shouldered shrug, trying to play it off. "It would get us what we both desire," he pointed out.

"Right," she murmured, eyeing him in suspicion, as if she was onto his tricks. "If you married me, then you'd *have* to go back to India, and plunge yourself into all the gory joys of warfare until your soul was gone. Meanwhile, you'd be sending all the gold you had won back home to

me, so that I could keep my estate intact, and maybe, just
maybe, one day, finally win my mother's approbation."

He went very still and slid her a wary look. "So, that's
what this is all about."

It was the first he'd heard about her mother, but the moment she said it, so many unexplained details about her
suddenly fell into place.

He was glad for the change of topic, relieved that it was
her turn to be embarrassed. She had turned away, looking
sheepish after having blurted out her careless admission;
her creamy cheeks were turning red.

"I shouldn't have said that," she mumbled. "It wasn't respectful."

"Don't worry. Your mother's not here, and I promise I
won't tell on you. Besides," he confided in a low tone, leaning closer to whisper in her ear, "I had one of *those* kinds
of mothers, too."

"You did?" She looked at him in surprise.

"Lily," he said slowly as he cupped her cheek, "anyone
who doesn't love you is a fool. Especially your mother. And
that goes for Lundy, too."

"What about you, Major?" she asked barely audibly,
with a daring lift of her chin. She gazed into his eyes. "Does
that apply to you, as well?"

"I'm no fool," he breathed.

The sweet, anguished longing that he read in the
lavender-blue depths of her eyes mirrored the burning need
that throbbed inside of him.

He gripped her shoulders, closing his eyes briefly, unable
to bear another moment of denial. "God—that's it—I can't
let you do this. I'm going to make a scandal of us that will
rock the ton to its foundations and shake you free of this
damned prison you've put yourself in—"

"No! Don't you dare do it!" Her cheeks were flushed
with passion as she planted her hand on his chest and
blocked him. "I won't marry you!"

"Why?" he demanded in outrage.

"Because the only way we could afford it is if you either
go to your family to help us, or return to India to fight. The

former I know you will not do—and the latter I cannot bear for you to do! Not when I've seen for myself the damage it's already done to your heart."

"I would do it for you," he whispered, aching for her.

She cupped his jaw and said with the most earnest gaze, "But I would never let you."

They stared at each other as time seemed to drop to a halt.

He couldn't help smiling at her, haphazardly. "What, you're going to protect me, then?" he murmured ruefully. This mere slip of a girl protecting him? It was the silliest, most adorable thing he had ever heard.

But something had registered in her eyes in answer to his question, as though his words had reminded her of some pressing fact. She lowered her hand from his cheek. "Look, Derek—I don't know why you came into the house today, and frankly, I don't think I want to know. But as for the reason I came in, well, I should probably warn you that . . . Edward bade me follow you."

"Well, now," he murmured, pausing to absorb this. "That was very foolish of him."

Though his heart sank a little and his male vanity smarted to hear that she had not pursued him of her own accord, preferably for amorous reasons, he appreciated the information—and his hunger for her was undaunted.

He ran his fingertip slowly down her chest. "Old Edward should've had a care for what might happen to his little spy if she were caught."

Lily shivered, her blue eyes darkening in answer to the searing awareness between them.

They had managed to resist it in the stable. But now it was just too strong. He could feel their mutual resistance failing, like a boulder rolling down a mountainside, faster and faster, gathering power, force, and speed.

Their separation had only sharpened their hunger for each other. He saw it in her eyes, and felt it in his blood. He bent his head slowly and pressed his lips to the curve of her neck.

Her whole body quivered with the most thrilling response. "Oh, God, please. Derek—don't. I want you so much. Don't compromise my reputation. It's all I have." She had gripped his shoulder, but he couldn't tell if she was trying to pull him closer or push him away. "I can't bear a scandal. I can't," she whispered almost frantically.

"Shh," he hushed her, unsettled by the near panic in her voice. God knew he did not wish to upset her.

Though it cost him a heroic effort to release her when his instincts told him that with a bit more effort, she'd be putty in his hands, he did just that.

He lowered his hands to his sides and took a slow step backward. "As you wish, Lily." Her trust was the most important thing. "I would never harm you or ignore your feelings or do anything to make you feel coerced." He swallowed hard, and added, "I'm not Edward."

"No, you're not," she echoed with a trace of bitterness in her breathy tone. "Would that you were."

"Well, go on," he said with a small nod toward the corridor. "Go on back to him. I shan't stop you."

She slanted him a wounded look.

Derek's pulse thundered as he held her in his gaze.

She made no move to go.

"But . . . if you want to stay," he added slowly, "you already know that I can be discreet. If this is all that I can have with you, I'll take it."

She stared at him with eyes of blue flame, and then she was moving toward him, reaching for him. She grasped the lapel of his jacket and hauled him to her suddenly. He went to her like a slave in her thrall; she curled her hand around his nape and pulled him down to kiss her in fevered desperation. He complied with swift and total willingness, starved for her lips. She wrapped her arms around his neck, rose on her toes a bit, and captured his mouth with a furious hunger that burned up his senses and melted all his wits. He caressed her, astounded by the explosive passion that came pouring out of the girl.

She cupped his jaw as she consumed his tongue in scorching intensity, clearly wanting, needing this as badly as he did. Derek groaned, tightening his hold around her slim waist.

Fighting this was futile. In this moment, there were no answers, there was only need, desire overwhelming all the reasons they both had to stay away from each other.

Passion took over. Want poured through him as they gave in to burning temptation. Her hands were all over him, and it was glorious.

Derek knew it was also insanity. Lundy had sent her and was waiting for her now. For God's sake, they were in the man's house. But she excited him so deeply that he was past caring. The despair of knowing she would never truly be his lent an edge of crazed urgency to their every touch.

With a quick glance out of the alcove to make sure the coast was clear, Derek spotted the next door just a couple of yards down the hallway. He began shepherding her toward it, never breaking their kiss. It led to a darkened parlor, a fact he had discovered a short while ago in his search for Edward's study.

He opened the door behind her and began pressing Lily into the room, his heart slamming in his chest. She stumbled along with him, eager to go as he backed her into the dim parlor, where the shades were drawn against the daylight.

Derek locked the door.

They crashed into the furniture, tearing at each other's clothes as they crossed the room, tangled in a blind frenzy of desire. His member throbbed like it would burst from his clothing as he pressed her down onto the wide, round ottoman. Sinking onto his knees before her, he nearly hesitated—and he was stunned by the unexpected depth of his reverence for her. He almost trembled to touch her, but her soft moan reaffirmed her need for him, and smoothly he lifted her skirts.

She fell back on her hands on the plush velvet ottoman, watching him as he kissed her chest all over and nuzzled her round, lovely breasts through the tight, tailored bodice of her gown. "You are so beautiful. Every inch of you." All the while, he caressed her fine legs and sleek hips beneath the voluminous folds of fabric, her skirts and petticoats hitched up around her thighs.

"Ah." She tipped her head back, reveling in his attentions. Her porcelain skin was flushed, her lips swollen and luscious pink from his kiss.

Staring at her in wonder, he bent lower and kissed her knee. A light, breathless laugh escaped her as he skimmed his lips slowly up her milky limb.

He left a love bite on the soft flesh of her inner thigh where only she would see it. It would fade in a few days, but till then, just a little something to remember him by. Then he touched her dewy core with his fingertip, reverently parting the delicate blond curls that veiled her womanhood.

His tender caress coaxed a restless sigh from her lips. Derek trembled, catching her scent. He moved closer, drawn by the warm, musky fragrance. Inhaling the natural perfume of her readiness for him drove him absolutely wild.

He dug his fingers into the yielding flesh of her hips, overcome by lascivious joy. Spreading her thighs wider, he bent his head and tasted her. She gasped the moment his mouth touched her. She was smooth and sweet and pebble-hard as he ran his tongue over and around her fiery center, plying her sweet core with kisses of the most artful variety. Drinking her in, he caressed her silky body again and again, adoring her innocence and losing himself in the bliss of devouring her.

Her sighs and soft moans and every rise and undulation of her hips told him just how she wished him to proceed. He made it his business to give exactly what she wanted. As he traced her hardened jewel with the tip of his tongue, gently, patiently licking away her inhibitions, he draped her elegant thigh over his shoulder, opening her more deeply for his thrusting tongue.

Before long, the last vestiges of her little ice-queen façade had melted away; she flowed wet and warm for him like a crystal-pure stream, and he drank deeply, exhilarated by each sinuous wave of her body rising to meet his kisses.

He yearned to possess her, to make every inch of her his, from her delicate toes to the tips of her ladylike fingers and the silken waves of her cool blond hair. But he doubted that would be permissible until after she was wed.

He could hardly bear to think of it and blocked it from his mind as her moans built in volume. Her fingers dug into his shoulders, his back. "Oh, *Derek*!" When he brought her to climax, her release was so deep that her nectar flowed onto his tongue. A swallow of it gave him ecstasy.

Before long, she lay back across the ottoman with a luxuriant stretch, then let out a soft, breathless laugh.

The breathless music of her satisfaction tickled his brain. He watched her, smiling darkly. Still on his knees in front of her, he fixed her skirts for her, making his darling lady neat and tidy once again.

"Oh, Derek. That was so unbelievably wonderful. Mm, I never imagined such splendid things."

"Still want to marry Edward?"

Drowsy laughter tumbled from her lips as she languished in the aftermath of pleasure. "You are impossible," she purred in a tone of utter feminine satiety.

"And you're beautiful," he murmured, gazing at her, and stroking her arm.

"Oh, we shouldn't be here, should we? I suppose we are both very bad."

"You, never. Me, perhaps. But nobody's chaining you here, if that's how you feel."

She came up on her elbows and slanted him an indignant look at his irreverent tone.

"There's the door." Then he smiled wickedly at her. "We both know you don't want to use it."

With a mild scowl, she heaved herself up to a seated position and draped her arms lazily around his neck, giving him a little chiding pout. "And here I thought we said good-bye last week."

"So did I. Yet somehow, here we are again. There doesn't seem to be much point in fighting it."

"No." She petted him, doting on him, apparently unaware of the lust still raging in his blood.

Derek soaked her in with his gaze, and then suddenly noticed the absence of an all-too-familiar detail. "No pretty diamond earrings today, Miss Balfour?" he whispered, ducking his head to nibble her naked earlobe.

She giggled and pulled back with a mysterious smile. "No, my Major. Not today."

"Is this your way of making sure I got the message that you were out of charity with me?" He offered her a penitent half-smile, considering how her diamonds had become the touchstones of their dealings with each other.

"Not exactly," she replied, a mischievous twinkle in her eyes. Then she shrugged. "I'm afraid they just . . . didn't match my gown."

"I thought you girls are fond of saying that diamonds go with everything."

"I missed you," she told him, changing the subject adroitly, stroking his hair. "It's like I'm sleepwalking on the days when I don't see you."

He shook his head, wanting her so badly. "I think about you all the time. I've been trying so hard to stay away from you."

They gazed at each other for a long moment.

"This wasn't supposed to happen, was it?" he admitted.

"I'm glad it did. Kiss me. Kiss me now." She pulled him closer and he did her bidding with a besotted smile on his lips.

He decided that this young lady had to come again. Yes. There had to be time for one more quick . . .

"*Mmm,* that's better." Her appreciative answer to his light kiss interrupted Derek's wayward thoughts. "It seems like ages since I've seen you. How *are* you?" she murmured. "And for that matter, how's your furry patient?"

"The horse?"

"Of course," she rhymed with a silly little smile.

"Worlds better. She even has a name."

"She does?"

He tapped her on the nose. "I named her Mary Nonesuch in your honor."

"I'm so flattered!"

"As you should be. I think you'll be impressed when you see Miss Mary again. Gabriel and I had her under saddle on the lunge line yesterday. A nice mover, in all, and I'm happy to say I should be able to deliver her to her new owner very soon."

"You've sold Mary Nonesuch?" she exclaimed with indignation.

"No, darling, I'm giving her to you."

Her blue eyes widened anew. "To me?"

He laughed softly at her expression of childlike amazement. "Yes, Lily, that was my intention all along. You will take her, I hope? She needs a good home. I can't risk giving her to someone who'll abuse her when I'm gone."

At the mention of his upcoming exit from London, her whole mien changed like the English weather. Her face fell, and a wistful sadness crept into her eyes.

"Oh, darling, don't look like that," he pleaded, his heart clenching.

"I can't help it." She turned away. "It isn't fair."

"Why isn't it fair?"

"Because you're going off to chase after fortune and glory and you don't even care what happens to me!"

"Of course I care."

She threw up her hands. "All this time, you've been browbeating me for being a fortune hunter, but I think it's all rather hypocritical of you, considering the first time we met, you specifically told me your whole purpose in going back to India was—and I quote—for 'fortune and glory.' Don't preach at me about 'chasing gold' when you're doing the exact same thing."

"Well—I suppose I did say that." He glanced at the floor and then eyed her warily. "But my situation is very different from yours."

"How so?"

He looked at her for a long moment, deliberating on how much to say. Then he shrugged and shook his head, casting off his caginess. He sighed and sat beside her on the ottoman. "When I was a boy, my mother was constantly pushing me to do better, try harder, achieve more. The worst possible fate for someone in my position would have been mediocrity."

"Your position?"

"Younger son. Even death would have been preferable to an ordinary life. The heroic ideal. She made it very clear, you see, that if I did not make something splendid of myself, fit to dazzle the world, I would be doomed to obscurity, and then—no one would ever love me."

He fell silent for a moment. He could feel Lily watching him, but he avoided her study, keeping his gaze cast down. "So, when I go and risk life and limb for 'Hindu plunder,' as you put it, it's because I'm only trying to be worthy of the thing I really want."

"And what is that?" she whispered.

He turned to her in silence and stared into her eyes. "Love."

"Oh, Derek." With a melting look, she wrapped her arms around him and the heavenly kiss she gave him could have told even the most virginal young man that she plainly longed to give herself to him.

Derek ached to receive the gift, but he knew full well that time was waning. Lundy would be watching for her, and others could be wondering where they both had gone. No, this was not the place . . . and he was not the man.

At least not as things currently stood.

He despised the thought of her going back to Lundy, but was expert enough to grasp which rules could be safely broken and which were ironclad. It was not permissible for him to enjoy her to the fullest until her future husband had known her first.

He felt his mood instantly darkening at that knowledge, but what could he do? As much as he burned for her, there were risks to be taken into account—risks to Lily, and to his investigation. Damn, he felt powerless to change any of it—and now he had bared his soul to her like a fool. To what end?

As far as he could tell, nothing was altered. They were still stuck in place. He still had not managed to dissuade her from her reckless course, nor could he bring himself to nullify her will and destroy her plans on his own initiative. Well, what did he expect? That one superior orgasm could change a woman's mind?

Meanwhile, lust still clouded his brain, and mixed with anger, it bubbled dangerously, a volatile brew. The fact of the matter was, he was upset—not because he could not make love to her, but because there would come a day when Lundy *would*. His little bride.

Feeling as though the whole thing was spinning too fast beyond his control, Derek clasped her upper arms and set her back from him, forcing an end to her kiss. He stared at her as he held her at arm's length.

"What's wrong?" Lily whispered as her shimmering gaze swept over the brooding look on his face.

"We need to stop," he answered hoarsely. Such heroic effort, such noble self-denial! he thought, mocking himself heartlessly as she looked at him in confusion. But really, his mother would have been proud. "You should go back."

"Oh."

He saw he had embarrassed her, and took pity on her innocence. "I wouldn't want to rush it with you, Lily. And I daresay we don't need one of Lundy's footmen walking in."

"No. I'm sure you're right. But, what of your needs?" she asked shyly. "I mean, if we don't—that is, won't you suffer injury to your, um, anatomy?"

He arched a brow. "Not unless you were planning on kicking me."

"No! Of course not." Her cheeks turned strawberry red.

Derek couldn't help smiling. "An injury to my anatomy, eh? And where did you get a daft idea like that?"

She dropped her gaze, hiding her maidenly shame behind her long lashes. "No place. It was just—something I heard."

"No, Lily," he said softly, finding her chagrin endearing. "Frustration is a part of life for all us randy males. You needn't do me any favors."

She sent him a strange, unsettled glance, murmured a terse, "Very well," and rose to go. Gliding over to a pier glass on the wall, she straightened her gown and smoothed her hair. "I wouldn't wait too long to get back to the party if I were you," she said over her shoulder. "Edward will be watching for you."

"And I imagine Fanny Coates is feeling lonely," he replied in a sharp-edged drawl.

But the second Lily turned and sent him a frown full of distress, her light-green skirts whirling gracefully around her slender form, he clenched his jaw, regretting his jealous remark.

She furrowed her brow, visibly trying to shrug off the small hurt and the jealousy that she, too, felt, it would appear. Saying nothing, she emitted an impatient exhalation and marched to the door.

Still throbbing with desire, Derek tracked her with his stare. "What are you going to tell Edward?"

"I don't know. I'll think of something." She hesitated, one hand on the doorknob. "I suppose I'll say you were with . . . some woman."

He gave her a cynical smile. "Why, that isn't even a lie." He did not know why he could not chase the churlish edge out of his voice, but he cursed himself for it again and dropped his gaze. Of course, he was frustrated out of his mind, but that was no excuse.

She sent him a piercing look. "I'm leaving now. Good-bye, again."

"Now that you got what you came for."

"Derek!" Again, she halted. "What is the matter with you?"

"Nothing. Nothing at all."

Only that I'm in love with you. The realization shocked him as it flashed across his mind.

He swallowed hard. And hoped she didn't hate him for taking this so poorly.

She stared at him from across the room, her expression slowly softening. A knowing look stole into her eyes, as if she could read his mind—his confusion, his dismay, his vexation with himself. His adoration of her. "Derek?"

He just looked at her.

"I lied to you about my earrings," she said gently. "Of course the diamonds would have matched my gown. The reason I'm not wearing them is because I do not have them anymore."

He furrowed his brow. "Why?"

She looked at him for a long moment, a mysterious smile tugging at her lips. "I gave them to that coachman that you horsewhipped in the street to make him drop the charges and keep you out of jail."

His jaw dropped. *"What?"*

He started forward, but blowing him a little kiss, Lily slipped out the door and closed it behind her with the quietest click.

Derek sat there in shock, unable to go after her yet on account of his massive erection. "Damn it—"

He glanced down absently at the straining cloth of his tan trousers and then, in longing disbelief, looked again toward the door through which she had vanished.

He barely knew what to think.

"Dear God," he finally muttered under his breath, inspired by that odd mix of fury and lust and delight that only she conjured in him.

She shouldn't have done it.

But he could have laughed aloud to hear that she did.

His heart surged into the empyrean. Dizzying heights.

"Well," he whispered into the empty air. "I shall have to get them back for her at once."

At last, he jumped to his feet, straightened out his appearance, then strolled back to the party like a man in possession of the most delicious secret in the world.

"Oof!" said Coachman Jones as Derek slammed him up against the wall of the tavern where he found the brute later that night, still celebrating his windfall.

It had been easy enough to hunt the man down.

The constables had told Derek the name of the man who had wanted to have him arrested, and military habits of observation had impressed upon his mind the name and address of the stagecoach company Jones worked for.

These had been painted in block letters on the side of the vehicle.

After leaving the Lundys' garden party in the late afternoon, Derek had gone to the company's bustling main yard and asked with a friendly smile where he could find the driver, Mr. Jones.

From there, it was a simple matter to locate the blackguard. About eleven that night, he found Coachman Jones getting drunk at his favorite tavern, still living high on the proverbial hog. Red-cheeked and greasy with the pub fare he had gulped down, Jones was dressed in a new suit of clothes and buying rounds of ale for all his cronies.

These worthies put forth a tepid show of loyalty, trying to interfere with Derek's intent to dole out justice. A bit of a brawl had ensued, but Derek welcomed the chance to let the warrior within flex his muscles after all this damned civility.

He sent his hapless opponents flying across tables, tumbling over wooden chairs, and sliding down the bar, their arms flailing. When they finally gave up and fled him, cringing, he tugged his clothes neatly into place and proceeded to teach Coachman Jones a lesson about taking advantage of a lady.

By the time the innkeeper trudged over with a loaded musket, warning Derek to vacate the premises, he went peaceably, having successfully obtained the name and location of the pawnshop where Jones had hawked Lily's earrings.

It was his next destination.

Considering the hour, the shop was closed, but the owner dwelled above-stairs and finally came hurrying down in answer to Derek's relentless pounding on the door and hollered demands for service.

The people passing by probably thought he was extremely drunk, especially since some ale had spilled on him during the tavern brawl and now he smelled of stale beer, but his mind had never been clearer.

It was diamond-sharp, with a white-hot focus on Lily

Balfour. Even when he was not consciously thinking about her, he could still feel her in his soul, his blood. The bond between them had taken on a life of its own and seemed to permeate every atom of his flesh.

He was simply not going to fail her in getting her earrings back. He understood exactly what her sacrifice for his sake meant, and every time he thought of it, he was amazed all over again; he could only shake his head at the sheer richness and joy that he felt.

As he paced outside the shop and waited for the owner to come down, he glanced around, marveling at the beauty of everything. The whole world seemed new, spangled with dancing moonlight. Even the narrow, dirty lane and shop's dusty windows glimmered with its magical silver glow.

Earlier today, upon his return to the garden party, Fanny Coates was the only one who had suspected the true cause of Derek's absence. After all, she had also been there the night he had disappeared with Lily during the concert at Lord Fallow's. But with a knowing laugh, the sophisticated lady had asked her taunting questions only softly, and Derek had admitted nothing.

Though he certainly did not regret the luscious diversion that had taken him off purpose today, the fact remained that he had failed in his mission to have a look into Lundy's files. He still needed that information. On the other hand, it surely wouldn't be long before Lundy started noticing the overly warm affection, if not the outright panting lust, between Lily and him.

Derek did not enjoy deceiving any man, but he supposed he had to pretend friendship a little while longer until he could finesse some answers out of her rough-mannered suitor. After all, once Lundy knew what was going on between the two of them, he was sure to slam the door on all of Derek's questions.

He already had a few ideas percolating in his brain about how to charm Lundy into tipping his hand. Edward liked his drink, and if Derek had to resort to getting the man thoroughly foxed in order to pump him for information about the committee, then so be it.

Through the glass windows just then, he spotted the branched lights of a candelabra traveling through the darkened shop. A moment later, the front door opened, bells jangling.

"I am truly sorry to take you from your leisure, sir," Derek said to the shopkeeper as soon as the little, rumpled man appeared, still hooking the curled arms of his spectacles over his ears. "A grave injustice has been done to a young lady of my acquaintance and, er, it is imperative that it be corrected at once."

"Ah. Very good, sir." The drowsy shopkeeper took note of Derek's gentlemanly clothes and aristocratic bearing and made himself instantly accommodating. "Come right in."

Before long, the shopkeeper had brought out the velvet trays of jewelry from his safe. With tremendous relief, Derek spotted Lily's great-great-grandmother's earrings at once and paid for them happily.

As he wrote the man a draught from his account, he offered up a silent prayer of thanks that someone else had not bought the earrings before he was able to rescue them. Now it would just be a matter of finding the right moment to give them back to her . . .

"Something else for a special lady, sir?" the shopkeeper tried to entice him, turning his attention to another tray of jewelry with an array of rings and bracelets, necklaces, earrings, and jeweled hairpins.

Derek hesitated with an almost bashful smile as the man directed his attention to the row of golden rings tucked in between the folds of velvet. He snorted. "I already proposed once today," he said in a breezy tone. "She laughed at me."

Besides, if he was going to buy a wedding ring, he'd hardly get it used.

The shopkeeper nodded, chuckling. "Maybe something a bit more noncommittal, then. Something sparkly." The man handed him a delicate silverwork bracelet studded with small clusters of diamonds and rubies.

"Hmm. Very pretty. But to tell you the truth, I'm not sure how she'd react," Derek mused aloud as he considered the bracelet, wondering if she'd be offended if he made a gift of jewelry to her after their episode on the ottoman.

Knowing Lily and her haughty Balfour pride, she easily might get angry, thinking that this was his way of "thanking" her for favors granted, rather than a simple token of his affection.

He put the bracelet aside. "Maybe I should play it safe."

"Funny. You don't strike me as the sort."

Derek laughed and fingered a jeweled hairpin, thinking it a somewhat more conservative choice, but the shopkeeper eyed it with a worried look. "Bad idea?"

"If it was my wife, she'd probably call it paltry."

"Oh. Right." Derek frowned. He was not rich like Lundy or Lord Griffith or even his father, of course, but he could afford to be extravagant—intelligently so—when it came to things that gave him particular pleasure. Like his excellent black stallion from Tattersall's.

He put the hairpin back and scratched his head, at a loss.

"I think we may have a few nice necklaces here that your young lady might enjoy—"

"Wait!" Perusing the velvet trays in the throes of indecision, Derek's gaze suddenly homed in on the largest, gaudiest, most hideous piece in the shopkeeper's collection. "Good God," he murmured in stunned recognition, reaching for it. "May I?"

The man nodded, slanting him a dubious look.

"I have seen this before." His heart suddenly pounding, Derek picked up the large, jewel-encrusted gold brooch in the shape of a rooster.

Mrs. Lundy's ugly rooster pin! he thought, mystified. But no, surely it couldn't be the same brooch. On the other hand, there couldn't be too many of these around Town. Well, blazes, if it was indeed Mrs. Lundy's, what on earth was it doing here? He glanced warily at the shopkeeper. "When did you get this?"

"It came in the week before last. Impressive, isn't it? One of a kind, I daresay. Are you, er, interested in the brooch, sir?"

"Actually, I'm more interested in learning the name of the person who brought it in."

"Oh, I'm sorry, I am not at liberty to say. It is our policy—"

"I understand—but I think I know who this brooch belonged to, and knowing how much it meant to her, I'm concerned that it might have been stolen. I mean—"

"Oh, sir, I am no fencing agent, I can assure you!" the shopkeeper countered at once, looking alarmed. "We do not take stolen goods in this shop!"

"Perhaps without your knowledge."

"Oh, dear."

"A simple yes or no would satisfy my mind. Was this piece brought to you by someone called Lundy?" Derek searched his face keenly.

Frowning, the shopkeeper gave him an uncertain look, then lifted the velvet tray and reached beneath it, taking out a slip of paper. He glanced at it, then shook his head. "No," he admitted in a confidential tone. "It came in from a Mr. Bates."

"Bates," Derek whispered, furrowing his brow.

Lundy's driver.

CHAPTER
∞ FOURTEEN ∞

Actually, Edward, I have no idea who that woman was.

Over the course of the next two days, Lily's conscience was uneasy about the performance she had given her suitor upon returning to the picnic, trying her best to look innocent.

On the other hand, it had not been entirely a lie. It was true—she barely recognized that wanton female in the darkened parlor as herself, Lady Clarissa Balfour's cool and proper daughter, writhing under Derek Knight's artful kisses. Good Lord, she'd have been disowned by her mother if Her Ladyship had caught wind of such shameless behavior.

As for Edward, well, he had tested her loyalty and Lily knew, even if he did not, that she had failed the test dismally. Worse still, she wasn't even sorry.

The alarming truth was, the only thing that had stopped her from making love with Derek in that darkened room was that she had been too ashamed to admit to him that she was not a virgin.

He cared for her.

His attachment to her had been written all over his handsome face. But if he discovered that she was not really as pure as he imagined, then Lily knew full well she might lose his affection. She wanted him so much that this now put her in an impossible situation.

At the same time, her intention to marry Edward was now caving in on itself in earnest, crumbling toward its hollow center. Everything felt so precarious now! She knew the time had come to change the set of her sails, just like Derek had jokingly said. But what she wanted most was for them to chart a new course . . . together.

Up until now, they had both had their schemes firmly in hand, and neither had been willing to compromise. But what had happened between them in that darkened parlor had made Lily see that what they could have together would be infinitely worth giving up some ground.

She still refused to pack up and move to India with him—she still believed that a return to war would be the worst possible thing for Derek—but maybe there was some way they could negotiate their way to the middle. There had to be some way to figure it out if they both put their minds to it. Recent developments, after all, were entirely encouraging.

Obviously, he did not need to attain fortune and glory in order to have love. Lily loved him already. She quite feared she had loved him from the first time she had set eyes on the exotic outsider at that masked ball weeks ago.

But if his beliefs about what he had to accomplish in life to be worthy of love had proved so false, maybe she, too, had misjudged her own set of obligations.

Maybe she *could* forgive herself for her past sins without first having to single-handedly save the family honor. Derek did not know everything about her, but after years of living in a state of self-reproach, the mere fact that someone as wonderful as he could care for her made Lily recall what was best about herself. It made her no longer so eager to punish herself for her sins.

And it made her see much more clearly that marrying Edward Lundy would indeed be the height of self-betrayal. Which was what Derek—and Mrs. Clearwell, for that matter—had been trying to tell her all along.

Unfortunately, she was not yet brave enough to cast aside her plans without first finding out if she and Derek would be in accord on this change of direction. He was the brave one. Before she dared let Edward go, she needed to talk to Derek and find out if he was willing for the two of them . . . to try.

The outcome she desired was in no way guaranteed, of course. This she understood well. She had already tried once to reach out to him the day she had gone to the stable, and though they had shared some confidences—and feverish kisses—he had soon ordered her to go away. It would take a lot of courage to put herself on the line again, but all she needed now was another chance to approach him with her questions.

She waited for her opportunity.

But then, the day after the garden party, Edward showed up at Mrs. Clearwell's house, and once more, Lily was seized with terrified guilt, thinking he had somehow heard about their adventures on the ottoman. Or worse—that the time had come for him to propose marriage!

But he had only come by to say that his mother had now left for Jamaica, and that for his part, he'd be going out of Town on business for a few days. Her heart thudding as loud as the bells of Saint Paul's, Lily had nodded gracefully and wished him a safe trip.

The moment he had left, she silently cheered the news, realizing that now she'd have the perfect chance to talk to Derek at the upcoming ball without having to worry about Edward seeing them together or getting in the way.

The future, the money, her mother's strict expectations— she'd put blinders on to all of it for now, until she learned what Derek wanted to do.

He had proposed marriage to her, more or less, but he had offered a similar cheeky proposal to Mrs. Coates the night of the concert at Lord Fallow's, so Lily knew better than to take that very seriously. On the other hand, she had come to realize that oftentimes his roguish jests were only a thin veneer for the deepest truth of his feelings.

Her uncertainty stretched her nerves thin, but at least the upcoming ball would give her a chance to speak to him.

The next night, as Lily got ready for the ball, her maid created an intricate style for her hair, pinning it up in coiled sections with an elegant array of jeweled pins, leaving wispy curls around her temples and her nape. For once, Lily took pleasure in the looks she had inherited from her mother. There had been times when she had cursed the face and form that had attracted the unwanted attentions of indecent and predatory males, but every day, that part of her life seemed to recede farther into the past; and now, anything about her that pleased Derek was worthy of her gratitude. Her heart was light.

A few hours later, she was strolling across the ballroom by her chaperone's side, covertly watching the throng of guests for any sign of her major, searching for him among the glittering crowd. She nodded to various acquaintances here and there, curtseying to a few of the highest-ranked notables as they passed, then had to whisk her skirts out of the path of some clumsy gentleman's thoughtless strides.

With disaster narrowly averted, she turned away, scanning the ballroom from behind the edge of her fan. Ruefully, she looked for any telltale cluster of beautiful women, knowing she would probably find the rogue at their center.

Instead, she spotted the *other* Major Knight leaning against one of the ballroom's Ionic columns.

Gabriel Knight was alone, lost in his thoughts, and apparently brooding in the middle of the ball. How different the two brothers were, she thought. Derek was usually the life of the party, while Gabriel just scowled in distraction and looked as though he wished he were somewhere else.

Lily nudged Mrs. Clearwell, then pointed out the elder Knight. Her sponsor gave her a rueful smile. "Maybe you and I can cheer him up."

"We can try," Lily said with a chuckle. As they walked toward him, her heart was already lifting. As close as the two brothers were, she was sure that if Gabriel was here, Derek could not be far off.

They greeted the elder Knight and exchanged a few pleasantries, but within moments, Lily could not resist asking. "Where is your brother tonight?"

"Actually, he is not here."

"Oh." She paused, startled. "Is he coming later?"

"No, apparently, he's gone out of Town for a day or two."

Lily stared at him. "Out of Town?" That was exactly what Edward had said of his own plans just yesterday. Suddenly, a knot formed in the pit of her stomach. "D-did he say where he was going, by chance?"

"Not to me. I had an appointment with my physician and when I got home, he had left only the briefest of notes. Some sort of army business, I should think. Is something wrong, Miss Balfour?"

"No. Thank you. I—" Her words broke off as Lily looked at Gabriel again, her sudden worry swiftly climbing into dread. This could be a coincidence, of course. But if Edward had found out about their parlor tryst . . .

Oh, God. Her mind began reeling as all of those inconvenient traits that she had chosen to ignore in Edward came flooding back to the fore.

The ruthlessness. The brutality.

"I say, my dear, you're as white as a sheet." Gabriel took her arm to steady her. "Are you ill?"

Lily swallowed hard. She pulled him aside while Mrs. Clearwell, unaware of her distress, exchanged greetings with some acquaintances.

"What is it?" Gabriel asked in a low tone, passing a probing glance over her panicked face.

"Major—I think your brother may be in serious danger."

"What?"

She cringed slightly with embarrassment, but forced herself to confess. "We were—together—when we shouldn't have been. If Edward found out—"

Gabriel's dark sapphire eyes narrowed.

Lily swallowed hard again. "Edward came to see me yesterday and said that he, too, was going 'out of Town' for a few days. If he found out about Derek and me—it might be a trap."

Gabriel gave her a calm nod, his rugged face deadly serious. "Try not to worry. My brother is quite able to take care of himself."

"You don't understand. Edward doesn't always—fight fair," she said with a gulp.

Gabriel gave her a bolstering smile. "Neither do the Marathas. Wait here. First I will check with his valet. Derek would've informed Aadi of his plans. He should be able to tell us where he's gone."

"Major, we have to make sure he's safe!"

"We will. Rather, I will. You stay here—"

"No—I'm coming with you!"

He frowned. "I don't know . . ."

"I know how to handle Edward."

He studied her a second longer. "Just one question. Does my brother know you are in love with him?"

She drew in her breath. "Has he said anything to you?" she asked gingerly, but Gabriel gave her a chiding half-smile.

"On second thought, I'm not getting in the middle of that. Come on."

Lily grabbed her chaperone's sleeve and pulled her away from the people with whom she was still engaged in conversation. Tugging her along, she hurried after Gabriel Knight.

"What's wrong, dear?" Mrs. Clearwell exclaimed.

"I'll tell you on the way," Lily said grimly.

In vino veritas.

In wine, truth—and so, Derek had turned to the venerable grape and the noble hops and barley to try to squeeze the truth out of Ed Lundy about the missing army funds.

Giving his "friend" Lundy the excuse that he was keen to escape the mounting pressures of the investigation for a day or two and to see a bit of England beyond the city, Derek had suggested this rowdy jaunt, and Lundy had agreed.

But considering his true, more underhanded intentions, the enterprise was proving to be a bit trickier than he had anticipated, not the least because, by this, the second night of their drunken bachelors' spree, after God-only-knew how many country pubs, bottles, and hours of overindulgence, Derek was, sadly, not unimpaired himself by the endless flow of liquor.

Which was to say, in fact, that Major Derek Knight was decidedly drunk.

Lundy was in considerably worse condition, laughing so hard he was wheezing and thumping the table at Derek's last sardonic remark. Derek had been relating an exaggerated version of his dread at being accosted in the street weeks ago by Lundy's henchmen. Lundy simply adored the story, practically falling off his chair and under the table, despite the tavern wenches' efforts to keep him propped up and spending freely.

The bevy of buxom barmaids at the smoky Bull's Head Inn had smelled money from the moment that Lundy and he had walked in and were even now doing their part to intoxicate the men further with their vulgar charms.

"God's bones, I thought I was in for a thrashin'!" Derek was saying. "Bloody welcome to London. Where the deuce did you find such a rugged assortment o' bruisers, anyway?"

"Ah, most of 'em have been with me from the old days." Lundy wiped away a tear of laughter and took another deep swig of ale. "Jones, Maguire . . ."

"Is it just me or don't they like anybody?"

"Oh, they'd probably like these pretty lasses," he replied with a lusty glint in his eyes as he perused the ample-bosomed redhead who was sitting on the table, trying to entice them by slowly hitching up her skirts to show them the embroidery on her stockings.

"What about Bates?" Derek asked, with no sign of his true intentions. "What's his story?"

Lundy gave a drunken wave of his hand. "Bates and me grew up in the same street since we were boys."

"Loyal, then?"

"Like a brother."

Derek nodded, lowering his bleary gaze and doing his best to hide his triumph at this information.

It was exactly what he had wanted to know—at last. Thank God.

Though bloody foxed, Lundy was still enough on his guard to have shied away from any sneaky questions regarding the committee. But just as Derek had hoped, the man had not anticipated this line of attack nor realized what it signified when he began asking idly about the people Lundy kept around him.

His henchmen.

Since Lundy's rough-looking driver, Bates, had signed for the hideous rooster brooch, Derek had reasoned that it was altogether possible that Bates had stolen the jewel from his employer and pawned it to pocket the money. But in affirming Bates's loyalty, Lundy had just given him strong reason to suspect that Lundy himself had given Bates the order to hawk his mother's jewelry. Which, in turn, suggested that Lundy's loud and constant show of opulence might all be a lie to mask the opposite reality.

God's bones, if Lundy was having financial troubles, it had serious implications for the missing army funds.

"You boys want another pitcher?" another sultry taproom angel interrupted, propping her hand on her waist. Her tightly laced bodice drew their admiration as she waited for their answer, swaying to the tune of the fife and drum from the rustic musicians in the corner and twitching her skirts in a flirtatious little dance.

She had her eye on Derek, who watched her in amusement, but Lundy waved a hand for her to bring it on. "Get us somethin' to eat, as well!" he ordered. "Lord, I fancy a big round arse like that on a woman," he added as she turned away. The barmaid squealed as Lundy slapped her rear end with hearty laughter to punctuate his point. He turned back to Derek, grinning.

Charming.

"More of a leg man, myself," he said dryly, but of course his mind was still revolving on the possibility of Lundy being behind the army fund's theft.

Perhaps he had skimmed the money and lost it, Derek mused. Or perhaps he had invested it in such a way that he was having problems liquidating it. In either case, he surely had to be scrambling to replace the borrowed funds, per Lord Sinclair's demand and promise of anonymity, to keep his neck out of the traitor's noose.

If his current suspicions were correct, then Lundy had obviously wasted Derek's time and played him for a fool, sending him all over Town to find the embezzler when it was Lundy himself all along. Of course, in regards to Lily, Derek had played Lundy for a fool, as well. His thoughts kept coming back to her, and at the moment, not just because he was besotted.

Why *hadn't* Lundy proposed to the delicious Miss Balfour yet?

Derek thought of all the times the obnoxious Bess Kingsley had intruded upon Lily's time with Lundy. The worst example had been at the garden party when Miss Kingsley had led Lundy away after that dashed bluebird had so amusingly sprinkled its good luck on Lily. Derek recalled his own displeasure with the way Lundy had taken Bess's side against poor Lily. What was that that her precious Edward had said?

"I have to go and talk to Mr. Kingsley. We've been workin' on a deal."

Suddenly a keen suspicion began taking shape in his head. A deal, eh?

If Lundy was indeed secretly embattled with financial problems of some kind, then perhaps the reason he hadn't asked Lily to marry him yet was because he was keeping his options open, waiting to see if he might have to cast Lily aside and marry Bess Kingsley for her dowry.

Good God, what if Bess Kingsley was Lundy's fallback plan?

There was only one way to find out.

"I am thinking of staying in England rather than going back to India," he announced all of a sudden, keeping his tone oh-so-casual.

"Really?"

He nodded. "Reckon I've given the army enough of my

blood and sweat. Time to settle down and marry a rich woman, what?"

"Aha, like the ravishing Fanny Coates?"

He snorted. "She's too smart to wed the likes of me. No, I was thinking of easier prey. I was thinking of offering for . . . Miss Kingsley."

"Bess?" Lundy cried, starting forward.

Derek nodded.

"You're joking!"

"Well, no! Not at all. Of course, she is a perfect nightmare, but I'm a younger son, Lundy. I'm not rich like you. Why shed my blood for fortune when seducing well-heeled members of the fair sex is such an easier and more pleasant way to make one's fortune?" He took a drink. "I must be practical, and her dowry's huge. Besides, it's a simple matter of confining her to the country house while I have my fun in Town. With Fanny Coates," he added with a rakish wink.

Lundy was staring at him in shock. "You don't want Bess."

"Why? You don't have designs on her, do you? After all," Derek continued smoothly, "you've got an understanding with Lily Balfour. Don't you?"

"Aye, but—"

"But what?"

"Nothing."

"You know, that's really a fine and noble thing you're doing, Lundy. Coming to her family's rescue with all their debts and their falling-down manor house. Most men would shudder at the prospect of shouldering such a large financial burden for the sake of a lady, but not you. I know you admitted to me that you only want to marry her to enhance your own prestige, but even so, she's lucky to have you."

"Yes, well, that's not the only reason."

"No? How now, old man, you're not in love?" Derek drawled.

"Hardly. I just want to get her in the sack," Lundy said with a laugh.

"I see," Derek answered coolly.

"Do you? Between you and me and the hole in the wall, I have always had a particular desire to roger a real lady, you know? Hard and fast, until she screamed out like a sailor's whore. Little fantasy of mine, you might say. Doesn't come much more blue-blooded than my haughty Lady Lily, and let's face it, how else am I going to get a lass like that in my bed? Her poverty creates my opportunity."

Derek stared at him in shock.

I think I may have to kill you for that, he mused, remembering her innocence, her delicacy, her grace and her trust, and the reverence with which he himself had touched her. He was outraged, but he realized that if he let it show, his true reaction would blow his cover.

When he observed the harsh glint in Lundy's eyes, it occurred to him that this could be the nabob's way of paying him back for Derek's fictitious designs on Bess Kingsley.

On the other hand, for Lundy to realize that that tactic would have any effect on him, he would've had to have noticed Derek's attraction to Lily.

Determined to remain calm, he willed his wrath aside with a bland smile. "Really, old boy," Derek said in a mild tone that belied the lethal rage that lay beneath it. "That's no way to talk about one's future wife."

Lundy laughed at him.

"I'll play a proper lady for you, Eddie," the redhead posing on the table offered.

"I doubt it, my dumpling. You've too much of a randy sparkle in your eyes."

"Have I?"

"Aye." Lundy hooked a beefy finger under her ribbon garter and roused a tipsy laugh from her. "Give us a kiss, love."

As he tugged the redhead lower to sample her wares, the brunette returned and suddenly fell into Derek's lap.

"Hullo. My name's Polly."

"Er, hullo." Derek paid her little mind as she began kissing his cheek and combing her fingers through his unbound hair, cooing her admiration in his ear.

"You're so lovely, Major darlin,' won't you come upstairs and have a bit o' fun?"

He could not manage to get her off his lap, but he made polite excuses in his state of distraction, still plagued by the question that lingered in his mind after Lundy's ugly words about what he'd like to do to Lily. *Was he only saying that to infuriate me, or does he really intend to use her that way?*

There was no way to be certain, but as he reached past Polly's waist to toy with the bottle on the table before him, he realized it did not signify either way.

Because in that moment he made up his mind that there was definitely, absolutely, no bloody way in Hell that he was ever letting Lundy within a ten-mile radius of her. Under no circumstances would he allow the crude bastard to lay a finger on her.

She was not marrying Lundy, period.

There was a shout nearby as the redhead climbed onto Lundy's lap, whereupon the pair tipped over their chair and went crashing onto the floor in a heap of drunken laughter, where they remained.

"Hell's bells!" the girl on the floor exclaimed indignantly a moment later. "The oaf's so drunk he's passed out! Eddie! Wake up!"

His only answer was a loud snore.

A roar of laughter erupted from the girls, the innkeeper, and all the other drinkers in the pub, but Edward Lundy was oblivious, sprawled, sans dignity, half underneath the table. His ear-splitting snores filled the taproom.

Wouldn't the other Distinguished Gentlemen of the Committee love to see this? Derek mused, but then Polly grew more demanding, draping one arm around his neck. Her other hand went a-roaming. "Major, love, let me give you one for free. You need it, I can tell. Besides, I think he likes me."

Derek plucked her wandering hand from his crotch.

"He, er, has a bit of a mind of his own. My dear Miss Polly—" He knew she was determined to persuade him, but Derek had Lily Balfour on the brain, and with Lundy passed out cold, there was little need to keep up the charade. "Perhaps you would go and fetch the landlord for me so I can see about getting a room for my unconscious friend."

"What about a room for you and me?" she whispered.

"I don't think so."

"Why not?"

"Because I'm married," he lied.

"Uh-oh, Major," Polly murmured, nodding toward the door. "I think your wife just walked in."

"What?" Derek looked over in question, then went motionless.

Lily was standing in the doorway, staring at him in disbelief.

"Good God," Gabriel uttered beside her in the doorway, but Lily just stood there with the color draining from her face.

She could not believe her eyes.

Edward lay in a snoring heap on the floor, while Derek appeared to have been cavorting with the painted harlot on his lap. When he looked over and saw Lily and Gabriel, a stunned expression flashed across his face—but he could not have been more surprised than she was.

At the moment, her cavalry hero was the very sketch of lawless, rakish debauchery, his clothes rumpled, his shirt open. His black hair flowed over his shoulders, long and messy and wild. Two days' unshaven scruff darkened his square jaw.

His silvery eyes were red and bleary with drink, but they widened in stunned remorse the instant he looked over and saw her. "Lily!" At once, he cast the tavern girl aside and swept to his feet, sending his chair clattering behind him with the violence of his motion. "What are you doing here?"

She shook her head at him, her relief that he was safe mingling with icy fury. "Obviously, wasting my time."

With that, she pivoted on her heel and walked right back outside, flinging the tavern door angrily out of her way.

Marching back out to the pub's surrounding yard, where they had spotted Edward's big, black coach from the road, Lily's mind was reeling.

But her heart—was crushed.

Mrs. Clearwell stuck her head anxiously out the window of her barouche. "Lily! Is he here? Is he safe?"

"He's here. He's safe. They're both here," she clipped out to assuage her fear. "They're drunk."

"Oh! Oh, dear . . ."

"Lily!" She heard his deep, drink-roughened baritone calling from behind her, but she did not turn around, striding toward the carriage. "Lily, wait! Would you just listen?"

She heard his swift, pounding footfalls as he ran after her, but when she felt his hand gently grasp her shoulder, she spun around and knocked it away.

"Don't touch me!"

"I can explain—"

"Oh, but there's really no need!" she cried, trying to sound nonchalant, failing because she was furious. "Please, don't let me keep you from your amusements, Major!"

"This is not how it looks."

"Keep your schoolboy lies to yourself," she replied in a withering tone. "I'm going back to London."

"Lily, would you just stop?"

"What for, you heartless bounder? What would be the point?" Tears flooded her eyes, and all of a sudden, she was so angry she could barely speak. "I have eyes. I can see that everything you said to me two days ago was only a game to you. Did you propose to her, too? Do you propose to different women every other day?"

He let out a frustrated exhalation and raked his hand through his hair. "Clearly, I am not at my best right now," he said through gritted teeth, "but God's truth, this isn't anywhere near as bad as it looks."

"Well, don't bother explaining." She shook her head at him. "I can't believe I trusted you. Good-bye, Derek. I've let you muck up my plans long enough, and frankly, you're more trouble than you're worth."

Anger flooded his silvery-blue eyes as she started to turn away. His hand shot out and gripped her arm. "You listen to me. Your 'plans' are over."

"You have no authority over me—"

"Lundy's bankrupt."

"*What?*"

"He's broke. I'm fairly sure of it, and if I'm right, then he's going to throw you over for Bess Kingsley any day now, for her dowry."

"That's impossible! How could Edward be bankrupt?"

"I don't know *how*! He probably overspent trying to impress Society. The house, the stables, the horses, the jewels." He furrowed his brow, searching her face, then he shook his head. "You wanted to know what I was up to when you stopped me in his house the other day. I lied to you—I had no choice. I was trying to get to his office so I could verify my suspicions by having a look at his files."

"And I'm supposed to believe you now?"

"Yes! Lily, you're the reason I'm doing all this," he exclaimed, gesturing toward the pub behind him. "I'm trying to get to the truth so that I can protect you! I brought Lundy here to get him drunk in the hopes that I could catch him in an unguarded moment and find out what the hell is really going on!"

"Did it work?"

Hands on hips, he heaved a frustrated sigh and shrugged. "Sort of. You're not marrying him, Lily. You're just not."

"I hardly need your permission."

"For God's sake, woman—listen to me. Wouldn't a shortage of funds explain why he hasn't asked you to marry him yet? As of tonight, I believe it's because he knows he might need to change course and wed Bess Kingsley for her dowry, not you." He paused while Lily stood there, at a loss, stunned, and struggling to absorb his revelations. "Considering how much you guard your reputation," Derek added, "personally, I'd suggest you start distancing yourself from Lundy as much as possible in Society. His troubles aren't over. In fact, they may be just beginning."

"What's that supposed to mean?"

"I can't tell you." When she rolled her eyes, he relented slightly. "Lily—it has to do with that committee that he serves on. The one I testified in front of, for the army. You're going to have to trust me on this. It's bad." He hesitated. "Very well, I think he migh have stolen some money from the fund."

Quite in shock and feeling much too vulnerable, she folded her arms tightly across her waist and turned away, shaking her head. "Well, isn't that just the old Balfour luck."

"Sweetheart—" Derek reached for her, but she pulled away.

"Leave me alone."

"I've been going out of my mind trying to find a way to keep you from getting dragged down in all of this."

"How can I be sure if you're telling the truth this time or if this is just some sort of sick game?" she demanded. God knew she had been through that before.

Indeed, this whole incident had called back much too vividly all the anguish and betrayal she had felt when she had learned that her "beloved" Lord Owen Masters was nothing but a two-faced fraud.

"A game?" Derek's cheeks had flushed with anger. "If I don't find that money, I don't get my post back! Do you really think I'd play games when my whole career is at stake?"

His words drew her up short, reminding her anew of his firm decision to go back to India—and her own foolish hopes in seeking him out earlier this evening. "No, Derek, I don't suppose you would," she replied in a taut voice. "I can't imagine anything that would make you risk your career." She shook her head and turned away, starting back toward the carriage. "I have to go."

"Lily, wait!"

She ignored him. "Please do not tell Edward we were here. I doubt he'll have any memory of it, but this has all been quite humiliating enough, as I'm sure you'll agree. Major, are you coming with us?" she clipped out, glancing past Derek to the elder Knight.

"I'll stay with my brother," Gabriel answered from a few yards back.

"I'm sorry to have dragged you out like this, Major," she added. "It seems my fears were quite unfounded."

"Can I call on you tomorrow?" Derek asked urgently, taking her arm to try to prevent her from leaving. "The day after?" he pursued at her unwelcoming look.

"I don't know," she replied.

He looked at her for a long moment, then shook his head. "Hold on," he muttered. "I had hoped to do this under better circumstances, but—here." He reached into his pocket. "Put out your hand."

"What is it?" Warily, Lily did so.

"I was keeping these with me for good luck, but since you're here . . ." Derek opened his fist and dropped her diamond earrings into her waiting palm.

Startled, she looked at them and then at him. Lifting them closer, she confirmed in a glance that they were indeed her great-great-grandmother's earrings that she had bargained away to Coachman Jones. "How did you . . ."

He gazed into her eyes. "Still think I'm playing games?"

She barely knew how to respond. "I need to think," she forced out, avoiding his searching gaze. "You'll hear from me when I'm ready to see you."

With that, she reached for the carriage door. Derek opened it for her and stood aside as she climbed in. Mrs. Clearwell slid over to make room for Lily, but the matron glanced at Derek through the window and shook her head at him in disappointment.

He dropped his chin and closed the carriage door for the ladies.

At once, Lily rapped sharply on the chassis to signal Gerald, the driver. A moment later, the barouche rolled into motion, leaving Derek behind, standing in the cobbled yard.

"Damn it," he whispered, then turned to his brother. *"What were you thinking?"*

"Don't take that tone with me. How was I supposed to know what you were about?"

"Why in the hell would you bring her here?"

"She was worried about you! She thought you were in danger—and when she explained it to me, so did I!"

"Damn it, Gabriel." He rubbed the back of his neck and turned toward the tavern once again, shaking his head.

"You know something, you're a fool if you go back to India when you've got a woman here who—" Gabriel's words broke off abruptly. He dropped his gaze with an exasperated huff. "Never mind. I'm not getting in the middle of it. Here." Reaching into his waistcoat, he pulled out a letter. "Aadi bade me give you this when I told him I needed to find you. It just came today. It's not from Colonel Montrose, but Aadi said you'd want it right away."

Derek took the letter with a terse nod of thanks and moved closer to the feeble lamplight that glowed by the tavern's front door.

The sender's name was not marked on the outside, but when he cracked it open, he saw that the very short note was from trusty Charles, his accountant.

Major,
   I found something. My search has led to a local ne'er-do-well by the name of Phillip Kane. When you return, please call on me and I will elaborate.
                              Yr Servant, etc.
                              C. Beecham, Esq.

"Good man," he murmured under his breath. The news was no doubt another nail in poor old Edward's coffin.

Gabriel looked at him in question as Derek folded the note and pocketed it.

"Come on," he said in an easier tone, clapping his elder brother on the shoulder and nodding toward the pub.

"Are you going to buy me a pint?" Gabriel asked wryly.

Derek looked askance at him. "After you help me get Lundy off the floor."

CHAPTER
∞ FIFTEEN ∞

"*I*'m here to collect the sorrel mare," Lily said to the grooms at the Althorpe's stable the next morning. She lifted her chin. "Major Knight gave me permission to take the horse out for a canter whenever I wish."

The pair of young grooms on duty heard the note of authority in her voice, glanced at her smart riding habit, and leaped to obey.

"I'll saddle the horse for you, Miss."

"Thank you. Are the Majors Knight at home?"

As one groom hurried off to saddle the mare, the other glanced into the empty stall usually occupied by Derek's big black stallion. "I don't believe so, Miss."

Good. If Derek had not showed up yet, then in all likelihood Edward would not have made it home by this early hour, either.

After all of Derek's shocking revelations last night, Lily intended to use this slim window of opportunity to find out for herself exactly what was going on. She had stewed and simmered all night long. By God, she would not be played for a fool. By morning, she knew what she had to do. Mere words, claims, from either man were not going to convince her anymore. She needed proof.

While Edward was still away, she devised a scheme to slip into his house, break into his office—the same feat Derek had failed to accomplish during the garden party—and either confirm or disprove the major's theory that the nabob was broke. If Edward was indeed going to jilt her in favor of Bess Kingsley, as Derek predicted, then this might be her last chance to find the truth.

As she paced the stable aisle restlessly, waiting for the groom to bring out her horse, she knew she was in a unique position to carry out this task. Long identified as Edward's future bride and lady of the house, the army of servants and all of his rugged henchmen would not be overly surprised to see her, just in case she was spotted; however, she was not going to allow that to happen.

She knew how to get into his monstrous castle-house unseen, and she knew where he kept his private papers. It was risky, but she was angry enough to try her luck. She craved answers. She had played the obedient young lady for much too long and could not stand it anymore.

Having shaped her scheme before breakfast, she waited until Mrs. Clearwell left for a morning call. Then she eluded the servants, letting them think she was still resting in her chamber behind its closed door. Meanwhile, she had slipped out the back, clad in her riding habit.

"Here she is, Miss. Neat and nice, fed and watered, groomed and shod and ready to go."

Lily turned around as the rhythmic click of hoofs sounded in the aisle behind her. Her jaw dropped when she saw the horse that Derek had promised her as a gift. She could barely believe her eyes. By God, it was a miracle!

After barely a week of Derek's skilled and tender care, the formerly battered, run-down horse glistened with rejuvenated health. Her red coat was as smooth and burnished as a new copper penny; her blond mane was braided with a bit of red ribbon in it to match the thick red saddle blanket, as soft as a cloud, which bore the monogram "MN."

Mary Nonesuch. Her namesake.

A wry smile played at Lily's lips as she ran her gloved hand along the horse's smooth, strong neck. "What a good girl. Do you remember me? Yes, you do, don't you? I gave you all those lovely carrots and apples," she murmured.

"He's taken good care of you, hasn't he? You look like the belle of the ball now."

Derek had bought soft new tack for the mare, as well as a lady's side-saddle of fine quality. Red embroidery adorned the rich brown bridle. Lily took a moment longer to let the horse get used to her, caressing her rounded cheek and scratching the now-bright white star on her forehead.

The sweet, calm, trusting expression in the mare's big, liquid-brown eyes belied the suffering she had endured.

With a tug at her heart, she nodded to the groom to let him know she was ready to mount up.

He assisted her into the side-saddle. Lily smoothed her skirts and gathered the reins, but was taken off guard by the incredibly empowering feeling of having her own horse beneath her.

When she was a little girl, she'd had a chubby dapple-gray pony to ride around Grandfather's acreage, but it had been years since she'd had the means to go where she wanted to go whenever she pleased. She could feel new strength and confidence rush into her. Where had it been all these years?

"Why, it's a match in heaven," the first groom said with an admiring smile as he took off his cap and raked his fingers through his tousled blond hair.

The other boy offered her a riding crop, but recalling the ruthless coachman's whip, Lily shook her head. "I think we'll get along just fine without it."

"You won't have her out too long, will you, Miss—?"

"Balfour."

The groom nodded. "Miss Balfour. Major said it's best to take it slow until she's stronger."

"I'm not sure how long I'll be, but I'll take care to rest her frequently along the way." With a gentle bump of her heel, Lily signaled the mare to go, but she looked back over her shoulder as Mary the Mare ambled down the stable aisle. "If you see the Major would you tell him I said—thanks."

"Will do, Miss."

Ducking out of the stable, they emerged into the day's golden sunshine, and leaving the Althorpe's yard, Lily took her easygoing mount out into the streets of London.

Free! Her heart soared inexplicably. Except for the absence of a groom or chaperone, she looked every inch the part of the fashionable young lady heading to Hyde Park for a genteel canter. But that was not her destination, so she lowered the veil that draped her smart riding hat to help conceal her identity in case she rode past anyone she knew.

Soon she was on her way, cantering the smooth-going sorrel mare out of the bustling city, toward the serenely wooded and garden-clad outskirts of London, where mansions like Edward's lined the Thames.

Along the way, she debated with herself a bit nervously about what she should do on the off chance that Edward arrived home during the course of her mission. She supposed she would think of something, but given the condition she had found him in upon walking into the pub, he'd probably need to spend the whole of today recovering in his room upstairs at the inn.

She hoped he was miserably ill. The lout deserved it.

Before long, Lily reached the tall metal fence that rimmed Edward's estate. Locating a section of fence that offered plenty of woodsy cover to hide her horse, she tethered her mount to one of the horizontal bars of the fence. Then she got up on the horse again and stood on the saddle, gingerly climbing over the barrier's tall wrought-iron spikes.

Jumping down neatly onto Edward's land, she fixed her skirts again, then began prowling toward the house, her heart pounding.

With both the master and his mother away, the staff must have been taking their usual tasks at a leisurely pace, for instead of the usual buzz of industrious activity everywhere, outside, the place was quiet.

Approaching nearer, she spotted a few of Edward's henchmen loitering by the stable wall, smoking and talking and playing cards. They didn't see her.

She darted around a large flowering shrub, making her way through the garden, toward the one door that she knew was probably open. The conservatory door, which led out onto the garden's flagstone terrace, was usually left propped open because in summer the glasshouse grew uncomfortably hot. Mrs. Lundy had often complained about the heat spreading to the rest of the house.

Sure enough, once she had the terrace gained, she was able to slip inside, dodging behind an enormous planter when a maid went hurrying by. The uniformed servant girl bustled past, heading toward the kitchens. Lily waited and listened, remaining crouched behind the planter until she was sure the girl had gone.

Once more, she was on her way, tiptoeing past the great hall, where two more maids were chatting idly as they dusted, and giggling over which of the footmen was handsomest. Padding through the empty dining room with all its glistening gilt, Lily turned the corner into the same silent corridor down which she had trailed Derek during the garden party.

Now that she knew his true intention that day, she was impressed to see how far he had actually come before she had so inconveniently interrupted him. Edward's private study lay straight ahead, at the end of the hallway. She spotted its closed door. But then she stifled a gasp, whirling into the same curtained alcove where Derek had accosted her, as one of Edward's fierce-looking henchmen crossed the intersection down the hallway.

She believed it was Mr. Bates.

Lily pressed herself against the wall, her heart pounding. Oh, perhaps this whole mission was a bit mad on her part—but it was too late to back out now. Her chosen destination was in reach, just a few yards away.

A wary peek around the corner of the alcove assured her that Bates had moved on.

Leaving her hiding place, she swept past the parlor where Derek had done such delicious things to her. An involuntary shudder of remembered pleasure raced through her, but she did her best to thrust it aside, intent on her mission. Moving with unhesitating stealth, her footfalls making barely a whisper over the polished floors, she reached the door to Edward's study. Opening it with ginger care, she peeked through the cracked door with one eye.

Empty.

Skirts whirling around her, she rushed inside and pulled the door shut, quickly locking it. Pressing a hand to her chest, she breathed a sigh of relief. Her heart was hammering so loudly she wondered how the noise of it did not alert the entire staff that they had an intruder. The only one who seemed to notice anything amiss was Edward's ferocious fight dog, Brutus. She could hear the black beast barking viciously from all the way outside in his cage next to the stable.

But other than a loud, impatient *"Shut up!"* nobody paid the barking dog any mind. Well, that hellhound's constant clamor was nothing unusual. Lily was only glad that they never let Brutus out of his cage. If he could kill his canine opponents in minutes, she would have hated to see what he could do to a person.

She wasted no time dwelling on the morbid question. The thick velvet curtains over the windows cast a shadowy midday pall over the room despite the brilliant sunshine outdoors, but the gloom was not dark enough to obscure the various places she'd need to search. She scanned the dusty, oak-paneled study with a glance.

A glass-doored cabinet housed the series of red leather-bound folios tied shut with black ribbons containing Edward's files—business correspondence and records and such. These ledger books were neatly alphabetized, each with a gilt-tooled letter on its spine.

But then her gaze homed in on the large metal safe by the wall. Now *that* was the logical place where Edward would store his most sensitive documents. She hurried over to check, but of course it was locked. The formidable iron door refused to budge.

Speeding silently across the room, she got right to work

searching the grand baronial desk for a key. Edward's desk was cluttered with an array of everyday items: a small hourglass, a supply of unsharpened quills, jars of indigo and sepia ink, wafers of sealing wax, a silver tray of powdered drying sand, a letter opener, a few writing pads, extra candles, and a large brass oil lamp.

With the mantel clock above the empty fireplace relentlessly tick, tick, ticking away the minutes, her search grew ever more urgent.

Aha! She suddenly discovered a small key tucked under the little tray of drying powder. She rushed back over to the safe, but before she could congratulate herself on her spy skills, she frowned.

The key didn't fit. *Well, what's it for, then?* It had to open something.

She turned and swept her gaze over the entire office again. Suddenly, she caught a glimpse of a folded piece of paper sticking out from beneath the leather desk pad.

It had been hidden before, but she must have moved the pad in her search, for it was visible now. At once, she strode over and slid the paper out from underneath it. She unfolded the paper and discovered that it was a tender farewell letter to "Eddie" from his doting mama.

Mrs. Lundy had left a heaping of affectionate advice on how her boy must take care of himself properly while she was gone. Get his rest. Eat his vegetables. Lily couldn't help but lift an eyebrow. The feared Edward Lundy might look like a ruffian, but there was a side of him that was nothing but an overgrown mama's boy. Twirling the mysterious key in thought as she read on, Lily came to a paragraph that made her wonder . . .

> *You must have faith and be strong until I return. Do your best not to worry overmuch, but take comfort in knowing that I, of all people, will not fail you. When that weasel of a solicitor hears that I'm on my way to oversee this matter personally on your behalf, he will not dare trifle with us a moment longer. You just keep your*

cards close to the chest, my dear, and keep them all busy in London. Never fear. I will be on my way back to you as soon as the sale is complete, and then Sinclair can go to the devil. I promise you, all will be well . . .

Lily frowned in puzzlement. *I thought she went to Jamaica for her gout.* But this would seem to hint at a completely different explanation. The rest of the letter contained nothing but more mother-hen fussing.

Finished reading it, Lily quickly tucked it back under the desk pad. Making sure she had put everything back on Edward's desk the way she had found it, she glanced around and realized the next logical thing to check was Edward's filing system of ledger books.

A daunting task. She suppressed a dull sigh, put the tiny key down on the corner of the desk, and went over to the cabinet. She reached for the small wooden knob on the glassed door, but as she opened it, the knob pulled right off in her hand. *Broken!* She stifled a curse as the tiny metal screw that was supposed to have held the knob in place fell to the hardwood floor with a small clatter.

"Blast," she whispered, bending down to catch it as it rolled away toward the base of the nearest bookcase. She glanced toward the door to Edward's study, praying no one had heard the small noise.

As she reached down to retrieve the stray piece, the collection of books arrayed on the low shelf at her current eye-level brought a wry smirk to her lips, for she noticed that the titles were in Latin. *Well, that is the height of pretension.* Edward hadn't a word of the Classical tongues. She doubted he had ever read an actual book in his life.

Suddenly, she frowned. Something looked weird about those books. They were too . . . perfect. She reached to take one off the shelf and gasped as she discovered it wasn't a real book at all. The unobtrusive row of seeming Latin titles were in fact only an artfully crafted plaster concealment.

Her jaw dropped when she gave the row of fake books a

tug and they popped forward, then glided up on a metal arm, revealing a metal safe within, long and narrow, fashioned to fit the shape of the hidden compartment. *Why, Edward, you devil!* Noting the keyhole in the middle of the safe, she snorted, got up, and hurried back to the desk, retrieving the tiny key she had found.

A perfect fit.

What she found inside the secret safe were more files. The *real* ledger books, she suspected. At first glance, they appeared identical to the ones on display so transparently in the glass case, but their contents must have been considerably more hazardous to have warranted this disguise.

She pulled out the first folio labeled "A–B" and set it on her lap, untying the ribbon. Opening the slim leather case, she began hastily riffling through the collection of loose papers and old correspondence. Nervous about her trespass and beginning to feel a bit desperate—after all, she didn't even know for certain what she ought to be looking for—she came to the end of the A's, started flipping through the start of the B's, and stopped cold.

Balfour, Lily.

She pulled a neatly fastened set of papers out of the file and stared at it, barely able to believe her eyes. Edward had hired a private investigator to look into her background!

Her mouth went dry. Her hands began to shake, and she rushed through the pages in stunned disbelief.

Good God, there were dates and details not just on her, but on her grandfather, his holdings, his date of death, the date of her parents' marriage, the church where she had been christened—even the name of her first governess!

Lily was horrified.

She knew the practice of investigating one's prospective spouse was not unheard of among the wealthy and the powerful, but being the subject of such an inquest herself was appalling to a private woman . . . with secrets to hide.

But slowly, her pulse slowed back to normal and her terror began to ease. By some miracle, there was no mention of Lord Owen Masters in the investigator's report. Her family's code of icy silence must have worked to guard her reputation even from a professional sneak.

It was bad enough that Edward's private investigator had managed to learn about the drunken duel of honor in which her hotheaded cousin, David, Pamela's younger brother, had thrown away his life. If poor Davy had not been so wild, he'd have inherited the title after Grandfather. But chasing his own destruction in the grand manner of the luckless Balfours, the lusty lad had called the wrong man a cheat at cards and had wound up dead, maiming his opponent, in turn.

Reading the account of her last male cousin's demise cast a cloud of darkness over her heart. If there had been more time, she would have pored over the Balfour file in detail, but then a new thought suddenly gripped her.

At once, she replaced the papers in the ledger book, retied its black ribbon, and hurried to put the folio away. Skipping over the other letters, she went straight for the "K–L" folio. *What if Edward, in his paranoia, had commissioned a similar report on Derek?*

After all, Derek was not the friend to Edward that he was pretending to be, a fact he had revealed to Lily outside the Bull's Head Inn. But did Edward know this, too?

If Edward was just playing along, aware that Derek was actually his foe, then that could spell trouble for the major. On the other hand, Lily's motives in checking for a file on Derek were not solely born of a noble desire to protect him.

She had been duped by a handsome liar once before, and after last night, finding Derek that way at the tavern, all of her scarred vulnerability in this area was on full alert. It was a slight detour from her purpose in coming here, but if Derek was a liar, it was best to face it now.

Edward's paranoia had provided her with a chance she might never get again, to discover any secrets about Derek that he might not have wanted her to find out . . .

She opened the K–L folio across her lap and turned through the entries.

Kane, Phillip. The first file in the ledger book was a thick one, full of financial-looking papers . . .

She turned past it.

Kingsley, Miss Elizabeth. Well! It seemed Edward really was considering marrying Bess, if he had gone to the trouble of having her investigated, too. Somewhat mollified that at least Bess had been subjected to the same indignity, Lily skipped the opportunity to peruse the private details of Bess Kingsley's life.

She turned another page and stopped.

Knight, Major D.

Gathering up her courage, she swallowed hard and opened his file. She did not know what sort of horrible thing she had been half expecting, but as her gaze traveled swiftly over the few pages collected, a quick account of his impressive military career and his various family connections, her eyes filled with tears.

Because it all matched exactly what he'd told her.

There were no lies here.

Even the story of his and Gabriel's battle against the royal guards at the maharajah's palace was there, unvarnished. The only thing he hadn't told her was just how steep the odds had been against him and his brother, which in turn led her to see what a very deadly warrior he must be when he was in his element. She blinked away her tears, smiling from her very heart, for she never would have thought of accusing Derek Knight of too much modesty.

Preparing to put the "K–L" folio away, she turned back to the first file and smoothed the pages to make sure it all looked neat and undisturbed, and it was then that the large sums of money noted on the entry under her hand drew her attention.

What is this? She narrowed her gaze and started more closely scanning the pages under *Kane, Phillip.* As the moments passed, her initial curiosity turned to rising disbelief. The file kept an account of enormous sums of money that had been paid out incrementally month after month to a firm called Warwickshire Canals & Co. The total came to more than 300,000 pounds.

Several letters from a Mr. Phillip Kane, President, described in long, tedious detail the progress being made on this extensive and apparently very ill-fated construction project. A quick glimpse at Mr. Kane's correspondence recounted an endless litany of problems that had come up along the way in the building of these canals—a flood, a spike in the cost of timber, a key engineer who dropped dead of a bad heart.

Lily shook her head, entirely taken aback to learn that Edward had engaged in this sort of long-odds speculation.

She knew he was experienced in matters of trade, but still, three hundred thousand pounds!

Not even the profligate Regent could snap his fingers at that kind of sum. She was obviously no expert in finance, but she could not imagine why or how Edward could have sunk such a fortune into these dubious canals and still have a roof over his head. A large roof, at that.

As she turned another page, she came down to the final entry, dated almost exactly one year ago—and winced, for there was nothing whatsoever to show for Edward's investment, nor much of an explanation from company president Phillip Kane.

The payments had simply stopped.

Hmm. She knew one thing for certain: Derek would want to see this.

All of a sudden, the sound of heavy, clomping footfalls in the corridor outside the office broke into her thoughts.

Lily looked up with a low gasp.

She froze, still holding the Phillip Kane papers. Someone was coming! The color drained from her face. *Edward!* A grouchy bellow to a servant removed any doubt who it was. He had come home!

In the blink of an eye, Lily folded the Kane papers and shoved them into the bodice of her neatly tailored riding habit. Scrambling to put the "K–L" folio back in its proper place, she closed the safe, locked the door, pulled down the false front of the books, and ran to the desk to put the key back under the tray of drying sand.

Then she whirled around, scanning the office with her heart in her throat, making sure everything else was in order. But how was she going to get out of here? There was only one door, no other exit, no place to hide.

She might be able to jump out one of the windows, but she realized there was no time to try. He would be upon her in an instant. Every second, the footsteps grew louder. Dear God, having discovered his theft, his treason, stealing from the Crown, Lily knew Edward might kill her if she did not think of something fast. She'd had no idea she was getting into something so far over her head.

Abruptly remembering that she had locked the door, she raced over and unlocked it to avoid raising Edward's suspicions when he walked in. Meanwhile, she concluded in a flash that her only hope of getting out of this unscathed was to fall back on the one strategy that, with years of practice, had become her forte.

She would put on her frostiest mask and hide in plain view.

When he opened the door, she was sitting on his desk in a pretty pose, her arms braced behind her, her legs crossed, the impatient swing of her top foot stirring the brown drapery of her riding habit.

She gave him an arch look when he hesitated in the doorway, his groggy and ill-tempered look turning to obvious bafflement to see her. "Lily!"

"So," she clipped out. "There you are. At last."

He cleared his throat a tad guiltily at her tone of wifely reproach. "What are you, er, doing here, my dear?"

"Waiting for you, of course!" she retorted with a chilly smile.

"Oh. Did you, uh, miss me?"

"Not in the least."

He cleared his throat and came slouching into the room, shutting the door behind him.

"Did you have fun on your *business* trip? Really, Edward. I am disappointed in you."

"How did you find out?" he mumbled, his head down.

"Word travels fast in the ton. But I had to see you for myself to confirm that these rumors were true. Well. It seems I have my answer. I shall be going now." She jumped off his desk and strode past him, making her way to the door with her nose in the air.

"Aw, Lily—don't go storming off." He reached out and grabbed her arm, halting her forward motion.

Damn! She had just missed making a clean getaway! She flicked a quelling glance down at the beefy fingers grasping her elbow. "Let go of my arm. You're going to give me a bruise." It took all her effort to maintain her high-handed façade, but she knew her ladylike aura of aristocratic frost was her best weapon in helping to keep his baser nature in check. Still, as her fear deepened, the disguise was wearing thin.

"Come, we don't get much chance to be alone," he wheedled her. "Stay and chat."

"I can't. I have to go." She pulled away in disgust, but he would not release her.

"Don't I get a kiss good-bye, at least?"

"Absolutely not." He leaned closer, and she grimaced at the smell. "You need a bath."

"Maybe you should join me."

"Edward! How dare you?" She let out a sudden gasp with astonished understanding. "You're still drunk!"

"Nay! Well, maybe just a bit!" His wheezing laughter confirmed her suspicions. "Give me one kiss and I'll let you go home," he teased, but a glint of lust had sparked to life in his eyes.

I've got to get out of here. This was getting extremely dangerous.

"Look at you, my haughty princess. I'm so pleased you came to see me. I think you really want to stay." Without warning, he slung his other arm around her waist and bent lower, inhaling the scent of her. "So lovely. Admit it, Lady Lily. You picked me for a reason. All the fine, lordly gentl'-men you could've had. I think you fancy a bit o' the rough."

"How dare you speak to me in such a disgusting fashion?" She tried to shove his arms off her waist, but his bearlike embrace only tightened. "God, you are so impossibly crude."

"Yes, but I'm exactly what you need. Come, Lily, my angel, just one kiss."

"I really do not feel like kissing you right now, Edward," she announced, struggling to keep her cool air well in hand. "You lied to me and you smell like a tavern floor."

"Aw, surely all my gold is worth that much to you, at least."

"You are behaving like a thoroughgoing boor!"

"One proper kiss and you can go. Come, I know you've got more fire in you than you gave me before. I can smell it in your blood."

She looked at him evenly, though inside, she was quaking—and revolted. But if this was what it was going to take to get her out of here in one piece, so be it. "Just be quick about it," she muttered, bracing herself as he leaned toward her.

"Ah!" In the next moment, his rough and slobbery kiss was upon her, rather like a pack of rabid hounds. He was stale and sweaty and he smelled like a dirty washrag, and if she were not so expert at controlling her reactions, Lily would have screamed, or at the very least gagged at the incursion of his tongue in her mouth and the wretched taste of his recent overindulgence. "Very nice," Edward rasped after a moment, but instead of releasing her, he came right back for more.

As he began groping her, Lily was shocked at his aggressiveness and tried to squirm free. He ignored her protest as she tried to push him away, but when he squeezed her breast, they both stopped short at the sound of crinkling paper.

Her eyes widened.

Edward pulled back a small space and looked at her in confusion.

Her face suddenly gone ashen, Lily panicked, pulling out

of his grasp and launching herself toward the door, but Edward grabbed her arm and yanked her back to him with a booming yell. *"What are you hiding?"*

"Nothing! Let go of me!"

With a wrench of her shoulder, he spun her to face him. "What are you really doing here?"

"I already told you—"

"Don't lie to me!"

"I don't know what you're talking about!"

"Oh, really?" He reached out and cupped her breast in rough insolence, his hand discovering not just yielding female flesh, but the rigid square of folded paper tucked inside the neat white buttoned shirt of her riding habit.

His eyes burned with fury when he looked at her again. "Damn you!"

"Edward—" She cried out as he grabbed the edges of her bodice in both meaty hands and ripped it open with a violent tear.

Lily instinctively tried to cover herself, but he had no interest in her body at the moment. He snatched the Phillip Kane papers out of the top of her chemise above her stays. Holding her in place against the wall with one hand clamped around her throat, Edward shook the folds of paper loose and saw what she had stolen.

Slowly, he turned to her in shock. "You lying little *bitch*." He threw her away from him, sending her tumbling onto the floor in a heap of brown skirts and ripped broadcloth, her hair falling from its tidy chignon.

He loomed over her. Lily cowered on the floor, trying to protect herself and hold her ripped bodice together at the same time.

"You barge in here and try to pretend that I'm the one who's caught for a bit of fun at a tavern? But you! You're the one who's caught, my haughty lady." He grabbed her by her hair and wrenched her head back, leaning down to snarl in her face, "You're goin' to pay for this."

"Edward, please!"

"Knight put you up to this, didn't he? *Answer me!*" he roared. *"Are you fucking him?"*

"No!" she screamed.

"Well, I don't believe you," he said quietly after a pause. "You've forced me to it, Lily. Now I'm going have to kill 'im."

"Edward, no!"

"Oh, yes. I see it all now. Nobody plays Ed Lundy for a fool. The both of you are going to pay." He released her roughly and stomped over to the door, throwing it open.

He bellowed for his henchmen.

Lily barely had five seconds to think of what to do before he was back, towering over her. For a second, she cowered in fear, expecting that he was going to start kicking her.

Every time she started to get up, he pushed her down again. "You stay right there, you filthy little fortune hunter. You stay on the floor, where you belong."

Lily flinched, and Edward laughed.

Bates came running and blinked when he saw her. "How the hell did she get in here?"

"You tell me!" Edward bellowed. "You fools let her pass!"

More of his thugs rushed into the doorway in answer to their master's wrathful summons.

"Jones, Maguire, search the property," Bates ordered. "Make sure she came alone."

"Yes, do," Edward added in sarcasm. "Incompetents," he muttered under his breath.

Lily could no longer hold her tongue. "Edward, there is no need to speak of killing Derek—"

"You little backstabbing harlot, think you can save your lover by lying to me?"

"If anything happens to Derek Knight, you'll be the first person the authorities will want to speak to," she shot back, thinking fast, "especially after your drunken spree with that rakehell—too much liquor has started many a duel, even between so-called friends. That's what they'll think." Her jaw clenched in determination, Lily climbed warily to her feet, on guard lest he try to knock her down again. Her heart was pounding and her chest heaved as she held her torn bodice together.

At least now she had his full attention.

"Then there's the small matter of Gabriel Knight, Derek's brother. He's said to be an even fiercer warrior than Derek is. All those powerful cousins of theirs—the Duke of Hawkscliffe, Lords Winterley, Rackford, Griffith—all of them. Don't be a fool," she warned Edward with total conviction. "If you strike him down, they will *all* come after you. You won't stand a chance."

He considered her words, then shrugged them off with a glower full of stubborn pride. "I'm not afraid of them." He glanced at Bates. "Ready the others. We're going after him."

"Ill-advised, Edward. Very ill-advised, unless you don't mind sacrificing a few of your boyhood mates to his sword." Lily nodded at Bates. "Derek Knight is a warrior with years of combat experience. You really think you and your little army of East End bruisers can take him down?"

He sent her an unpleasant smile. "We'll manage."

Her desperation climbed as Edward turned away and headed for the door with a curt order for one of his men. "Tie her up and don't let her out of your sight."

"Edward, wait! If you would just calm down, there is another way to get rid of him!"

He paused, his back to her. He seemed to debate with himself in annoyance, then turned around and looked at her impatiently. "Very well. I'll bite. How?"

Lily's mouth had grown so dry she could barely force the words out. "Capture him, but don't kill him. Throw him on a ship bound for India. Then he'll be out of your way and no one can accuse you of murdering anyone."

He stared at her, deliberating. "Kidnap him."

"Precisely. Anyone who's ever met the major has heard him say he can hardly wait to go back to India. So, let him. They'll just assume he got tired of waiting and decided it was time to get back to his troops."

Edward approached her once more with a menacing stare. "I have an even better idea. I deposit the two of you in a room at some unsavory hotel, each dead of a gunshot wound to the head. They'll call it a lovers' quarrel. Murder-suicide. A very scandalous end for such a fine lady, no?"

She flinched, but checked the dread that the bloody image inspired. "Frankly, I like my idea better."

He narrowed his eyes, scrutinizing her, then he began laughing quietly at her feeble jest and turned away once more. "Let's go," he said to his men.

Her frayed control snapped at the ease with which he ignored her.

"Edward!" she wrenched out with a sob. Panicked, she rushed after him and grabbed his arm as tears flooded her eyes. "Spare him! I'll do anything you want!"

"Well, now." He turned to her with a sinister leer. "That is an interesting offer, Miss Balfour."

Her heart in her throat, her body suddenly gone ice cold, Lily forced herself to hold his gaze.

"Exactly what are you willing to do?" he asked, mocking her.

She did not answer.

"I'll not marry you."

"I know."

"On the other hand . . ." He cupped her chin and tilted her head back, inspecting her face as though she were some wretched Roman slave girl for sale in the shadow of the Colosseum. "I daresay I could find a use for ye."

His men joined in his jeering laughter.

"What do you say to that offer, my proud Miss Balfour? Your services as I please for the major's life?"

Lily said nothing, but lowered her gaze, turning scarlet. Her lack of outrage at his indecent words was enough, she trusted, to signal her submission to the hideous pact.

She could feel Edward's gaze consuming her. "Boys, I'm feeling magnanimous. I think we can spare the major, after all."

"Oh, come on, Ed!" Bates protested. "There's no need to make bargains with the likes of 'er! You can have the wench whether she's willing or not!"

Edward cast him a swinish smile. "Not much sport in that, eh?"

Lily held her breath, fearing her fate, but noting the fleeting look of uncertainty in Edward's eyes.

There was lust and violence there, but also, the slightest glimmer of heart. Perhaps he wondered what his mother would have to say about all this. Perhaps a part of him did not *want* to kill Derek despite his hotheaded first reaction.

Edward looked away, quick to conceal the glimpse of humanity. "No," he ordered in a gruff tone. "We'll put him on the first ship bound for India. No sense tangling with the whole Knight family, like she said. Nor do I fancy a visit from them Bow Street blackguards, either." He looked at Lily from her head to her feet. "You'd better make this worth my while."

"Well, I don't like it," Bates grumbled. "Damn lot easier just to kill the bastard. If Knight's as practiced with a weapon as she claims, then how are we supposed to get close enough to restrain him?"

Edward glanced at Lily. "He'll come to her, won't he, love? Little virgin and the unicorn, eh? You want him to live, you help us take him nice and easy."

She cried out in fright as Edward grabbed her arm again and dragged her toward his desk, pushing her down into the chair and then slapping a piece of paper before her along with a quill pen.

"Go on," he ordered. "Write him a nice little love letter telling him to meet you tonight . . ."

Lily missed the rest of Edward's cold words as she gazed at the sharp letter opener tucked away in the cubbyhole of the desk directly in her line of sight.

For a second, she wondered if she could stab him with it, fight her way out of here. But that was absurd.

In her fantasies, maybe, the little girlhood dreams she had spun at the garden folly, but in real life, she was no warrior. Not like Derek. She had her wits, he had his sword, and between the two of them, that would have to be enough.

"Tell him to come to the mews behind Mrs. Clearwell's house. We don't want to arouse our fine warrior's suspicions."

"Oh, Edward, please," she breathed, and looked up to search his face in guarded pleading.

"Do it!" he roared at her, bringing his fist down on the paper before her.

She jumped. Handling the pen like a foreign object, clumsily dipping it into the ink with trembling fingers, she began to write, her tears spilling onto the page.

For she realized now that after the angry way they had parted, Derek was going to walk into that dark alley tonight and think she had betrayed him.

CHAPTER
⚓ SIXTEEN ⚓

"It really is the most curious thing," Charles was saying to Derek, who leaned against the opposite wall, arms folded across his chest, his brow furrowed in thought.

He had come to the solicitor's tidy Whitehall office directly, even before traveling on homeward to the Althorpe. He had a bit of a headache from his excesses outside of Town and was in need of a heavy meal, but this had been too important to delay.

"Why such a respected and dignified peer as Lord Sinclair should have made a payment from his accounts to an infamous scoundrel like Phillip Kane, well, it quite baffles the understanding. I know not what it signifies, but I had a feeling you would want the details, such as they are."

"Oh, yes, Charles. You were quite right to send for me."

"Here you have it." Charles glanced at his notes. "Five thousand pounds, dated almost exactly two years ago."

"Hm. Five thousand pounds is no trifling sum." He took a swig of water from his canteen, still a bit dry-mouthed after his excursion to all those pubs. "So, what do we know of this Phillip Kane fellow?"

"Ah, his name was quite familiar to those of us in legal circles, for he was constantly running afoul of the constabulary, getting into all sorts of trouble. Somehow he always delivered a fine cock-and-bull tale to explain his latest mischief, and he'd tell it with a smile. Half the time, his smooth talking worked, too, even on the magistrates. He had a charming air. Good-looking fellow, flamboyant, with the manners of a gentleman—but thoroughly dissipated. An adventurer, always on the make with some new scheme. Pity he didn't deign to turn his talents to honest measures, but he seemed to feel the world had wronged him."

"How?"

"Well, he was rumored to be the bastard son of some high-ranking aristocrat, by an opera girl," Charles said with a grimace of distaste. "He grew up around the theater world and learned all of its vices at an early age."

"An actor?"

Charles shrugged. "I never heard of him taking to the stage himself, but whatever skills he picked up among their breed seemed to serve him best with the ladies and at the gaming tables. He had a reputation as a womanizer, but mainly he was known as a cardsharp. It seemed to me quite plausible that Lord Sinclair could have paid him to settle a gaming debt."

Derek shook his head. "Lord Sinclair doesn't touch the cards. They would've never appointed him to the committee if he had any history as a gambler. All that money under his care . . ." He paused. "Of course, His Lordship could have paid Kane off on behalf of a younger male relative, a son or nephew who might've been stung by this sharper's gift with the cards and the dice."

"Ah, that could be." Charles nodded, pursing his lips. "Do you wish me to look into it, Major?"

Derek waved off the offer. "I'll do it. I think it'll be extremely enlightening to have a little chat with Lord Sinclair about his dealings with this man. I'd also like to talk to Phillip Kane, if you know where he can be found."

"The boneyard, I'm afraid."

"He's dead?" Derek asked in surprise.

"Quite." Charles handed him a newspaper clipping that proved to be an obituary. "It was all a bit of a mystery, actually. To be sure, Phillip Kane made a great many enemies in his short, colorful life. Whatever he had done this time, or whomever he'd crossed, it was enough to inspire him to flee to France. Apparently at Calais it was not long before he resumed his usual mode of life, but the French must not have enjoyed being abused by his various talents any more than our gambling set here in London did, for within a few weeks, his landlady found him dead in his rooms. Poisoned."

Derek raised a brow. "Poison? Hmm, a woman's weapon. Revenge perhaps from some heartbroken former conquest?"

"Certainly I could believe that, but there were plenty of people who would've wished him dead." Charles shrugged. "I remember the case well, for those of us in the legal world rather knew it was bound to happen sooner or later, only a question of when and how. One of the newspapers had sniffed out a copy of the local prefect's report, and as I recall, nothing was taken from Kane's rooms. No sign of a struggle. The most popular theories in circulation were that it was either a former lover or a suicide."

"No note to justify the latter?"

"No. Eventually, when a few months passed and nothing was ever found—and with no one who seemed inclined to lament the scoundrel's passing—the case faded into obscurity." Charles sighed. "Well, if Kane had had the courtesy to be murdered in England, it would have been easier to pursue, but his dying abroad, well, there was also the slight complication that solving it would have required our English and French justice officials to work together, and neither side was inclined to be too friendly about sharing information."

"How convenient for whoever killed him," Derek said softly. Then he paused. "When did they discover his corpse? How long ago did this happen?"

Charles glanced at the papers. "More than a year now. Fourteen months, to be exact."

Derek nodded, mulling it over. "Very well. Excellent work, Mr. Beecham. Perhaps Lord Sinclair can shed further light on the matter. I shall pay a call on him on my way home."

"Is there anything else I can do for you now, Major?"

Derek smiled. "Just keep looking over those books as

much as the Bank will allow it. Let me know if you find anything else."

Charles smiled and gave him a slight salute.

Derek paused on the way out, with a sudden last question. "Did the London rumor mill ever posit what 'high-ranking aristocrat' might have fathered Phillip Kane?"

"There was an active theory about, one I heard whispered at the Temple Bar."

"I had no idea you lawyers were such gossips."

Charles laughed. "Apparently an earl had quietly paid Kane's legal debts after one of his arrests."

"Who was it?" Derek asked, fascinated. "Surely it wasn't Lord Sinclair?"

"No, but now that you mention it, it was another member of your committee. Or ex-member, I should say. Lord Fallow."

Derek stared at him. Lord Fallow, their host the night of the garden concert where he had walked down to the river beside Lily.

Lord Fallow—Ed Lundy's loyal patron.

"I thought . . . Lord Fallow had no son," Derek said slowly. Somewhere along the way, he had heard that the lack of a son was partly why the noble lord had taken the lowborn Lundy under his wing.

"Yes, well, according to the world, he did not," Charles replied. "His Lordship certainly never acknowledged Phillip Kane as his own. Of course, with the way Kane conducted himself, I'm not sure I would, either," he muttered. "I wouldn't place too much faith in the veracity of this claim, though, Major. 'Twas only a rumor, one that Kane may easily have started himself just to cause trouble. This was the same man who claimed that Her Royal Highness, Princess Charlotte, God rest her soul, had winked at him once when the royal chariot passed him on Pall Mall."

Derek's lips twisted at the outlandish tale.

Charles frowned. "Of course, if it were true . . ." His words trailed off as he eased down into his seat behind his desk, frowning.

"If it were true," Derek said, "then Phillip Kane would've had a very strong reason to hate Edward Lundy."

Charles murmured his agreement.

Mystified, Derek nodded at him and then walked out of the office, pondering it all the way to Lord Sinclair's.

When he reached the earl's home, a post-boy ran over, offering to hold his horse's bridle for a shilling. Derek accepted his services, warned him about the horse's temperamental nature, then strode up to the earl's front door and banged the brass knocker.

When the butler appeared, he was no more pleased to see Derek than he had been last time and informed him that the earl was not at home.

With one eye on the butler and the other on the boy doing his best to keep the black stallion under control, Derek shrugged off his hopes of a visit for the moment and decided it could wait. He left his calling card instead, eager to get home at last after the strain of his revelries away from Town.

Returning to his horse, he tossed the boy the promised shilling and mounted up again. But as he rode away, he felt the hair on his nape bristle up with the instinctual perception of eyes on his back. Suddenly, he could feel somebody watching him.

He glanced back casually at Sinclair's house and spotted movement in the upper window. Just before the curtain swung back into place, he glimpsed a portly figure staring out the window.

Looking ahead again, he scowled. *Lying bastard. Sinclair's at home, he just didn't want to see me.* Of course, it was no surprise. He was not exactly the chairman's favorite person.

No matter. He would track the earl down later someplace where he could not run for cover, then he'd ask his questions. Preferably after a meal, a bath, and at least a few hours of sleep.

When Derek brought his black stallion into the stable at the Althorpe and handed him over to the grooms, he found the two lads grinning from ear to ear.

"Your lady friend came, Major."

"She took the mare."

"Lily?" he exclaimed. "I mean—Miss Balfour?"

"Aye, that's 'er."

"She told us to tell you thanks, she did."

"Thanks?" he echoed. Well! He had told her he intended to give her the horse, and after her displeasure with him due to finding him half drunk at that tavern last night, it seemed she was quite content to collect her present, thank you very much and au revoir. "Did she, she say anything else? Like . . . if she might be coming back at all?"

"No, sir."

"Just—thanks."

He sighed, then scratched his scruffy cheek, in need of a shave. "If she happens to bring the horse back, would one of you lads be so good as to come and let me know?"

"Aye, sir."

"Thanks." Upon returning to his apartment, he gave Aadi and the other servants a similar order. Then he went into his chamber and crashed down onto his bed. He was asleep in minutes.

Without dreams.

A knock at his chamber door some time later roused him. Derek blinked his way back to consciousness, certain he'd only just closed his eyes.

When he raised up a bit, he saw his brother poking his head in the door, waving his mail with a rare grin. "Special delivery for the major."

Derek shot upward. "Colonel Montrose?"

"Better," Gabriel replied. He walked in and tossed the letter onto Derek's stomach.

He picked it up at once and tore it open, silent as his gaze scanned the few lines. "It's from Lily."

"I know. What's it say? You're forgiven? She hates you?"

"It doesn't say," he answered, rather wide-eyed with the sudden wake-up after such a deep sleep. "She wants to see me."

"That could be very good. Or very bad." Gabriel

laughed wickedly, gave him a knowing look, and then withdrew, leaving his "little brother" to agonize privately over what the maddening lady might have to say.

Ten P.M, her missive ordered him. Derek scowled. *You mean I have to wait?*

When the appointed hour of their secret rendezvous arrived at last, Derek looked into the pitch-black mouth of the alleyway ahead and took an instant dislike to the place.

He wasn't sure why he was seized with such a strong gut reaction to their designated meeting point, but when you served in combat long enough . . .

Something didn't feel right.

His first thought was for Lily's safety. Damn it, what was she thinking, a young lady alone, loitering out here after dark? Even genteel Mayfair had its footpads. And worse.

If anyone dared hurt her . . .

"Lily?" He swept the inky gloom with a slow, careful glance, and only then got down off his horse, his movements cautious, watchful.

He could not see her. But he thought he heard some small noise ahead.

Bloody hell.

Either he was being insanely overprotective, or there was more than one person in that alley.

Overprotective.

That had to be it. This wasn't India.

This was civilized London, and all the world was not a war, a battle. Only in his head.

Nevertheless, his hand passed in a habitual caress across the hilt of his sword. Pistol at the ready, on the other hip. He glanced at his horse, consulting the animal's keener senses; the black stallion's ears swiveled and his nostrils flared.

With measured paces, he walked his horse forward. The slow clopping of the tall black's hoofs over the uneven cobbles of the narrow lane reverberated off the brick walls of the stables and carriage houses crowding in on both sides.

The alleyway was thick with shadows, but the sky above

was silken black, an invisible cloud cover casting a filmy veil over the crescent moon and blocking out the stars.

Gleaming green eyes in the gloom heralded the presence of a cat. A gray tabby went gliding by in furtive fashion, low to the ground and hugging the wall as it prowled for mice.

Ahead, a single rusty lantern, feebly beaming, hung from the corner of the carriage house. Lily suddenly stepped into view, her blond hair shining in its pool of light, a dark woolen cloak wrapped around her.

Derek's pulse climbed. In spite of himself, a smile broke across his face at the sight of her.

Thank God.

"There you are," he called softly in greeting, leaving his horse at the hitching post. But he looped the reins only loosely around it—just in case they had to ride out of here in a hurry. "I've been thinking just now about wringing your neck. You had me worried, girl."

She did not smile at his jest. Her expression was somber, her elegant face stark and pale beneath the lantern's golden orb. She glanced around uneasily, clutching the cloak around her shoulders.

"Are you all right?" he asked in concern, drawing off his riding gauntlets as he walked toward her.

"Derek!" she screamed a split-second before blinding pain exploded through his skull.

He pitched forward, caught himself hard on his hands and knees. Dark battle-honed instincts roared to life. Still stunned by the blow to the back of his head, he reached for his sword, but three men were piling on him, shoving him down onto the ground on his stomach and wrenching his arms up behind his back.

He thrashed ferociously.

"Greetings from India, Major," some rough voice mocked him. He heard a puff of breath as a powdery dust of ground chili peppers was blown into his eyes.

Blinded, his eyes on fire, he yelled her name in agony, but couldn't see the next punch coming. A fist from the darkness slammed into his jaw, wrenching his head to the side.

He felt around for his weapon until somebody stepped on his hand. He belted out a curse as the boot heel ground down on his knuckles.

"Lily! Answer me!" he shouted.

"Derek!"

"Take my horse and go!"

"Oh, she'll be stayin' with me, mate."

"Lundy?" His chest heaved. He shook his head, struggling to see.

In the background, he could hear Lily screaming. "Leave him alone! You said you wouldn't hurt him!"

"Lily!" he called, thrashing again.

"Don't fight them, Derek! Please don't fight!"

Her words seemed strange. They brought his situation into focus. An ambush. Lundy. He'd been lured by the perfect bait into a trap.

He had just one question. "Why?"

"As if you need to ask, you two-faced bastard."

"I don't understand," Derek ground out.

"Don't you? You never should've involved her in our business, Knight. Did you think I wouldn't find out?"

"So, it was you who took the money all along."

"Let me tell you something, you cocky bastard," Lundy growled. Derek could not see him. His eyes were two fiery holes in his head. But the nabob's voice was very near and low, and his next words stunned Derek nearly as much as the blow to the head. "Lord Sinclair told me it was all right to borrow against the fund. Just to borrow!" Lundy vowed. "It's not like I was stealin'! I've already got the means to put the money back. It's just a matter o' waitin' now, but you couldn't be patient, could you? Not you! Typical hotheaded cavalry officer! You think you're so much better than me. Well, you go back and you fight your little war, and you remember all the while that Lily's going to be with me. In my bed. Taking everything I give her."

"If you hurt her, Lundy, so help me God"

"Don't you threaten me."

Derek wrenched out a low cry, curling around the blow when Lundy kicked him in the stomach.

Again, he was unable to see any of it coming. *God damn it.* "Lily!" he screamed out, maddened by the need to hear her voice and know she was safe.

"Shut him up!"

"Derek, please, don't fight them!" Her call fell like soft cool water on his burning face.

"You listen to the little lady, Major." Bates had hold of him now, judging by the voice. "She's got good advice for ye there."

Still struggling, he was gagged with a foul cloth while two others held him down and clapped his wrists in irons.

"Get 'im in the coach," Lundy grunted. "Maguire, bring his 'orse."

Bates and Jones hauled Derek roughly to his feet. He tried to resist with sharp and angry movements, nailing one of them in the stomach with his elbow, but all it got him was a hearty punch in the gut from Bates.

Lundy's ex-prizefighter coachman nearly knocked the breath out of him. "Hard or easy, Major," Bates said evenly. "It's up to you."

The gag across his mouth muffled the obscenity with which he responded. The next thing he knew, he was thrown into a vehicle. At once, it started away.

Back at Edward's castle-house, Lily was locked in a Gothic bedchamber on the third floor to await her fate.

Meanwhile, they had imprisoned Derek in the large metal cage normally reserved for Edward's vicious fight dog. After chaining Brutus to a tree below Lily's window, Edward had ordered his men to drag the cage into the stable, the better to conceal its new occupant, their prisoner. Lily could see the stable from her bedroom window, but she had not caught another glimpse of Derek since they had arrived an hour ago.

For a while, she had paced back and forth across the eerie, dark-paneled room, pounding on the heavy wooden door for them to let her out, but nobody came. Below her window, Brutus barked incessantly, perhaps spooked by the wind, which had picked up. Gusts rattled the window panes now and then as Lily curled herself into the window seat and stared out anxiously into the pitch-black night.

She could not stop thinking about Derek. Indeed, she was half frantic with concern over his welfare. How badly was he hurt? They had hit him so many times. That first blow to the head had looked awful, but the spice powder in his eyes was their cheap way of rendering him a more manageable foe. That had to have been extremely painful.

She hoped it had worn off by now.

For as long as she lived, she would never forget those excruciating moments in that alley. She could still recall in detail the cautious way he had approached, like he had sensed something was wrong. But he had come anyway. Why? Out of concern for her?

The thought of what he had just gone through and being unable to go and check on him was driving her mad! If only there were some way to make him understand she was trying to save him, not destroy him. She had done what she'd had to do to save his life.

The ghostly reflection of her face in the window pane wore an expression of despair as she stared out toward the stable. She touched the glass, wishing there were some way she could get to him.

The flickering flames from the candelabra were superimposed over her image in the glass like golden tears, but when the window's mirrorlike reflection also showed her the huge canopied bed behind her, a frightening fortress-mound of sharp carven spires, Lily looked away.

Her skin felt ice-cold, but her heart was still numb to her fate. She had agreed to this devil's bargain because there was no other way. She had to save Derek. What other choice had she had? At her wits' end, she dragged her hand slowly through her hair. Perhaps it was best if Derek never knew . . .

The sound of shuffling movement in the hallway outside the locked door of her chamber broke into Lily's thoughts just then. She whirled around and stared at the door, her heart suddenly pounding in dread.

Edward.

The blood drained from her face. Oh, God, had the time come already to fulfill her end of the bargain?

She knew that Edward had been holed up in his office in a late-night meeting with the corrupt East India Company sea captain whom he was bribing to smuggle Derek out of England. They must have arrived at some agreement. It sounded as if their meeting was done.

Holding her torn riding habit together, Lily moved away from the window and prowled toward the center of the dimly lit chamber, prepared to meet her fate with her head held high. She was not going to hide by the wall, cringing. She was a Balfour, by God. She would not give this low brute the pleasure of seeing her cower.

Perhaps Derek's brash courage in the midst of being beaten by several men had inspired her to go down fighting. Hearing the jangle of metal as the big, awkward key plundered the lock, she did her best to force away an unnerving flash of terror over what would soon befall her.

But when the heavy door swung open with a ponderous creak, it was not Edward who appeared on the threshold.

One of his surly underlings came slouching in with a tray of horrid-looking food for her very late supper. Lightheaded with the sudden relief, Lily kept her gaze down and her arms folded tightly across her chest as she waited for her acting jailor to leave again. It occurred to her to rush past him and escape out the open door, but she didn't dare try it. If she caused trouble, they would take it out on Derek.

Even if, by some miracle, she could find a way to escape, she and Edward had a deal. She didn't dare go back on her word while Derek was still in their grasp.

So she held her ground in chilly silence, barely breathing until the burly servant was out of the room and locking her door once again from the hallway side.

She closed her eyes with a shaky exhalation. Good Lord, that was close. Well, her fate had not been averted, only postponed.

Knowing that Edward was bound to come soon, she had

no appetite for the food that had been brought to her, even less so when she lifted the tray's lid. Underneath it she found a disgusting bowl of cold, congealing pea soup with a gnarled hambone sticking out of it, a hunk of hard bread, and some watered-down wine. Curling her lip, she replaced the lid without interest and returned to the window.

Beneath the swathe of heavy velvet curtains, she sat down on the built-in window seat and stared out again toward the stable. But when her gaze moved beyond it to the sculpted grounds of Edward's estate, her thoughts drifted back to the night of the masked ball, meeting Derek for the first time at the garden folly. Under its silly pineapple roof, she had thought at first that she had wished him into being.

And now look at them.

Oh, if only I could do it all over again, she mused in a rising wave of sorrow, *I'd have gone out on the lake with him in that gondola.*

If she had known she would fall in love with him, she would have let him ruin her then and there.

Derek's makeshift jail cell was not tall enough to allow him to stand up straight, so Lundy's henchmen had provided him with an empty crate to sit on.

Once he was in the cage, they had freed his hands long enough to let him flush his eyes with water, warning him that if he misbehaved it was Lily who would pay for it, but he had no sooner blotted his face than he was manacled again.

Well aware of the threat to her, he had he stood obediently and let them do it.

Now he sat on the wooden box, leaning back against the metal slats of his cage, his legs stretched out before him, his wrists still bound behind his back.

His head was throbbing from the blow to the back of his skull, but his outward stillness concealed a brooding rage.

If anyone had hurt her, they would pay.

Derek wasn't even sure how this turn had come about. What had happened while his back was turned? Something must have set Lundy off.

He hated to think that Lily might have used the information he had confided in her last night to do something she ought not to have attempted. Something rash.

All he knew was that he had to get her out of here.

How?

Well, he'd just have to figure something out.

He had heard he was being shipped off to India, to be smuggled out of England in the cargo hold of one of the Company's many merchant ships. But these lads didn't know him very well. He was not about to go back and tell Colonel Montrose he had failed. He still had his orders: to find out what had happened to those army funds and get that damned river of gold flowing to the troops so they could beat the Maratha Empire for once and for all.

He was not about to let the likes of Ed Lundy stop him from carrying out his duty.

One step at a time. First, he would have to get rid of the shackles. This might require a bit of finesse. Lundy's three main henchmen had been ordered to guard him.

An ugly trio. He studied them through bloodshot and aching eyes. Bates was the leader; Jones was naught but a mean-eyed thug; Maguire was the youngest, about five-and-twenty. He was missing a finger, courtesy of Brutus the dog, if Derek recalled correctly from a prior—and friendlier—visit to Lundy's stable.

Having secured their prisoner, it was barely an hour before the three resorted to warding off boredom with a game of cards. They huddled around the light of the lantern that Maguire had placed in the center of their makeshift gaming table, a warped board resting atop a crate like the one they had given Derek.

From his shadowed cage, Derek studied them for a long moment, his raw stare unnoticed. The men were soon caught up in idle argument over their game.

The three of them and the cage with its keen metal lock were all that stood between Derek and his freedom, but he reflected that he had never killed an Englishman before. He had never anticipated having to use his warrior training on his fellow countrymen.

If they were smart, he thought, they would know when the time came to stand aside.

"Gentlemen, pardon me for disturbing your game. I don't believe it was your intent to kill me," he said in a rather breezy tone, "but this gash on the back of my head has not stopped bleeding even now. Might I trouble you for a length of bandage that I may bind it?"

The request and his polite tone seemed to startle them. Then Jones began laughing. "Got 'im good, didn't ye, Bates?"

"Nothin' personal, Major," Bates said with a modest chuckle. "I never 'ad nothing against ye."

"Yes, of course," Derek answered in a gentlemanly tone. "Maguire, get him a bandage and a wet cloth, too. No harm in letting the blackguard clean 'imself up. Took quite a beating, he did, and took it well."

"Yes, sir." As Maguire got up and went into the tack room, Derek stood, ducking his head under the low top of his cell. He moved to the slatted metal wall of the cage nearest the men as Maguire came back with a clean white cloth of the sort normally used for bandaging horses' legs.

"I'll wet it for 'im," Jones said wickedly, taking the cloth from Maguire. The thug went over to the nearest horse's stall, dipped the rag in the animal's water bucket, and then wrung it out with one hand.

Bates's magnanimity did not extend to stifling Jones's humor. He and Maguire both laughed at this cheeky insult as Jones brought the still-dripping cloth over to Derek.

"Are you going to unlock these shackles, or would you like to clean the wound for me, as well?" he asked mildly, unable to take the rag from the man, considering that his hands were still manacled behind his back.

Jones scoffed. "I ain't doin' it!"

"Don't look at me!" Maguire said. "I ain't touchin' 'im."

"Ah, ye both can hang, ye useless pair o' . . ." Still muttering under his breath, Bates trudged over, taking the key to Derek's manacles out of his pocket. "Turn around, you coxcomb. You try anything, we shoot you. Understood?"

"Quite."

A moment later, Derek's hands were free. He rubbed his chafed wrists a bit, thanked Bates for this favor like an agreeable captive, and accepted the cloth with its share of horse slobber mixed with water.

So far, so good.

He returned to his seat on the wooden crate, where he tended the lump on the back of his head in watchful silence until the men largely forgot about him again.

With a careful survey of his surroundings, he searched for any way out. Damn it, if his head were not thumping so badly, it might have been easier to come up with a plan.

"Awful quiet over there," Jones remarked after a while, glancing warily in his direction.

"Aye," Bates agreed, "too quiet. If you're scheming something, you may as well forget it. Unless you want another thumping."

"Or a bullet in the heart," Jones muttered as he took another swig from his bottle of whisky. "Don't care what kind of bargain your little miss made with the boss."

Derek moved forward, his gaze homing in on Jones suddenly. "What?"

Maguire began laughing. "Rather a shame, ain't it, seein' as how she's a lady and all?"

"Was," Jones corrected.

"Aye, was. Until now!" Maguire agreed.

They both started laughing, taunting him.

"Boss said he'd have her one way or another, didn't he?"

"Smart man, our Mr. Lundy."

"That's why he's rich and we ain't."

"What . . . bargain?" Derek asked again in a deeper, nigh sinister tone. The hair on the back of his neck stood on end. He could almost feel his blood beginning to curdle in his veins.

Their hilarity expanded.

"He wants to know what bargain!"

"I'll bet 'e does! Don't you worry your pretty head about it, Major Knight."

"Aye, it's only the reason you're still breathing," Jones said under his breath, flashing a dark grin.

Derek got up and went to the edge of the cage, gripping the bars. "Bates." The single word, fraught with desperation, expressed his demand for answers, but Bates hesitated.

"You might say your young Lily promised Mr. Lundy certain favors," Maguire piped up.

"It were sweet, weren't it, the way she pleaded for this blackguard's life?" Jones taunted, but Bates reached across the table and smacked him in the head.

"That's enough! Shut yer maw! He don't need to know the rest." He turned to Derek, cutting off his questions before he could ask them. "Never mind about it!" he ordered. "The little fool brought it on herself."

"Burglary's a crime, you know," Maguire chimed in. "Mr. Lundy could've turned her over to the constable."

"Burglary?" Derek looked at them as horrified understanding dawned.

"You two, not another word!" Bates ordered, pointing in his underlings' faces.

Derek was too wary of them to beg for information; it would only give them something more to use against him. But he was beginning to piece it together.

And he blamed himself.

Oh, Lily. He closed his still-stinging eyes with a thousand curses speeding through his mind. His head throbbed harder. *I will get us out of here.*

Think.

He needed to create a diversion.

He had to get out of this cage, and one of these men was going to have to be a pawn in his escape.

Longing to tear them and especially Lundy apart, somehow Derek found the self-control to approach them once again with a calm, steady demeanor. Resting his elbows on the bars of his cage, he cleared his throat. "Sure could do with a drink." He watched them with a keen stare.

"I'm not surprised, after hearing that news about your little girly friend," Jones said with a callous chuckle.

"You're a pain in the arse, you are," Bates muttered at Derek. He nodded at Jones. "Give 'im some of your whisky."

"The hell I will! Give 'im yours!"

"Do it," Bates repeated, giving Jones an icy stare. "It's proper-like. Ask the soldier." He nodded toward the cage. "An Englishman does not abuse his prisoners. We ain't savages."

Debatable, Derek mused.

Jones snorted, but seemed to recall that Derek had dedicated his life to defending the same England they called home.

Derek hid his satisfaction.

Giving Bates a disgruntled look, Jones kicked his stool away as he rose. He swiped the tin dipper that Maguire had been drinking from.

"Hey!" Maguire protested, but Jones ignored him, pouring a splash of his whisky into the cup and then slouching over to deliver this to Derek.

Derek waited calmly as Jones approached. He could feel the savagery that years of war had taught him, alive, surging in his veins. A dark power, his to use. He didn't really want to hurt the man, but if it came down to it . . .

Lily was all that mattered at the moment.

Perhaps Jones noticed the strange look in Derek's eyes, for he hesitated slightly and hung back, reaching out almost gingerly to hand him the cup.

His fears were well founded.

Derek disregarded the cup and grasped Jones's forearm, yanking him forward so he smashed his face on the bars and let out a bellow. Derek spun Jones about-face and with a wrench of the man's shoulder pulled his arm high behind his back. He thrust his left hand through the bars, catching Jones about the throat in a choking headlock.

"Unlock the cage if you want him to live."

It happened so fast that Bates spit out his mouthful of whisky while Jones flailed in astonishment, and Maguire stared, slack-jawed.

"*Do it!*" Derek roared. They didn't move fast enough.

"You want to see me break his neck?" He began to squeeze, and Jones's face started turning scarlet, strange choking sounds tumbling from his lips.

Jones's one free hand scrabbled at the arm around his throat, but Derek ignored his struggles, only applying more pressure. "You let me out or I'll kill him."

"Why, you damned colonial." Bates shot to his feet and reached for the nearby pitchfork. "You let him go or I'll skewer you." Bates angled the pitchfork through the slats and stabbed at Derek with it.

Derek arced his body out of the way, but when Bates took another vicious jab at him, trying to poke him full of holes, he had no choice but to release his hostage, grabbing the handle of the pitchfork instead. He wrenched it out of Bates's hands and pulled it into the cage. In the next instant he had spun it around, prepared to use it as a weapon, but Jones, now freed, wanted his blood.

Jones marched over to his cast-off coat and pulled a horse pistol out of the pocket. "You're a corpse, you bastard," he said in a garbled tone, still rubbing his throat, panting.

When Derek saw Jones load a powder slug into the muzzle, he knew he had only seconds to react.

Angling the pitchfork through the bars of his cage just as Jones raised the pistol, Derek gripped the pitchfork like Poseidon's trident and hurled it as best he could from his cramped, bent position.

The pitchfork sailed; his aim was true.

Jones's gun went off as he threw himself out of the pitchfork's path. His shot flew high, dinging off the metal bars, but as he fell, he stumbled over their makeshift gaming table. The board tilted on impact, hurling the contents of their table into the air.

The light playing cards fluttered down in a colorful shower, but the oil lantern and two open bottles of whisky catapulted three or four yards through the stable and landed in a tall, round pile of loose dry hay.

Maguire cursed in astonishment as the haystack burst into flames.

* * *

Inside the dim Gothic chamber, Lily lifted her tear-stained face from her arm when she heard the commotion below. She had lain down in the small cubbyhole of the window nook and must have drifted off. She barely noticed the smell of smoke at first. But then a new set of sounds besides the incessant barking of Edward's vicious dog gradually invaded her awareness. Yells and animal screams from the darkness outside. *What the deuce—?*

Rallying herself from her despair, she pushed up to a seated position and peered through the glass.

At once, her eyes widened at the scene of mayhem below. The stable was on fire!

Smoke was pouring out of the horses' stall windows and in one spot, flames had begun shooting through the roof. Horses were running free, careening in all directions in terror of the blaze.

Edward's men were working frantically with cloths pressed over their nostrils and mouths. Some plunged back into the burning stable to rescue more of their master's horses, while others rushed about with buckets of water, trying to put out the blaze. Their efforts were pitiful compared to the ferocity of the fire.

With one awestruck look, she was sure that Edward's fine stable was going to burn to the ground, but only one question screamed through her mind.

Where is Derek?

Lily did not see him.

As she pushed the window open, her gaze probed the clouds of drifting smoke.

Where could he be? Dear God. She gripped the windowsill. *What if he's still inside there?*

Something deeper than logic assured her that this was the case, and in a heartbeat, she knew she had to help him.

At once, she was on her feet. She flew across the room and fought against the heavy locked door, pounding her fists on it, shouting for any servant within earshot to let her out.

Nobody came.

Enraged at her situation, she gave up this futile aim and marched back to the window, knowing she'd have to take matters into her own hands.

It was a long way down, with a vicious dog waiting at the bottom, but as she leaned as far out the window as she dared, surveying her prospects, she spotted an ivy trellis a few feet to her right. If she could inch her way over to it, it could serve as a ladder that she could climb down—but then, what to do about the dog?

Now it was clear to see why Edward had ordered the dog tied there—to prevent her from even trying to escape.

Should she risk it?

Brutus would tear her apart before she set foot on the ground. *Ah!* With a swift glance over her shoulder, she recalled the tray of food the servant had brought up.

When she threw the lid aside, she found the food looking even more disgusting than before, clotted and cold. On the other hand, the fight dog was probably not a picky eater. Grimacing a little, she plucked the greasy, dripping hambone out of the soup bowl, shaking clumps of pea soup off it.

Then she went back over to the window, certain that this was madness. At the same time, she knew she had to act. When another glance in the direction of the stable failed to reveal any sign of Derek, she knew in her soul that if she didn't help him, nobody would. They were not going to risk their lives to save a man they had wanted dead in the first place.

Her mind made up, heart slamming in her chest at the recklessness of her mission, Lily tucked the slimy hambone into her torn bodice with a grimace and set out for her descent down the steep wall of Edward's mansion.

Crouching on the window seat, she climbed gingerly out the window. Turning by degrees until her back was pressed to the exterior wall, she slowly traversed the narrow platform of decorative masonry, feeling her way along with each agonizingly slow sideward step. A brief glance down made her dizzy.

She prayed hard not to slip. By the time she gained the top of the trellis, her knees felt wobbly and her palms were slick with sweat. It didn't make the climbing easy, especially with a greasy hambone shoved down her dress!

"Ow," she muttered when she pricked herself on a rose's thorn on her way down the wooden latticework.

Brutus suddenly noticed her coming.

Chain links jangled below as the dog lost interest in the crazed horses rushing free about the grounds and trotted over to the wall, where he began barking anew.

Lily whimpered as the dog leaped up at her, his powerful jaws snapping shut on thin air mere inches under her feet. How was she to go down there when this monster was already trying to eat her?

She shrieked when Brutus's next attempt succeeded in tearing the long, graceful train of her riding habit. She held on tight to the trellis as the dog fell to earth again with a mouthful of fabric.

Hanging onto the trellis for dear life, she called to the dog in what she hoped sounded like a friendly tone. She slid the disgusting hambone out of her bodice and waved it toward the dog, making sure the black beast saw it.

Brutus stopped barking long enough to sniff the air.

With a frightened glance over her shoulder, Lily calculated exactly where to throw it—as far as the dog's chain would reach in the opposite direction from where she needed to go.

Provided the monster took the bait at all, she'd probably have only seconds to jump down and escape the circumference of his leash.

What if the chain that held him broke? What would stop him then? Nothing, she realized. If that happened, then she was dead. A bad way to go, too. But it wasn't as bad as burning alive.

Derek. She had to think of Derek. She knew he was waiting. She could feel him in her heart. Every second counted now.

With one last terrified glance toward the stable, she held

out the bone, making sure she had the fight dog's attention. "B-Brutus! Here, boy! Look at this! This is for you! Yes! Easy now. There's a good boy!"

The dog made another high vertical leap, but this time Brutus was aiming for the hambone rather than her.

"Good boy—go fetch!"

She hurled the bone.

The chain links clanked as Brutus raced after it.

With barely a glance, she jumped off the trellis, landed in a knee-jarring fall on the grass, picked herself up, and raced toward the stable. Instinctual dread cut off her breath at the sound of chain links rushing after her.

She stumbled, tripping on the torn hem of her skirts, and rolled ahead just to keep moving.

An ear-splitting bark rushed at her like a cannonball.

When she looked up through the tangle of her hair, she was on eye level with the dog. Brutus was almost upon her. He was coming straight at her, his slavering jaws wide. He seemed to think he was in the dogfight pit.

But a sudden jolt to his collar stopped Brutus cold. The chain pulled taut as the dog reached the end of his tether; his killer jaws slammed shut mere inches from Lily's face.

The chain held.

Slowly, still terrified, she backed away.

Good Lord, how could I ever have thought about marrying a man who would keep such a pet?

As it sank in that she was still alive, that Brutus had not eaten her, Lily shoved herself to her feet and kept running toward the stables.

No one paid her any mind until she neared the burning entrance. Already she could feel the radiating heat from the towering flames. The thick smoke invaded her nostrils.

She could hear Edward's booming voice before she spotted him. From behind the screen of billowing smoke, he sounded panicked. "Capture those horses before they run away! I'll have your heads for this!" Through the shifting smoke, she caught a glimpse of him. He was pacing back and forth, his hands clapped to his head.

He stopped again to scream at his henchmen. "Put the water on there. There!" He pointed frantically to a section of the wall that had flames shooting out. "Faster, you useless bastards!"

Lily wanted at all costs to avoid him, but she would have to pass him to get into the stable. She pressed on, hoping to sneak past him, but suddenly, in the chaos, they nearly collided.

Edward stepped out of a billow of acrid smoke and grabbed her arm with a snarl every bit as vicious as his dog's. "What are you doing out of your room?"

"Let go of me! Where's Derek?"

"In Hell, for all I care!"

"He's still in there, isn't he?"

"Forget about him!"

Lily struggled to shake off his grasp. "Let me get him out!"

"He deserves to burn! Look at what he's done to me!" Edward flung a furious gesture at the stable.

"I'm not going to let you kill him."

"Hold still, damn you!"

There wasn't time to fight—and with Derek's life at stake, there certainly wasn't time to fight honorably. Lily drew back and kicked Edward in the groin as hard as she could.

He let go of her arm with a garbled roar, dropping to his knees and hunching over his nether regions. Lily pulled free and ran into the burning stable.

Another newly freed horse came charging out of the smoke, nearly trampling her in the middle of the stable's main aisle, but Lily dodged out of the way. Then she moved on, using her sleeve to try to filter the air, veiling her nose and mouth from the choking smoke as best she could.

"Derek! *Derek!*" She screamed his name repeatedly. She could only see a few feet ahead through the smoke and was already perspiring in the radiating heat. "Derek! Where are you? Can you hear me?"

Then, over the crackle and hiss of the fire, she noticed a

rhythmic banging sound deeper in the stable—a powerful clash of metal banging.

Derek.

Thank God he was conscious—and fighting like hell to kick out the door to his cage, by the sound of it.

"Derek, I'm coming!"

"Lily?" The banging stopped. She heard the sound of coughing. "Lily!"

As she pushed on deeper into the burning stable, she could start to make out the square silhouette of the cage in the middle of the aisle ahead. Fury poured through her for what they had done to him, but she forged on, absolutely determined to get him out.

She spotted a moving shape in the smoke ahead, down near the floor. Through the haze of gray smoke, the picture came clearer with her every step. He had paused in his assault on the cage's door and had crouched down low to catch a few breaths of the better air nearer the ground.

"Lily!" He straightened up as best he could in the too-short cage as she ran to him, closing the distance between them.

Behind the grid of the cage's bars, he looked appalled to see her. "What are you doing in here?"

"Rescuing you!"

"You've got to get out!"

"Not without you!"

"It's too dangerous! Watch—the bars are hot," he warned as she started to reach toward him. His chiseled face was drenched in sweat as he searched her eyes fiercely, his own red-rimmed. "Look up. Lily—the ceiling's on fire. Any second now, the roof is going to cave in. I want you out of here. Now."

She ignored him, glancing around. "I don't suppose they left the key?"

He shook his head. "No. Sweetheart," he said in a softer tone, stopping her. She was astonished by how calm he was. He swallowed hard. "There may be no way out of this for me. You need to go."

"No," she uttered, shaking her head. "No."

"Please." He reached carefully through the bars and touched her hand. "Just save yourself—"

"No!" she repeated more forcefully. "I'm going to get you out of here! I'm going to prove to you that I didn't lure you to that ambush to betray you—"

"I would never think that. I knew it wasn't your fault."

"You did?"

"Of course, right away. Now listen to me. You need to go."

"I will not leave you—"

"Lily," he whispered, staring at her, "I love you."

She drew in her breath and turned to him in amazement. "Derek." Tears rose in her eyes. She reached her hand carefully through the bars and took his hand. "I love you, too."

New resolve flooded her as she stared at him. By God, she was not going to let the man she loved die while there was breath left in her body—especially not like this. It was too unfair. He had not survived so many battles to die here, trapped like an animal.

"I am not going to let this happen to you," she ground out so fiercely that he looked startled.

Clenching her jaw, she pulled away from him and ran into the smoke, infused with wild new courage.

"Lily, look out!"

She glanced up at Derek's warning, her gaze homing in on a burning beam overhead. She leaped out of the way just as it came crashing down.

"Are you all right?" Derek called in a shaky tone.

Her pulse pounding, Lily nodded. "Fine!" She knew she had to think of something fast. The stable was coming down around them. Time was running out. "Keep working on the door, all right?"

"I'm not sure there's any point." When she glanced over at him, Derek held her gaze with a soulful stare. "Please—"

"Don't even tell me to go!" she retorted before he could give the intolerable order. "Whatever happens," she vowed, "I am not leaving you."

She knew what it was like to be left behind when you

needed someone the most. With that, she rushed into the billow of smoke ahead . . .

And came back a moment later wielding a long-handled shovel that she had found lying amid the rubble.

"Good!" Derek exclaimed, coughing, waving her over. "Give it to me and get the hell out of here."

Lily marched back to the door of the cage and just looked at him. "Stand aside!"

"Lily—"

Crash!

"Jesus," Derek muttered, backing up a bit.

Swinging the long-handled shovel again with all her strength, she bashed the metal edge of it against the cage door.

The door jumped, but the lock still held.

She banged it again.

Derek watched her in grim silence, no longer protesting. Perhaps he realized that he wouldn't have been able to get a good arc with it anyway inside the small, constricted space. But he was probably praying as hard as she was.

Lily struck the locked door of the cage again and again— harder, faster, more furiously—and still it held, until she let out a scream of sheer fury and blasted it one more time with all she had left.

The metal hinges gave way with a groan.

She threw the shovel aside as Derek kicked the door open and rushed out into her arms.

"Let's get out of here," he murmured. Lily nodded as she realized she was shaking. Holding onto each other, they started toward the stable's main exit, but the way was blocked. Derek glanced around, his eyes narrowed against the smoke.

She still could not believe how calm he was, but then, with his vocation, he was probably quite used to smoke-filled scenes of chaos and destruction.

"There." He pointed through the smoke. The blaze had not yet reached the last stall in the aisle, emptied like all the rest now that the horses had been rescued.

The open window offered them their best and probably last hope of escape.

Racing through the stable, they ran to the end box stall. Derek threw the door open. They sped across the hay-strewn floor to the horse's window. Then he lifted her easily up onto the broad window sill.

Lily jumped down onto the grass just a few feet below. Derek was right behind her, leaping out of the window, grabbing her hand.

With the whole of Edward's property in chaos behind them, they fled into the darkness.

CHAPTER
∞ SEVENTEEN ∞

"*T*hey're shooting at us!" Lily cried, glancing over her shoulder when a mighty cracking sound ripped through the night.

"Get down!" Derek shielded her with his body as they continued running across the manicured grounds of Edward's estate. "Keep going. We should be out of range soon."

Hunching down a little, they pressed on, racing toward the high wrought-iron fence that girded Edward's property.

Edward's fine horses were careening around the park, zigzagging this way and that, some of them bunched into a loose herd, others following their own paths. Not far ahead, a ghostly gray leaped over a clump of azaleas and galloped on.

"I could catch one of these horses to get us out of here," he murmured.

"No need; the sorrel mare is tethered in the woods. Besides, there's a fence."

"All right. Come on, sweet," he urged her as Lily coughed, her lungs still aching from the smoke.

When another clipped report rang out, the top ball of a boxwood topiary near them burst into a shower of leaves.

"Climb!" he ordered, cupping his hands to give her a leg up as they reached the wrought-iron fence.

Wasting no time, she stepped into the makeshift stirrup of his hands and grasped the bars, pulling herself up. Gingerly scaling it, she made sure her long skirts weren't hooked on the blunt spikes that lined the top of the fence before landing none too gracefully on the other side.

"You wouldn't have brought a water canteen, would you?" Derek asked as he climbed over the fence as smoothly as though he did this sort of thing every day.

"Afraid not," she murmured, watching him in wonder as he jumped down with the stealthy grace of a big cat. "You must be parched."

"I'll live. Let's find your horse."

"This way, I think . . ."

They hurried through the woods by the side of the road. In the darkness, along with her memory being somewhat blurred by the wild events of this day, it was hard to remember exactly where she had tethered Mary Nonesuch.

Derek stalked beside her in patient silence. Now and then he called softly to his former patient. Lily could feel the protectiveness fairly emanating from him.

"There she is," Derek said suddenly, pointing to a large shadow among the trees.

They rushed over to the docile mare. Though she had pulled free of her tether, she hadn't gone far. The placid horse whickered and came toward them.

Derek tightened the girth and lifted Lily into the saddle. "Now, go."

"What?"

"She's not strong enough to carry us both very far."

"Yes, she is!"

"Don't argue with me. Ride on. They're going to come after you, and I'm going to stay here and stop them. Go to Gabriel—"

"No! I came too close to losing you already. Come with me. Damn it, Derek, you're hurt, you're unarmed, and you're ridiculously outnumbered—"

"Lily, I can—"

"I know you can! But I don't want you to. You have nothing to prove to me! I just want you with me. Please, Derek. I can't lose you."

He glanced at the sky, the moonlight silvering the elegant

line of his throat. "Lily, if he forced himself on you, he's got to die—"

"No. It didn't happen."

Slowly, he leveled a piercing gaze on her face. "Are you telling me the truth?"

"Yes." She admitted in a shaky tone, "He pushed me around a bit and made some threats, but I got out of there before anything worse happened. Derek, please. You have to come with me or I shall go mad. We've got to get out of here—together."

He looked at her in exasperation. "We're not going to get very far together, Lily. The horse is too weak."

"Then we'll get as far away as she can manage to take us and hide. Give her a chance, Derek. She's stronger than you know. She might just surprise you. Now, for heaven's sake, I saved your bloody life—get on this horse!"

He gave her a sardonic look, then shrugged off his protests and relented, springing up onto the mare's back behind her. Reaching around Lily, he took the reins with one arm hooked around her waist, holding her securely. Wasting no more time, he urged the mare on quickly through the woods until they came out onto the road.

"Come on, girl. Let's just hope you're faster than you look." He nudged Mary Nonesuch into a swift canter, and they were off, sweeping down the country lane.

The sorrel mare seemed to sense their desperation, and, as if ignoring the still-healing sores on her back, she strove heroically to give them all she could, stretching out her canter to an all-out gallop through the darkness.

Frankly, Lily was more worried about Derek. "How's your head? Your eyes?"

His answer was a noncommittal grunt. "So, you thought you'd break into Lundy's office," he said in soft, terse displeasure by her ear. "Not one of your better ideas, darling."

"Well, I know that now, don't I? But before you scold me, I learned a few things that you'll want to know."

"Like what?"

"Mainly, that you were right. Edward's in deep financial trouble—and I discovered why. He speculated away three hundred thousand pounds in some canal-building scheme."

"Canals?" he echoed, mulling this. "Well done, Lily."

"There's more. Mrs. Lundy did not go to Jamaica for her gout. I found a cryptic letter from her in Edward's office that hinted at some sort of trouble with his plantations there."

"The plantations. Of course." Derek paused. "Lundy must be selling them. You see, once he thought he had me down, he admitted he took the money. But he claimed he had already taken measures to replace what he had 'borrowed.' Sending his mother off to sell his plantations quickly and quietly would have been a good start at replacing the sum."

"It would certainly draw less attention than if he began selling off his properties here. Everyone would soon know he was in dun territory, and then whatever social rank he'd gained would have been lost."

"Don't forget, he also had changed his marriage plans, choosing Bess Kingsley and her dowry over you."

"Right," Lily answered grimly.

"He was selling off some jewelry, too," Derek murmured. "Probably hoping he could keep himself afloat until his mother came back and his marriage went through. Thus the wild-goose chase he sent me on."

"Hm?"

Derek snorted in disgust. "He kept trying to point me toward every man on the committee other than himself."

"Well, that fire at the stable will have been his undoing," Lily said. "I saw him back there. He kept groaning he was ruined."

"Then that means he's at his most dangerous right now," Derek murmured. "His back is to the wall. He's got nothing left to lose."

"God, you could have died." Leaning back against him a little, she reached up and touched his face. "I'm so glad you're all right."

"Thanks to you." He kissed her fingers as she caressed him. "I can't believe you saved my life," he whispered.

"I'm just happy I succeeded."

"You were astoundingly brave in that stable tonight, do you know that?"

She smiled.

He kissed her cheek as they rode on. "I meant what I said back there, Lily," he whispered. "I love you."

She rested her head against his cheek, nestling against him. "I love you, too. And I know you meant it. You always say exactly what you mean, don't you?"

"Afraid so."

"It's one of your loveliest qualities."

"Then in that case, you won't mind my asking why you smell like ham?"

She let out a wry snort. "Never you mind it, you rogue! It's the price I had to pay to save your hide."

"Oh, I don't mind. It just gives me one more reason to want to eat you."

"You are such a nasty man."

"It's one of my 'loveliest' qualities." With a wicked laugh, he urged their flagging horse on. "Come on, girl. No slowing down yet."

"Keep going, Mary. We need you."

"She can't keep up this pace much longer. We have to get off the road now," Derek said. His voice turned grim. "They're coming."

"Can you see them?" Lily asked with a fresh wave of fear, craning her neck for an anxious look behind them.

"No, but Mary can hear them," Derek answered, nodding at the horse's ears. Lily marveled at his ability to read the animal's subtlest cues, but then, he was used to relying on a horse to save his life in all of those cavalry charges. "Hold on."

Derek pulled on the reins, letting their blowing mount slow to a bumpy trot. Turning the horse off the road, he urged the animal down the embankment and into the cover of the trees.

Lily did not know whose property they were on, but for

several moments more, Derek guided Mary Nonesuch through the rolling countryside, moonlit meadows interspersed with thickly shadowed groves.

Derek hurried the mare over the next rise, then, a few hundred yards from the road, they sought cover in amongst a stand of trees. Derek slipped down from the saddle and beckoned to Lily to crouch lower over the mare's withers. He went forward to hold the bridle and keep their horse quiet and still.

Holding her breath, Lily waited, watching the road. She was nervous, but Derek's nearness made her feel safe. He reached over and laid a comforting hand atop hers as Edward's men came thundering into view on the section of road that they had just evacuated.

There were four of them, racing closer, coming around the bend. But while Derek and Lily watched in tense silence from their little grove, the brutes never paused.

Instead, they went barreling on toward Town, kicking up a great cloud of dust in their wake.

Lily did not exhale until Edward's henchmen were well out of sight. *That was too close.*

Derek was also silent as he watched them pass. He waited a couple of moments more, making sure they showed no signs of coming back. At length, he turned to her with a rueful smile.

"I think we're in the clear." Releasing the horse's bridle, he approached her. "I think we could all three do with a bit of a respite before we move on?"

As Lily nodded in fervent agreement, a raucous flurry of quacking reached them from the wooded area across the field. They both turned to look, then exchanged a puzzled glance.

"That sounded like a duck," Lily said.

"Ducks mean water," Derek answered with a wily smile. "Come on."

Lily jumped down off the horse and walked beside him as they left the grove and crossed the moonlit field. Derek glanced back at the road, but there was nobody on it. Lily was glad to put more distance between it and them. The farther they could get away from Edward's men, the better.

He was right, she thought. They could both use a break to sit and rest a little, hopefully find some water to drink after that torturous fire, and regroup before figuring out their next move.

With the trusty Mary Nonesuch between them, they walked up a gentle rise, and when they went down the other side of it, they could no longer see the road at all. It was now perhaps a quarter-mile behind them.

Before long, they entered cautiously into the woods. Lily took Derek's hand, letting him lead her through the darkness. Overhead the swaying branches creaked, but in moments, they came to a clearing.

"Those are ducks, all right," Derek murmured.

Lily and he exchanged a fond smile, and then both paused, staring at the huge, tranquil lake before them.

A large, disgruntled clan of ducks was indeed in residence, trying to bed down for the night among the clumps of pussy willows around the grassy banks, only they couldn't stop bickering long enough to settle down.

Farther out on the water, however, all was serene. Starlight sparkled on its dark, glassy surface, beckoning to them. After the ordeal of smoke and flames, the cool lake looked like heaven.

"Have you ever seen anything more beautiful than that?" Lily whispered, watching the ripples passing over the shimmering water, driven on by the playful night breeze.

"Yes."

When she glanced over at Derek, he was gazing at her.

She smiled at him with a blush rising in her cheeks.

He smiled back. But the lake was more temptation than Derek could resist after nearly being roasted alive.

He let go of her hand, stepped back, and pulled his shirt off over his head. "I'm going in," he announced with great gusto.

"Oh!" Lily blurted out, blinking at the dazzling sight of

his magnificent body, each sculpted ridge of muscle kissed by moonlight.

"You're coming with me," he informed her, then gave her a wink and strode ahead.

"I—" Lily started to point out it was improper, but then she recalled her hesitation on the night of the masked ball.

She had refused him then when he had asked her to go out on the lake with him in a gondola and take a moonlight swim. *Naked,* as he had so roguishly specified at the time.

But she was no longer that woman, that tense, frightened creature in a cage.

Knowing him had changed her. Because of him, she no longer had to hide.

Fate had given her another chance, and this time she refused to waste it.

"Well?" Derek prompted from the water's edge, where he stood on one foot to pull off a boot.

She flashed a cheeky grin. "Well, yourself, Major." With that, she pulled away the last ribbon holding up her hair; she shook out her tresses as they tumbled free around her shoulders and strutted past him toward the water, starting to take off her dress.

He watched her go by, his mouth agape, then he let out a wicked *"Yes!"*

She shot him a sparkling glance over her shoulder as she bared it.

He was watching her in amazement, his rapt gaze trailing eagerly down her body. Lily thrilled to the desire in his stare, but as she looked toward the water again, she realized exactly where all of this was headed . . . and she remembered the secret she had sworn she'd never tell.

She stopped, both hands still holding onto her torn bodice.

Her former scheme to lie to Edward about her lack of innocence was one thing, but this was Derek. She longed for total union with him; she felt so close to him right now after all they had just been through. And she trusted him.

Hopefully not in vain.

She knew then that the moment of truth had arrived. She wished she could deny it. Surely this was not the time to burden him with something so dire after he had nearly been burned alive. But they could not be one until she had confessed her terrible secret. And they had to be.

They both craved completion in each other's arms.

There was no way around this. She loved him and respected him too much even to try to deceive him.

But dear Lord, what was he going to say?

She did not know, but somehow she summoned up all her stoic Balfour resolve.

If he could not love her because of this, it was best to know it now. If he was going to reject her for her fall from grace, she would just as soon keep her clothes on and retrieve whatever broken pieces of her heart were left after he shattered it.

Facing the lake, her back was to Derek, but she could still feel him watching her.

"What's wrong, beauty?"

She said nothing for a moment, closing her eyes. *Dear God,* she prayed, *please don't let him hate me.* Oh, this was much more terrifying than rushing into any burning stable.

"Lily?" He had walked over to her and now laid his hand gently on her shoulder, turning her to him. "Darling, what's wrong?"

She looked at him and found herself awed anew by his wild male beauty. His long, tangled hair was blue-black in the indigo night; silver shadows sculpted his angular face and stone-carved body. His pale eyes gleamed in the moonlight. She touched him in helpless wonder, running her fingers down his smooth, gorgeous chest.

I want you so much.

"What is it?" he whispered, gazing at her in concern.

"Oh, Derek," she breathed, then shook her head, casting about for her courage. "There's something that I have to tell you, but I . . . I don't know how."

He captured her hand where it rested on his solar plexus and lifted it to his lips. "Lily, I love you. You can tell me anything. Whatever it is, I'm here for you."

She stared at him with a wince of uncertainty, and then lowered her lashes. "Very well."

He studied her, waiting.

Lily squared her shoulders. "Edward wasn't the only one who was duped by a fraud. I was, too, when I was just fifteen. He said he loved me, and I believed him." She braced herself and said quietly, "I am not a virgin, Derek."

He was perfectly still.

"That is why I chose a man like Edward," she forged on in a shaky tone. "I knew I could trick someone like him. Lie to someone like him. But not to you. I love you so much." Without warning, tears misted her eyes. "I have so much respect for you, Derek. I only wish I was worthy of your respect, in turn—"

Her words were cut off as he pulled her into his arms and hugged her. He cupped her head under the crook of his chin, and his whispered words were fierce. "I have *always* respected you, but never so much as right now."

Tears flooded her eyes as she wrapped her arms around his waist and held on tight. "I don't want to lose you."

"You're not going to."

"If this changes how you feel toward me, I'll understand—"

"It doesn't change a thing." He captured her face between his hands and tilted her head back to meet his intense stare. "I would still die for you."

She looked into his eyes and sobbed once, most ungracefully.

"Shh," he whispered, pulling her close again.

She shed her tears against his warm chest while he held her in tender silence, petting her head to comfort her. But she could feel him brooding on her confession.

"Who hurt you, Lily?" he murmured at length. "Tell me his name."

She glanced up at him warily. "Why?"

"So I can do what must be done." The peculiar tone of his voice sent chills down her spine—a calm, soothing surface with an undertone of cold murder.

She pulled back. "That was not the point of my telling you."

"If this bastard hurt you, he needs to pay."

"Grandfather already dealt with him."

"An old man?" he cried angrily.

Lily flinched.

"Sorry," he amended, restraining his fury with visible effort. "How?"

"He made him leave England and told him that if he ever came back, he'd be killed. He fled to the Continent—where he's probably seducing young Italian girls right now like he did me."

"I would not have left him alive. Didn't anyone insist he marry you?"

Lily swallowed hard, remembering her heartbreak at the news. She had been so thoroughly deceived. "He already had a wife, as it turned out. And two babies."

Derek cursed under his breath.

"Grandfather spared his life for their sake."

"Why?" he bit out. "Because he saw what growing up without a father did to you?"

Lily looked at him imploringly.

His answering stare gentled; he must have realized how much his anger was upsetting her. When he spoke again, he had chased the edge of bitterness from his voice. "If you don't wish to reveal his name, at least tell me what manner of man he was—what manner of man with a wife and children goes out and seduces a fifteen-year-old girl?"

When he put it like that, Lily suddenly wondered what she was protecting Owen for. The strength in her balled up like a fist in her middle. *You're right.*

"His name was Lord Owen Masters." She turned to Derek. "He was twenty-six, the younger brother of a marquess. He was visiting one of the local gentry in our village. That's how he first saw me. I was sitting up in a tree reading a book." She paused, allowing herself to remember.

Where shame had been before, now suddenly there was grief. But Derek's nearness steadied her.

"He thought my reading a book up in a tree was very amusing and struck up a conversation." She shook her head. "I had never been outside my village before. What did I know of highborn London rakehells and their charms?"

"No wonder you despise their breed."

"He told me I was pretty. He came up into the tree with me."

"Like a snake," he muttered.

"Yes. He asked about my book and then he wanted to know everything about me."

"I'm going to kill him," Derek said amiably.

"Oh, Derek, he was vile, but I'm the one who was stupid and gullible and naïve."

"You were a little girl! Surely you don't blame yourself?"

"Of course I do, as well I should."

"I don't believe my ears."

She stared at him. "I let him have his way. Not once, but twice before my mother discovered the affair."

"Did you even understand what he was doing?"

She just looked at him. "N-no, but if it wasn't my fault," she said haltingly, "then why would my mother have screamed at me so much and threatened to throw me out on the street?"

"Oh, darling," he whispered, moving closer. "I see why your grandfather left you Balfour Manor." He shook his head. "Lily, your mother's reaction was hugely wrong. You mustn't believe her." His eyes narrowed with a brooding look. "I've seen men like this. I've gone to school with them, I've served with them. Whoever he was, this man singled you out because your father wasn't around to protect you."

"No." She flinched and looked away as though he had struck her. "Please don't say that, Derek."

"Why? It's true and I think you know that."

"You can't blame my father, it's *my* fault!" she wrenched out.

"No." He gazed into her eyes. "It's the man's fault, and your parents'."

She shook her head.

"You were innocent," he said softly. "You were just a girl. I know how frightening it must be to realize that. That there truly are vicious people out there in the world, people with no conscience who would do such a thing. And to be made a victim of something beyond your control that is terrible."

Lily wept softly until he wiped her tears away.

"But you've got me now," Derek told her in a harder tone. "And if anyone ever tries to hurt you again, they're going to have to get through me first."

Lily trembled as she gazed at him, longing to believe. "You're going to kill half the world for me, eh?"

"If they annoy you, yes."

"My soldier."

"Actually, I'm interested in a new career." He cupped her cheek.

"Oh?" she whispered unsteadily. "In what field?"

"This one will do," he replied with a glance around at the moonlit meadow around them. "Whatever keeps me close to you."

She pulled back a bit and looked at him uncertainly. "I thought you were going back to India."

"Change of plans."

"Since when?"

"Since now."

"Do you mean it?"

"Do I look like I'm joking?"

Her heart quaked. "Maybe you should think about this. Take a day or two and—"

"What is there to think about? Did you stop and think before you rushed into that burning stable to save my life? Or when you gave up your most prized possessions to keep me out of Newgate? No, Lily. My mind is made up. I may not be a rich man, but everything I have is yours, and if I have to pick up a hammer myself to fix your damned roof, I'll do it. I'm yours—" He bowed his head. "If you'll have me."

She stared at him in wonder. "Are you saying . . . ?"

"Marry me. I know we can make it all work out, as long as we're together."

"*Oh, Derek.*" She flew into his embrace and pulled him down to kiss him with pure joy. "I love you."

"I love you, Lily." His arms wrapped around her waist and he lifted her off her feet a little. "Thank you for trusting me with your confidence."

"Thank you for being worthy of it." She kissed him again. "You taste like smoke."

"You taste like smoked ham."

"Disgusting."

"I don't care." He laughed.

"Just kiss me."

She did.

"You know," he drawled after a long moment, "for our honeymoon, dear, I have always wanted to see Italy."

"Derek!" She couldn't help laughing through her tears as she tilted her head back and looked at him, shaking her head. How Grandfather would have loved him!

"Hm?" he asked, gazing down at her with an innocent lift of his eyebrows.

"Oh, nothing, you impossible creature," she murmured. "More kisses, please."

He smiled and obeyed.

"*Mmm,* Derek," she purred after a moment, plucking at the waistband of his trousers. "We've got to do something about all these clothes."

He nodded, gazing at her with a ravenous smile. "Agreed. Time to go for a swim?"

"Oh, yes. I think so."

Exchanging another eager kiss, they stripped with speedy efficiency, watching each other like hungry diners waiting for the chef to quit explaining his delectable creations so they could indulge. Lily freed her arms from the tailored sleeves of her torn bodice. Her fingers trembling with anticipation, she unfastened the side buttons at her waist.

Derek had a head start on her, already rid of his shirt and boots. He peeled off his snug breeches and flung them aside. Staring avidly, she watched him rid himself of his short drawers. He slid her an impossibly seductive smile as he turned away, and then walked in all his naked glory into the water.

Lily watched him, wide-eyed.

Heart racing, she hurried to follow him, fighting her way free of the intricate lacing of her stays. At last, she let her riding habit fall away and stepped out of its pooled fabric at her feet.

Ahead of her, Derek waded into the water, testing its depth. Then he dove forward, disappearing with a splash. He came up for air a few seconds later with an "ah" of manly relish.

"How is it?"

"Blissful." He flung his head back, smoothing his hair out of his face with both hands.

Lily marveled at his biceps.

He cupped his hands and drank a few swallows of the water to relieve his thirst, and then splashed at her.

She grinned.

"I'm *waaaiting*," he called softly.

"Coming!" As she lifted her chemise off over her head and paused to drop it into the pile of her discarded clothing, she heard the low, almost pained exclamation that escaped his lips at the sight of her nude body, though she did not know the word he had uttered or even what language.

She glanced at him. He was standing in waist-deep water in the moonlight, his stare devouring her. Dressed in nothing but her diamond earrings, Lily tucked a lock of her hair shyly behind her ear and slowly walked toward him. She could not believe she was standing outside in nature totally naked.

Scandalous!

Wonderful.

Never before had she felt so free, with nothing left to hide. All her skin tingled with heightened sensitivity. She could even feel the zephyr's softest current whispering past her sides.

He moved forward, the silvered water rippling around him as he came toward her, offering a gallant hand to assist her down the gentle slope into the lake. Smiling wide, she trod carefully over squishy mud and slippery stones.

"There you are," he murmured.

The water was cold, but after the fire had nearly melted them, it felt glorious. Lily laughed.

The next thing she knew, she had dunked herself under the surface and came up breathless and exultant. It was like washing the past away with all its hurt and shame, becoming fresh and clean and new.

Derek flicked water at her and Lily in turn duly splashed him. "Excuse me, I saved your life and this is my thanks?" she scolded.

He laughed. "Come on, I'll take you for a ride." He pulled her toward him through the water. She clasped her hands around his neck as he indicated, and then he swam, Lily floating along over his back.

"My sea horse," she whispered in his ear.

"Down we go."

She held her breath and hung on tight; his powerful strokes sent them gliding through the water's silent world, trailing bubbles. When they came up for air, she let go of him, treading water across from him. "Can you touch the bottom here?"

"Yes." He stood firmly. The water was up to the middle of his chest. "Come here. I'll hold you."

It was an invitation she was happy to accept. She smiled and swam over to him. He gathered her into his embrace. Lily lay back luxuriously across his arms, buoyant on the water, her hair floating around them like pale seaweed.

His eyes smoldered as he watched her in tender amusement. "My water lily." Droplets glistened on his body as he leaned down to claim her lips.

The water was cool, but his kiss was hot; his skin was slick as she curled her arms around him. Drinking in his kisses, she ran her hand down the smooth, hard curves of his chest and arms. He moaned softly with pleasure at her touch. Holding her, his arm hooked across her bottom, their wet naked bodies pressed close, warm skin and cool water. She felt intoxicatingly, exhilaratingly alive.

Derek paused to gaze at her. His wet hair was blacker than the night, slicked back from his forehead. His pale eyes captured hers in a hungry stare. His lips were plump with her kisses and moisture gleamed along his square jaw. She looked into his eyes in longing, and he smiled.

Bending near again, he began kissing her whole face, her brow, her eyelids. He nibbled at her cheek and chin, teething her lower lip gently, drawing her mouth open to consume her tongue. Lily's chest heaved. Her fingers dug into his broad shoulders.

Derek kissed his way down her neck. Her nipples were hard, and as she arched back a bit in the water, his tongue played over them. He licked and drank the water off her skin, his exquisite mouth sliding along her body. "You should always be naked," he murmured. "Like Lady Godiva."

"Only if you join me."

"With pleasure." Then his wicked smile faded to a look of rapt intensity as he visibly savored her caresses.

Lily's hands glided over his sleek, sun-bronzed body, the corded steel of his sinewy arms, the rippling muscles of his abdomen. He looked into her eyes, his own dark and stormy with passion. Silver starlight glided over the sleek contours of his body. He watched her with a smoldering gaze as she reached below the water's surface and grasped the rigid length of his arousal, stroking him.

She could feel him throbbing in her hand as he accepted her worship. She gave him the deepest possible kisses, even sucked on his tongue as she pleasured him, entranced by his masculine grace. The solid power of his hardness, so thick in her grasp, told her how much her touch excited him. She thrilled to his response and persisted dauntlessly until he stopped her with a groan and gathered her near.

"I want you."

She brushed her cheek hungrily against his. "Make love to me."

He took her face between his hands briefly and kissed her again and again. He went slowly toward the water's edge. There, he got her up onto the banks and laid her down on a bed of velvet grasses.

He rose out of the water and leaned over her, braced on his hands. She enfolded him between her thighs and groaned with needy pleasure as she took him in. His big, swollen member filled her to the brim. Breathless, Lily raked her fingers down the muscled wall of his chest. He licked his lips and lowered himself to kiss her.

She grasped his nape, taking his tongue and his cock inside her in ravenous need. His hand was so warm, cupping her breast artfully. She wanted him in her over and over again, this beautiful man, her true love. Wrapping her thighs around his waist, she hooked her heels together behind the small of his back and arched beneath him.

"Ah, you're rather a naughty one, aren't you?" he purred in great approval.

"I want to give you pleasure."

"Oh, you do, Lily. You do. I knew you were passionate, but I never guessed this much." When he moved down and kissed her again, she ran her hands down his lean sides and molded her palms over his sleek buttocks and his hips, drawing him in more aggressively at the same time she arched to meet his thrust. "You want it harder, love?" he asked in a taut growl.

"Yes," Lily whispered.

"I can do that." He had been holding back, she realized, gallant as he was, protective of her supposed sensibilities. But she was going mad for him. Sensing the wild degree of her desire, he took her mercilessly, ravishing her.

It was nirvana.

Placing his thumb lightly on her pleasure center while he took her, he made her toes curl with the delightful sensations. Their damp bodies slapping, his loving was bone-jarring, fierce, and sublime. As her strength ebbed in the sheer luscious delight of his taking, her hands slipped weakly from his neck.

She clasped her wrists loosely above her head and let him do with her what he willed, her whole body subject to his every whim. He cupped the bare cheeks of her bottom in his big hands, the better to feed her quivering passage with his massive erection. He was trembling with arousal. Her breasts rocked to and fro as he took her; his lips chased them in hot, playful courtship.

His fevered panting filled her world.

Lily made not the slightest protest when he shifted positions, eager to accommodate whatever wicked notion had inspired him. He knelt behind her, turning her and pressing her forward onto all fours. When he took her from behind, Lily knew she had no further claim whatsoever to call herself a lady.

Happily, though, she did not care. They were as randy as two animals in a field, naked and unself-conscious, absorbed in their mating and lost to everything else.

She reached up behind her and caressed Derek's cheek. He kissed her shoulder and pulled her up onto her knees, never leaving her body. She parted her legs wider, all but sitting on his lap, leaning back against him. He slid his hands around her waist, touching her body everywhere, Her chest heaved as did his.

He was so deep inside of her now that if he moved a fraction of an inch more, she would scream. "It's never been like this for me before," he blurted out in a ragged whisper at her ear.

"What do you mean?"

"I don't know. You could make me lose control. I love you."

"Derek." She curled her fingers loosely in his long hair. "You're an angel."

"I want to come inside you."

"Yes," she panted.

"You could make me explode, the way you move."

She smiled with the heady knowledge that she pleased him.

"Turn for me," he breathed. "I want to kiss you when you come."

She turned slowly to face him, straddling his lap.

Gently she welcomed him again, relishing her impalement on his tremendous shaft. "Mm, Derek, you are very well made," she remarked in an admiring whisper.

He kissed her softly in amusement, his passion deepening with every stroke of his tongue on hers. His desire was robust and virile, full-bodied, and his need was strong. She burned to slake it.

The position he had chosen for their climax was wonderfully intimate. They were both sitting, facing each other, she on his lap, he with his arms wrapped around her.

The world beyond the few-feet circumference of lake and stars and grass around them had ceased to exist. There was only each other. They had defied death and certain doom together, and now must answer instinct's demand to affirm their mutual survival and their bond—and indeed, the fact that they had found each other at all.

"I love you," she whispered.

"I love you, too. I can't believe you saved my life. How can something so fragile-looking and sweet be so brave?" He kissed her hand. "Lie back for me, darling. Let your man complete you."

His heavenly words alone could have brought her to climax, but he was right. She craved his love—and release from this delicious frenzy. He wanted to give. She needed to receive, and only he would do.

He laid her down in the same position from which they had started and he loved her with every stroke of his magnificent body on hers, heightening her satisfaction. Tender and thorough, attentive to her every desire, he was a lover beyond her wildest fantasies. Weeks ago, she had given him a kiss, a bold, handsome stranger in a garden folly. Now she gave herself to him in total, mind and body, heart and soul. She had never thought she would trust again—but then came Derek Knight.

"Come for me, Lily. Come for me." His gentle urging and his velvet gaze were all it took to coax her surrender.

"Oh, Derek."

"That's right, darling. I'm here for you. Let it all go."

She obeyed. She closed her eyes and relaxed into the beauty of the silken fire sweeping through her. Desire consumed her. Derek drove her to the edge with his intoxicating rhythm and then she was falling into ecstasy. He watched her surrender in stormy, loving reverence and then gifted her with his own. Dimly, distantly, she heard the escalation in his deepening moans.

As he lunged against her bucking hips, her splendor-dazzled eyes were opened to mere slits as she watched him arch his head back with a grimace of pure rapture. His seed flooded her core in massive pulsations. *"Oh, yes."*

As the powerful surges of lightning-like pleasure racked them both with sweet convulsions of release, the shudders gradually eased, their violent flashes of brilliance simmering down to a warm, heartfelt glow.

It spread through her entire body.

Derek was panting as he laid his head on her heaving chest. Lily wrapped her arms around him in weary devotion and looked up at the stars, flat on her back in the meadow on that summer's night.

She let out an idle laugh of sheer, joyous astonishment. He joined her, understanding the noise without need of explanation.

How fortunate they were, she thought as she dragged her lips along his hairline, amazed to think that Derek Knight was hers and had just made love to her beneath the stars.

No fortune. No gold. Not even any clothes to hamper them. No worldly possessions in sight, but they had escaped with their lives. They had each other, and that was all they needed.

In this moment, they had everything.

"What do you mean, you lost them?" Ed Lundy demanded, glaring at Bates.

Bates started stammering excuses, but Lundy barely heard, shaking his head at him in disbelief. Didn't any of these fools seem to grasp that his bloody world was caving in?

His stable was ashes, his horses were loose, his prisoners had vanished, and he could all but feel the cold hand of doom tapping him on the shoulder, whispering in his ear that he was done for.

His fears swam around him in the night. His mother might not get back in time with the proceeds of his land sale, and if he did not replace the money he had borrowed from the committee's treasure trove, then he'd be hanged.

Hell, he'd be hanged anyway, for even if his mother somehow rushed back magically in the blink of an eye, he had another problem, for in the meantime, he had committed more crimes. He had kidnapped two people, one of whom had half an army for a family. If the law didn't get him, all those fearsome Knight brothers would. Damn, he should have killed the major when he'd had the chance! But the truth was, he hadn't had the heart—and didn't that prove that he really wasn't such a bad fellow?

Merely an ambitious one who had aimed a bit too high in life and got in over his head.

He was shocked, though, that little, fragile Lily Balfour had rescued her cavalry hero. Well, good riddance to her, too! The fact of the matter was, he felt a hell of a lot easier with Bess.

But even if he married Bess tomorrow, his long-simmering problems had just exploded like so many spewing volcanoes around him. He had thought he could keep them all under control, but now he barely knew which one to cork up first. Everything had gone to Hell at once.

His furious, panicked confusion made it difficult to make a plan for how to proceed. Downing another large swig of whisky from his flask did nothing to help clear his head, but it was time to recognize that he was in serious trouble and he needed help.

God, he wished his mother were here. She had a hard-headed side few people ever saw. Sainted woman, so strong in a crisis. If she were here, she would know what to do, but of course, she was already on her way to do whatever she could to save him.

He thought of going to Lord Fallow, the closest thing to a father he had ever known, but he could not bear to face his mentor's fury and disappointment at his bungling. He dreaded telling Lord Fallow how completely he had let him down. Still, Lundy knew he was in over his head and had no choice but to seek help. So instead of approaching Lord Fallow, he did the only rational thing he could think of and sent Jones out to summon Lord Sinclair.

It was the dead of night, but too bad. The message he had sent with Jones would make the old man understand the critical nature of the situation.

God, he thought as he paced and waited and barked orders at his useless men until he was hoarse, this was not going to be pretty.

He had dodged the chairman's laborious inquest and Knight's tricky investigation at the same time, like some poor bounder trying to cross a patch of quicksand. No wonder he drank! It was enough to wreck a man's nerves. He swallowed another gulp of whisky and thought, *Well, I led them on a merry chase for as long as I could*. Obviously, however, his only hope now was to come clean.

Though he was backed into a corner, Ed Lundy had not yet reached the end of his tenacity. He had not come so far in life just to give up. He knew full well that Lord Sinclair would have no choice but to help him, for the chairman's own reputation rested on the credibility of the committee as a whole. That was the way it worked in London, the gentlemen's club that Lord Fallow had helped him get into.

Sinclair wouldn't like it, but he'd have no choice but to help him cover it up. Lundy was sure of it.

When the chairman arrived, relief washed through him. The portly old earl marveled at the fire and his horses galloping everywhere, but Lundy hurried him inside to explain the situation.

Though he cringed over the shameful confession he had to make, Lundy felt better knowing that at least now someone had come who would tell him what to do, how the hell to handle the situation. Sweating profusely, he showed Lord Sinclair into his office, sat him down, and told him the whole, sordid story.

How Phillip Kane had sweet-talked him into investing in nonexistent canals, promising huge returns through an "exciting" new speculation company with opportunities for profit that no one else had been told about yet. As the candles burned lower, he revealed every detail of how this silver-tongued snake-in-the-grass had lured him into taking part in the scheme in the hopes of tripling his investment in just a few years. He had made it all seem like such a sure thing that Lundy had concluded he had to sign up before he lost out.

"I was going to replace it all as soon as I was able. I was going to use the money to make more and then put it back before anyone noticed," he continued. With the enormity of the bills he already met faithfully month after month, Lundy had not wanted to part with any of the possessions that had helped him gain the ton's acceptance— the sprawling mansion, the opulent stables, the horses who ate better than he used to as a boy, nor even his expensive porcelain doll and bride-to-be, Lady Lily.

But before long he discovered that his pride had done him in. His greed had got the best of him.

As it turned out, there were no canals.

There was no such company.

And after swindling him out of a kingly sum, Phillip Kane had nipped off to the Continent to live the high life.

Lundy had immediately hired an investigator to track Kane down, but when his former Bow Street man found the blackguard, he was already dead. Lundy was not about to make a stink about the theft at that point, for fear that he would be accused of murdering him!

"I know this is terrible, sir," he admitted while, sitting across from him, Lord Sinclair shook his head in fretful silence, his clasped hands resting over the silver head of his walking stick.

"Dear, oh, dear."

"I never meant any harm. You said it was all right to borrow from the fund as long as we put it back before anyone noticed. I tried! I'm still trying, and I will replace the sum I took—but surely you can see it's not my fault! It's just that the timing was disastrous! How was I to know there'd be another war?"

"Now, now, calm yourself."

Lundy lifted his flask for another swallow, but it was empty. He threw it aside with an angry curse.

"There, there, have a drink, my boy," Lord Sinclair said with a paternal air, reaching into his waistcoat. He pulled out his very own flask and offered it to him. "It will help to calm your nerves."

Lundy was startled, indeed, touched by the gesture. He lowered his head. "Thank you, my lord," he mumbled as he accepted it. "You're very kind."

"Not at all. Now, then, we must find a way to put it right." There was something strange in Sinclair's gaze as he watched Lundy toss back a swallow of his whisky. "You mustn't worry your head. You're young! How were you to know? You've mucked things up rather badly, but now that at least you've told the truth, it will all be sorted out soon."

"Do you really think so, sir? Can we fix it?"

"Oh, yes, dear lad. I know it for a fact. You relax. I know just how to make all your problems go away."

Relieved by his confession and touched by the old fellow's reassurance, Lundy pursed his lips together and nodded earnestly. "Thank you, my lord. Thank you." He attempted a trace of a sheepish smile and added, "Good whisky."

Lord Sinclair smiled sagely. "Drink up."

CHAPTER
∞ EIGHTEEN ∞

"So, what do we do now?" Lily asked as they dressed again hastily out in the field.

Derek turned to her with a dazed smiled as he fastened his breeches, still a bit lost in his thoughts.

He had been looking around at the sky, the lake, and the cool, breezy meadow, taking a moment to imprint it all on his memory. Savoring the moment was a habit born of knowing every day could be your last, but he marked this night in his mind as his greatest victory, the night that he had won his greatest prize.

He was looking straight at her, her skin aglow after their lovemaking, her hair wet and rumpled, the same ethereal, pale shade of the golden moon.

No citadel stormed, no foe defeated, no army scattered before his forces could compare to the quiet triumph of this love.

In the past, whenever women had started to get too close, or seemed poised to slip past his defenses, he had always chased them off with a simple question, all the while longing for a lover who would prove her devotion by pledging to follow the drum, to follow him anywhere.

But tonight Lily had done more than that. Indeed, she had surpassed his wistful fantasies. The girl had been prepared to die with him in that stable rather than leave him behind. She had told him her deepest secrets and had given him her all. Perhaps his proposal had been a little spontaneous, but he was absolutely sure she was the woman he was meant to marry.

Sweeter still, he knew he was in love. This condition, he now understood, was easily as dangerous as any cavalry charge, though in a wholly different way. But he wasn't afraid. He had never felt stronger before in his life.

And to think when he was young his mother had always warned him not to count on anyone ever loving him, a younger son, unless he first attained great fortune and glory in battle. Tonight Lily Balfour had dispelled that painful myth. Her trust was more treasure than any mountain of Indian gold to him, her love all the glory that any man could desire.

All of this reminded Derek that his new top priority in life was to ensure that Lily was protected.

This dark business with Lundy was not over yet.

Lily would not be totally safe until Derek had seen it through to the end.

"You're staring at me."

Her pert comment drew him from his thoughts. "You'd better get used to it."

She put her hand on her hip and gave him her adorable little scolding smile. "Did you even hear what I just said?"

"Of course I did, my love."

She lifted her eyebrows. "Well?"

"If you'd repeat it, I'd remember better."

She snorted. "Oh, I was only saying how unpleasant it is that Edward's completely out of control and trying to kill us. Hm?"

"Ah, no worries," Derek replied in a breezy tone. "You and me against him? He's the one who ought to be afraid." On his way to check on the horse, he paused to help Lily wiggle back into her smart, tailored riding habit.

When she pulled up the sleeves, he frowned at her torn bodice, reminded anew of how close Lundy had come to harming her.

"You're glowering," she murmured, then cupped his cheek. "I'm all right, darling. Honestly."

"Maybe so, but I'm not about to let half of London view

the snowy bosom of my beloved," he drawled. He untied the strip of black cord with which he had bound back his hair, crooked his finger at her to come closer, and then used the cord to tie the two sides of her ripped bodice back together.

She caressed his chest with a dreamy, sated smile. "You fix everything."

"At your service, madam."

"Mm, really?" she answered wickedly.

He gave her a cheeky bow and continued ahead to check on Mary Nonesuch, grazing in contentment nearby.

Lily followed him, still working on her buttons. "So, what do we do now? Mrs. Clearwell must be mad with worry."

"Well, we can't contact her yet, I'm afraid. Lundy's probably got men stationed outside both our homes, waiting for us to return."

"Oh! You're right. We'd better not. Maybe we should go to the authorities and tell them all that's happened?"

Derek shook his head. "No, Lundy's back is to the wall. I think we've got to be very careful how far we push him right now. If we go to the constables, they'll rouse a hue and cry to go and take him, but considering his army of hirelings, things could turn very bloody, indeed. And if Lundy gets killed, I'll never be able to track down the rest of the army's money. Besides, he's not allowed to die until I've paid him back for what he did to you."

"Just don't get yourself killed," she warned. "I can't do without you, you know."

"How sweet." He leaned over and stole a kiss.

Lily sighed, swaying a little on her feet with drowsy contentment, but Derek steadied her again and then smiled in amusement as the funny little thing shook herself briskly back to business.

"Maybe we could get Lord Fallow to come and try to reason with Edward," she said, "calm him down. Aside from his mother, the earl is the only person Edward truly respects."

"That," Derek replied, "is actually a very good idea.

Lundy obviously isn't going to talk to us, but Lord Fallow might just succeed in getting the cretin to spill his guts."

"Oh, but what if we tell Lord Fallow all this and he doesn't believe us? If only we had some proof! I wish I had succeeded in stealing those papers about the canal scheme. I almost had them!"

"Can you remember anything specific about them?"

While he got the horse ready to resume their journey, she ticked off what she knew. "The name of the supposed firm was Warwickshire Canals and Company. The total sum that Edward lost was some three hundred thousand pounds. The payments stopped without explanation a little over a year ago. Oh—and all the correspondence was conducted by the company's supposed president, Mr. Phillip Kane."

"Phillip Kane?" Derek exclaimed, turning to her in astonishment.

"You know that name?"

He furrowed his brow. "Unfortunately, yes." He paused. "Charles found a significant payment to Phillip Kane while he was searching Lord Sinclair's financial records."

Lily tilted her head in puzzlement. "Why . . . might Lord Sinclair have wanted to pay off Phillip Kane?"

Derek was silent for a long moment.

"I don't know, but you were right," he answered grimly. "We need Lord Fallow to reason with Lundy, and we need him fast. He may be our only hope of getting answers out of the blackguard. Ready?"

She nodded. He set her up on the mare's back as before, and swung into the saddle behind her, gathering the reins. "Let's go."

"Who *are* you two young people, and why the devil are you bothering me at this hour?" Lord Fallow demanded, roused from his bed, still in his nightcap and dressing gown. "It's the middle of the night! You had better have a very good explanation—and so had you!" he warned his butler, who gave him a cringing look of apology.

"We're very sorry to disturb you, sir," Derek stared at

once. He refreshed the earl's memory about who each of them was and their prior invitation to his home on the night of the garden concert. Then he got straight to the point. "I'm afraid it's a bit of an emergency, sir. It concerns your protégé, Mr. Lundy."

"Edward?"

"My lord, something's very wrong with Edward," Lily chimed in. "He attacked me in a most unspeakable fashion and then abducted Major Knight most violently. We got away, but now he's trying to kill us!"

"Surely, Edward wouldn't—" he started, then reconsidered. "But why? What did you do to him?"

"We discovered serious misconduct on his part regarding the army funds entrusted to the Appropriations Sub-Committee," Derek clipped out. "To try to silence us, he took Miss Balfour prisoner. I was to be thrown into the hold of the first ship bound for India, where I couldn't cause him any trouble."

"Oh, dear." The earl's lined face had paled.

"We got away, but Edward's men are still chasing us," Lily said. "That's why we came here. We know how much Edward loves you. We were hoping you might be able to reason with him. With Mrs. Lundy in the West Indies, you may be the only one now who can calm him down."

"She's right," Derek agreed. "We don't need the situation to escalate any further. Will you come with us?"

"Yes, yes, let me get dressed. Make yourselves at home, I'll be right back. Fenley, bring them something to eat."

"Very good, sir," the butler replied.

"And rouse whatever male servants can carry a weapon," the earl added.

"Sir, I'd recommend we bring no more than three or four of your men," Derek interrupted. "We'll be outnumbered, but any more than that could set him off."

The earl nodded and the butler turned to them, but Derek had one more question.

"Lord Fallow?"

"Yes, Major?"

"Lundy told me that Lord Sinclair once took him aside privately and explained that the committee members have a certain privilege over the money placed under their control. That they were at leave to borrow discreetly against the fund like their own personal bank, as long as no one found out and they put the money back in short order."

"*What?*"

"Is it not true?"

"Absolutely not true! It is expressly forbidden in our by-laws!"

"You're sure?"

"Of course I'm sure. I'm the one who wrote them!"

"But an unofficial policy, perhaps?"

"Never. Not while I was chairman, anyway," he said warily. "I am certain Lord Sinclair would realize such a practice was highly unethical."

"But why would Sinclair lie to Edward?" Lily asked softly. "As the head of the committee, wouldn't any short-fall in the fund ultimately land at his feet?"

"Not if he had a suitable scapegoat," Derek murmured in a grim tone as the whole thing came clear in his mind. "An outsider. Somebody no one had accepted from the start. Someone they all would like to see knocked back down to where he came from."

"Oh, Edward," Lily murmured.

"I sent him right into a trap," Lord Fallow uttered with a stricken look.

"We must hurry," Derek told him in a steadying tone. "Now that you've confirmed my suspicions, I'm afraid Lundy's life may be in danger."

He didn't want to frighten either of them, but he saw now who had killed Phillip Kane.

What else was the chairman to do with his unpredictable co-conspirator once the brash young gambler had outlived his usefulness?

And if he had killed once, the second time was easier.

"We have to get to him before Sinclair does," he said guardedly. Of course he was not eager to save the lout, but if they could get Lundy to tell his side of the story, then Lord Sinclair would know he was caught and might finally be persuaded to admit where he had hidden the army's missing sum.

Lord Fallow appeared shocked by Derek's implication. "Major, I've known Sinclair all my life, from our school days! He was never the most agreeable chap, I admit, and in truth, I always rather felt he quite disliked me for some reason, though I never wronged him. I am stunned to hear he might have stooped to this corruption, but I could never believe he would do murder."

Derek started to answer, to counter the earl's optimistic view with news of the payment to Phillip Kane that Charles had found in Sinclair's records. But then he remembered the rumor that Lord Fallow might have been Phillip Kane's unwilling father, and he held back his words.

Fallow would need a clear head to deal with Lundy. He did not need the information right now that Sinclair might also have murdered his natural son.

It was then that Derek realized fully that Lundy might not have been the only target of this operation.

If Sinclair had been harboring some sort of long-held grudge against his old schoolmate, this whole scheme could have been but a hateful, cruel, and cowardly way of striking at the innocent Lord Fallow.

"Better safe than sorry, sir," was all he said in answer.

"Yes, well, I suppose you're right, at that."

"Sir," he added, "I shall want to borrow a few weapons, if I may—just in case."

Lord Fallow frowned, but nodded and gestured his permission to his butler. "Let the major arm himself."

"Very good, sir."

The earl nodded firmly and then hurried upstairs to dress.

The butler sent the night porter to the kitchens to fetch some food for Derek and Lily, then showed them to the mansion's armory where countless swords, rifles, and muskets were on display, arrayed in starlike designs all over the walls.

When he unlocked the earl's fine gun case with its selection of gleaming rifles, Derek smiled. Little Matthew could have Gunter's. This was *his* confectionery. "The ammunition is kept elsewhere, Major. I will bring it."

"Don't be stingy," he murmured.

The butler nodded, then hurried off to fetch it and to wake a few of the male servants who knew how to use a weapon.

After selecting his sidearms, Derek escorted Lily back out to the soaring statuary hall with its Grecian busts and vast checkerboard floor.

While they waited for their food, he pulled Lily close and hugged her, saddened to think of the wound Lord Fallow had in store if Phillip Kane had indeed been his son. What a snake Sinclair was!

Lundy had proved a snake, as well, and when Derek looked at Lily, he shook his head at how she, too, had been the victim of a selfish, skulking fraud. *There are snakes all over this garden Earth.*

And then there were the flowers.

"My sweet Lily," he whispered as she turned her face up to search his eyes.

"Are you all right? You seem quiet."

He mustered up a weary smile. "Hungry."

She gave him a cheeky grin. "Maybe they'll bring us some ham."

He laughed, adoring her, and lightly tweaked her nose for her impertinence.

A few minutes later, the porter brought back some bread and ale, cold slices of meat, and cheese. "I hope this will do for now, sir. Considering the hour, it was the best I could find."

"We'll take it," they said in unison, famished all the more from their little swim—and other exertions.

Sitting on the pristine marble stairs, they devoured the food, and when Lord Fallow returned, it was time to go.

The men were armed, and two of the earl's carriages waited outside to take them to Lundy's.

Lily turned to Derek. "Do I get a gun?" she asked with an eagerness that simply tickled him.

"Darling, don't be daft. I'm not letting you go back there—"

"Derek!" She glanced self-consciously at the others. "I mean, Major!"

"No, Lily, to Lundy, you're a target—"

"My dear young people," the earl interrupted, still buttoning his sleeves at his wrists, "Edward is certainly not going to harm anyone in front of me."

"You see? Even His Lordship knows," she protested. "Edward is always on his best behavior in front of Lord Fallow." She clung to Derek's hand and gave him a beseeching look. "Please don't leave me. I have to be with you."

Well, he thought, *she's safer with me than if I leave her here and Lundy's hirelings find her.* "Very well," he conceded as he cocked his rifle with an ominous click. "But you stay right beside me."

She smiled from ear to ear. "If I must."

When they passed Lundy's henchmen fleeing down the road in the opposite direction, Derek knew something must have happened at the estate. Maguire and Jones didn't even stop to confront them.

Derek and his party did not bother to chase them for now, but they were all the more determined to find out what was going on.

By the time they arrived at Lundy's estate, the black of night had turned to gray with a hint of dawn gathering in the east.

The gates were open and an eerie, tomblike hush hung over the grounds. The place appeared deserted except for the horses and the dog.

Brutus was still chained to the tree and had barked himself hoarse by now. He started up with his usual noise when he saw them but soon gave up with a cough and sat on his haunches, merely watching them as they all got out of the carriages.

Meanwhile, Lundy's prized bloodstock grazed in clusters here and there. The fire was out, but smoldering plumes of smoke still rose from the ruined stable, their delicate spirals rising from the burned-out hulk, blending into the gray mist.

"Look." Derek pointed. "That wasn't here before."

There was a strange carriage parked outside the house.

"Someone's come," Lily murmured while Derek kept her behind him. "Do you think it's Lord Sinclair?"

Suddenly, they heard an abrupt crashing sound and a garbled yell of pain from within.

"Edward." Lord Fallow started forward, recognizing the voice of his protégé. He turned to Derek. "You two had best stay here for the moment. I will go and talk to him."

"Call for me if he gives you any trouble."

The earl nodded, beckoned three of his four men, and strode ahead. Derek watched as Lord Fallow banged loudly on the front door and called Lundy's name before opening it.

He was rather surprised that it was unlocked.

The earl and his three servants slipped inside.

Derek, Lily, and the fourth servant waited outside. Derek scanned the neo-Gothic monstrosity, its windows dark. The house also looked deserted. Even the servants seemed to have fled. What had happened here? he wondered. But when another thunderous crash sounded from somewhere in the house, one of the earl's men poked his head out the door.

"Major!"

"Let's go. Lily—" He started to tell her to stay outside with the remaining servant, but when he glanced over, the man was vacantly picking his ear. Derek furrowed his brow. *On second thought*—"Stay close to me," he murmured, taking her hand.

Leaving the servant behind to guard the carriages, Derek and Lily hurried inside.

The man who had waved them in led them toward the chaos.

Lord Fallow was waiting for them near Lundy's office, the very room that Derek had tried to break into on the day of the garden party.

"He's locked himself in there," the earl murmured. "He won't answer. I can't get to him."

"Is he alone?"

"I don't know, but he let out a scream a minute ago that raised the hair on my arms."

"Did you see anyone else? Sinclair?"

"No. I almost told my men to break the door down, but God only knows what we might find."

"I'll do it," Derek said grimly. He turned to Lily and pointed to the door of the parlor they had visited during the garden party, a wordless order to her to hide in there.

She nodded and obeyed.

When he heard the parlor door's trusty lock click home, he approached the study. Hearing a low moan of pain from within, Derek brought up his weapon.

Nodding to Fallow to move out of the way, he kicked the door open without warning and aimed the rifle at Lundy's head.

But then he saw he needn't have bothered.

Lundy had clapped his hands over his ears at the bang of the door and let out a garbled cry.

"My God," Derek breathed as the others rushed into the room behind him.

Lundy stumbled past his desk, slowly lowering his shaking hands. "Quiet, quiet," he panted.

"Edward," Lord Fallow murmured in wonder, gazing around at the chaos in the room.

By the feeble glow of a candle that Lundy could not seem to look at directly, as though the small light agonized him, Derek's gaze swept the room. The office had been ransacked. The contents of Lundy's desk had been swept aside and scattered all over the floor.

"He's stone drunk," one of Fallow's men muttered as Lundy lurched across the room.

The earl himself seemed to reach this same conclusion. "Edward, this is no time for overindulgence!"

"You go to Hell," Lundy wrenched out, fairly spitting the words at his startled benefactor.

"Edward!" Lord Fallow exclaimed in bewilderment.

"You should've left me in the gutter where I belonged. I saved your life, and this is my thanks?"

"He's not drunk, my lord," Derek said in stoic calm. "He's been poisoned."

"Poisoned?" Fallow echoed.

"Where's Sinclair?" Derek demanded, slowly lowering his gun.

"Dead!" Lundy gestured toward the fireplace, where Derek now noticed the portly crumpled figure lying inert by the foot of the hearth, half-covered in scattered files. "Aye, I did it. Don't bother arrestin' me for it. I'll be joinin' 'im soon enough."

"What did you do to him?"

"Threw him across the room! He didn't get up—hit his head. Too good a death for him, the snake." His words had barely ended when Lundy let out a shriek and arced with a wild grimace, falling against his desk, his head jolting back. He fell to his knees.

"Edward!" Lord Fallow ran to him, trying to help, but Lundy warded him off.

"Don't touch me—it hurts!" he wrenched out, gasping for air as the horrible convulsion passed.

"Nightshade," Derek whispered.

"Is there nothing you can do?" a soft voice murmured from the doorway.

Derek froze, then closed his eyes, realizing Lily had come out of her hiding place. God, he did not want her to see her former suitor's agony. "You should not be here."

"Can't you help him, Derek?"

"I wish I could."

"Lily?" Lundy asked weakly. "I can't see. Are you here?"

"Edward."

Derek put out his arm and stopped her on her way toward him. "Don't."

"Derek, he is dying. No one deserves to die alone. He is no threat to me now. It's all right." She removed his hand from her way and went over and knelt down beside Lundy, wishing she had some way to comfort him. "Oh, Edward."

"I'm sorry for what I done to you," Lundy groaned. "You always was too good for me."

"I'm sorry, too, for the way I chased your fortune."

"Well, it's all gone now. Tell my mum—good-bye."

Tears rose in Lily's eyes as another fierce convulsion wracked him. Derek drew her back, pulling her away from the sight. Lily turned her face into his chest as Lundy screamed.

He held her while Lundy died before their eyes.

After a moment, perhaps his anguished spirit left their midst, for the heavy sense of suffering ebbed from the room.

The others stood in hollow silence, staring at the corpse. His eyes were wide, his face frozen in a grimace of pain.

Derek looked at Lord Fallow. The earl seemed to have aged ten years in the past ten minutes. Reading his face, he could tell that His Lordship had begun to put two and two together.

Derek set Lily aside with a kiss on her brow and stalked over to the prostrate form by the fireplace.

Moving a few of the files and scattered papers off Lord Sinclair, he noted a small pool of blood beneath the chairman's balding head and felt for a pulse. When he touched the man's neck, Sinclair began to stir.

"He's alive."

"Not for long." Lord Fallow stalked over and slapped Sinclair awake, then grabbed his arms, wrenching him up to a seated position to stare in his face. "Open your eyes, damn you! I want you to see my bullet coming."

Derek reached out to stop him. "My lord—"

"Stand aside, Major!" Ashen-faced and shaking, Lord Fallow thrust his pistol into Sinclair's face. "You murderer. Traitor! You killed them both, didn't you? First Phillip, now Edward! You killed them both! My son and one who was like a son to me. Why, why?" he wailed.

In the quiet as Lord Fallow waited for his answer, Derek could hear Lily crying softly.

He looked at her with a gaze that begged her to leave.

But she stayed.

"Go on, shoot me, you arrogant son of a bitch," Sinclair muttered. "Prove to everyone you're not the saint that you pretend to be."

"*What?*"

"I'm so sick of you, Fallow. I'm so sick of everyone fawning on you, and hearing your name uttered in such reverent tones. 'Ah, Lord Fallow, such a virtuous man!'"

"What are you talking about?" he cried.

"To hell with you if you're too stupid to understand how much I despise the sight of you. Just get it over with. Pull the bloody trigger."

Lord Fallow looked horrified and bewildered. "What did I ever do to you?"

Sinclair said nothing.

Fallow looked at Derek, at a loss.

He shrugged. "Jealousy? Some people don't need a reason to hate. It's in their nature. Please, my lord, put your weapon away. He does not deserve your bullet," Derek said evenly, prepared to stop Fallow by sterner means if it came to it. "No doubt he would prefer it to a trial before the House of Lords and the noose he's got coming. Don't give him what he wants."

"You're right." Fallow trembled, but Derek's words finally sank in. Slowly, he put his pistol back in the holster. "Quite right, Major. A quick end is too good for the likes of him."

"Ah, the good man Fallow doesn't disappoint," Sinclair hissed in poisonous bitter mockery.

"Good man? Do not call me good!" Fallow shouted, grabbing Sinclair's collar. "I abandoned my son, the one that you killed. I ruined him with my neglect. And look where it's led." He released him roughly. "Good man? I am a failure, guilty of the cruelty that only a parent can give. And now God's paid me back for it."

"Sir," Derek whispered as Fallow broke down weeping.

"Phillip. Edward . . ."

Derek gestured to Fallow's servants. They stepped forward and gently collected their old master, taking him back outside. Derek tried to wave Lily out of the room, too, but she shook her head and remained firmly planted.

Her loyalty moved him. He gave her a tender look, ordered Fallow's men to bring the constables, and then turned his attention to the chairman.

"You're caught, Sinclair," he informed him. "Your only hope of leniency now is to tell us where you've hidden the money you stole."

"I stole?" he retorted sardonically as he sat up, leaning against the empty fireplace.

"Oh, yes. Need I remind you that treason is the sort of charge that could get your family stripped of its title forever? Lord! Could you stand to see your firstborn son reduced to a mere commoner?"

Sinclair's eyes flared slightly.

"Appalling possibility, isn't it?" Derek drawled. "I take it you failed to think that far ahead. Or perhaps you merely assumed your scheme would never be found out."

He scoffed. "What scheme?"

"Taking a cut of the army's money for yourself. Three hundred thousand pounds, to be exact."

"I did nothing of the kind."

"Of course you did. And I know how you did it. Lundy and Phillip Kane were merely your instruments. But now it's all come to light."

"Oh, really?"

"Shall I explain? It's really not that complicated. You, with all the business savvy, set up a fraudulent company and hired Phillip Kane with his acting skills to pose as its director. He probably thought he'd be getting a nice, big, juicy cut of that money, but instead all he got was this." He pointed to Edward's corpse, already rigid from the nightshade. "I'm not much of a gambler, but if I were, I'd have to bet you planned to eliminate Kane from the start, as soon as he had served his function."

"Major, your accusations are ludicrous."

"No. Because, you see, my lord, we found the payment you made to Phillip Kane in your financial records, and God knows he had reasons of his own to hate his father's protégé. Both of you must have been consumed with jealous hatred." Derek paused before moving on. "To help coax your mark Edward into taking the bait, you made sure to plant the lie in his brain that borrowing from the fund was a common practice among the Gentlemen of the Committee, as long as the loan was kept discreet."

"You must have been smoking your Indian hookah pipe this evening, Major, really."

Derek smiled. "Generally, I avoid the stuff, my lord. God, it must have been torture, sitting on top of all that gold for so long and not being able to touch it. And then Fallow had the gall to introduce someone like Lundy into your elite circle. The nerve!"

Sinclair glared at him.

"Living in Fallow's shadow all your life was bad enough, I'm sure. But then he added insult to injury when he expected you and the committee to accept this lowlife," Derek taunted. "Edward Lundy didn't belong. He wasn't one of us, one of our class, was he? He was not a gentleman, and you were not about to let him become one. This time, I think, Fallow had pushed you too far."

Sinclair refused to talk, but his eyes confirmed it.

Derek was determined to make the earl betray himself. "But you were so clever. You set it up so that if anyone even discovered the theft, you'd pin the whole thing on Fallow's creature, and distance yourself from any whiff of wrongdoing by nobly pressing on with your charade of an investigation.

"Once the deed was done, you sent Kane off to France, but then you double-crossed him once he'd served his purpose. Of course, it wasn't as though you could have let him live. He was too reckless, too unpredictable. Not too scrupulous, either. Not a gentleman like you. He could've blackmailed you with the whole scheme someday. He could've slipped up and told someone. So you killed him before he became inconvenient. But, really, Chairman. Nightshade?"

Derek paused.

"No one deserves such a horrible death. A bullet would

have been kinder for them both. But I guess you were too cowardly to confront either of them, man to man. Big, strong, young men. They would have bested you. That was why you chose the poison."

"Your whole theory is very amusing, Major. But you're quite mistaken. I never poisoned anyone. Lundy drank the poison by his own hand in despair over his ruin and guilt for his theft. Having already made up his mind to die, he summoned me here so he could confess. When I tried to stop him from taking his life, he threw me across the room. I struck my head, as you can see, and then blacked out."

Derek narrowed his eyes. Sinclair must think him an idiot soldier indeed if he expected him to believe that cock-and-bull tale. Not even a madman would choose such an excruciatingly painful mode of suicide.

But he decided to give Lord Sinclair a craftier answer than simple negation. "So," he murmured, "it's your word against Lundy's, then?"

The chairman snorted in disdain, as if there could be no question about which man the world would believe.

"Perhaps there's a chance you're telling the truth," Derek conceded mildly. "Let's find out." Glancing around, he spotted a silver flask on the floor.

"What are you doing?" Sinclair watched him uneasily as Derek walked over to the flask, still keeping his pistol trained on him in case he tried anything.

"I'm going to get you a drink, my lord." Pulling his handkerchief out of his coat pocket, he used it to cover his hand and bent down, carefully picking up the flask. "It's almost empty, but I think there may be a few drops left."

He holstered his pistol as he returned to the chairman, who had begun to cower.

"That's not mine."

"It bears your monogram, an S. The better to deceive your victim, no doubt. Lundy didn't have the slightest inkling, did he? Not until it was too late. You knew he would fumble it sooner or later and call on you—and you were ready. You snake!"

Still sitting on the hearth, Sinclair started backing up against the fireplace. "Stay away from me."

"What's wrong? If your flask didn't poison Edward, then take a sip and prove it. You look like you could use a draught." Derek gripped Sinclair's chubby face, forced his head back, and started to pry his mouth open. "Cheers, Sinclair! Have a drink!"

Lily shrieked while Sinclair fought him, but Derek knew exactly what he was doing.

"All right, all right! I'll tell you everything! For the love of God, get that evil stuff away from me!"

"Where's the money? Tell me now!" Derek roared, not relenting. He was not going to let Sinclair retract his confession as soon as he let up the pressure. The correct location of the money would stand as proof of his guilt. *"Where did you hide it?"*

"It's in a bank in Scotland," he choked out, thrashing against his hold.

"Where?" Derek boomed at him. "Answer me, you bloody thief!"

"The Royal Glasgow!"

"Under your name?"

"No," he gasped. "No. I used—Fallow's."

Derek released him, shaking his head in disgust. "Now, then. You see? Telling the truth isn't really so hard."

"Go and wash your hands," Lily ordered him in a shaky tone.

Steadying himself from his burst of wrath, Derek took a deep breath, nodded, and rose. He gave his pistol to Lily as he passed her. "Hold him there a moment. I'll get Fallow's men."

Sinclair had to be contained, but Lily was right. Even a tiny drop of the nightshade could make a man deathly ill if it seeped into the skin. A larger dose would render him as dead as Lundy.

He called to Fallow's servants to come back, then went to find some soap and water.

"The constables are on their way, sir," the footman reported when he ran in.

"Good. See that they arrest that viper. He's confessed," Derek said. He looked at Lily. "I'll be right back."

She nodded, still aiming Derek's pistol straight at Sinclair's chest with both hands. "You'd better not move, old man," she warned. "I may be a lady, but I'll shoot!"

Hm, Derek thought, rather tickled by her ferocity. *I think I am a bad influence on her.*

As he turned to leave the room, his glance happened upon Lundy's corpse. He winced a bit, though death was nothing new. He wouldn't miss it, he concluded, having made up his mind as of tonight to give up soldiering.

Oats and barley? God only knew what the future might hold. He went off to wash his hands of the whole bloody business and wondered how he'd fare as a civilian.

CHAPTER
∽ NINETEEN ∽

Recalling the day he had found Lily searching for bridal patterns and fancy white cakes, Derek knew how much having a proper wedding would mean to her, so he insisted on giving her enough time to arrange a day for them that she could look back upon when they were old and gray, and smile.

The wedding night, now, that would be *his* responsibility.

He was doubtful, but Lily swore that she could have everything ready within a few weeks with Mrs. Clearwell's help. Derek told her to make the wedding as she liked and he would pay for it.

He finally got around to telling her about the modest fortune he had built up over his years of service in India, as well as the very respectable inheritance he would receive from his father. In reality, he was welcome to ask for it to be released to him at any time.

He explained that of course he was not a millionaire like Lundy had been before he had ruined himself, but he wanted her to rest assured she would be very comfortable.

While she set up the wedding arrangements, Derek didn't mind waiting for the big day. The best thing about being engaged to Lily was that he could see her whenever he liked without having to leap at chance occasions or contrive silly excuses to be near her. He took advantage of this luxury to the full, and they were frequently together.

In the interim, the fates of many ran their course.

With the charges brought against him, Lord Sinclair was accorded the courtesy of house arrest while awaiting his trial in the Lords. But after the money had been found in the Royal Glasgow Bank just where he said it would be, he hanged himself rather than face the public spectacle.

This inclined the Regent to allow Lord Sinclair's son to inherit the title rather than stripping it from the family. The son had had nothing to do with the theft.

Lundy was examined by the coroner and buried, his properties put up for auction. Lily dutifully sent off a heart-wrenching letter to his mother, but Derek doubted the woman would return to England anytime soon.

Bess Kingsley also disappeared from Society after Edward's death. Derek heard a rumor that her ironmonger sire had hired her a strict new governess and shipped her off on a Grand Tour in the hopes of refining her manners.

As for his trusty accountant, there was talk that the noble Charles Beecham, Esquire, should be knighted for his services numerical to the Crown. The authorities were disposed to turn a blind eye to the slightly sketchy means he had used to review Sinclair's records, considering the large sum of stolen money that had been recovered. And with the whole of the Knight family seconding this effort, he might well be Sir Charles soon.

The constables were still searching for the rough lads Bates, Jones, and Maguire, but Derek had a feeling they had fled the realm.

Lord Fallow had a beautiful marble headstone erected over the previously unmarked grave of Phillip Kane, posthumously acknowledging his natural son. He then offered himself as the patron of a local orphanage. Society buzzed with mixed sympathy and surprise to hear how the old, soft-hearted earl went two or three times a week to read stories to the children.

Meanwhile, once the stolen money was returned to the total sum of three million for the war, Derek was summoned to the Admiralty and entrusted with the intelligence of when and where the navy flotilla would set sail to transport the army's gold to India. To avoid trouble, it was not information the government cared to make public, but he was personally invited to take passage on one of their ships if he wished to return to his post now that his mission was complete.

He still had not heard from Colonel Montrose.

He had canceled plans to repurchase his commission, but he couldn't help but feel a bit put out as he returned to the Althorpe from his visit to Whitehall. Communication from India to England took a long time, and often, sent letters did not make it out of a war zone at all. But he couldn't help wondering if his regiment had simply moved on without him, that maybe he hadn't mattered back there as much as he always thought he had.

For all his supposed glory, it left him feeling like nothing but one insignificant little cog in the wheel of the empire. It irked his pride, but he had a new purpose in life now, a new cause, and her name was Lily.

Pulling the front door of his apartment shut behind him, he spotted the silver tray where the mail amassed each day and merely scowled at it. He had donned his uniform for his visit to the Admiralty and glimpsed himself in it in the mirror above the console table, but soon it would be time to take it off and hang it up for good.

Sauntering into his rooms, he was puzzled to find the place deserted. Aadi did not appear to greet him, nor was there any sign of Gabriel.

Where is everybody? he wondered.

And then he heard the music.

The silvery warble of the sitar started up from somewhere outside and was joined a moment later by the tabla drums.

He glanced out the open window and spotted the Indian servants practicing their musical skills. Derek took comfort in the familiar sounds, but it made him ache a bit for the home he'd left behind so hastily. But as he turned to lean against the window, intent on listening further, he suddenly noticed the flower petals strewn along the floor.

His eyebrow arched up instantly.

Well, well. What have we here? Pushing away from the wall, he discovered a pink flowery trail, followed it around the corner of the hallway, and saw, ahead, that it led straight to the closed door of his bedchamber.

His blood heated in curious surprise as he walked toward the door; his pulse started pounding in time with the drums. He smelled incense burning as he neared his chamber door. As he slowly opened it, he immediately spotted the little candles burning here and there around his room.

The shades had been drawn against the light.

When he stepped inside the room, he found Lily reclining on his bed in a sensuous pose. Her eyes were lined with thick black kohl like those of a temple dancer. Her hands and feet were adorned with intricate henna designs; a golden chain around her waist was all she wore, and on her forehead a jeweled bindi gleamed.

Derek's jaw dropped.

A warm, seductive half-smile curved her lips, rouged to match her nipples. "*Namaste*, Major."

Gulp.

He barely had the presence of mind to close the door behind him.

His body instantly responded. He glanced absently at the door to make sure he had closed it all the way, then looked at her again in pure, lusting astonishment.

She was a creature spun from his most secret fantasies, an exquisite harem girl, golden-haired and milky-skinned.

He could not take his eyes off her.

"Is it my birthday?" he asked hoarsely, barely daring to blink lest the vision dissipate.

"I wanted us to have some . . . very special time together before everyone starts arriving in Town for the wedding."

By "everyone" he suspected she was referring to her mother. Thus her extreme naughtiness now.

Derek was enchanted.

"Besides," she added with a seductive smile, a goddess waiting for him, "if the major cannot go to India, then a bit of India can come to him." She pushed up onto her knees with a sinuous motion and held out her arms to him.

Derek walked to her, roughly yanking his black uniform stock off from around his neck, then taking off his sword-belt, dropping it behind him.

His heart slammed behind his ribs.

"*God*. Look at you." When he touched her, he felt the slickness of her body covered in jasmine-scented oils and shuddered. "You are just *full* of surprises, Lily Balfour."

From beneath her lashes, she peered up at him in sizzling invitation.

He clasped her nape, staring at her through glittering eyes. Then he lowered his head and claimed her mouth. She tilted her head back and parted her lips wide to receive his burning kisses, returning them with all of her fire.

Rock-hard for her, Derek broke off the kiss, panting and eager to explore her. She watched his hands caress her, but she closed her eyes with an impatient sigh as his slippery touch rode over the thrusting peaks of her hardened nipples.

When she drew the opening of his shirt apart and kissed his chest, it was almost more than he could bear.

He lifted her face and took her mouth again fiercely. Then she was kissing him like she was lost in it, cupping his face, trembling. He slipped his finger under the golden chain around her hips and used it to tug her closer.

Still fully clothed but so ready for her, he unbuttoned the placket of his breeches and pressed them down around his hips. She helped him, then reached down with one henna-painted hand and with a decidedly possessive squeeze, grasped his furious erection. He groaned as his English harem girl began to stroke him.

There was so much he meant to show her. Eastern tricks. Techniques, positions. *Later*.

He had to have her, now.

Clasping her bare waist, he laid her back across his bed. She licked her rouged lips in anticipation and watched him through heavy-lidded eyes. He leaned down to mount her and she lifted her hips to take him in.

"Ah," she whispered as the thick, throbbing head of his shaft entered her wet core.

He had been tense and irked and, oh, God, this was exactly what he needed. He held her waist, wanting to jam himself into her without delay, but he did not wish to hurt her with the epic size of his arousal. He had never been this excited before in his life.

His pounding pulse ticked off the seconds as he gave her a moment to inch her way down the big, hard cock between her thighs. He watched her in agonized desire as she closed her eyes and smiled in wanton satisfaction when she had finally taken him in to the hilt.

Once, twice, buried deep inside her, he pleasured her with deep, slow strokes, but then she licked her lips and ran her hands down her body, and Derek simply lost his mind. He ravished her, taking her with the force of a battering ram. She bared her teeth with a wrenching groan, loving it.

Derek loved *her*. Time lost all meaning; his barbaric passion for her ruled his senses. His chest heaved. His blood was on fire, damp with a lover's sweat beneath his uniform. His hardness swelled even more as he leaned down and pinned her wrists to his bed.

"Oh, God—Derek!" Her blissful little scream was music to his ears as his shaft continued pumping her with a deep, relentless rhythm.

He bent his head and captured the wild, panting breath that accompanied her orgasm, inhaling it in Tantric fashion, blowing his air softly into her mouth in return.

She was thrashing, nearly sobbing with release beneath him. Her jerking movements brought him to the edge. Then she ripped her nails down his chest, and a low shout tore from him like a war cry. He came to her from the very depths of his soul. His climax seemed to last forever.

At length, however, the mind-splitting pleasure eased, and he collapsed on her, winded and quivering.

And nowhere near done with her yet.

Later, as they lay naked together, Lily rested her head on his chest, slowly caressing him in the afterglow of passion. Derek's thoughts drifted back to his visit to the Admiralty, then he mused that while he might have had trouble parting with his uniform, she had stripped it off him rather handily. He told her about the navy's offer to carry him back to India.

She moved up onto her elbow and looked at him warily. "What answer did you give them?"

"What do you think?" he countered with a lazy half-smile. "I said no thanks."

She stared somberly at him.

"What is it?" he murmured, caressing her cheek with his knuckle.

"You're really going to stay with me? You're not going back to India?"

"Of course I'm staying with you. Get that fear out of those big, blue eyes. I'm not going anywhere, sweeting." He smiled at her. "You *own* me now."

"Because I saved your life?" she asked, bracing herself with a stoic look. "Because you think you owe me?"

"No, because I love you, you little silly-head. And because you need me. And I need you. I really need you." He moved closer, giving her a meaningful kiss and tempted to roll her onto her back for a third round.

But she stopped him. "Derek, please be serious."

He paused, meeting her troubled gaze.

"I know how much the army means to you," she said. "We've talked about it many times. Your decision to give it up and marry me seemed really sudden that night at the lake, and I just want to make sure you've thought it through and won't regret it."

"Regret it? Are you mad? No, darling. I've done my time for King and country," he said softly. "My decision might've seemed sudden that night, but the truth is, it's been . . . bubbling along under the surface for quite a while now, though I didn't want to admit it." He shook his head. "Gabriel and I have been talking about this for some time and I see now he was right. I'm ready for a new sort of life. As an old married man," he added, tickling her waist.

She jerked away and then pinched him in retaliation.

Derek laughed. "As Gabriel once pointed out, soldiering

is all I've known, all I've tried. Who knows? I might be good at other things."

"Oh, you'd be good at anything you put your hand to," she said with certainty. "For my part, I'd be very happy to think of you doing something safer. If anything ever happened to you, I don't think I could survive it."

"Well, you don't have to be afraid," he whispered, and capturing her chin on his fingertips, he gave her a soft kiss.

"You won't change your mind?" she murmured, opening her eyes again with a dreamy look. "You're here to stay? Because if I let myself count on you and you leave . . ."

"Oh, Lily. You're breaking my heart with your uncertainty. Of course I'm here to stay. You have my word." He leaned back against the headboard and gathered her into his arms, holding her again. "And if my word's not enough to put your mind at ease, then know that I have reasons of my own for this change of plans."

"You do?"

He sighed, nodding. "I know now that going back to the army would not be good for me." He was not too keen to discuss it, but as his future wife, she deserved to know more about his private demons. "Do you remember the day you came to see me at the stable?"

"After you rescued Mary Nonesuch? Yes. You asked me to shoot you," she added wryly.

"So I did. And you asked me how I live with all the things I've done. Do you remember what I told you?"

"Yes. You said you just don't think about it."

"Exactly. But you see, that's not always a practical solution. It's not always possible. Sometimes—" He hesitated. "Sometimes I think it's got me by the throat."

She went very still, listening to him. He stroked her hair as he held her. Its softness soothed him.

"I realized something when I was stuck inside that metal cage. Two things, actually. First, the reason that I was so hell-bent on getting back to the war was because you can't think about anything but the job at hand in the thick of the fight. There's no time for pondering anything else. That kind of introspection can get a man killed. So you stay numb. You fix all your focus on the victory, and do what you have to do. Then you get somewhere quiet and it all starts leaching out, coming back again."

He fell silent for a long moment.

"I thought if I could get back to that hell as quickly as possible, immerse myself in it as usual, that my . . . difficulties would be all the sooner ended. But in reality, I know perfectly well I would only be making the problem worse. Masking it with outward activity and all the while heaping up even more gruesome memories that I'd have to deal with eventually. Maybe Gabriel was right—he usually is. Maybe I came out a little worse off than I knew and should quit while I'm ahead." He glanced at her. "That's what you were trying to tell me all along."

"Yes."

"Well, I guess I finally got your point. Sooner or later, I'd have to come to terms with this. Now that you've come into my life, I'd much rather go through it all with you by my side."

"I'm here for you," she whispered.

"I know. It helps more than you realize." He kissed her brow.

"Anything at all that I can do for you, you let me know," she ordered him tenderly.

"Just be you, be my darling Lily. And don't stop loving me."

"Sweetheart." She moved nearer, wrapped her arms around him, and held him like she'd never let him go.

Derek closed his eyes, wonder-struck all over again to think of how he had gone so quickly from his own private hell to this heaven.

"What was the second thing you realized when you were trapped inside that cage?" she murmured, holding him. "You said there were two."

"Yes." He gazed into her eyes for a long moment. "With that fire closing in, before you showed up, I realized I could not stand to die without ever having had the chance to know real love."

"But you know it now, don't you?" she whispered, caressing his cheek. "We both do."

He nodded, and kissed her, and then he laid her down to make love to her again.

Two days after their "very special time" together, Derek met his future mother-in-law. And was promptly stunned by the immediate change that came over Lily with her mother's arrival in Town.

The Balfour ladies had come to London.

His bride's initial hope of having their wedding in her little village church had been nixed by Lady Clarissa's horror at the thought of Knight family dukes and marquesses laying eyes on the decrepit Balfour Manor.

Derek's sister, Georgiana—who was of course behind Lily's first delightful foray into Indian culture—hosted a dinner party to help the Balfours and the Knights become acquainted.

It did not take long for Derek to see that Lady Clarissa Balfour was a force to be reckoned with.

Dear Lord, he had been through battles that were easier than that dinner party. Lady Clarissa seemed quite at home in Griff's opulent mansion, but when it came to Derek himself, he sensed she was less than impressed.

Aunt Daisy was a sweet but anxious, fluttering old thing who took one look at little Matthew and fell completely in love with him. Meanwhile, Cousin Pamela fascinated Derek. He made Griff list for her all the museums, art galleries, and intellectual societies of London that the budding writer must visit while she was in Town. She just kept staring at the two of them like she couldn't believe anyone would actually want to talk to a plain spinster like her, let alone take an interest in her stories.

While Derek befriended the other two, Lily did her best to manage "Mother." Within a few hours of observing mother and daughter together, his protective instincts were already on high alert.

By the time the evening drew to a close, Lily and he were both drained and strangely exhausted by the visit. They took a stroll in Hyde Park together to unwind, telling the others they had to sort out a few more wedding details.

They walked in silence for half a mile, too spent to summon up a word. Fortunately, being together had a way of restoring them.

"So . . . ," Derek said in a cautious but amiable tone when he had finally rallied the strength to speak again, "your, er, your mother's going to live with us?"

Lily bit her lip and looked askance at him. "Well, she lives at Balfour Manor, and we're going to live at Balfour Manor, so . . . ?" She shrugged.

"Right." He stroked his mouth, then thrust his hands into his pockets as his gaze slid to the ground.

"Is that going to be a problem?" she asked anxiously.

Derek did not want to cause trouble by criticizing her mother. After all, maybe he had not given the woman enough of a chance yet. "No, no. Not on my part. Can we put her in the wing that has the bats?"

"Derek." Lily sent him a stern look belied by the sparkle in her eyes.

"Sorry," he drawled. "I don't think she likes me."

"Well, I do." Lily took his arm, tucking her hands in the crook of his elbow as they ambled on through the deepening twilight. "Darling, I know Mother can come across as rather—aloof at first. She just needs a little time to get used to you, that's all."

"If you say so."

"Don't worry. I'll protect you from her," she teased.

He arched a brow. "You're the one I'm worried about. I can see you walking on eggshells around her. I can't be that tactful."

"Can't or won't?"

"Grrr."

"Won't you try, for me? At least a little? Come, darling. She's my mother."

"All right," he muttered, sending her a doting half-smile. "She brought you into the world, and for that, I am in her debt. So I will be an attentive and obliging son-in-law. For as long as I can stand it," he added wryly.

What he did not say aloud was that he had not forgotten what Lily had told him about her mother blaming her for the debacle with Lord Owen Masters. Hard-hearted woman, he was not inclined to sympathize with her.

Protecting Lily was his new purpose in life.

The next day, while Lily and her mother, aunt, and chaperone frittered about with the last wedding bits, and while Pamela went off exploring London's cultural attractions by herself, Derek lounged around the Althorpe drinking tea and reading the family authoress's latest handwritten manuscript. A fortnight ago, before the Balfour ladies had left home, Lily had written to her cousin, told her of Derek's interest, and asked her to bring her best Gothic tale for him to read.

He finished it in three hours with a grin from ear to ear. Having met the writer, having seen the gleam of longing in her eyes when he told her how she ought to have it published, having watched her shake her head sadly, reminding him that this was not permitted, he knew what he must do.

Perhaps he could have a new career as a literary agent, he thought, tickled with his inspiration as he swept up the manuscript into a neat leather folio and, a short while later, marched grandly into the hallowed offices of John Murray, Publisher.

He refused to go away until Mr. Murray himself came out and met him. Though it took all his charm and a passing mention of every lofty family connection he possessed, he finally coaxed the renowned publisher into reading Pamela's book.

It was much too entertaining to be hidden away in a drawer.

As far as Lily was concerned, the real moment of their marriage in the truest sense had been the night she gave herself to Derek. The Sunday wedding was more for the families' sake. She aimed for the casual elegance of a morning affair, and being an essentially practical woman, she was used to working hard to achieve elegance even on a slender budget. Reining in Mother's slightly more pretentious tastes was more of a challenge.

On some points, she could do naught but give in. It was a matter of choosing one's battles. With that in mind, she had negotiated with her mother, agreeing to hold the ceremony at the ultra-fashionable St. George's Hanover Square in exchange for Lady Clarissa's permission to invite their estranged kin to her wedding, the new Viscount Balfour and his wife.

It had been Derek's idea, thoughtful man. As Lily told her mother, it was the right thing to do.

With the glamorous Knight family heavily involved, the wedding would be covered by the Society pages, and to leave Lord and Lady Balfour out would have been an unforgivable snub. Though the title ought to have gone to Papa, the new Lord and Lady Balfour had never done anything to Lily, or to her mother, for that matter. The bad blood in the family was even older than that. Nobody even remembered anymore what all the fuss was about.

The new Lord Balfour had seemed agreeable enough in their brief meeting, she insisted; he had given a perfectly nice eulogy at Grandfather's funeral. Her mother finally relented and Lily sent off the invitation. A few days later her kinfolk sent back a positive response.

Before long, the momentous day arrived. Lily went to her wedding surprisingly serene. Let the Society columnists critique her as they may, she was at peace with her choices: pink roses and baby's breath, a string quintet playing Bach, a simple gown of pale blue silk with a snowy-white veil and gloves. She also wore the sapphire earrings that had been Derek's engagement present to her.

He had said they would need new traditions to start their new life together, and maybe someday their great-great-granddaughter could wear the jewels to a masked ball and—Lily had finished his sentence—kiss a handsome stranger in a garden folly.

Cousin Pamela, her bridesmaid, looked stunning in dark blue satin. London life agreed with her.

Derek and Gabriel, his groomsman, both wore their indigo cavalry uniforms. The brothers stood up at the front of the church watching Pamela and then Lily walk in.

Since her father was gone, she had borrowed theirs.

Looking very stately indeed in his swallow-tailed morning coat, Lord Arthur escorted her down the aisle and handed her over to his son. He glanced from Derek to Lily, a bit misty-eyed. Then he withdrew and sat down by Mrs. Clearwell, who was already bawling outright.

The ceremony reached its climax in the quiet solemnity of the heartfelt vows they exchanged, standing hand in hand. As Derek placed the plain golden wedding band on her finger, tears rose in Lily's eyes, and when he reverently lifted the veil away from her face so he could kiss her, she remembered the night at the garden folly and how she had refused to let him raise her mask and see her for who she truly was. Now he knew.

He knew her to her very soul. And he loved her.

Lily knew that she would love him always.

She barely heard the reverend's words as he pronounced them man and wife. As he leaned down to claim her lips, Derek also looked a little dazed from the intensity of his feelings.

She floated more than walked back outside, and it was here that her guests discovered the one whimsical touch she had been unable to resist. Three cages full of white doves were released when the wedding party came out.

They went fluttering up into the sky, like all their bright new hopes taking flight. Lily had chosen doves, the symbol of peace, now that her warrior had found a home.

From there, it was on to the lavish breakfast reception at Knight House. True, she did not know Derek's cousins very well, but when a duke and duchess offered to host one's wedding reception at their glorious Town palace, it was not the sort of favor any sensible person declined. It was more than just a kind gesture, after all; it was a signal to Society that trumpeted the newlyweds' inclusion in their exalted London clan.

The champagne flowed while the wedding feast was

served. The cake awaited, a wonder to behold with its white tiers, its sprinkling of edible silver glitter, and its gardenlike profusion of pink and purple rosettes. Lily could not stop staring at it.

"I think it's too pretty to eat," she declared as Mrs. Clearwell joined her.

"Where is your husband? Oh, the sound of it! Your husband! You cannot know what a triumph this day is for me, my dear, you simply cannot know." Mrs. Clearwell took a large gulp of champagne.

Lily wondered how many flutes of it she had already swallowed. She spotted Derek charming everyone, as he was wont to do. He was talking to Lord and Lady Balfour, being an attentive host, and, she realized, going out of his way to make the outsiders feel welcome. Darling man, she thought as she beckoned him over.

"What is it?" he asked, joining her with a kiss on the cheek.

Lily gestured to her chaperone. "Mrs. Clearwell has something to say to us."

"I must give you my final words of advice, my dear young people!" Mrs. Clearwell whispered loudly.

"Yes?" Lily asked, waiting, all ears.

"We shall be happy to have them," Derek replied a bit more skeptically, putting his hand on Mrs. Clearwell's back to steady her. "Are you feeling quite all right, my dear?"

"I may be slightly tipsy," she admitted. "But I have cause to celebrate. Besides, I'm off duty, aren't I? My chaperoning work is through." She sobbed loudly into her handkerchief. "Oh, I'm just so happy."

"You were a wonderful chaperone," Lily said, patting her arm.

"You were a wonderful charge." She blew her nose and pulled herself together. "Now, then, listen well, for my advice is true." She gathered both of them closer. "Follow your heart—trust it, my children! It knows more than your head ever will. It led you to each other. Trust *yourselves*. It is the only way you then can trust each other. There will be bad times, to be sure—there always are. But never give up. And whatever happens, never let each other go."

"We won't," Derek assured her softly, but Lily just hugged her, too choked up to say a word.

A short while later, Gabriel came over and asked for a word with Derek.

"You made a beautiful toast," Lily said to her new brother-in-law, who smiled modestly.

"I'll return your husband in a moment, Mrs. Knight." She beamed at her new title.

Derek followed his brother toward one of the balconied windows. "What is it?" He furrowed his brow. "You're not going to subject me to more marital advice, are you? I've been getting it all day—"

"No," Gabriel said with a wry laugh. "Actually, I have a favor to ask of you."

"Oh, you're a fine one," he exclaimed. "Asking me for favors on my wedding day? I suppose that means I can't refuse."

"Exactly."

"What can I do for you?"

Gabriel paused, his stare intensifying. "I want you to take over the role of Father's main heir."

"*What?*"

"I don't want to do it," he said. "I don't want the burden."

Derek stared at him in shock. In all his life, he had never heard of his ultra-responsible elder brother shirking his duties. "But, Gabriel, you're the firstborn."

"So? It's not like there's a title to consider. Father can leave his fortune to either of us. I've spoken to him and he's agreed to my plans. I had Charles Beecham draw up the papers. All you have to do is sign—and then, congratulations. You can be the firstborn, so to speak. I hope it pleases Lily. And her mother," he added ruefully.

"Gabriel, why are you doing this?" Derek asked in deepening worry. "This is your birthright. I can't possibly take it away from you. Have you lost your wits?"

"No, of course not. I've never been saner in my life. Will you do it or not?"

"Well, I will do whatever you ask of me, but—" His words broke off, for he was thoroughly stymied.

Obviously, this would change his situation, his future prospects. He would draw a larger income from the family's holdings, one that could support a wife and children much more lavishly. As the designated heir to a nabob as rich as Lord Arthur Knight, all the merchants in England would give him virtually unlimited credit. He could live as he liked, and he knew how to manage the finances every bit as well as Gabriel did.

But he couldn't help frowning. "Is this your way of trying to rescue your little brother once again?"

"No. Well, maybe in part."

"Gabriel—"

"Derek, I want you to do this for me. You don't understand. I have more pressing matters to attend to. I can't be burdened with all of these material concerns."

"What's going on?"

He waited for some other guests to pass by to avoid being overheard and then leaned closer and lowered his voice. "You were there when I was struck by the arrow. You saw what happened to me." Gabriel stared at him with feverish urgency.

"Yes."

"Death came for me," he said barely audibly, "but I slipped through his fingers. There has to be a reason why. There is something I'm supposed to do. I can feel it. But I don't know what it is yet. I have to find it. I have to be ready. There is some new fate in store for me, and when the time comes, when it reveals itself, I will have to be ready to go. I cannot have these worldly impediments weighing me down."

"Go where? I don't understand."

Gabriel's stare intensified. "Into the light."

"Oh, God—"

"Derek, my death was only postponed—"

"Don't talk like that! Your end will not come about for another forty years!"

"Maybe, maybe not. All I know is that next time, I intend to be ready."

"What do you mean?" he asked uneasily.

"Derek. This is what I didn't want to tell you when you were still hell-bent on being a soldier. When I died—"

"Gabriel."

"When I died," he repeated insistently, "I caught a glimpse of the place where I was going. And let's just say it wasn't pretty."

Derek's eyes widened.

Gabriel leaned closer. "I was shown all the death that I had dealt out in the field of battle, all the agony I had caused my fellow man, the blood I spilled. I have renounced it. All of it."

Derek swallowed hard, wondering if Gabriel's vision could be real.

"My mind is made up. I have put down my sword. I will not fight again, and I have no use for these worldly possessions. You have married. I will not."

"You're giving up women, too?" he exclaimed.

"My fate is coming, Derek." His brother grasped both of his shoulders and stared fiercely into his eyes. "If *you* don't understand this, no one will. Somehow I have to clear the slate. I've been given a second chance to make up for all the blood I've spilled, and when my destiny presents itself, I must not hesitate. You must take care of Father and Georgie and the others. Promise me."

Derek eyed him warily. "You can count on me, but—are you sure about this?"

"Dead sure."

"Very well, then. I will do as you ask."

Gabriel smiled guardedly and gave him a nod of thanks. Relief flickered in the depths of his dark blue eyes. He walked away abruptly, and as Derek watched him vanish into the crowd of guests, he could only wonder uneasily if his idolized brother was a little mad after his ordeal—or all too sane.

*   *   *

Lily had hoped that the picture-perfect weather on the day she brought her husband home would have shown off Balfour Manor in the most favorable light. But as they got out of the carriage, the brilliant sunshine had the opposite effect, illuminating every flaw and bringing its decrepit truth to light.

Her heart sank a bit as she gazed at her home after having been away long enough to view it with fresh eyes.

It was a sad and gloomy place.

She looked askance at Derek, cringing to see what his reaction might be. He studied it with a trace of worry in the quirked set of his lips. She'd be worried, too, if she were in his shoes. As the new man of the house, all her family's headaches rested on his broad shoulders now.

"It actually looks better in the fog," she said.

"Hm."

"What do you think?"

He turned to her with a smile of slightly forced enthusiasm. "Picturesque."

"Well, it's not exactly the Pulteney Hotel."

He quivered. "God, don't mention that place. You'll get me started," he murmured.

She laughed wickedly as he put his arm around her shoulders. When he ducked his head to whisper a low growl into her ear, Lily would have blushed if she were still able to, but she had lost that ability sometime during their honeymoon.

Ah yes, she still recalled every detail of the glittering suite that Derek had reserved for their three-night stay at London's most exclusive grand hotel.

If it were not for the fine room service, they'd have surely starved, for they had barely left the bed.

On the fourth morning, she had emerged from their hotel room a vastly more experienced lover, having had her introduction to the Tantric arts. Breath and energy, chakras and complicated positions inspired by yoga. In short, the erotic mysteries of the East were not all that mysterious anymore.

Although Lily had relished her husband's masterful control, she was well aware that he had learned these delectable skills for the same reason he had once believed that he must attain fortune and glory in order to win his chosen lady's love. But his chosen lady loved him well before she had ever heard of the Kama Sutra, and so all his study might as well have been in vain—except that it was an extremely pleasant way to spend a night.

Beside her, Derek took a deep breath and braced himself, still staring at the house as though it were a Hindu fortress he had been ordered to storm and conquer. He gave Lily a brave squeeze around her shoulders. "Let's go."

Derek refused to flinch when he saw the house.

He told himself it wasn't half as bad as he had expected.

It was worse.

He met the staff, who came outside to greet them: a lovelorn footman who seemed to worship Lady Clarissa, an ancient groundskeeper who looked like he might keel over at any moment, a plump terse housekeeper, and an exhausted-looking maid. He gave them each twenty sovereigns, which included their back pay and a good deal extra for their loyalty. They nearly broke down in tears.

Doing his best to hearten them, he suggested to Lily a stroll around the grounds and into the village after the long carriage ride. She hastily agreed, perhaps not overly eager for him to view the interior yet.

He was dreading it, but there would be time for a thorough inspection of the place. Soon he would figure out just what he was dealing with. It was not encouraging, if the stable was any sign of things to come. The dilapidated barn was barely fit for a goat, but Mary Nonesuch and the black stallion accepted the indignity without complaint.

Lily, Aunt Daisy, and Cousin Pamela—who still knew nothing of his visit to John Murray, Publisher—escorted them down the two little streets that comprised their tiny village. They stopped at the church, where they paid their respects at her grandfather's grave. Lily pointed to her father's monument, though she said his body had been interred in India.

Meanwhile, Aunt Daisy drifted over to stand by a third Balfour headstone. Derek walked over to her and wondered why she had tears in her eyes. Then he looked at the grave and saw it read *Davy Balfour, 1796–1816. Beloved son.* He winced, noting the year and short span of the lad's life, barely twenty when he had died.

Derek put his arm around Aunt Daisy's plump shoulders and gave her a kiss on the head.

"I am so sorry," he said softly. No wonder she was always such a wreck.

He was beginning to think that all these Balfour ladies needed rescuing.

"My little boy." Aunt Daisy leaned her head against his shoulder with a small sniffle. "You and Lily be sure and have lots of sons for me to play with, won't you?"

"I assure you, my dear, we are already hard at work on the matter."

Aunt Daisy laughed at his sober tone and smacked him, which he deserved. But having restored a bit of a smile to her face, he let the ladies lead on back toward the grounds.

Lily gazed at him in tender thanks.

His air of calm assurance did not waver, although the interior of the house proved just as dark and dismal as he had expected.

For the following fortnight, Derek strove to get his arms around the whole of the renovation project, inspecting the manor from its damp root cellar to its bat-infested attic, from its sinking foundations to its holey roof and half-rotted beams. The crumbling mortar of all twenty fireplaces needed replacing. In several of them, the bricks had already caved in. Water damage had stained and warped the plaster throughout the top floor where everyone had their bedrooms. No wonder poor Pamela was constantly sneezing, with all of the mold.

Modern water closets and kitchen plumbing would eventually have to be installed to make the place properly inhabitable. They were also in desperate need of a new stable and outbuildings.

Agricultural improvements throughout the acreage would be required to make the fields productive again. The ground wasn't even ready for oats and barley yet.

The few tenants, long left to fend for themselves, came to complain to him that their cottages also needed mending.

Once Derek grasped the full magnitude of all the problems at Balfour Manor, he had to take deep breaths to restore his calm. What the hell was he supposed to do?

Yes, his prospects had improved considerably as Lord Arthur's newly designated heir, but he had to be responsible. He was not about to burn through his father's entire fortune, which was what it would take to put this place to rights.

But even more disconcerting were the changes he observed in Lily. Ever since they had come here, the unhappy influence that this place exerted on his bride became more marked. Derek was worried. It was his duty to protect her, not just in body but in spirit and emotions. He did not know how he was supposed to do that in this place.

He did not know how to fight ghosts, and this crumbling manor house was full of them.

For example, every time Lily went up or down the drive, she had to pass the tree where Lord Owen Masters had first approached her. Derek had asked where that had happened, and when she showed him, he had wanted to chop the thing down, but Lily said it wasn't as if the big, old tree had done something wrong. "It does not deserve a death sentence, Derek." Of course. It was only a tree.

Maybe so, but when Derek looked at its knobby old trunk, he saw the faces of ghouls grinning at him, ghouls who preyed on little girls.

That was the first moment that he knew deep down in his survivor's core that he had to get her out of here. This eerie place had her under its spell, and somehow he had to save her.

Then there was the sad, pathetic ruin of the garden folly that her father had left unfinished for his daughter—another painful memory that she had to face every day. If Langdon Balfour were alive, Derek would have liked to punch him in his aristocratic nose. The garden folly was just one more thing Derek wanted to fix for Lily, to help rebuild and mend her heart. For his part, he would make sure the job was finished this time, and done properly.

But for now, he debated with himself on what to do.

It could not be good for Lily to have to see, every day, these constant reminders of the losses and betrayals she had suffered. Yet the most damaging influence of all came from her mother. By God, he thought, Lily should not be anywhere near that harpy except for the briefest possible visits. The woman was poisonous.

Working on her embroidery in the drawing room, Lady Clarissa would send small jabs of insult and criticism at her daughter all the day long, intimidating Lily and wielding the weapon of guilt on everyone around her. For God's sake, why wouldn't the girl stand up for herself?

Though Lady Clarissa didn't dare try her tricks on him, Derek was careful about intervening—he knew quite well that to offend a first-rate manipulator like her would only end up making *him* look like the villain somehow. But he wasn't sure how much longer he could bite his tongue, seeing what all this was doing to his wife.

Subjected each day to her mother's cruel comments and this place, and the Gothic weight of the past that permeated Balfour Manor, Lily grew quieter, more subdued, withdrawn. Every day she seemed like someone more removed from the fearless goddess who had saved him from the stable fire. She had become almost mousy. It was difficult to watch. His beautiful wife was becoming a hollow-eyed stranger.

To Derek, it would have been easier to nurse her through a bout of the flu. This inward infirmity in her he did not know how to heal.

He knew he had to get her out of here before she faded away like a ghost herself. He had to save her, break her out of this cage and free her, just like she had done for him.

But the cure he had in mind—well, he thought grimly, she wasn't going to like it.

In fact, she was going to hate it. She might even end up hating *him*. But so be it. He would do whatever was necessary to protect her. That was his most sacred vow.

His mind made up, Derek wrote to Charles Beecham to get the wheels in motion for the sale of Balfour Manor.

He did not know yet when or how he would tell Lily they'd be moving soon—to wherever she fancied.

He only knew he had to save his wife.

CHAPTER
∽ TWENTY ∽

The ghost of guilt, familiar guilt, whispered its silent curses in her ear later that night as Lily watched her weary husband drag himself into their bedroom, his big, strong body moving slowly, stiffly, after another sixteen-hour day of backbreaking work.

Waiting in her bed for him, dressed in a sleeveless white chemise, Lily watched him, privately stricken to see what she was putting him through.

Although dauntless Derek never uttered a complaint—indeed, he seemed to be taking it in stride—still, he must think that marrying her was akin to indentured servitude or a sentence of hard labor in the penal colonies of Australia.

He peeled off his dirty work clothes and washed himself without a word.

Soldiering on.

Lily felt the sting of tears behind her eyes and had to blink them back. Oh, what was she doing to him?

When he came over and sat on the edge of the bed, she knelt behind him and rubbed his shoulders, kissing his neck in wordless apology. He sighed as she worked out a knot at the base of his neck.

He didn't have to say it. She knew he hated it here and soon he'd probably start to hate her, too.

She could tell he was not happy. How could he be, working like a dog, subjected to all the tension of life around Lady Clarissa? By now, Derek was probably wondering why he had married her, and coming home to Balfour Manor, remembering the sorry little person she had always been here, Lily had begun to wonder that herself. How had someone as flawed as she managed to snare such a god for a husband, anyway?

Derek had promised he wasn't going to return to India, but by now he was probably wishing he could. A part of her was terrified, perhaps irrationally, that he was going to leave her, after all, just like her father.

"You all right?" he murmured, reaching up to clasp her hand on his shoulder as if he could hear her churning thoughts.

Lily paused. "I'm fine," she said in a tentative tone. Whining would only make her look worse. "How are you?"

"I've been better," he admitted with a weary smile in his voice.

"Oh, Derek," she breathed, sliding her arms around his neck. She held him; he leaned his head against her cheek.

"Mm?"

I'm so sorry for all this. She stroked his long hair, pondering her unformed questions, then moved back and let him lay his head on her lap, caressing his cheek and his chest. She took a deep breath. "What's on for tomorrow? Pamela and I want to help."

"Oh, God." He groaned to be reminded of it. "Some fire hazard in the kitchens has to be taken care of first. But the most important thing is that tomorrow night I've got to patch up those roof holes where the bats got in."

"At night?"

"You have to do it at night while they're out flapping around, so, that way, when they come home in the morning, they can't get back inside."

"How clever."

He smiled sagely.

She stared at him for a long moment, feeling as if her heart would burst. "Darling, I'm so sorry about all this," she blurted out. "And I'm sorry about Mother. I know she's driving you mad. She's just used to ruling the roost, you see? And now you're here and she can't push you around and she doesn't know what to do."

"I just don't like seeing her intimidate you." Derek laid his hand on her knee. "I know she hurts you, darling. She's been beating you down for years with her fault-finding, hasn't she?" he asked tenderly.

"I've learned to know when to ignore her."

"But you shouldn't have to live that way," he protested in a soft tone, looking into her eyes. "There is nothing about you that deserves unkind words. Lily, I love you. When I married you, I took a vow to protect you, not just in body, but in spirit, too. If she's going to be nothing but a harmful influence, there's going to come a point where I've got to say, no more."

"You are so sweet."

"Why don't you ever stick up for yourself around her? Someone ought to put her in her place and I think that someone should be you. I will do it gladly if you wish, but I really think it would be the best thing for you, and maybe the best thing for her, too."

"What are you suggesting?" she asked in amusement. "That I have a shouting match with my own mother?"

"Aye, let her have it, girl. It's the only way she's going to learn that she can't walk all over you."

"Oh, Derek, I don't think I could ever do that. It wouldn't be, er, ladylike." She couldn't help smiling sheepishly at him.

"You never had a problem standing up to me," he reminded her, then he flexed one bulging arm before her eyes. "Aren't I a bit scarier than she is?"

Lily admired his biceps with a lavish caress, running her palm along the smooth, stony mass of muscles. She smiled at him with desire fluttering to life in the pit of her stomach. "Good point."

He cupped her cheek. "You're not a little girl anymore. Remember that. You're a grown woman. A beautiful, luscious, fully ripened . . . woman," he finished huskily as he trailed his fingertips down her neck and then brushed her loose, flowing hair behind her shoulder so he could better view her breasts.

Lily trembled as his light touch glided down over her nipple, and moaned softly when he slipped the strap of her chemise off her shoulder. He bared her breast and leaned lower, capturing her nipple in his mouth.

In a moment, he moved up to kiss her lips. She slid her arms around his neck, lying back and wrapping her legs around him as his tongue caressed hers.

"Are you too tired—?" she whispered, but he smiled wickedly against her mouth.

"Never."

He reached down and stoked her desire to new heights with his deft fingers, and then went down on her, as well, pleasuring her with his clever tongue. But once they began making love, she spared him the exertion, letting him lie back and enjoy while she rode him.

"Take this off," he ordered thickly, sliding her chemise higher. Still straddling him, Lily paused and slipped the simple garment off over her head. An almost pained look of appreciation etched his face as his hands followed his gaze. "God, I'm a lucky man."

She was moved to hear that he still felt that way.

Leaning down to kiss him, Lily gave him her all, loving him with a smooth, gliding motion until she had brought him to a powerful climax to replenish his body and soul.

"Oh, Lily, darling, come to me," he groaned.

"I love you," she whispered as she achieved release atop him seconds later.

They lay together afterward, their bodies still joined, his big member lying semi-hard inside her. She rested on his chest and closed her eyes with a peaceful sense of well-being. Everything made sense again. His love had such a power for chasing off her fears.

In his arms, awash in the afterglow of love, it seemed as though nothing could ever assail them.

But this was only the calm before the storm.

* * *

The following night, Lily and Pamela crept up into the bat-infested attic with Derek, and while its winged residents were out dining on moths, they helped him fix the roof. All three wore triangular-folded handkerchiefs over the lower part of their faces like a gang of bandits to avoid breathing in the dust of bat guano or the unhealthy black mold eating away at the beams.

It was no job for a lady—nor for a gentleman's son, in fact—but after exclaiming over what a disgusting, or rather "macabre" task they had ahead of them, they got down to work. Lily kept the lanterns glowing so Derek could see what he was doing. He had brought up a ladder and climbed onto the roof for a closer look at the problem. Now he handed down the manor's loose roof tiles like some unenviable dentist at work on a giant, extracting so many black, broken teeth.

While Lily made a pile of the old tiles, Cousin Pamela dutifully handed new boards up to him through the largest hole in the roof.

Derek kept banging away with the hammer.

Sometime after midnight, they started getting punchy, helping Pamela plot her next novel.

Derek had proposed a story about a young man who visits a strange castle and learns it's infested with ghosts that he must somehow fight. Lily suggested an exorcist, but Pamela said that only worked on demons.

"Maybe he could have some special tool to fight the ghosts with," Lily suggested.

"Like what? A magic hammer?" Derek replied with a grin, leaning down through the hole to show them the one in his hand.

"Would you be careful? If you fall, I'll kill you."

"That's what he could do! He could die," Derek exclaimed. "If he was dead, he could fight the ghosts as a ghost himself."

"But then they'd have to find a way to bring him back to life," Lily reasoned. "How's that supposed to work?"

"I don't know. You'd have to talk to Gabriel," he muttered, but he did not explain.

"I like this idea," Pamela mused aloud. "I'll start on it first thing tomorrow!"

"It *is* tomorrow," Derek replied from up on the roof.

"Oh, yes. Can you see our bats flying around from up there?"

"No, but if I do, I intend to tell them as their landlord that their rent is overdue."

By morning, Derek had sealed the bats out of the attic and they were swooping around outside the house in a bit of a panic. The servants had arisen for their daily duties; the footman and maid helped the three of them carry out the tools and nails and piles of refuse from their project.

"Eh, that was so disgusting."

"Be sure and wash up well. Bats can carry diseases, which is why I didn't really want you to help, but so be it. I'm glad that you did. Thanks, ladies."

"We're the ones who should be thanking *you*," Pamela answered, but Lily merely gave him an adoring smile.

"Oh, there you are!" Aunt Daisy came rushing across the entrance hall below as they made their way down the stairs to put their things away.

Derek and the footman were carrying the ladder, Lily held several doused lanterns, while Pamela had the last board that hadn't been needed.

Aunt Daisy fluttered about in a state of agitation. "Hurry, daughter, oh, hurry!"

"What is it, Mother?" Cousin Pamela asked in concern, setting the board down carefully at the bottom of the stairs, leaning it against the newel post.

"Something's come for you—a letter! Here! Oh, quickly!"

"Is it from that poet fellow you met at the literary society, hm?" Lily teased, giving her cousin a knowing look.

"No!" Aunt Daisy exclaimed, waving it like a winning slip in the parish lottery. "Dear heaven—it is from a publisher!"

Pamela gasped aloud. "What?" She flew over to her mother and gripped the sealed letter in both hands. "Murray! John Murray, Publisher. Oh, dear God, he publishes

Lord Byron a-and Sir Walter Scott! But how could he even know about me?"

Derek cleared his throat, lowered his head, and feigned innocence.

"You didn't!" Pamela's jaw dropped as she turned to him.

"Why not? The tale was good enough. My dear, you can never succeed if you won't even try."

Pamela turned to Lily, her face white. "I-I can't. I can't open it. Lily, you read it. I can't bear to see what it says."

Lily set her lanterns down, took the letter from her hyperventilating cousin, and sent her husband a dubious look, for this was the first she had learned of his mischief.

He gave her a nod full of cavalry confidence.

Lily cracked the letter open, but her eyes widened as she read the letter.

"What's it say?" Pamela squeaked.

She looked at her in amazement. "Mr. Murray wants to publish your book."

Pamela screamed.

"Wait! There's more." Lily gripped her arm and glanced again at the letter. "He wants to know if you have any more you might be interested in selling!"

Pamela shrieked again and burst into tears.

Then everyone was hugging her, cheering. Aunt Daisy was crying and prattling on incoherently about how proud she was of her daughter. Lily was jumping up and down, while Derek clapped the footman on the back and beamed with pride. But then, into this clamor of rejoicing, a cold voice gusted in like the frigid north wind.

"What is the meaning of this?"

Everybody stopped.

"Oh, Clarissa," Aunt Daisy spoke up bravely, though her voice was barely a whisper, "Mr. Murray of London wishes t-to publish our Pamela's books."

"Really?" Mother breathed, turning her needle-sharp glance toward the authoress. "Pamela, I am shocked at you! How could you risk the family's reputation this way?"

"I'll use a pen name, Aunt Clarissa, I-I swear."

"No! It is out of the question, and I am stunned you would dare contradict me in this manner."

"It wasn't her doing," Derek announced in a bristling tone, stepping forward. "It was mine."

"Ah, I should have known," she said with dripping sarcasm.

"Mother," Lily warned.

"Don't 'Mother' me!"

"Oh, please, everyone, please stop!" Aunt Daisy wailed. "I feel the palpitations coming on!"

Lady Clarissa ignored her and refocused her anger on Lily, her blue eyes flashing dangerously. "This is all your fault, you selfish girl! You're the one who got us into this, marrying this pretty fellow instead of keeping your word and taking your family duties seriously. But then again, knowing you, you probably had no choice."

Lily stared at her in hurt shock.

Derek drew off his work gloves. "Did you just insult my wife's honor?"

Lady Clarissa looked away with a nonchalant shrug. "If the shoes fits."

"Madam," Derek addressed her, "go upstairs and pack your bags. You are leaving."

"Oh, I see!" she mocked him. "You're going to throw me out of my own house?"

"It is not your house, Lady Clarissa," he reminded her succinctly. "It is mine. And I . . . want . . . you *out*!"

Lady Clarissa jumped as he bellowed the last word in drill sergeant fashion. She stared at him, looking like a breeze could have knocked her over. "Well!" She glanced at Lily, who was standing there frozen in shock. "If that's how you all feel," the queenly woman clipped out. Then she snapped her jaw shut, whirled around, and flounced out with her chin high.

Everybody turned and looked at Derek in amazement.

He glanced around at them with no signs of remorse.

Lily gazed at him uncertainly, then shook her head and

ran upstairs to check on her mother. The woman probably didn't know what hit her.

When Lily reached her mother's grand but frayed and dusty bedchamber, she found her angrily packing her things.

Or at least making a show of it.

"Mother?"

"Don't talk to me, you little traitor," she said under her breath as she tossed another armful of threadbare clothes into her portmanteau, which lay open on her canopy bed.

"Mother, please. Derek just wants everyone to get along. You don't really have to go—"

"As if you care what happens to me!"

"Don't be like that. Please, calm down. Shall I bring you some tea? It'll be all right—"

"No, it *won't*!" she shouted, turning to Lily with eyes wrathfully ablaze. "You've ruined everything! This is all your fault and you can't even be bothered to care! What were you thinking, bringing home someone like him? He doesn't belong here! A half-pay officer? He's not at all what we agreed upon! Do you have any idea how completely you've let us all down, all because, once again, I presume, you were *incapable* of keeping your legs crossed?"

Shame flooded Lily at those cruel words. Head down, her heart reeling from the blow, she had not noticed Derek leaning in the doorway. But then she heard his deep, steadying voice, reminding her of who she really was.

"Lily Knight," he said softly from across the room, "you are the bravest woman I know. Are you going to stand there and take that?"

He was right.

Through a sort of fog, she recalled the stable fire, and how she had fought like mad to save him. Could she not summon up just a little of that defiance now to fight for herself?

"I'm right, aren't I, Major?" her mother drawled, interrupting Lily's reeling thoughts. "You only married her because you had to, for honor's sake."

Derek shook his head in stony silence, refusing to rise to the bait.

Lily knew he was also silent because he wanted her to be the one to speak up. Her heart was pounding. She barely knew where to begin, there was so much anger bottled up inside her. "You just can't stand to see me happy, can you?" she ground out, startling even herself with the vehemence of her tone.

Slowly, she lifted her head and looked her mother in the eyes.

Lady Clarissa regarded her in aloof amusement, one eyebrow raised. "Ah, what's this, a show of spirit from the mouse?"

Lily flinched. "I am so sick of you hurting me. A mother is supposed to love you, but all you ever do is mock me and find fault. I've tried so hard to win your approval. For years I've tried, but you know what, Mother? I give up," she declared, tears filling her eyes. "Nothing I do is ever going to be good enough for you, so what's the point? You've been ashamed of me since the day Lord Owen Masters wrecked my life."

When her mother rolled her eyes, Lily's temper snapped.

"Where were you when he was preying on me?" she shouted at her. "Absorbed in yourself! I was fifteen years old, Mother! Only a child! I didn't know anything—I didn't understand! That bastard all but raped me, but you didn't even care how it had affected me. Instead of helping me or comforting me, all you did was scream at me and worry about how we would cover it up! Well, maybe *you* deserve some of the blame," she said coldly. "You were my mother—you were supposed to be protecting me. My father was dead—mainly because you drove him away."

These last words startled Lily even as they came tumbling out of her mouth.

They were the truth that no one had dared speak in so many years.

"You and Grandfather. You both pressured him into leaving for the money's sake and he died."

Lady Clarissa's eyes had filled with tears, but she was silent and stock-still.

"Well, you're not going to drive my husband away, too," Lily finished in trembling shock, her composure hanging by a thread. "You can live in proud, stiff misery if you want, and I know, misery may love company. But I'm not going to join you in it anymore." She glanced over at Derek. He sent her a steadying nod. She looked at her mother again, her heart pounding. "I intend to be happy," she said, "and if you can't live with that, then Derek's right, and you should go."

Lady Clarissa took a deep breath, avoiding Lily's gaze. She turned to her portmanteau and closed it, fastening it with a click. "You're right," she said at length, still staring at the distant wall, refusing to look at Lily, as though her daughter's face were a mirror that revealed too many unflattering lines. "You're quite right," she clipped out. "I failed you. I failed your father, too, and now I have to live with my regrets."

Lily trembled, waiting for her mother to look at her, but instead, Lady Clarissa picked up her valise and walked out the door, apparently persuaded to accept her banishment.

Derek stopped her by the doorway with a gentle hand on her shoulder. "My sister, Georgiana, has already made a guest suite in her home ready for you and the others. Have the footman drive you there. She will be expecting you."

"I see. You've been planning this for some time."

Derek said nothing.

Lily closed her eyes, holding back sobs by sheer dint of will, and then her mother was gone.

She heard Derek's approach heralded by the squeaky floorboards. Then strong arms wrapped around her, and she broke down against his chest. He held her close.

"*Brava*," he whispered. "I love you."

Lily wept.

"You needed to do that."

"Yes."

"Do you feel any better yet?"

"No. Not yet."

"You will. I promise," he breathed and he kissed her head again.

"She—didn't react very well."

"You said your part. That's the important thing."

"I suppose."

"I'm proud of you. I know how hard that must've been."

"I'm not as brave as you," she whispered.

"Oh, yes, you are."

She glanced up at him with a wry but tremulous smile. "Do you really think so?"

"I'm living proof of it, my dear. I'll tell you one thing. She heard you. I think you're going to start seeing a change."

"I hope you're right. I don't know why she has to be so cold. I don't think she quite knows how to love."

"But you do."

"Yes. I do." After a moment, she let out a small laugh and shook her head, beginning to feel better. "I can't believe you threw her out."

"Aunt Daisy and Pamela will ride with her to London. Georgiana was happy to offer a few rooms in that palace of hers for a while."

"Well, that's wonderful," she forced out with a sniffle. "Pam will be able to meet with her publisher, and Aunt Daisy will love seeing Matthew again. Maybe Mrs. Clearwell can find a nice rich gentleman for Mother."

Derek succumbed to a reluctant laugh. "Oh, my darling, she's not a miracle worker."

"Oh, you are bad."

He captured her face between his hands and bent his head, pressing a gentle kiss to her lips. "Lily?" he whispered after a moment. "You know I love you, right?"

She lifted her lashes and gazed dreamily into his silvery blue eyes. "Yes."

"Good. Because, darling, there's something that I really need to tell you."

*   *   *

Derek knew the moment of truth had come.

Ah, bugger.

Damned nuisance, those bloody moments of truth.

"I love you," he told her again. It was true, but perhaps he was stalling just a bit.

"What is it, darling?" Her eyes flew open wide. "Oh, God, you're going back to India!"

"No! No, no, of course not. Come, sit down, sweeting. You've had a bit of a shock."

Though that was nothing compared to the shock she had coming.

He led her out of her parents' bedchamber, a room that frankly made him uncomfortable, and drew her gently into the threadbare settee under the mullioned windows at the end of the long, darkly paneled corridor.

They both sat; Lily gazed at him earnestly, folding her hands in her lap in that gentle way of hers that did strange things to his insides. He laid his hand over both of hers.

"Is something wrong, husband?"

"No." He took a deep breath and reminded himself he would have done much more than this in order to protect her. He just hoped she didn't want to plunge a dagger in his chest when she heard the news. "Uh, firstly, I am glad to report that our finances are in excellent order."

"Oh." She furrowed her brow, then nodded. "Good."

He swallowed hard. "Gabriel asked me to accept the role as Father's main heir."

"*What?*"

"He said he no longer wanted to be burdened with the responsibility."

She paused, frowning. "That doesn't sound like him. Is he all right?"

Derek shrugged. "I don't know. He usually knows what he's doing. But as you can imagine, this will be a great benefit to us," he added.

She considered this revelation with a look of increasing surprise. "Are you saying I managed to marry a rich man, after all?" she exclaimed.

He laughed. "Quite."

"How clever of me! Why, you dickens!" He was relieved to see her loosening up after that row. "Why didn't you tell me this before?"

"Gabriel could still change his mind, though God knows, his temperament is that of a mountain. Even so, there's plenty to go around, so I'm not worried."

"Were you afraid I was going to go spend all your new inheritance?"

"No." He touched her cheek fondly. "I was afraid you'd tell your mother, and then she would."

"Ah. Well . . ."

They exchanged smiles of glowing attachment.

"At any rate, my coming up in the world," he said dryly, "is not the only part of our circumstances that's undergone a change." As he gazed at her, his expression sobered.

"What do you mean?"

Derek willed himself to maintain the most soothing possible tone of voice. "We're going to be moving."

"Moving?" She went on her guard. It was the subtlest shift, like a wall coming up behind her eyes.

"Yes," he murmured, lightly holding onto her hand. "I would like you to start thinking about what sort of house you'd like to live in—I mean, your ideal."

She seemed confused. "But I already have a home. I live in Balfour Manor."

"No, darling," he said softly. "Not anymore."

"What?" She yanked her hand out of his hold.

"We can't afford this place—"

"But you just told me you're rich! I know the house is run-down, Derek, but now you can hire the workers—"

"No."

He looked into her blue eyes and refused to waver, despite her panicked look of heartbreaking betrayal.

"I'm taking you out of here," he told her very gently. "This place is bad for you. I can see what it's doing to you, even if you cannot. Lily, I'm your husband and it's my job to protect you."

"Protect me?" She rose and glared at him in shock.

"The house is rotten and there are bad memories for you everywhere."

"But Balfour Manor is mine! It's mine! You can't sell it out from under me, you wouldn't!"

"It's ours."

Technically, it was *his* now that he'd married her and he could do with it what he wished, but there was no point in mentioning that. She knew it full well. She just didn't want to admit it. Now she was shaking her head at him like he was Judas. "I don't believe you. This is what you warned me *Edward* would do. Edward! And now you, acting just like him! How could you do this to me? Balfour Manor is my home, the only home I've ever known! It's been in my family for three hundred years, and now you're going to sell it to some stranger? Chop it up and hawk it away? How dare you?"

"I'm doing this because I love you. I know you're upset, but this house is dangerous, Lily. I'm not going to raise my children here."

"How could you betray me this way?"

His words did not quite seem to be sinking in. "I'm not betraying you," he said calmly. "I'm going to take you somewhere you will be happy. I can't stand seeing you like this. I don't want you breathing this air."

She folded her arms across her chest and paced back and forth across the corridor, shaking her head. "I don't believe you've been scheming all this behind my back. That's why you said Georgiana had her guest rooms ready for Mother, isn't it?"

"Yes."

"So, your *sister* knew you were selling *my* house before you even told *me*?"

"Just try to listen to the plan."

"Oh, the plan?" she spat.

"Charles Beecham has arranged an auction at the end of the week. That's why I've been trying to do at least the most obvious repairs, to help get a good price."

She shook her head at him with eyes full of accusation, but, grimly, he forged on.

"I tried to interest your kinsman first in the hopes of trying to keep all the Balfour properties together, but not even he wanted the place."

"So, that's why you wanted him to be invited to the wedding!"

"Once we have a buyer, then we'll arrange a suitable length of time to move your family's personal effects out of here. I will see that your kinswomen are set up in suitable living quarters, perhaps in a house near Mrs. Clearwell's. Would that please you?"

She didn't even seem to hear the question, but turned to him sharply. "Are they going to tear the house down?"

Derek squared his shoulders. "Depends on who buys it."

Fury rushed across her countenance at his response. He was not surprised. He knew this was the one possibility she did not want to contemplate, above all. She stared at him in withering silence for a long moment.

"Well, let them just try to get me out of here," she vowed. "They're going to have to rip this place down with me still inside, because I'm not leaving. Balfour Manor is my home, and I'm *not* going to let you destroy it." With that, she pivoted on her heel and walked away, slamming their bedroom door farther down the hallway.

Derek lowered his gaze and took a deep breath. "Ah, bloody hell."

Ah, well. At least he had broken the news. He had waited until the auction was just a few days away because he knew it would be best to have it over quickly.

Like a post-battle amputation.

Deciding to let her mull it over for a while, he jogged downstairs to see the ladies off.

They took the news better than Lily did.

Pamela and Aunt Daisy seemed almost happy to hear it. Truly, they were ready to fly out of this cage. Lady Clarissa barely seemed to absorb what he was saying; Derek got the feeling she was still in shock. That her daughter's angry tirade was finally sinking in.

As their shabby black carriage pulled away, he watched it heading down the drive, past that damned tree. They were on their way now, he thought, confident they would be fine once the upheaval of the move settled down. After all, they had not stopped talking about their visit to London for weeks, musing about the people they had met and the places they had gone, all of them, starved for life and color and activity. In London, perhaps they would not be so haunted by the dead Balfour males in the parish graveyard.

Once they had gone, he braced himself to return to the bedroom, but discovered his wife had barricaded herself inside. Of course, it would have been an easy matter to knock a hole through the worm-eaten door or the ancient plaster, but he didn't dare.

He knocked on the door like an oh-so-civilized gentleman. "Lily?"

"Go away! I'm not speaking to you!"

"Fine, I'll speak, you listen." Somehow it was easier to spill out his heart to a plain brown door. "I can't stand to see what's happening to you here. I love you so much, and I feel like I'm losing you—to this place. It changes you in ways I don't understand. I want to help you."

No answer.

"Lily, your coming back here is as bad for you as going back to the battlefield would have been for me. We both have our ghosts. You weren't about to lose me to mine, and I owe you the same loyalty."

"Loyalty?" she yelled in a fury through the slab of wood that separated them.

"Of course! I would do anything for you. Anything," he added in a choked whisper. "The last thing I ever want to do is hurt you. And I know you're angry. I understand that. But whatever you might think, I'm doing this because I love you. Someday you'll thank me."

Silence.

"Can't you say something?"

"I hate you."

"No, you don't," he told her wryly. "You love me. You know you do."

"Go away!"

"Fine. I'm going to go find some food. You want something to eat?"

A wordless yowl of rage was her reply.

Oh, dear. It seemed he lacked a proper terror of her fury. "Lily, it's as plain as day that you are not happy here. So why do you refuse to sell this place? It doesn't make any sense! Why were you willing to go to such lengths to save it? Tell me that. Why were you willing to marry someone like Ed Lundy to preserve it? With all its rotting beams and caving-in fireplaces? Why does it matter so much?"

"It just does!" she wrenched out.

The answer sounded like something he would have expected from a little child.

That was when he started to suspect what was really going on inside that head of hers, whether she knew it or not.

"Well," he said evenly through the door, "hate me all you want, but I'm not letting you go. Mrs. Clearwell's orders."

"Oh, shut up."

He smiled in spite of himself. The reminder of her chaperone's advice on their wedding day had to soften her up at least a bit. "Darling, I'm going to buy you the most beautiful house you ever saw," he promised her. "What would you like? A garden? A ballroom?"

"But I want *this* house!" she wailed, twisting the heart in him with her tone of youthful despair.

Bloody hell. The tears had started in earnest now. He could hear her crying in there. "Lily, let me in. Let me hold you."

"No. Just go away! I can't believe you did this to me, you traitor."

Despite his certainty that he was in the right, hearing her crying and knowing that he was the reason made Derek feel approximately one inch tall.

Damn, but there was no helping some people!

He shook his head, half distraught himself, and left her to weep her tears in privacy. He knew her, and as much as he wanted to break down the door, he knew it was important to give her time and not lose faith. So with all his military discipline, he made himself wait one half hour and did not come back until he had washed himself from the dirty attic job, changed into clean clothes, and procured a tray of food and tea for both of them.

He carried it up to the door, knocked gently. "I'm back."

No answer.

He frowned. "Lily?"

This time, when he tried the knob, it turned, no longer locked. He opened the door and peered cautiously into the room, and there was his wife, sitting crumpled on the floor below the window, crying with her arms wrapped around her and a look in her big blue eyes like a fractured little girl.

Oh, God. Derek closed the door behind him. "Do you want some tea?"

"I figured it out," she said in a shaky tone.

"What's that?" He set the tray aside and went to her. "What did you figure out, love?"

"Why this place mattered so much." Her teeth were chattering as if she had caught a chill.

"Why?" he whispered, crouching down before her.

"I-I guess a part of me thought my papa might still come home. And we ought to be here to see him when he came b-back or he wouldn't know where we went. He might not be able to find us again." Twin tears fell from her eyes. "But he's not coming back. I know that, of course. I guess I always did. But it still hurts."

"I know, sweetheart." Derek reached for her and pulled her into his arms. She draped her arms wearily around him, crying.

"Shh," he breathed as he held her on his lap. "I'm here."

For a long time, she cried until all of the tears were out of her. Derek still stroked her and comforted her until she lapsed into spent silence.

He was unsure how much time had passed, but beyond their bedroom window, twilight had come.

"I'm sorry for all the things I said."

He kissed her brow. "It's all right."

"You forgive me?" she whispered.

"Always. Do you forgive me?" He looked into her eyes.

"You were right," she said barely audibly. She nodded, lowering her gaze. "This place. I needed to be free."

"You are now." He threaded his fingers through hers.

"Derek?"

He looked at her in question.

"Take me out of here," she whispered. "Can we leave? Can we just go now, before I lose my nerve?"

He nodded, rose, and helped her up. "Let's go."

They went outside to the stable, where he saddled the horses and that night, they rode back to Town. He cradled Lily before him while he rode on the black stallion with the sorrel mare, Mary Nonesuch, comfortably tethered behind.

They cantered through the darkness heading toward London with no firm destination in mind. As long as they were together, they had all that they required.

They had everything.

⮔ EPILOGUE ⮔

*L*ily's ideal house summoned up images of taking tea in a pleasant summer garden. Warm golden tones on the walls cast a hazy glow over airy interiors, filled with soft, plump furniture clad in muted floral chintz. Plants in pots flourished everywhere, thanks to the abundance of light through the tall, arched windows.

The white cottage they had found was perfect for them: not too big, not too small. Just far enough away from Town for tranquillity—they could see cows grazing in a meadow from their bedroom window—and yet near enough to partake of London's endless amenities.

And it was new. Everything worked just as it should with barely a squeak in the light hardwood floors. It had good copper plumbing, a modern w.c., and a roof that was snug with no drafts. From the day Derek bought the house for her, to Lily, it was a little slice of heaven on earth.

It was home.

A place of safety. A place of joy. Above all, a place of love.

Balfour Manor was no more. An architect had bought it at the auction and had taken it down, sending the best parts off to his various new projects.

The Balfour ladies split the proceeds from the sale among themselves, and with astonishing speed, the alteration in their circumstances drastically changed their lives.

Mother moved into an elegant little house on Mrs. Clearwell's street. Upon her reentry into Society as a still-beautiful and independent widow à la Fanny Coates, Lady Clarissa soon found herself hotly pursued by some of the ton's wildest young bucks. Around them, her stiff-necked propriety couldn't last long. Constantly surrounded by lusty and high-living, amorous younger men, she had no time anymore for criticizing Lily or anyone else. She was too busy having the time of her life.

Cousin Pamela also had her share of admirers. She had already jilted the poet—thereby providing him with an abundance of new material to sob about in his verses, no doubt—and was on to the next companion, an aspiring composer this week, Lily believed. Upon her arrival in London, Pamela had ditched her spectacles, procured a daring short haircut, and took to wearing red. John Murray, Publisher, had arranged for six of her novels to be printed over the course of the next two years. As for Aunt Daisy, she had no shortage of Knight children to play with. Her current favorite was the ducal daughter known as Baby Kate.

The Balfour ladies were so busy—and so happy in their new lives—that Derek and Lily were largely left to themselves, which suited them quite well.

Derek had finally received the long-awaited letter from his old commander with news of his men. Ironically, Colonel Montrose reported that the Maratha Empire was defeated after only four months! It was all over even before the navy treasure ships had arrived, and as for Derek's men, they had seen no action. His former regiment had been stationed on the other side of India when the first shots were fired and "all the fun" was over by the time they reached the front. The ferocious Baji Rao was dead and the British colonies were safe again.

Derek had laughed at the letter, then forwarded it on to Gabriel in his lonely, rural hermitage so that he, too, could read the news—never mind the fact that the firstborn Knight did not seem to care for any reminders of his old life or the affairs of the world. Gabriel kept to himself out there, waiting, according to Derek, for some sort of divine signal that would reveal his future destiny.

Derek and Lily, of course, had no further questions

about *their* destiny. They had found it months ago one night at a masked ball.

"Lily!" She heard her husband calling from outside and went to the window, but when she saw Derek down in the garden, amazement struck her. She opened the window with an incredulous smile.

"Look! It's done! I just finished it!" Beaming with pride in his handiwork, Derek gestured to the whimsical white garden folly that he had just finished painting. "What do you think?"

Lowering her hands from her mouth, Lily uncovered her radiant smile. Her answer was a little strained, though, from the lump in her throat. "It's perfect! You're perfect, Derek!" she called. "It's beautiful!"

He grinned and beckoned to her. "Come have a closer look!"

"I'll be right there!" She pulled the window closed against the coolness of the parti-colored autumn day, then hurried out of the room, crossing the upstairs hallway. She lifted the hem of her skirts as she went rushing down the stairs to join him, her face beaming.

Maybe her wishing powers still worked, after all, she mused. You never knew. You just never knew.

Read on for a special note from the author . . .

Gaelen Foley
writes to you about

HER EVERY PLEASURE

The next seductive adventure in
the Spice trilogy!!!

Dear Reader,

Thank you for joining me on the heartfelt journey of this story. While I hope Derek and Lily's tale will linger in your memory, in the meantime, I'd love to share with you a little bit about *Her Every Pleasure*, the exciting finale in the Spice trilogy. (The first book, if you missed it, was *Her Only Desire*, starring Derek's sister Georgiana and Lord Griffith.)

In *Her Every Pleasure*, we delve into the heart of Gabriel Knight—a battle-weary warrior seeking redemption. What he finds instead is an exotic beauty asleep in his stable one morning, who pulls a knife on him when he startles her awake! As a hardened soldier who's had men flee from him in terror on the battlefield, Gabriel finds the threat from the "mere slip of a girl" rather amusing. Mostly, he believes she is there courtesy of his brother Derek, who threatened to hire a "gorgeous wench with no morals" to take care of him—and to put an end to his sexual fast. He thinks that's why this beautiful firebrand has invaded his lonely rural hideaway.

But is he ever wrong!

His "gorgeous wench" is in fact a rebel princess on

the run; a driven, dynamic young royal who has grown up in England ever since Napoleon conquered her family's kingdom. With her father and two elder brothers mysteriously murdered, Princess Sophia is now the royal heir, and she is determined to claim her rightful throne and bring peace to her war-torn land.

Attacked en route to a secret meeting with the British Foreign Office, Sophia is separated from her bodyguards, escapes in the fray, and hides in Gabriel's nearby stable, disguising herself as a commoner to elude the villains. According to her security protocol, she must stay put until her men find her again.

Princess Sophia is as amused by sexy Gabriel's mistaking her for a lowly peasant girl as he is by her quick ability with a knife—so she decides to play along. After all, the mysterious, blue-eyed warrior makes it clear that he has no intention of giving in to this delicious temptation that his brother has supposedly sent his way.

(Ha!)

Merry mayhem ensues as Gabriel discovers his new "servant girl" doesn't have the slightest inkling of how to cook, clean, or wash clothes and really hates taking orders. She's much better at giving them, and as a seasoned military officer, so is he. And yet their sizzling attraction is undeniable.

As you can probably tell, I can't wait to write this book! It's shaping up to be one of my grandest adventures yet, moving from the majestic castles of Regency England to the sapphire waters of the Mediterranean. I hope you'll be as swept away as I am by this passionate tale of a rebel princess and the powerful warrior destined to become her champion.

Of course, it makes me a little sad that *Her Every*

Pleasure will be my last Knight family book, but there are many more stories to write and wonderful new characters to discover.

For those new to my Knight family series, please visit my website at www.gaelenfoley.com for the full rundown on all the previous Knight family novels, starting with *The Duke*. They're all still available. You'll also find lots of writing craft and history articles on my website, including the big reader favorite, my extensive Regency glossary. Consider it your go-to destination if you wish to familiarize yourself with some of those obscure nineteenth-century terms that pop up in Regency tales. And if you do visit, why not drop me an e-mail? I love hearing from my readers!

Thank you, as always, for spending time in my little corner of the Regency world. I hope you enjoyed your visit. It's a pleasure and a privilege to entertain you!

With warmest wishes,
Gaelen Foley